# Victoria Fox

# WICKED
# AMBITION

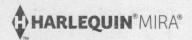

Published in Great Britain 2013
Harlequin MIRA, an imprint of Harlequin (UK) Limited,
Eton House, 18-24 Paradise Road,
Richmond, Surrey, TW9 1SR

© Victoria Fox 2013

ISBN 978 1 848 45232 9

60-0613

Harlequin's policy is to use papers that are natural, renewable and recyclable products and made from wood grown in sustainable forests. The logging and manufacturing processes conform to the legal environmental regulations of the country of origin.

Printed and bound by
CPI Group (UK) Ltd, Croydon, CR0 4YY

For Chloe Setter

# ACKNOWLEDGEMENTS

Thank you to Madeleine Milburn, a diamond among agents, who championed these characters long before they arrived in this story. To my brilliant editors at MIRA, Jenny Hutton and Sally Williamson: I'm so grateful for your direction and support. Special thanks to Kim Young for her early feedback on this book and for everything she gave to the others. To Tara Benson and Claudia Symons for their passion, their ambition and for Gin School; and to the rest of the team at Harlequin UK, especially Mandy Ferguson, Jason Mackenzie, Nick Bates and Tim Cooper. To Rebecca Oatley, Pally Kaur and Lisa Wlodyka at Cherish PR—it's going to be so much fun.

Shout-out to Bernie and Matthew Strachan for keeping the bonkbuster dream alive; to Chioma Okereke for her solidarity; to Jenny Dodd for wine and chats; to Ian and Katharine Stonex for their encouragement; and to Mark Oakley for everything in between.

Finally, thanks to Toria for knowing Jax and Leon from the beginning. They made it!

# Prologue

*Palisades Grand Arena, Los Angeles*
*Summer 2013*

IF NOT VICTORY, REVENGE!

It was printed in hot-pink marker on the back of the cubicle door, the lettering neat and precise. Ivy Sewell reached to touch it, her fingertips tentative, tender almost across its surface, as she might in another life have caressed a lover's cheek.

Her hard blue stare locked on to the affirmation. Ivy's was a malice years in the making, a shoot green in youth that had turned black through adolescence, insidious and strangling as a weed, so that tonight, here, at last, the instant of her retribution had arrived. In the wings, the truth gasped its final throttled breaths; the old order shrugged off a wilted coil. She was deadly. Lethal. Toxic. *Poison.* And the world prepared to feel her wrath.

There would be before tonight, and after tonight, and

nothing would ever be the same again. In the eleventh-floor washroom of LA's Palisades Grand Arena, on the most televised event in the entertainment world calendar, vengeance was their apocalypse.

Ivy carved a painted fingernail, danger red, into the print, gouging a nub of plaster.

IF NOT VICTORY, REVENGE!

Victory had never been hers. But revenge? Revenge was in her blood.

From inside the stadium she could hear the muted thrum of beats and the united roar of the fans. Ivy imagined the cries were for her, urging her on, baying for the carnage she was about to unleash. She released her breath, tasting salt and iron, her tongue flicking across the split in her lip where she had bitten too hard in anticipation.

Three women.

Each was here to claim the spotlight. Each was an international superstar, a glittering icon with the world at her feet. Robin Ryder, UK talent-show sensation, the rags-to-riches sweetheart rescued from oblivion. Kristin White, global pop phenomenon with the voice of an angel, who had ditched the princess act after tragedy struck. And Turquoise da Luca, America's number one female vocal artist and now tantalising toast of Tinseltown.

One of them was going to perish.

At the mega-event better known as the ETV Platinum Awards, Ivy Sewell was concerned with one target and one alone: her twin. The hated sister, born identical and torn towards an opposite fate, who had claimed everything Ivy herself should have been, who had snatched it all from her grasp, who had turned her back and slipped so seamlessly into a life of opulence and glamour, forgetting where she had come from or what had gone before.

Ivy shoved the bag into the trashcan, forcing it down with her fists. Later, when it was discovered, they would know how clever she had been. In it lurked the disguise she'd worn, the orange T-shirt with its Burger Delite! logo emblazoned across the front...a whole person, just like that, folded away in a sack. She stared indifferently at the hands that would carry out this great execution. Wrists pale and brittle, like branches in winter; the fingers thin.

Only when the bullet entered would it be over. Only when that flawless skin was ruptured, that smile erased, that heartbeat frozen, one and the same as hers and yet a universe apart, would it be finished: one life in exchange for another.

A rapturous cry exploded. The show was beginning, the stage lit up to welcome the players, the kings and queens of twenty-first-century music, the alphas and the studs and the bitches and the beauties with their diamonds and their hundred-thousand-dollar gowns.

Ivy closed her eyes. The letters were emblazoned on her lids, bright as fire.

IF NOT VICTORY, REVENGE!

The curtain was up. And now it was show time.

# PART 1

One year earlier

# *1*

Robin Ryder was seeing stars, weightless and electrified as she flew towards the raging sun of her orgasm. Fuck the wardrobe her stylist had spent hours perfecting; fuck the producer's countdown mere minutes away; fuck everything except this glorious, glittering fuck.

'Does that feel good?' the man breathed, gripping her waist and pulling in deeper. Robin, on top, ground against him; the slippery, yielding leather of the seat was soft and sticky beneath her knees, and she threw her head back to moan her reply.

Backstage in the VIP suite, ahead of a live Saturday night broadcast of *The Launch*, she was riding this guy like it was the last ride of her life. What she was doing was reckless, it was sinful, but Robin had never been able to play by the rules. She was a judge and he a contestant; it was all kinds of wrong and yet all kinds of right. RnB tunes filtered through the music system, and at the bar an empty magnum of Krug nestled on a bed of ice. As Robin held tight she decided she would definitely, oh *definitely*, be putting him through this week.

'I'm there,' she cried, 'don't stop, I'm there!'

'Me too,' the guy choked, driving in hard. 'My God, you're so fucking hot.'

The throne-like chair was a prop, used in the early audition stages: when a judge liked what they saw they hit a lever, prompting the seat to rush forward on a pair of rails. Thankfully for Robin the gimmick had been relegated backstage once the live nights began—she'd proved a hit during those first weeks where her inclination to back everybody had her getting motion sickness every ad break. After all, *The Launch* was where she herself had begun: now she was the nation's darling, drawn from obscurity, a rough diamond polished through song. Robin had risen to fame through the very show she was tonight judging.

The public loved Robin's voice, raw and sensuous, somewhere between pain and deliverance. They loved how she wore her heart on her sleeve. They loved her guts, and her honesty. They loved her story—loved that she'd been hurt and wanted to seize her dues. Over twelve months Robin had soared to a dizzying stratosphere, invited to every party, on to every red carpet, booked for every event. Her gift was undeniable and her smile lit up a room.

'Do you want it?' the contestant was panting, his sweat-slicked six-pack glistening in the half-glow. 'Right there, do you want it?' He was this year's favourite, tough guy with the voice of an angel—and a heavenly body to match.

She came in a crash, a bursting galaxy of dazzling confetti as she writhed on the brink of paradise. Sex was Robin's release. It enabled her to feel that warmth, that closeness, without risk of being wounded. You got what you came for and you left. She didn't get why people wanted to stick around afterwards anyway; she had never understood this sleeping-in-each-other's-arms thing. She'd got this far alone and she didn't need anyone else.

'That was amazing,' he groaned, cradling her, kissing her over and over as she gasped through the aftermath of her climax.

She had barely had time to fling a shirt over her nakedness when the door opened. Robin didn't know which happened first: the contestant's face dropping as fast as his pants had ten minutes earlier; or her attempt to dismount disastrously striking the switch that jolted the chair meteorquick towards their visitor like some sort of warped sacrificial offering.

'Oh,' said their caller, as Robin scrambled to conceal herself. Instead of a mortified exit (which would have been the polite thing), he stood there, an infuriating grin on his face.

Light flooded the room. 'Shit, man,' gabbled the contestant helpfully. 'Shit, shit, shit.'

'Do you mind?' she raged, so mortified she couldn't bear to turn round.

'Sure.' She could hear the smirk in his voice. 'Guess I'll come back later.'

It was a miracle she made it through the show without punching him.

Leon Sway, Olympic sprinter, was guesting on tonight's panel. Since the summer Games had decreed him a World Personality, the athlete was hotly in demand for every broadcast going. Leon was mixed race, with close-cut black hair, strong cheekbones and an all-over movie-star look: it was little wonder he had been gracing billboards across the globe with a ream of sponsorships and modelling contracts; and now here he was making a star appearance on the adjudicating *Launch* line-up—what the hell did he know about music?

'I've been a fan of yours from the start,' Robin told a quivering choirgirl after an impressive rendition of Adele. 'That was a brilliant performance; I really felt it. Well done.'

'Sure that's not all you felt?' came the murmur from her neighbour, just loud enough for her to hear. She tried not to scowl—either that or turn to Leon and chuck her glass of water in his face. It wasn't in Robin's nature to wish for the ground to open up and swallow her whole, but tonight had to be the exception. As the acts ran through their numbers and the board delivered their verdicts, she tried not to dwell on what parts of her anatomy might have been unveiled before they'd even been introduced—not easy with Leon's supercilious bulk to her left, interspersed with a hot flash of shame every time she recalled his untimely intrusion.

'Do you think she can win?' asked a producer mogul who had been tagged as her rival on the show. 'With those nerves I can't see her pulling off any live gigs.'

'This is a live gig, isn't it?' Robin snapped. She could sense Leon watching her. Why did he have to be such a smug, full-of-himself…? Ugh, she couldn't even think of the word.

'Well, yes…'

'I absolutely believe in her,' commented Robin, battling through her disgrace. 'This is where I got my break and it took me time to grow, of course it did. If she were cutthroat at this point you'd be tearing her apart for being difficult to work with. Which is it going to be?'

The arena shouted its approval. Robin's image filled the screens on either side of the stage, the people's champion: she was petite, her hair chopped short but with a trademark sweep still long enough to obscure her eyes, which were cat-like and aglow with dramatic make-up. Hers was a cautious demeanour that belied the tough, attitude-fuelled work that had made her name: Robin's music spoke of more years lived and more experiences earned, and had consequently secured her the first ever talent-show-spawned album to be nominated for—and win—a Brit Select Award. The victory had made Robin Ryder, at just nineteen, the hottest thing on the UK scene. She believed in putting everything into her art, the offering up of her heart and her soul, because for a long time she had imagined that both those things were damaged beyond being any use to anyone.

When the time came for *that* contestant to take the spotlight, she grimaced. Leon couldn't resist fixing her with a stare throughout the entire introductory VT.

'It wasn't for me,' he judged afterwards. 'It kinda felt like you were distracted.'

'I disagree,' put in Robin. 'For me it was a very focused, determined performance.'

Leon turned to her. 'Are you complimenting his performance?'

The blush threatened to engulf her. 'Sure,' she managed, the double entendre squatting resolutely between them. 'I am.'

'Focused *and* determined—that's how you like it, then?'

She returned his glare. 'Who doesn't?'

The host, confused, went to ask another panellist their view.

'It seemed like he had something else on his mind,' Leon steamed on before he could, 'something more interesting than being up on that stage. Don't you feel that's an issue?'

'Whatever drives him is fine by me,' she replied stiffly, knowing that every word she uttered was laced in innuendo. 'After all, what would a *sprinter* know about vocals?'

It was a cheap shot, she ought to know better, but humiliation had forced her into a corner. A blood-hungry cheer erupted and she could all but hear the producers salivating.

'Well, he is the bookies' favourite,' supplied the mogul.

'Not just the bookies'…right, Robin?' Leon joked, a crescent-moon dimple appearing on one side of his all too slappable face. His insinuation was obvious. There was a horrible silence. Robin's cheeks flamed. She tried to think of something to say and nothing came. She was so angry she could scream. This was *live TV*!

'Ex*cuse* me?' she spluttered.

But the presenter moved on, instructed to sever it at the point of maximum speculation.

Afterwards, everyone assured her that it hadn't sounded that bad. Robin wasn't stupid. It would be all over the papers tomorrow thanks to that insufferable bastard Leon Sway! The contestant looked hopefully at her as she fled: that was the end of him.

Her car took her straight to Soho's Hideaway Club, where she found scant solace in ordering the strongest concoction she could find. Her band met her there.

'I don't want to talk about it,' she said, before Polly, her bassist, had a chance.

Polly was American with a peroxide-blonde beehive. 'All right,' she said as they settled in a booth. 'But just to say—'

'Don't say anything.'

'It could have been worse.'

'Could it?'

'*Did* you screw him?'

Robin was aghast. 'Who, Leon?' she demanded, outraged at the thought.

'No!' Polly named the contestant. 'Although Mr Sway, well, you have to admit—'

'I'm warning you: don't even go there.' She downed the drink. 'Anyway, what difference does it make? Everyone thinks I did, so I did. Isn't that how it goes?'

Within minutes a tower of frosted glasses was deposited in front of them, together with several giant bottles of part-frozen vodka. An accompanying note read:

*Want a winner on your team?*

Her manager Barney signalled across the space. 'Hey, Robin, check out your secret admirers.' Close to the neon-bulb-strewn bar, just decipherable through the low-lit shadows that gave way to pockets of absolute dark, Olympian Jax Jackson, officially the fastest man in the world, was partying with a harem of lovelies. Two Olympians in one day? Some luck that was. Jax raised a glass and Robin prayed he wouldn't come over: thanks to Leon he probably thought it was a free-for-all.

'If we accept these you don't have to do anything in return, right?' Matt, her drummer, was already pouring. He winked at Robin when she raised her middle finger. 'What? Girls never buy me drinks; it's not like I know the rules!'

Robin tossed back a syrupy shot, then a second, then a

third. Polly threw her a glance and she matched it. What was wrong with having fun? She was young and free and famous, and didn't need anyone to tell her she deserved a break.

'What?' she countered. 'Aren't we partying?' Matt grabbed the second bottle and filled the glasses and everyone went in for a sticky collision before the liquid vanished.

'Sure,' said Polly, not sure at all. What Robin had gone through didn't go away; you had to deal with it before you could move on, not get trashed till you forgot. 'You earned it.'

'Nah, *we* earned it,' corrected Robin, putting one arm round Polly and one round her manager and pulling them close. 'We're family, aren't we?'

*Family.*

Even as she said the word she could hear how hollow it sounded.

## 2

Five thousand miles away and several hundred feet above a Hollywood theatre, Kristin White and her boyfriend were making a surprise landing at the premiere of *Lovestruck*.

'Jesus Christ, what the hell was that?' Scotty panicked, clinging to the door of the chopper as it began its shaky descent. Kristin giggled and put a comforting hand on his knee. Out of the window they could see the red carpet splashed beneath them like a river of fire, the upturned faces of fans and paps dozens-deep, gazing awe-struck at the approaching marvel.

Scotty gripped her fingers, white-knuckled, and gulped.

'Relax,' she soothed, leaning over to kiss him.

'I am relaxed,' he warbled.

'You're James Bond,' she calmed him, 'remember?'

'Yeah.' Scotty closed his eyes, holding tighter. 'I'm Bond. I'm James fucking Bond.'

When the helicopter touched ground, Scotty was so relieved he grabbed Kristin and embraced her passionately. 'Wow,' he raved, 'that was totally wild!'

It wasn't like Scotty to initiate a PDA and Kristin trembled with joy, filled with the brilliance of the moment. Here they were at the peak of their careers, crazy famous and crazy in love. Her tummy lurched at his kiss more than it had at any point over the last half an hour.

'Check out the reception,' Scotty rhapsodised. 'This is sick!' He took her hand with a reassuring squeeze and said, 'You look really beautiful tonight...you know that?'

She glowed.

By the time the door opened Kristin could scarcely hear what her boyfriend was saying because the screams were so loud. Thunder rushed at them, crashing in waves, a wall of sound so solid and suffocating that the whole impression was one of being underwater.

'Scotty, I love you! Scotty, marry me! Scotty, over here!'

Kristin took Scotty's hand in hers and held firm as they posed and turned for the circus of cameras. The paparazzi lining the passage shouted their names, encouraging them to stand separately, together, to kiss, the latter of which sent the fans demented, crying out for Scotty once more and snapping him frenetically with their camera phones.

Dating the subject of a gazillion teenage fantasies was never going to be easy. Kristin tried not to get jealous. *You're my only girl*, Scotty would promise. She trusted him.

A stylist was on hand to rearrange her dress, a pretty lilac fishtail with capped lace sleeves, offsetting to a T her tumbling flaxen waves and creamy porcelain skin.

'Kristin, hi, this is some arrival!' *Entertainment Now!* caught her for an interview. 'Would you answer some questions for our viewers?' Scotty was happily dragged off to sign autographs. A girl fainted and had to be removed from the throng.

'You've written the soundtrack for this movie,' the reporter enthused. 'How has it been collaborating with the film industry? Are there any more projects in the pipeline?'

Kristin delivered the quarter-smile. One of the first things her mother had coached her in was that there was a complex spectrum of smiles and each one meant a different thing, and the quarter was coy, a little bashful, promising more than she was prepared to say. Her mom had worked hard to get Kristin to where she was today: pop princess, the angel every little girl dreamed she would one day grow up to become, strumming on a guitar or gliding across a piano and singing gentle songs about true love and knights in shining armour who whisked their beloveds from towers in the sky. Scotty Valentine as her steady completed the picture.

'The movie's fantastic,' Kristin gushed. 'It's been a magical experience.'

'You and Scotty look blissful. Has he been supportive through the process?'

Kristin stole a glance in her boyfriend's direction. Scotty was talking into someone's cell, now in his comfort zone and a pro at pleasing his crowd of devotees. She had to remind herself that he was her guest tonight, not the other way around. Kristin had her own following—her last four consecutive singles had shot straight to number one; her trio of albums had gone platinum, selling in excess of sixty million records; and she had claimed more than eighty awards—but Scotty Valentine, with his mop of blond hair and huge, puppy-like blue eyes, was that thing to which, when done right, there was and never would be an equivalent: lead vocalist in the most outrageously popular boy band in US history, a five-guy line-up with the slick tunes and the heart-throb status to take it all the way.

People had thought the boy band was dead…and then along came Fraternity.

'He's been great.' Kristin expanded the smile, unable to help how elated the truth made her. 'He's absolutely, amazingly perfect.'

Scotty was her muse, her inspiration and her reason for everything. Everyone said they made a bankable duo as if in some way that took away from the genuine feeling they had for each other, but Kristin knew it was special. She had never been in love before. Scotty was her first. Being one of millions worldwide who felt the exact same way was just something she'd have to get used to. Couples in the fame game appeared and vanished quicker than a fast-food order, but what made their relationship different was that they had ridden the wave together—they had known each other since they were seven years old, novice entertainers on *The Happy Hippo Club*. Best friends first; it had made sense that once the innocence of childhood affection wore off they would upgrade to the next level. Kristin had liked Scotty for ages before it became official, admiring him from behind a line she could not cross, until a nudge from their management had finally sealed the deal. It was a true romance, like something from a fairy tale—and Scotty her treasured Prince Charming.

The golden couple was ushered off the carpet. Away from the cameras Scotty's smile wavered. He still looked peaky from the helicopter.

'Are you OK?' she asked, concerned.

'Yeah. Feel a bit sick, that's all, all the adrenalin...'

'You poor thing.'

Scotty allowed himself to be comforted.

'I'm so glad you're here,' she whispered, inhaling his scent.

He took her arm. 'Do we have to stay for the whole thing?'

'Why?' Kristin asked, disappointed. 'Do you have some-place else to be?'

'Of course not!' It came out a touch sharply, before he corrected himself. 'I mean, forget it, baby; it's fine. It's just that whole act out there, it's kinda exhausting.' He consulted his reflection in a gilded drinks font. 'Do I look OK? Not too pale?'

'We're sitting in a theatre,' Kristin teased, 'in the dark. Does it matter?'

In the event Scotty fidgeted all the way through the boy-meets-girl romance to which Kristin had arranged the score: he never had possessed a long attention span. The movie starred two of Hollywood's most coveted teen actors; the pretty-faced guy was plastered across every bedroom in Young America. Maybe that was why Scotty got jittery whenever the shot lingered on the actor's face. He didn't like it when a challenger arrived on the scene.

It didn't matter. Kristin would never notice another guy while he was around.

The arrangement sounded good and she was pleased with how they had fed it into the final take. At the reception she was congratulated by a mob of industry players.

'Talk about making an entrance!' they flattered. The retelling of the helicopter story, from which he omitted the finer points of his anxiety, cheered Scotty. Kristin loved seeing him in his element, smiling and charming, her favourite boy in the world.

She was chatting with the director when Cosmo Angel, A-list action hero whose wife had taken the part of the young mom in the movie, collared her with an alligator smile.

'You really write all those songs yourself?' he leered.

'I sure did.'

Cosmo was ridiculously hot but there was also something dangerous, almost unpleasant, about him. Some women liked that, but Kristin wasn't so sure. Cosmo was of Greek descent, hairy like a wolf, with a full mouth, and thick, bristling eyebrows that met in the middle. His presence was massive, oppressive, looming. He looked as if he could hook an arm around your waist and crush you to death like a snake.

'Well—' Cosmo stepped closer and she noticed how musky and exotic he smelled, an aroma that matched his brooding looks, sort of smoky, not like Scotty, who was vanilla-clean like freshly washed laundry '—you know how I like to see young talent emerge...'

'Thank you,' she said carefully, 'I appreciate that.' She wasn't about to tell him that twenty-two years felt like longer when every waking hour as far back as she could remember was spent in preparation for How To Be a Star. Hence learning to play three instruments by the time she was eight and taking her Grade 9 piano before any of the other kids in her class had learned their times table. No wonder *The Happy Hippo Club* had snapped her up.

Scotty joined them. He and Cosmo shook hands and Kristin watched them talk, for a second feeling dislocated from everything and everyone around her, as if she were a stranger to her own life and looking in through a window. Some days she felt fortunate. Others she didn't know how she had ended up here or even if it had been her choice at all.

It was crazy, but this was her world. She had never known anything else.

Thank God for Scotty. So long as he was around she'd be just fine.

# 3

'*Baby, you know what I am; I'm a wild girl, wild girl...*'

Turquoise da Luca, undisputed queen of the US charts and in possession of the goddess-like status that meant she was known only by her first name, ground to the pulse of her latest single. They were shooting the video for 'Wild Girl' in a downtown Los Angeles warehouse, an army of hot male dancers mirroring Turquoise's every move.

'*Honey, you can't tame me, I'm a wild girl, wild girl...*'

The wind machine picked up and Turquoise's silky mane of ebony hair blew about her face, relinquishing flashes of the pale emerald eyes that had inspired her name. She could feel the energy of the troupe at her back, the force coming off each choreographed routine as the guys relied on her lead, surrendering to the next arrangement and powerless to stop the rush. Every movement was executed with the slickest measure, every twist and step in sync, and as Turquoise sang to the recorded track she counted the metre in her head like a dual heartbeat. When she fell into the final position she knew it was nailed.

'That's the one!' The director incited a celebratory round of applause and Turquoise joined in, congratulating her team. Performing was her ultimate. When she was up on-stage, in front of a camera, giving it her all, she was liberated. She was somebody else.

Shrugging on a robe, she disappeared into her dressing room. Several of the company gazed longingly after her, bathing in the residual mist of intoxicating perfume. Not only was Turquoise one of the most renowned chart-toppers in the world, she was also one of its most staggeringly gorgeous women: a vision of never-ending honey-tanned legs and a waterfall of liquid jet hair that descended to the impeccable swell of her ass. She attracted stares wherever she went. Of supermodel-height but with the curves of an exotic Amazonian princess, Turquoise wasn't just beautiful; she was astonishing. Lithe and graceful, supple as a panther, she was that rare thing: more radiant in real life than she was on film.

She'd just had time to kick off her stilettos when there was a knock at the door.

'Hey.' Her visitor rested one arm against the frame. 'I had to see you.'

It was Bronx, her principal dancer. Originally trained in ballet and tap, Bronx had a soaring frame that combined polish and poise with sheer brute strength. They had met on her first video, before she'd hit the big league, and after every encounter, even now, she berated herself. Turquoise knew she couldn't give him anything more. If Bronx found out about her, if he knew what she'd done and who she really was, he would never want to see her again.

'Aren't you gonna invite me in?'

'My schedule's off the wall,' she replied. It wasn't a lie: she had a fashion gala still to make and an industry party in New York tonight; there was a flight to catch.

Bronx was undeterred. 'I don't know about you,' he said, 'but all that sweat and grease back there left me feeling kinda hot…'

'We've talked about this,' she told him. 'It's not going to—'

Bronx kissed her, finding her tongue with his and flattening his body against hers. His dick was rock-hard. For an instant she responded, unable to resist the promise of his body.

'You're gorgeous,' he whispered, trailing his hands across her contours, from her shoulders to her breasts to the dip of her hips, 'so damn gorgeous. I can't help it, being with you all day like that and wanting you every second—'

'Don't.' Turquoise pulled away.

'When're you gonna see you and me are made for each other,' he murmured, 'that it's meant to be?' She pushed against him but he didn't stop.

'I said, *don't*!' Turquoise bit down hard, tasting blood. It had been a dumb idea to fall into bed with one of her performers, indiscreet and unprofessional and not at all what she was about. Bronx was a good man, true and noble and sincere, and those were the precise reasons why there could never be a future between them. Everything he was, she wasn't.

*Secrets*. They would be the death of her.

'Jeez!' Bronx pulled back, putting a hand to his mouth.

Pain made him angry before he checked himself. He couldn't understand it, had tried and failed and tried again and would never quit trying because he adored this woman, plain and simple. Fame and riches didn't matter. If anything, he preferred it when they forgot all about Turquoise's celebrity, just the two of them in bed, she in his arms, fast asleep, breathing gently. He loved the way her eyelashes rested on her cheeks, the softness of her skin, the bead of perspiration that gathered in her philtrum when they made love. Those nights when she would moan in her sleep, in the throes of a private torture, and would wake in the small hours and stand alone by the window, arms folded, head tilted against the wall, pale and silent and closed off in the moonlight.

Why wouldn't she let him in? What was she hiding?

'What's up with you?' he asked gently.

Turquoise was shaking. She hated how that happened, the trembling, but it did, every time she wasn't in control. 'Leave,' she managed.

'Can't we talk about this—? When can I see you?'

'I'm sorry.' She closed the door on his objections, collapsing against it and sinking to the floor, her head in her hands and the thick threat of tears in her throat.

It was minutes until the shivering subsided. Dragging herself together, Turquoise began to remove her clothes and make-up, gesturing robotically, stripping herself bare.

Why couldn't she let go? Why couldn't she move on? Bronx had never hurt her; she knew he never would. Yet every time she wasn't the instigator she felt pinioned, backed into a corner against her will, the rising panic, the gathering dread, and worst of all the dead certainty that she couldn't get away…

It was over. It was done with. Nobody had to know.

Turquoise da Luca was a superstar now. What did she have to be frightened of?

After the commotion of the shoot, the quiet of her personal space was both necessary and frightening. When she was busy, her mind didn't wander: she was Turquoise, A-list diva, shatterproof, a twenty-six-year-old woman grown out of that past. When she was by herself, she remembered. The last thing she wanted was to remember.

She steadied herself against the dresser, her knuckles white. And yet…

She saw too much of the devil responsible. Charming his fans on TV, amiably chatting in gossip columns, inciting adulation on a string of blog posts and starring in a catalogue of acclaimed movies, his pristine white grin gleaming like an infinite taunt…

*Cosmo Angel.*

Hollywood royalty. Twenty-first-century idol. *Bastard.* An actor so spectacularly handsome it seemed impossible he was made of flesh and bone.

She knew what he was made of. She knew what lay beneath.

Cosmo had ruined her. He was evil. As long as he was breathing she knew there was no escape. She could play pretend but it would always be there, prowling beneath the surface, a swamp-like creature scourging the depths, choking her, suffocating her, making her pay.

Turquoise confronted the mirror, its frame spotlit with glowing pearls, the array of war paint scattered at its base: the tools of her disguise.

She stared at her reflection for a long time, not moving,

until she began to see someone familiar looking back. A young girl, fear in her eyes, too afraid to object and too timid to speak out, beseeching, *Why didn't you save me sooner?*

*I couldn't. I didn't. And I'm sorry.*

There was a brief, sharp knock and her assistant came in, chattering about the car that had arrived for the gala. The spell was broken. Just like that, Turquoise was rescued.

*4*

A monumental cheer went up as Robin departed the couch on a weekend talk show. Since the wrap of *The Launch*, and in particular the hysterical rumours she had endured about a certain male contestant, she was frontline on every major TV channel.

'How about that—Robin Ryder, ladies and gentlemen!'

She turned at the green room and waved. The slot had gone great, the funnyman host's wisecracks matched evenly by her quick humour and steady banter. As usual she'd been asked about her unorthodox childhood, and was able by now to rely on the stock phrases settled upon by her management. At first it had been painful dredging all that up, it wasn't as if she wanted to be reminded every day, but in surrendering those facts to the public, in sharing them, the shame had lessened and the impact was gradually relinquishing its hold.

In her dressing room she changed out of the gown her stylist had picked and swopped it for a bold-print playsuit

and leggings, which she teamed with lace-up boots and a
pink bolero. A slick of lipstick and she was set. It was eleven
p.m. and the night was young. She was meeting her girlfriends at London nightspot Kiss-Kiss, and rumour had it
that supergroup LA hip-hop crew Puff City would be there.
Robin was a disciple of their work; it was brave and righteous and took no prisoners, everything she aspired to in
her own music, and their main man Slink Bullion was a legendary producer and collaborator. She wanted to sound him
out about a joint project. Her people had said they would
speak to his, but nothing could convince Robin that there
was a better way than talking face to face.

When she arrived, the club was hammering a dirty,
sexy stream of beats, and was packed with grinding bodies. Robin was taken through a concealed entrance towards
an alcove. Kiss-Kiss had been built on the relics of an old
church. From vaulted ceilings dripped bruised candelabra,
huge colour-stained windows depicted rock gods old and
new, while a glittering altar boasted a fearsome set of decks
from which bled the new religion: music.

Robin spotted Polly's beehive right away and her friends
Sammy and Belle. It had been difficult to form bonds with
people in her old life, moved as she was from place to place,
and it was only when she'd quit the system and gone it alone
that she had been able to make her own choices. That had
brought with it a whole heap of struggle but at least it had
been a struggle she'd had a say in—and through it she'd met
Sammy and Belle, people who knew her before all this took
off. Sammy had been the one who had encouraged her to
audition for *The Launch* in the first place.

'Check out the bar,' said Belle as she sat down. They

already had a rainbow of free drinks on the go and Robin helped herself. 'We're in for a treat.'

'What is it?'

'Jax Jackson and Leon Sway.'

She couldn't believe it. 'You have to be kidding me.'

The last thing she wanted was to encounter that self-righteous idiot, and enduring the attentions of Jax Jackson wasn't far behind. Jax might be an Olympian but he didn't do it for her: he was a notorious womaniser and by all accounts a chauvinist. The fact he had the Hugh Hefner bunny tattooed on his bicep along with the strapline *Come and Play* said it all, really.

'I thought those guys were sworn enemies,' Robin observed. Leon was silver to Jax's gold: the men were archrivals, on the track and off. Word was they couldn't stand each other.

'Maybe they called a truce,' suggested Sammy.

Polly scoffed. 'Gimme a break: you should see how much coverage they get in the States. It's insane. They're, like, hotter than Hollywood. For the first time Jax has got some stiff competition. Testosterone, girls: he's freaking about the guy on his tail—'

'Stiff competition? A guy on his tail?' Robin prompted the others to giggle. 'Now there's a story I'd be interested in.'

'Jax'd sooner die,' commented Belle wryly. 'Talk about macho alpha bollocks.'

The same went for Leon, evidently. Robin was filled with fury remembering his indiscretion. She tried to see through the wall of people. A cluster parted just long enough to award her a view of Leon on the periphery of the group. He was wearing a grey T-shirt beneath which she could detect the lines of his muscle, the hard strength of his stomach and the clean, swift strokes of his arms. His green eyes caught the light.

'Pretty, isn't he?' said Belle.

'If you like egotistical, tactless dickheads.'

Sammy grabbed her. 'Let's go say hello.'

'Uh-uh, no way.' Robin kicked back. It was tempting to stride over and explain to Leon exactly what she thought of him, but she refused to give him the satisfaction.

Jax Jackson came into view, making a chump of himself as a Nicki Minaj track came on and drunkenly he toasted the air. Jax was a couple of inches shorter than Leon and more hulking. Not that she was making the comparison.

'Why not?' Polly teased. 'Jax has already made it clear he's a fan...'

'He bought us a drink,' she said, recalling his come-on at the Hideaway. 'Big deal.'

'Bet you'll go over when you see who they're with.'

'Who?'

'Puff City.'

Robin baulked. 'No way.'

'Yes way. Go ahead, check it out.'

Sure enough, at the bar with Jax was the inimitable Slink Bullion. He was wearing a baggy white sweater and reams of gold jewellery. The Puff City crew skulked behind. Robin recognised Principal 7, the esteemed white rapper filling Eminem's shoes, and G-Money, who was cool in a preppy way and whose real name was Gordon or something.

Downing another shot, she stood and closed the gap between them.

'Hi.' She interrupted the exchange. Jax was momentarily

irritated by the disruption before succumbing to a smile. Annoyingly Slink was dragged off by his girlfriend.

'Hey, lady, it's you.'

'Yeah, it's me. And it's not lady, it's Robin.'

'Kinda thought you blew me off the other night, Robin.'

Jax towered over her. His frame was extraordinary, huge and light and built for speed. He was smirking in the way of a man who imagined every female to want to fall in a faint at his feet. She scouted for the rest of Puff City but they'd melted away.

'I didn't know the drinks came on condition,' Robin retaliated.

'They didn't. But here's another chance to give me your number.'

'Thanks, that's sweet.'

'We've been hearin' a lot about you.' Jax grinned. 'Seems like you're the place to be right now, a hot little hotel in paradise. I wouldn't mind a trip there myself.'

'That's disgusting.'

He held his hands up. 'Just sayin'. And you should know I don't mind a challenge. Hell, I *like* it. It don't happen often but when it does, I'm there like a bitch in heat.'

'I'm feeling better by the second.'

'Back off, Jax, she's not interested.'

Robin turned to find herself face to face with Leon Sway. The surprise of him at such close range tied her tongue in a knot. Before she could slam her brain into gear, Jax said:

'What's it t'do with you?'

'You're drunk. Step away.'

'Nah, *you* step away.' Jax pushed him. His fists on Leon's

chest elicited a *thump*, rock on rock. Leon squared up to him, spoiling for a fight.

So now he was playing the hero? If she weren't so livid she'd have laughed.

'Get used to it, man,' taunted Jax. 'You're a second-rate citizen around here.'

'Funny, I thought I almost beat you.'

'In your dreams, punk—that ain't *never* gonna happen. You hear me? *Never.*'

'You keep telling yourself that.'

'Don't need to. Facts speak for themselves.' Jax shoved him again. Leon returned it, harder. Jax lost his footing and flailed embarrassingly against the bar. Disgraced, he took a wild swing at his rival, swiping at air as Leon evaded the impact and delivered in return a clean punch on the jaw. Jax fell backwards into his assistant's arms.

The assistant stooped to gather his ward, securing Jax under the armpits. Jax staggered upright and shrugged himself free, mouth curled, jabbing a finger in Leon's direction. 'I've got your number, asshole,' he hissed, trembling with fury. 'I'm comin' for you. Know your place. The man Jackson don't forget, you got that?'

Leon looked blank. 'I'm terrified.'

'You should be.'

'Good of you to intervene,' snapped Robin when Jax had been steered away, 'but I was handling that myself.'

Leon drank from his bottle of beer. 'Thought you could use a little help, that's all.'

'I don't need your help.'

'Then should I get you a drink?'

She laughed. 'Good one.'

'What's funny?'

'What's *funny*,' she explained, 'is that your messed-up idea of a pick-up is running my name into the ground in front of the entire nation—on *prime-time TV*.'

He held his hands up. 'I'm sorry about that. Really. I was just messing.'

'Just messing?' She couldn't believe his audacity. 'D'you know how much stick I got? And out of interest, what the hell has it got to do with you who I hook up with?'

Leon grinned. 'I didn't exactly ask to walk in on you…'

Embarrassment soaked her. 'Yeah, well, try knocking next time.'

'Sorry. I know I should have left it. It's just it was kind of irresistible.' There was that maddening smile again. '*You're* kind of irresistible.'

She was momentarily thrown. 'I bet you reckon anyone can jump on, right?' she blustered. 'Well if you think I'm going anywhere *near* you, you are *seriously* mistaken.'

Leon regarded her, amused by some hidden joke, in a way that might have been sexy were he not such a categorical prick. Leon Sway had one of those textbook-perfect faces, the nose straight, the green eyes sparkling; white teeth and smooth skin, the right angle square-sharp where his jaw met his neck. Clean-looking. Way too conventional and boring for her.

'OK,' he said eventually, 'can we start again?'

'Start what again?'

'Whatever this is that's going so spectacularly wrong.'

'Let me give you a clue. This? It's nothing. It's less than nothing.'

'Hey, cut me some slack. I haven't had a lot of practice with this fame stuff.'

'Really? Aren't you meant to be Sexiest Man in the World or some such bollocks?'

As soon as Robin said it she regretted it. Leon had been awarded the title in a women's magazine. Bringing it up made her sound as if she had a schoolgirl crush, which she most definitely and emphatically *did not*.

'I'll go for "some such bollocks",' he replied. 'If you get over your problem with me.'

'I don't have a problem.'

'You do, because everything I say you're hating on. Why're you so defensive?'

'Don't presume to know anything whatsoever about me.'

'I might make less mistakes if you gave me an easier time.'

'I'm not easy.'

'I never said you were.'

'You might as well have done.'

A muscle twitched by his eye. 'Let me take you to dinner.'

'Dream on.'

'I'm not kidding. I want to make it up to you.'

Robin sighed. With his rumpled T-shirt and steady grin and boyish bravado, Leon was the kind of person she would never in a thousand years be able to relate to. He was probably from some over-achieving American family who baked cookies and sat around a campfire singing and played tennis on a private lawn in summer. He was rich, clearly, and her guess was he always had been. That upbringing, the kind of anchor she herself had always yearned for, was exactly why he was able to make her feel so small.

'Don't bother,' she threw back, moving to go.

'Look,' Leon said, less patiently, 'I'm trying, OK? I'm only being friendly here.'

'Make friends with someone else,' she said, and turned and walked away.

# 5

Kristin loved kissing her boyfriend. Scotty Valentine's lips were pink as candyfloss and just as sweet, his tongue soft and hesitant as it explored her mouth. She could spend hours simply kissing, running her fingers through his caramel hair and staring into his Pacific Ocean eyes.

They were in her bedroom, making out to a Turquoise ballad. Kristin took Scotty's hand and guided it to her breast—he never instigated it, he was too gentlemanly—and lifted to meet his touch. She peeled off her T-shirt and the lacy sweetheart bra beneath. Scotty had only seen her topless once before and looked as uncomfortable now as he had the first time.

'It's OK,' she murmured, reaching into his jeans. 'My mom's out...'

Dutifully Scotty tended to her nipples, nuzzling and licking till she started to sigh, then he dropped a chain of kisses across her stomach and in doing so reversed his crotch out of reach. She drew his head back up to hers, looping one arm round his neck and the other between his legs. Nothing. That was why, then. She inhaled his scent. It didn't matter.

'Sorry,' Scotty mumbled, sitting up. 'Don't know what's wrong.'

'It's fine,' said Kristin, covering herself because she still felt shy around him. She hoped it was fine. Last time Scotty had been unable to get a hard-on and while he assured her it had nothing to do with her and he thought she was gorgeous, it couldn't help but sting.

'Just tired,' he informed her, zipping his flies.

'We don't have to have sex,' she ventured. 'I could, you know...'

'What?'

'Help you along?' she muttered uncertainly. 'And then...?'

He looked at her as if she'd just suggested defecating on the carpet.

'I've got to go.'

'Have I done something wrong?' Awkwardly she fumbled into her T-shirt.

Scotty grimaced. 'I feel like I'm being hassled all the damn time,' he complained, 'for sex. You want it every day! I'm not a machine, Kristin.'

She was confused. 'But we haven't even got that far...'

'Don't you think maybe if I could *relax* a little more I might find it easier?'

'I'm sorry,' she stumbled. 'I thought you were relaxed.'

He pouted. 'Having my nuts attacked every waking hour isn't my idea of relaxation.'

She wondered if he found it weird, the whole ex-best-friends thing. She should try to be more sensitive. 'OK. Let's just chill, then. You don't have to leave.'

'I do,' he said dejectedly, 'I need some me time. Everyone wants a piece of Scotty Valentine, don't they? Why can't people just leave me alone?'

Kristin swallowed her dismay. It was the pressures of his work. Fraternity had been gigging flat out and Scotty was exhausted. So what if she was desperate to consummate their affair? Love was patience. Fifteen years they had known each other; what was a little longer?

'D'you know what it's like living my life?' he bewailed. 'All the expectation, it's bringing me down. How am I supposed to meet it?'

'You're not.' She touched his face, turning it towards her. He'd gone salmon-pink. Kristin understood he was ashamed and it was self-defence that made him lash out. When would he realise he didn't need to pretend with her? She worshipped him no matter what; without the band, without the ten million Twitter followers, just Scotty, the boy she adored.

Tentatively she kissed him. Slowly but surely he started to return it, leaning her back on the bed with a refreshed energy. Abruptly he flipped her round so she was on her stomach, and fiercely tugged down her knickers. For several seconds Scotty kneaded her ass, the breath catching in his throat, before, with a blinding sense of relief, Kristin felt his erection charging against her, prodding for entry. She parted to receive him, telling herself to stop because he needed to use a condom, but before she could speak she realised he was going for something different. Too tight, too sore, giving way to a splinter of disabling pain. She gasped in shock.

'Wait,' she breathed, attempting to pull free and turn on her back. It was a tricky manoeuvre but with some fumbling she managed to hook her legs round his waist and guide him in…but the throb in his jeans had totally evaporated. Totally. Scotty collapsed on to her, deflated, and she stared at the ceiling, eyes wet with tears, tracing circles on his back.

'I'll call you later,' he mumbled eventually, getting up and grabbing his things. Bewildered, Kristin hugged her knees to her chest.

'Scott,' she tried, 'we can talk about this…'

But he was gone before she could say goodbye.

At lunch, unable to ease her mind, Kristin took a swim in the mansion pool. Was it such a big deal? she wondered as she ploughed through her twentieth length. Scotty wanted to give it to her another way. That way had got him hard. Plenty of girls did it. Just because she hadn't, it didn't make it wrong. If that was Scotty's thing then perhaps she should give it a go…

Lemon sun bounced off the patio, hot and sweet, blazing down from a flawless blue sky and reflecting off the glinting rock lagoon and sharp green lawns. When Kristin had started raking in the big bucks, her mother Ramona had wasted no time in securing them a prime piece of real estate. The imposing mansion (referred to as The White House) was enormous, comprising fifteen bedrooms, twelve of which were never used, a rooftop gym and home movie theatre. Out front, Corinthian pillars bragged the remarkable entrance. Inside, photographs of Ramona as a young fashion model adorned the walls.

Kristin was desperate to move out. She wanted to live with Scotty, like a proper couple, and get engaged and get married and have kids. But she had made a promise to herself that she would stay until her little sister turned sixteen. United, she and Bunny were an allied force against their mother. Bunny couldn't do it on her own; she needed her: without Kristin she would get extinguished like a beetle beneath Ramona's Louboutin.

The main door slammed, followed by a flutter of animated chatter. Kristin dried herself off, wrapped a towel around her waist and crossed to the house.

Bunny was galloping out to meet her, dressed head to toe in sequins and a wig better suited to a forty-year-old transvestite. At thirteen she wore full make-up, her nails painted and her eyelashes huge, and was struggling to balance on the four-inch stilettos that were preferred by the pageant organisers. She was small for her age: apparently her petite stature was a hit with the judges. Bunny White was a teen beauty queen, the best known in the state.

'We won!' she squealed. 'I did my hula dance and then I had to catwalk and *then* they asked me what I wanted to be when I grew up! I said a singer, like you. Then they asked me who I loved best in the world and I told them Joey from Fraternity because *all* the girls said Scotty and I wanted to be different, and I couldn't say him because he's your boyfriend.'

'Hey, slow down!' Kristin embraced her. 'That's amazing, I'm so proud.'

'It was me and Tracy-Ann in the final,' Bunny rattled on. She smelled of perfume and the drench of hairspray clamping her style into place, and her skin was clammy with Bronze Baby fake bake. 'Mom thought it was over when my wig fell off and I cried but she made me go back on and then Tracy-Ann fell over and that's when Mom said she knew we'd won!'

On cue Ramona White emerged from the mansion, consummate mother and manager, stepping into the sunlight in her sharply tailored suit and enormous Prada shades. Her silhouette was twig-thin and her hair was pulled back in a savagely tight chignon.

'Congratulations,' said Kristin flatly.

'Shouldn't you be writing?'

'Day off.'

'Is Scotty here?'

Bunny suffered a chronic blush and Kristin stifled a laugh. She found her sister's infatuation funny. Scotty had been part of the family for years. Ever since *The Happy Hippo Club* days he'd come round for dinner when Ramona was out, making the sisters laugh over pasta with his goofy impressions, or ride his bike over on a Sunday to watch TV and eat popcorn, or bake cookies with Bunny at Thanksgiving, or pumpkin pie at Halloween. When he'd become Kristin's boyfriend her sister had nearly fainted.

'He left.'

'Why?' Ramona enquired. 'Did you fight?'

'No.'

'You've got to keep a man happy, Kristin. Otherwise they'll walk.'

*Like Dad did?*

'Bunny, get upstairs,' their mother directed, 'and start scrubbing that make-up off.'

'Can't I wear it a bit longer?'

Ramona slid her daughter a look. Bunny retreated without another word.

'She gets to take a break now, right?' Kristin asked.

Her mother lit a cigarette, scissoring her way to a lounger, where she elegantly collapsed, drawing sharply on it. 'Do you think *I* get a break?' she retorted. Ramona's cat Betsy, a white fluffball with one of those squidged-up expressions that looks like it's been hit in the face by a sledgehammer, leapt on to her mistress's lap and licked its lips.

'HAIRS!' Ramona cried, outraged. Immediately the cat was tossed to the ground. 'Betsy needs a trip to the beautician; this moulting's going to be the death of me!'

'Bunny's a kid,' Kristin persisted, as the white fluffball shot through the patio doors.

'And so were you when you started on your journey.'

Kristin disliked how Ramona made out as if it were *her* journey, as if Kristin hadn't had it shoved on her as the only way of life available. Some days she grudgingly admired her mother's resolve: yes, they'd come from little, and now, thanks to her child star exploding, had more wealth than they knew what to do with. Most, she hated how she had never been allowed to grow into her own person before being told who she was expected to be. Their mother's ambition was ruthless. She would stop at nothing to see her two girls succeed.

'This is good for Bunny,' pronounced Ramona in her don't-you-dare-argue-with-me tone. 'It's character building. She's got to get used to the pace.'

'What if she doesn't want to?'

The shades came down a fraction. A pair of glinting grey eyes narrowed over the top.

'Why wouldn't she?'

'I don't know. She might want to try something else? Being a teacher, say, or a vet?'

Ramona snorted, as though those professions were so far beneath her that she could scarcely deign to look; professions that actually *mattered*, because while Kristin's music was enjoyed by many it didn't contribute to the world, not in any practical way.

'What my daughter *wants* is to be famous.' Ramona slipped the shades back into place. 'You heard her. She *wants* to be exactly like you.'

'Wrong. That's what you want.'

'You're giving me a migraine, Kristin. Haven't you got an album to write?'

She didn't need to be told twice. Storming indoors, Kristin struggled to control her temper. No one made her angry like her mom did.

She flipped open her cell. She longed to call Scotty; he'd make her feel better. But something told her no. After today, if Scotty needed space then that was what she would give him. She would give him anything, because without him she was lost.

Bunny White's bedroom walls were plastered with posters of Fraternity.

Her infatuation covered every scrap. Fraternity pouting sincerely to camera; Fraternity leaping into the air, their matching grins sparkling like islands in the sun; Fraternity with their arms slung round each other's shoulders; Fraternity in black and white with their tops off. Like every girl Bunny's age the five-piece was the apex of teenage idolatry. They were cute, they were funny; they sang about love and cuddling and kittens and birthdays. Bunny adored them with every ounce of devotion her little heart could carry.

Scotty Valentine was her favourite. She could never tell Kristin how much it stung when she saw them together, and though she had tried not to care—really she had—she just couldn't help it. Naively she had imagined that Scotty would one day turn into *her* boyfriend. He might have started out like a big brother but over the years her hazy worship had blossomed into a killer crush that was picking her apart day by day. Age gaps didn't matter so much the older you got, and in a few years he might have started seeing her in a new way.

All her life Scotty had been there, perpetually out of reach, exotic and elusive, the boy against which all others were measured and could never hope to compare.

She pretended that Joey was her number one. Joey was the cute, mischievous member of the group, and she *would* say yes if Joey asked her on a date, like, obviously she would. But Scotty, with his perfect smile and dreamy eyes, was her ultimate. When she was alone she fantasised about Kristin being out when he came to the mansion, like he had in the olden days, and how they might hang like they'd used to, and he would remember what a cool girl she was and how grown-up she was now and then maybe when he left he'd lean in and…

Bunny had never kissed a boy before. The very thought of touching Scotty was enough to drive her crazy with cloudy, indistinct longing. It made her blood race and her head feel like it was about to explode. Would she ever experience it for herself?

She settled at her Pretty Princess table and began removing the grips that held her wig in place. Her mom had secured them viciously, jamming each one into her hairline till it made her scalp throb. Before long, if she kept on winning trophies, she would be just as rich and pretty as her sister and boys like Scotty would start to notice.

Her best picture of Scotty was a close-up headshot. It wasn't very big and she kept it in her coral beauty drawer, right at the back where no one would see it. Bunny reached in now and extracted it, tracing her finger around his jaw and pressing the image to her face so she could kiss it. Scotty smiled back at her, a glint of promise in his twinkling blue eyes. He was at the beach in the photo and you could tell he was shirtless, even though it was severed at the neck. His collarbone was deeply tanned with the lightest smattering of freckles.

Bunny kissed the image one more time before replacing it. She could hear her mom and sister arguing downstairs and wished Scotty would come and take her away. Humming Fraternity's number one smash 'I Dig U', she imagined him scooping her up in his strong arms and driving her off into the sunset. Maybe he'd come on a horse and where they would end up or what they would do she wasn't entirely sure. All she knew was that she wanted Scotty Valentine. She wanted him so badly it hurt.

Soon she'd be vying for the coveted title of Mini Miss Marvellous. It was an international competition for which she and her mom had been preparing for months. Ramona promised it would be her launch, and the battle that propelled her to stardom.

Then, she'd be a woman. Fraternity—and Scotty, always Scotty, despite everything that told her it was impossible—would finally be within reach.

# 6

Turquoise da Luca had been to every major city on the globe, but New York remained her favourite. It made her feel plugged in and part of something crucial, an integral cog in a great and glorious machine. The party she had attended on Friday provided the perfect excuse to hang for a few days and tonight she was catching up with A-list actress Ava Bennett. The women had met at a film premiere two years ago and had swiftly become friends.

'You look gorgeous,' Ava told her as they were seated for dinner, tossing her sheet of shimmering platinum hair. Turquoise had chosen her usual spot in Giovanni's, a cosy, family-run Italian on Waverly Place. 'Who're you fucking?'

Turquoise nearly spluttered out her martini. 'Excuse me?'

'That glow,' Ava said, mercifully stalled while a deferential waiter came to take their order. Once he'd gone she elaborated, 'It's written all over your face. Who is he?'

'There *is* no he,' Turquoise lied, deciding that Bronx

didn't count. There was no relationship on the cards so why waste time talking about it?

'You're lying,' observed Ava slyly, but Turquoise knew her friend wasn't any the wiser. She was a good liar. The best.

'Tell you what—' Turquoise raised her glass and they clinked '—let's talk about you.' She loved hearing about Ava's job and, no matter how famous she herself became, she would always attach a certain enchantment to the movies. 'How's work?'

'Ah, you know.' Ava waved a bejewelled hand. 'Promotion for *Lovestruck*'s going through the roof.' Ava was playing the young mother in a new teen romance. Songstress sweetheart Kristin White had penned the music and it was causing quite a stir. 'Cosmo's been insufferable about this script he's writing, mind you. He's being ever so secretive.'

Turquoise's heart pounced. It was easy to forget that Ava was married to her nemesis.

When her friend and Cosmo Angel had first got together Turquoise had tried to cut contact, feigning illness whenever Ava wanted to meet or claiming her diary was against it. But Ava was a loyal companion and hadn't given up, and short of explaining why she had embarked on the avoidance campaign there wasn't a great deal she could do. It meant that on occasion she was forced to see Cosmo, to shake his hand and exchange empty pleasantries as though they were strangers. Never would she risk going closer. Never would she visit Ava's house. Never would she spend any more time with the man than was absolutely necessary.

'He's writing a script?' Turquoise ventured, relieved when

their appetisers came and hoping that might change the subject. Her throat had closed. She couldn't eat.

'It's a break from acting. He wants to give something back. You know, get creative.'

*He sure knows how to do that.*

'What's it about?' The words were like glue on her tongue. Even as she asked she had the horrible sensation of already knowing the answer.

'This is the thing,' Ava exclaimed through a mouthful of basil gnocchi, 'he refuses to say! It's centred around a murder; that's all he'll give me.'

'What kind of murder?' Her voice was tiny.

'Beats me.' She laughed. 'Ask him yourself.'

Turquoise averted her gaze. She scrambled for something to say. It was horrible deceiving Ava, they were close, but she had vowed to take the truth to her grave…the truth of what she'd done and where she'd come from…the truth of what happened.

Secrets she couldn't tell a soul.

*Especially when Ava was Cosmo's wife.*

Fortunately Ava changed tack for her. 'You seen this?' she asked, producing a paper from her purse and tapping its front page. On it was an image of Jax Jackson pumping iron.

The article was about the athlete landing yet another brand affiliation. Its headline read: JAX 'THE BULLET' JACKSON FIRES A WINNER.

'Two words for you, honey,' said Ava. *'Hot. As.'*

Turquoise disagreed. 'I hung with him once. He's not all that.'

'Really? Where?'

She batted off the question. 'I can't remember.'

'Well, *I'm* sure getting an introduction. See if that drags Cosmo out his office!'

'Jax is a fool.'

'Imagine it, though.' Ava leaned in, a wicked smile on her face. 'He's got to be an animal between the sheets, hasn't he?'

'Hmm.'

'Not that I'm complaining. Cosmo's a tiger.'

Turquoise excused herself to visit the bathroom. She almost tripped in her haste to reach it and only when she was alone could she steady her breathing and get a grip of the thumping in her chest. She closed her eyes, stars bursting in her vision, images from the past rushing back though she tried with all her might to stifle them.

*Cosmo can't hurt you now. You have to get a hold on this; otherwise it'll kill you.*

Maybe that was what she deserved. She deserved to die and if it weren't by electric chair then it would be by her own conscience.

*He made me. It wasn't my fault.*

Or was it? She had been seventeen, old enough to know her own mind.

*Stop. STOP!* She put her face in her hands, pressing her temples till they ached.

What if it came out? What if the facts escaped? Every hour of every day she lived in terror of that revelation and what it would mean. Armageddon: the end of her world.

*It won't. Cosmo has his own reputation to protect. He's the only one who knows...*

Turquoise drew air in and out, in and out, slowly, till her

pulse regained its rhythm. Gradually light seeped through and her goals readjusted. The first was to get through dinner.

Cosmo Angel had known her a lifetime ago. He had known her when she was a girl, vulnerable, weak. When she was someone capable of...

He didn't know her now.

She made her way back through the restaurant and greeted Ava with a smile.

*Grace Turquoise da Luca was born in Hawaii in 1986, the only child of religious parents. When she was a baby her father took her mother for a drive in the country and they never came back. The car was found battered and burned at the foot of a ravine and despite efforts to ascertain the truth of what happened, no definitive clues were found. Some said her father had been cursed by debt and had decided to end it; others that it was an act of God for having birthed Grace two months before they were married.*

*Grace had no memory of them throughout her childhood, save for photographs and scraps people told her. Her mother had been a striking woman, very dark, and her father 'a stubborn man'. That was all she knew. Her parents were strangers.*

*After their deaths she stayed with a village woman, a friend called Emaline, because it was believed further disruption would damage her beyond repair. There she passed a safe, happy few years; she went to school, she made friends and she listened to the records piled high at home. Wonderful old-world singers like Billie Holiday, Ella and Etta, as well as Emaline's own voice as she sang softly with a guitar on the veranda, sipping lime cordial.*

*For her eighth birthday Emaline gave her a guitar of her own. From an early age Grace Turquoise knew that music would be her life-long obsession.*

*On rainy nights they would sit side by side on the couch, the fire burning, a woollen rug across their knees and Emaline's arms safe and warm as she pulled the child close to kiss the top of her head. They would watch black-and-white movies together, get lost in worlds of romance and betrayal, lovers and wars, glamour and fantasy. Emaline would whisper stories about when she was a girl, and how one summer she had run away from home and spent long hot weeks acting for a theatre until her father had found her and brought her home. Grace's imagination had been filled with the glittering characters Emaline had played, the handsome leading men she had known, and how Emaline had dreamed of some day becoming a Hollywood actress. 'Do you know what I believe?' Emaline whispered into Grace's hair one sunset. 'I believe that's going to be you one day. My little star.'*

*Soon after her eighth birthday Grace was sent to live with her uncle on a farm in Pennsylvania. Ivan Garrick hadn't seen her mother in years but it turned out he was her only living relative. Grace didn't want to go. She didn't want to leave her friends or Emaline. She didn't want to live with someone she had never met. But that was the law and she could do nothing to dispute it. When she turned up on Ivan's doorstep she was frightened.*

*But Ivan was a kind man. He was fifty or thereabouts and admitted to having had a dispute with her mother, after which he had been cut out of her life. He had always longed to meet Grace and had petitioned long and hard for her cus-*

*tody. Like her he had no surviving family and so they had to
stick together, he said. Blood was blood, he promised. Lots
of things happened in life but that could never be changed.*

*If her parents had been devout then Ivan was in another
league. Every day he spent hours at church, talking with
the pastor and praying for his sins. Grace couldn't understand. Ivan was a gentle, lonely man and she couldn't imagine him sinning any more than she could Emaline refusing
her a kind word. Bad people existed but Ivan wasn't bad.*

*A short time later, they received word that Emaline had
passed. Grace travelled alone to her funeral and cried as
she had never cried before. Ivan organised her return ticket
and was waiting at the station to meet her when she arrived.
'You're home now,' he said.*

*Sometimes Ivan disappeared at night. She would wake
to find the big house empty and pad through its dark chambers, calling his name. The next morning he'd stay asleep
until the afternoon, and would emerge looking tired and
haunted. Those days he prayed the most.*

*Grace settled into her new life and concentrated on her
music. At ten years old she learned to read compositions; at
twelve she was strumming on the guitar Emaline had given
her and at fourteen she realised she had a voice to go with
it. Ivan would ask her to sing and would sit and watch her,
telling her how beautiful she sounded and what a lovely
young woman she was becoming. Grace liked it when he
said that. Not a girl any more but a woman. It made her feel
grown-up, ready to embrace the exciting life ahead of her.*

*Soon after, she became a grown-up for real. Playing out-
side one day, she felt wetness in her skirt and when she went
to the bathroom she found blood. Her first thought was that*

*a monster had crawled inside her; the monsters Ivan talked about that he promised the Lord would protect them from. She shook in his arms, and Ivan had to explain as best he could that this wasn't a disease but a natural progression— one he had, in fact, been counting on.*

We've been waiting, *he told her.* Fear nothing, my angel. You've arrived.

*It was six months before his meaning became clear. The last six months of innocence.*

*It happened on a Tuesday night. She would always remember the moon, crisp and white like a marble in the sky. Ivan crept to her bedroom and told her to come outside, there was something she needed to see; it was a present he'd bought for her. He was sweating and his fingers trembled, waxy in the dark, but she'd thought it was the puppy she'd longed for and so in her nightgown had descended the stairs and pushed open the door to the yard.*

*Outside was a circle of people, dressed in black robes and hoods that covered their faces. They were chanting. At the centre a fire sparked and burned, hot and red and orange, an angry fire that told her this was wrong. Something was wrong. They wanted to hurt her.*

No, *she wept,* I don't want to.

I don't want to. *It became her mantra for the years ahead. But nobody listened.*

*And they didn't listen then. Grace struggled to break free but they pinned her down, tying her wrists above her head and looming like giants, the chant building and gathering pace, becoming frenzied and wild. Through the vestments she recognised the pastor's eyes, flashing grey and watery with lust as he knelt between her legs...*

*Her agony shattered the night.*

*The next day, she ran. In a sense the ordeal was the anaesthetic she needed. All Grace could focus on was escape, numb to everything but the terror she had endured and the lone goal of freedom. Ivan was sloppy, a careless, cowardly man. He'd underestimated her spirit. She packed a small bag and left the next afternoon, walking the road out of town, walking and walking until she didn't care any more if her legs gave in and she lay down and died. She thought of Emaline. It made her cry but it also made her strong. Emaline's voice told her to keep going and not to give up. Songs she loved played in her head, all the women she'd grown up with walking alongside her, holding her upright and pushing her on.*

*Some time before dawn a car picked her up. 'Hey, baby, you wanna ride?'*

*The guy in the driver's seat was young. He had a nice smile.*

*Grace Turquoise pulled open the door. Sleep rushed at her like a tidal wave and she embraced it, secure in the knowledge that now she was saved. Now it was over.*

*But she was wrong. It was only just beginning.*

# 7

Robin was wired when she came offstage. She had performed her breakout single 'Lesson Learned' at the annual Palace Variety to rapturous reception.

'They're loving you, babe,' encouraged her manager Barney when she stepped into the wings. 'Twitter's going off the wall.'

'One more time for *Robin Ryder*!' The host's voice boomed through the studio.

'Wanna go out?' Robin headed to her dressing room, Barney in close pursuit. 'I've got an invite to Level 7, the new place off Poland Street. It's worth checking out.'

'Are we celebrating?'

'We're always celebrating.'

'We will be when you hear who I've been talking to.'

She turned. 'Who?'

'I've just taken a call from Arcadia,' announced Barney triumphantly. Arcadia was Puff City's management. 'They're interested in a partnership, Robin. Slink Bullion likes what he sees. Your profile's rocketed and they want a piece of it.'

She was elated. 'That's the best news I've had all week. Get us a meeting?'

'You bet I will.'

Robin pushed open the door with her name on it. The first thing she noticed was the enormous bouquet of peonies and roses on her make-up table, wrapped in brown paper and tied with a purple ribbon. There was a card sticking out of the top.

'What's this?'

'They got delivered to the office,' said Barney. 'I had a runner bring them down.'

'Why?'

'Some kid dropped them by. He said to make sure you received them, or the guy he worked for wouldn't be happy.'

She turned the card over. It read:

*But I want to be friends with you*

Robin frowned. She pretended not to know who it was, but she knew straight away.

'Who're they from?' asked Barney.

'I have no idea. There's no name.'

The last words she'd thrown Leon's way. *Make friends with someone else.*

'It's a fan,' she said dismissively. 'And I'd rather this stuff got filtered.'

She had decided not to tell Barney about the creepy stuff she'd been receiving in the mail recently. Last week a weirdo scrapbook had arrived filled with cutouts of her image and

inscribed with the note: *I'm closer than you think*. Before
that a ream of paper, in which her name was reproduced
over and over, line after line, page after page, like something from *The Shining*. She thought the handwriting was
the same on both but couldn't be certain.

It was freaky but there was no point mentioning it. Some
fans were nuts; it went with the territory. She could take
care of herself.

'I thought you preferred to see everything?' said Barney.

'Not any more.'

Seizing Leon's bouquet, she crossed to the wastebasket
and dropped it in.

Barney was shocked. 'Can't you take them home? They're
hardly offensive. You never know, they might brighten up
the place…'

Robin tried to imagine the arrangement in her flat. It
didn't work for a second. Her first-floor space in Camden
was minimalist to the extreme, the walls blank, the bed un-
made and the cupboards empty. All she had in the fridge
was a half-drunk litre of Coke and some leftover Chinese
noodles. A single coffee cup rattled round the kitchen.

'I don't like flowers,' she said. 'They're sickly.'

'I think they're pretty.'

'You would. And anyway, I don't want a stranger's shit
in my space.' Especially when she didn't have her *own* shit
in her space. Other people's houses were stamped with their
history, mementoes of a time gone by, but Robin's displayed
evidence of nothing but the necessities of here and now. It
came from a life of being constantly uprooted, spat in and
out of the system like an unwanted toy—and Robin *had*
been unwanted, she was unwanted by definition. Why else

would she have been given up? Her own mother hadn't wanted her.

At four days old Robin had been left in a bin in an East London park, wrapped up in a plastic bag. She hadn't been Robin Ryder then, she'd had another name, one the hospital had given her, but they had never found the woman responsible and Robin had long ago given up on dreams of reunions and forgotten sisters and brothers, replacing that need with the iron resolve that she would never rely on anybody ever again. When things got tough, people abandoned you. It was a fact of life. The only person you could trust was yourself.

So she didn't need Leon Sway or his stupid dumb flowers.

'Let's go,' said Robin, pulling on her jacket. 'First round's on me.'

*'Encore, encore, oui, oui, oui!'* The girl arched her back, craving his touch with animal reflex. She had never had a lover like Leon Sway. *'Vous êtes magnifique!'*

Leon hardened for what time he'd lost count, pulling the girl on top of him and kissing her fiercely. Their tongues entwined, hungry for more.

She gasped as he filled her. Strapping his powerful hands to her waist, the girl rocked back and forth, marvelling at Leon's physique, the immaculate, glorious body of a world-class player. Every tendon and sinew was a model of perfection, the summit of strength and beauty; a machine shaped and honed for the sole purpose of winning. Her palms were spread across his pecs, dwarfed by the canvas of his chest, as she moved to his rhythm, quickening and quickening as their hips locked and Leon pulled the hair from her face as she sweated and pulsed on top of him, loving the muscle and the tenderness and how one was indistinguishable from the other, until, in a crescendo, they both reached their pinnacle.

At twenty-four, Leon was one of the greatest American athletes of all time.

Without contest he was the greatest lover.

'That was amazing,' she moaned, her accent thick. She collapsed on to him. Leon held her, trailing his fingertips down her arm and listening as her breathing slowed to sleep. It had been too long in the run up to competition. All that effort and fury, all the passion and drive, had nowhere to go once the finish was crossed. Desire, the simmering volcano Leon had held at bay through months of training, of replacing his urges with the promise of victory and the unwavering commitment that required, fired his run from the splinter of the starting pistol. But now it was over? Another person's skin; their warmth: the softness of a woman.

He closed his eyes, trying to picture anything else but what he always did:

Another man's tread crashing over the line before his.

As the sun swam into the darkened room, Leon rolled over and checked his watch. Eight-thirty. He needed to be at the airport. He had been putting off returning home, knew he had his reasons but that didn't make it right. Somehow there was always a TV appearance to be filmed, a gala to be attended, a photo shoot to make... Each day brought with it a fresh deluge of offers: luxury watch brands pursued him as the face of their sports range; global drinks manufacturers were desperate to secure his allegiance; designer labels coveted him to front their new campaign. Just yesterday he had been stripping off in a Paris studio, replacing a soccer legend as the face of an underwear giant. His almost naked pose, a vision in black-and-white of rippling torso and bulging crotch, had been blown up to the size of an airbus and would already be winging its way across the Atlantic for its debut in Times Square.

Quietly Leon extracted himself from the bed sheets and parted the blinds. The French capital was spread before him, the glossy River Seine and the glinting Eiffel Tower, in the bronzed early morning like a jewel city. Imposed against its skyline was his own reflection: dark hair, almond skin, green eyes that had stared down a legion of opponents... except one.

The tyrant he couldn't defeat, the rival he hated: Jax 'The Bullet' Jackson.

Swiftly Leon showered and dressed. As far as he was concerned, Rio couldn't come around soon enough. Bring on the competition—because next time, he would win.

He packed his belongings, checking his phone for a missed call or a voicemail. Nothing. Robin would have received the flowers by now: he had put his digits on the back of the card and wondered if she'd make the move. Leon couldn't get her out of his head, ever since they'd met— since before they had met, if he were truthful, because he'd noticed her in the press, admired her from afar, and when he'd been offered the spot on *The Launch* he had taken it partly as a way to meet her. He could never have guessed that their first encounter would be quite so memorable.

Robin wasn't his usual type, if he had one, but then she wasn't his usual anything because she wasn't at all...usual. He kept replaying that initial face-to-face (though he could think of other ways to describe it); the VIP room he'd been told was empty, the glimpse of Robin's smooth back, the delicate, bare shoulder, and the curve of her waist beneath the hastily pulled-on shirt. She thought he'd seen more but he hadn't—honestly he had been as embarrassed as she, and had tried to make light of it but instead it had backfired. How Leon wished he could go back to that night and play it differently. Robin was sexy and feisty and rude and wilful and she fascinated him. Was it the attitude that came off so brutal, yet in a dropped gaze betrayed her fragility? Was it the big fringe, beneath which shone those huge, careful eyes? Was it the way he had seen her laughing with her friends before she'd come over in the club, a generous smile that he suspected she saved for people she loved? He had to see her again. They had to start over.

'Hey.' Leon woke the girl, brushing her hairline with his thumb. 'I gotta split.'

She smiled. 'Is it too much to ask for a second date?'

'Never say never.'

'Last night was *incroyable*. So was this morning.'

He kissed her.

She tried to pull him back but he resisted. There were things he had to get home to; people who needed him. He made for the door.

*This is a long game*, his coach always said. *Never lose focus.*

Leon didn't intend to. It was time.

Los Angeles: back to the streets where he grew up. Back to where it began.

# 8

Kristin flew with Fraternity to Tokyo. The boys were running a PR tour for their new album and that meant she and Scotty were being separated for long periods of time. She liked to come along where she could, and luckily the trip fell on an opening in her schedule.

Asian fans were like none other in the world. She knew this from her own forays into the East, but that was nothing compared with the frenzy that the boys incited. The instant they exited the jet a crush of groupies descended, brandishing their camera phones and howling their exaltations. A vast number were wearing Fraternity baseball caps, a different colour for each band member. There was red for Joey, the cute one; green for Doug, the indie one; purple for Luke, the one who could play guitar; yellow for Brett, the one with the best six-pack…and blue for blue-eyed Scotty. Most of the caps were blue.

As the band was ushered through Arrivals, Kristin saw this was only the start of the Fraternity merchandise. Scotty

Valentine bum bags adorned the crowd. Scotty dolls were waved manically in the air. Scotty key rings hung from Scotty wallets as the writhing masses clamoured for autographs with Scotty pens. Faces were painted with love hearts accompanied by Scotty's name. T-shirts with the band splashed across them were worn by every schoolgirl, some lifted and tied in a knot to show off a smooth pale belly, the navel pierced. There was enough Fraternity merchandise in Narita Airport alone to sink a tanker.

They were performing at the Tokyo Dome. Kristin was in the VIP section and looked on as the boys opened with 'I Dig U', sending the fans into paroxysms, especially when Scotty came forward to kneel to the crowd and croon the bridge: *'Girl, I've been waiting my whole life to find you, now let me put my arms around you and hold you tight, oh, baby, right through the night...'* The fans were screaming so much that Kristin was surprised they could hear the music over the top. But the show was slickly rehearsed and she was impressed at the boys' flawless dance moves and ability to harmonise while their heart rate had to be spinning through the roof. Towards the finale Brett and Doug took their tops off. This was impromptu and drove the arena wild, with one girl falling into a seizure and having to be lifted over the barriers to safety. Teenagers clasped each other, wailing and snotting and crying, reaching out desperately to touch their heroes. When the rest of the guys followed suit, Scotty included, revealing their chiselled pecs and golden tans (she suspected at least three of them waxed—Scotty did, at least), Kristin thought the crowd might evaporate in a puff of smoke. Fortunately the encore was forthcoming and minutes later they were whisked offstage.

'Superstars, every last one of you!'

The man who had put Fraternity together was waiting with congratulations. Fenton Fear, the fabled label owner and moneymaker, had been responsible for a glut of staggeringly successful pop groups over the last twenty years, each one manufactured by his own fair hand. Tagged 'King of the Charts' for his seemingly failsafe formula for securing a hit, with Fraternity he had hit on his biggest jackpot yet.

Fenton embraced all his boys heartily and graciously kissed Kristin hello. At forty-something he was a good-looking older man with a thick head of sandy hair and a moustache that tickled Kristin's cheek. She had always liked Fenton; he was a rock-solid businessman with a kind, receptive ear to his clients' wants and needs. Moreover he seemed to genuinely care about the boys, especially Scotty, so they already had that in common.

'I need a shag after that,' pronounced Luke. 'Someone sort me out?'

'No such luck,' answered Fenton disapprovingly. 'Press conference downtown in half an hour, get showered and get going.'

'Serious?' There was a smatter of grumbling as the boys wiped their torsos down with a towel. Kristin went to cuddle Scotty and he gave her a brief, limp hug.

'When aren't I?' challenged Fenton. 'Let's rock it.'

'I might head back to the hotel…' said Kristin, squeezing Scotty's hand as the rest of the group trailed after Fenton. She waited for him to object.

'Sure,' said Scotty non-committedly, already chasing in their wake. 'Later.'

Kristin took a car to the Mandarin Oriental. She felt

uneasy about Scotty's behaviour. Ever since that day he'd tried to have sex with her back in LA. Was he embarrassed? Had he gone off her? But he had to still be interested if he wanted to do *that*...didn't he?

On the drive she received a message from Bunny. Her heart lifted. She'd been loath to leave her sister with Ramona—their mother's pageant obsession was spiralling out of control—but had promised Bunny that when she and Scotty were back they'd take her out, anywhere she liked, to do things that normal thirteen-year-old girls did: not tottering about in high heels while a sweaty middle-aged man appraised her chest-to-leg ratio.

Can't wait 4u to come home ☹ Scotty OK?

She tapped back:

Guys fine. Big sell-out gig, you'd have loved.
Won't be long now. C u soon ☺ xx

Bunny was forever asking after Scotty. Kristin liked that her two favourite people got on so well. She remembered her own enchantments at thirteen—being so young you could never hope to disguise how you felt, no matter how many blushes you thought you hid.

Even so, Scotty had been alarmed when they had gone into Bunny's room one day and he'd seen the pictures of him strewn from wall to wall. Kristin had been searching for a bracelet her sister had borrowed and he had followed her in.

'What the fuck is this?' he'd demanded, disturbed. 'A fucking shrine or something?' Scotty had never used to be so easily riled, or used such bad language. Since they'd got together he'd become so…ratty.

Kristin had found what she'd come looking for. 'She's only a kid, Scott,' she'd told him, closing the door softly behind her. On it was a sign that read STRICTLY NO ENTRY!

'Don't you think it's messed up?'

'Not really. She's one of about a trillion so you'd better get used to it.'

He'd shuddered. 'Girls are weird.'

Kristin remembered his words as they pulled up outside the hotel. A doorman helped her with her bags and within minutes she was safely ensconced in her suite, where she ran hot water and salts into a roll-top bath. Sitting on its edge and guiding her hand through the steaming, fragrant water, she decided to try not to think about Scotty. Just for tonight.

When Scotty Valentine was a boy, he had never imagined he would be waking up at twenty-two with a multi-million-selling album to his name and more wealth and fame than he'd thought possible. Spending his formative years in *The Happy Hippo Club* had groomed him for a life of entertainment, but he couldn't have expected anything remotely on this scale.

On his sixteenth birthday the record execs had come knocking. Kristin had already been signed to her label, so had a couple of the other guys, and the pressure was on to get selected. Producer Fenton Fear had been among them, casting through the assembled boys like an emperor through his minions. He had been assembling a band, already had four in the bag…but who would be his missing link? Scotty had auditioned on the spot, posing for a variety of modelling shots, in one of which he'd had to pout in a too-big tuxedo and clutch a bad-tempered rabbit that kept nipping his fingers. 'Can you sing?' Fenton had asked, with an expression that implied it didn't matter if he could or not. But Scotty had surprised everyone: he possessed a rich if inconsistent tone that could be worked upon, and that same tone would soon overtake the other band members and cement his place as lead vocalist in Fraternity.

In a matter of hours Scotty had been settled on: the sublime addition that completed Fenton's picture. 'You're it,' Fenton had said, as Scotty basked in the sunshine of his praise, enjoying the lunches Fenton took him on to discuss their world domination plan, the lavish spa treatments whenever Scotty needed some down-time, the city breaks Fenton paid for when a change of scene was in order. 'You're the most perfect creature I've ever seen.'

Now, at a press conference at the Tokyo Grand Hyatt, only half listening as Luke took the first of the questions, Scotty felt insanely insecure. He craved those early days when he had been the apple of Fenton's eye. Fenton had barely glanced at him all afternoon. On the flight from LA he had chatted with the others, ignoring him, and had barely caught him for a word even after the explosive success of their show. What had changed?

He knew what. It was that Kristin had insisted on tagging along. Scotty had told her no but she'd gone on and on, and in the end he had been forced to capitulate. How could he not? There was no way he could arouse suspicion, especially after the other week's disastrous sexual episode. The fact was he didn't *want* to make love with Kristin. He'd *never* wanted to make love with her. When he saw her body, he was cold—and she knew it. There was only so long he could stall the process before she started asking the questions that mattered.

Fenton needed time together; Scotty got that. He needed it, too. Tokyo had been the perfect opportunity to release their urges, and then Kristin had ruined it all.

'Would you say that success has strengthened your friendships or challenged them?' A journalist stood to deliver the question, holding out her Dictaphone.

'Aw, we're all buddies!' Doug enthused. 'It's another family, we're just like brothers, so, yeah, some days we fall out, but nothing serious…' He jostled with the others. Scotty made a good fist of joining in but it took every ounce of will he had.

It was such a mess. The label was to blame, deciding that Scotty and Kristin would make the perfect couple, and who cared if Scotty actually wanted to or not? Kristin was like his sister, he felt nothing sexual for her whatsoever, and, while they had shared history and of course he was *fond* of the girl, that was strictly as far as it went.

Fenton had broken off their secret affair in accordance. If the matter were ever discovered there would be outrage, and four traumatised band members and an army of hysterical teenage girls would be the least of their worries… for Fenton had signed Scotty when he was sixteen, and the industry wasn't to know that they hadn't begun sleeping together until two years later. That spelled interference with a minor. But Scotty knew it was more than that. Fenton thought that Kristin would turn him, that after everything he'd wind up finding happiness with a woman. Scotty had asked himself the same. Who knew, maybe if he liked girls after all, wouldn't that be so much easier? But he didn't. He never would.

And he hadn't got over Fenton. He would never get over Fenton. He was in love. The snatched nights they shared, so few and far between, were the hours he lived for. Several times Scotty had suggested they jack it in, Fraternity, their careers, and run away, but Fenton couldn't. Scotty had his whole life ahead of him, he said: what was he doing anyway with a forty-three-year-old man with a gut and a reliance on hair plugs? Scotty was beautiful, Scotty was his angel, and sooner or later Scotty would wise up and move on. He knew that was how Fenton saw it, and however many times he reassured the man that it was him he wanted, hair plugs and all, insecurity and self-loathing eternally got in the way.

Worse was the fact that Fenton refused to let him split from Kristin. *You need a girlfriend, Scotty. I don't have a wife. Don't get caught up in that rumour mill...*

'We'll take a question from the back,' directed Fenton from his chair at the side of the panel. 'The woman in the grey jacket, please.'

'Scotty, I'd love to know: is there a wedding on the cards for you and Kristin?'

Scotty was so deep into his thoughts about Fenton that the rehearsed response failed to trip off his tongue. 'Er,' he stalled. 'No. Absolutely not.'

The woman seized on it. 'Trouble in paradise?'

'No, we're very much together.' *Pull it back, Scotty, you're good at this.* 'We're both so busy at the moment, but that doesn't change the fact we're totally in love. Who knows, maybe some time next year.' He flashed the Valentine grin. 'If she'll have me!'

Everyone laughed, and Scotty with them. Nobody saw the fleeting glance he threw Fenton's way, so brief it was hardly there, a promise that he hadn't meant it, that it was Fenton he adored and craved and it always would be. But Fenton didn't look back.

# 9

Turquoise hit London for a charity gig. Hyde Park was teeming with crowds, the festival spirit so indigenous to this country, as girls in torn vests perched with sunburned shoulders on their boyfriends, waving plastic pints under a warm autumn sky. Balloons were released into the air along with the heady smell of pot. Nearer the front the fans were younger, bright-eyed and awestruck, holding aloft banners that rippled in the light breeze.

TURQUOISE IS MY IDOL. I HEART KATY. ROBIN RYDER ALWAYS.

Her set flew. New single 'Wild Girl' was an uncontested hit. Turquoise ran an extended version and by the end was throwing the mic to the audience, getting their arms in the air and waving along so the throng of gold shook before her like a field of corn. Cameras flashed as she powered to the bass, her silver catsuit teamed spectacularly with her whipping stream of hair and impressive five-inch heels that miraculously she managed to dance in.

One thing Turquoise had nailed beyond reproach was stage presence. It didn't matter if her arena was a hundred or a hundred thousand, she unleashed fury and energy on her routines that was unrivalled by anyone else in the business. Undisputed mistress of bringing a crowd together, she infused every show with a sense of togetherness and shared purpose that had them rallying for more, but matched this with an illusion of intimacy, as if she were performing for each person individually and giving them their own experience to cherish.

Six sequences weren't enough and so as encore she performed a ballad, her first number one on both sides of the Atlantic. It was called 'The Best of Me' and proved why Turquoise deserved every ounce of her mega celebrity. She wasn't just a killer performer or someone who could hold a tune; she could *sing*, in a way that demanded quiet from her listeners, the same seductive still that settled every time it was just her and a microphone and a voice, no frills, no extras. She didn't need it. To anyone who believed that commercial success couldn't be married with honest, inherent talent, it was the only response she needed.

*'Nights I still think of the pain you put me through; never gonna know what it took to forget you...'* Turquoise would always be fond of the song, it had been her revolution and the birth of her star, but it was too close to home to ever be easy. Perhaps that was what had made it special. People recognised the sentiment and identified it with their own lives, taking it to their hearts and making it one of the biggest-selling singles of the noughties. She lived on the principle that it wasn't possible to write a good song unless there was a piece of you in it, unless you had given something in ex-

change. But anger was a more straightforward emotion to represent—passion, rage, uprising; all the sentiments that powered her dance tracks.

Sadness, regret...*guilt*. Those were the hard ones to bear.

Afterwards, Robin Ryder took the stage. Turquoise liked Robin's style; the girl had swagger and wasn't afraid to use it. 'Lesson Learned' was a catchy, urban record overlaid with Ryder's trademark London chorus. Turquoise felt fortunate to be working at a time when there was such exciting talent pushing through the industry.

'You did a great job out there.' She introduced herself once Robin's set was done.

'Thanks. Compared with you, it was average, I'm sure.' With candour, Robin added: 'I'm a bit star-struck.' She smiled. 'It was you and Slink Bullion that made me want to do this. You both got me through a tough time in my life.'

Turquoise was humbled. 'You know Slink?'

'No,' Robin admitted, 'but we're in talks to team up.'

'Between you and me, Puff City aren't the easiest crew to work with.'

'Oh?'

'Can I grab you for a moment?' Turquoise's manager intervened.

'Are you staying in town?' asked Robin.

'Just a flying visit.'

'I'm in LA next month. Shall we make a date?'

'I'd like that.' They kissed on both cheeks before Turquoise was pulled away. 'I'll have my assistant get in touch.'

Turquoise's manager was a woman called Donna Cameron. She was Australia-born but hadn't been back in twenty years because when she did 'life stood still'. Her books were notoriously sparse: she represented just a handful of clients, all of them major.

'You hungry?' Donna asked.

'Not especially.'

'OK. We'll do drinks, then. Nobu?'

'Who with?' Turquoise was tired and had been looking forward to an early night. Her return flight to LA left at dawn.

Donna smiled with controlled pleasure. 'Sam Lucas,' she revealed, tagging the famous movie director. 'He wants to cast you in his new project. He doesn't care what it takes, he says, it has to be you. Turquoise, this is the golden opportunity.'

It was. They had been talking about a move to the big screen since last year. Turquoise had reached the pinnacle of success in her music and now there was nowhere to go but sideways, expanding her empire and building on the fan base she already had.

'It's the right project?' Her heart ached with pride when she thought of Emaline, how they had watched their old movies in the fading afternoon and dreamed of Hollywood.

*That's going to be you one day. My little star...*

'Sam and his group are in London,' said Donna. 'He can give us the script tonight. From what I've been told, it's tailor-made. This is a classic empowerment story and you're the one to tell it. It's going to appeal across the board. It's a big budget production and they've got some huge names attached. Cosmo Angel, for one.'

Turquoise froze. Her mouth went dry.

'Tell me about it,' commented Donna. 'If I wasn't twice

divorced I'd seriously consider marrying the guy. If he wasn't with Ava, of course.' She winked.

'Cosmo's in the movie?' She could barely stand to say his name.

Donna shot her a quizzical look, perplexed that at her stage in the game Turquoise should get misty-eyed about even the biggest hitters on the A-list.

'He's your love interest.'

She couldn't do it. There was no way.

'It doesn't sound like a role he'd want to sign.' Turquoise tried to imagine Cosmo as a man subjugated by a woman, and couldn't. He would always be the victor.

'Is everything all right?' Donna was concerned. 'I thought you'd be pleased.'

Turquoise opened her mouth to respond. No words came. How could she begin to explain? Where would she start?

'I don't know if it's the best thing for me right now,' she offered weakly, thinking only, *I have to get out of this; I have to get out of this.*

'But we've cleared it.' Donna was trying to understand. 'We've talked this through before, Turquoise. Hollywood has always been on the cards, hasn't it?'

'Yes. But…'

'At least come meet Sam, see what they have to say?' She gave Turquoise's arm a reassuring squeeze. 'I know you're tired,' she said kindly. 'You've been working all hours; it's no wonder you're finding it tough to summon enthusiasm for a new project. Let's ride out tonight. Once we have the facts we can make an informed call. Sound all right?'

Turquoise found herself nodding. There was nothing else she could do. 'Fine.'

She would figure it out. She *had* to figure it out. Because one thing was certain: she was never going near Cosmo Angel again as long as she lived.

*Grace Turquoise da Luca should never have said yes to the ride. If she hadn't, she might have had a different fate. She might have perished on the road, just lain down and waited for dreams to take her, or surrendered to delirium and stumbled out in front of a truck. Or she might have made it to the next town and found help. She might have been rescued. She might have got into a car with anyone else but Denny Malone.*

*Denny was twenty-three and had a haggard, drug-addled face that made him look ten years older. His had been a tough life and he had the livid white scars on his arms to prove it.*

*They arrived in Denny's home city early morning. Grace drifted in and out of sleep, startled awake then shivering back to oblivion. Denny had an apartment and he told her to shower. He didn't offer her a phone call, but then whom would she have rung?*

*'Can I have some clothes, please?' she asked, trembling cold and wrapped in a towel.*

*'Lemme get a look at you first.' Denny was on the couch, smoking. He narrowed his eyes and flashed her that smile. 'Drop it.'*

*Grace Turquoise wished she had never become a woman. She wished she had never found the blood in her knickers, because it meant she had to do things she didn't want.*

*'Bit thin,' he diagnosed when she was stripped. 'Good tits though.' He told her to come over and roughly he clasped*

*her ass, patting it when he was done like a piece of meat.
'We'll give you a couple of months then you're ready to go.'*

*Ready to go where? She didn't know. She was scared.*

*Six weeks later, she was getting sick. 'What's wrong with
you?' Denny demanded. 'You ain't knocked up or something?' He took her to a friend of his who worked out of
a backstreet surgery. There, the man prodded her insides
with coarse, long fingers that hurt when they went all the
way up. She wept and bled, and bled and wept, and prayed
a miracle would happen and Emaline would appear next
to her, holding her hand and kissing her head like she used
to do when there was a thunderstorm and she woke from
a nightmare.*

*Now, there was no waking up.*

*The abortion set back Denny's plan, but two months later,
after her fifteenth birthday, Grace Turquoise was sent to her
first client. He was a bald, overweight businessman with a
lust for young girls, and as he ordered Grace to undress,
drooling with anticipation and sucking wetly at her nipples, she closed her mind and body to everything except the
house where she grew up, the rustling palms and the ocean
breeze, Emaline and her lime cordial and all the songs they
used to sing. When the man pummelled into her, just as the
pastor had done that horrifying night, Grace accepted that
this was the world. This was what men did.*

*Denny was pleased with the twenty dollars she produced.
He kept it all and said that next time, if she did another good
job, he'd let her take a piece.*

*Her next call-out was a young guy, in his twenties, who
wanted to watch her play with herself. She hadn't done that
before and had to be shown how. Then he crouched over her*

*and dangled his thing in her mouth. That was worse than the pummelling and cost him thirty dollars, which Denny kept all over again.*

*'I don't want to do it any more,' she told him. 'Please don't make me.'*

*Denny was counting out a stack of cash. She'd seen other girls at the apartment, sent to do the same things. They were older than Grace and she didn't want to end up like them. 'You wanna hit the streets, go right ahead,' he growled. 'Ain't no easy ride out there.'*

*One of the girls, Cookie—'not my real name, honey, but then whose is?'—was sent out with her one night. A twitchy Vietnamese man met them at his hotel room and tugged his penis while he watched them make out. Cookie made her swallow two tiny pills that made everything fuzzy and not so bad, even when the man had sex with them both, one then the other then Grace again until he spurted all over her, and afterwards Cookie hugged her and told her to forget, not to worry, because it was just a job and you had to leave it at the door.*

*They were a popular duo. Denny was raking it in. He'd started giving Grace a percentage of her earnings, enough to buy food. Grace preferred doing things with Cookie because she was gentle, and sometimes when Cookie kissed her down there she got a tingle that made her lift her back and forget for a second that there was anyone else in the room.*

*'Call this number,' Cookie instructed her the day she turned seventeen. 'They specialise in girls your age. Get shot of Denny, he's a bad lot.'*

*Grace did as she was told. She spoke to Madam Baby-*

*doll on Cookie's phone, sent her photograph and a week later was packing her scant belongings and catching an overnight bus to Los Angeles. She felt nothing about leaving Denny. She hated him.*

*Madam Babydoll ran a different ship. She employed sixteen carefully selected girls and housed each in her mansion in the hills. Grace couldn't take in the world she had entered. It was dazzling with sunshine and promise. This was where people went to make their dreams come true. Was she leaving her nightmare at last?*

*Not quite. Madam Babydoll provided under-eighteen girls to a moderate rank of Hollywood star. Lily Rose, a sugary-pretty Californian with a deep golden tan, explained to Grace how important it was to make a good impression, because you never knew who was going to strike it big one day. Grace couldn't work out why Lily Rose was here because she had a family in LA and she dressed smart and spoke nice.*

*'Why are you doing this?' she asked her once. Lily Rose shrugged. She'd just returned from an encounter with an up-and-coming producer. 'I could go home if I wanted,' she mused, 'but this is way more fun. Some day I'm gonna be an actress, just you watch. The way I see it, it's an opportunity to get noticed. My clients never forget who I am.'*

*The clients were cleaner and richer than Denny's, but they didn't treat her with any more respect. She came to learn that actors were the worst. They were preoccupied with seeing themselves, whether it was having her against a mirror or recording an encounter to watch afterwards— Madam Babydoll permitted this only if her girl could verify its deletion—while Grace sucked and licked till they came.*

*They wanted her to worship their bodies, and, while it was preferable to having her own attacked, the younger and more virile could take hours and she often left sore and stiff, forced to wait days before she could work again.*

*Others had perversions. The older ones, mostly, who were married or had kids and wanted her to dress as a schoolgirl; or who wanted to dress up themselves and be held. Some brought wives and she'd play with them both. But Madam Babydoll paid out sixty per cent of every cheque, and soon Grace Turquoise had several thousand in the bank—enough to quit, if she'd wanted, but she didn't know what else she'd do. Over four years she had seen it all. She'd had sex with countless men and women and had learned to view the ordeal as simply her trade, her talent, the thing she had been trained to do. She hadn't sung a note in years.*

*It was a Friday in June when Madam Babydoll told her she had a 'very special' client to visit. The girls were envious. Was it someone important, someone famous?*

*She was instructed to wear a black coat with nothing underneath except a lace thong. As Grace Turquoise headed to the rendezvous, hair immaculate and lips perfectly glossed, the professional that Denny Malone had groomed and Ivan Garrick before him, she could never have imagined who would be waiting for her, or what he would ask her to do.*

# 10

Robin's *Beginnings* tour was to be her first foray into America. She hadn't realised the extent of what her team had planned until she sat in on a meeting at Barney's Kensington office.

'This is the stage set.' A Perspex model was deposited on the table in front of her, over which the show's art director peered for her reaction over steel-rimmed glasses.

'Wow.' It was the only word that sprang to mind. The stage backdrop was ink-black save for a white imprint of Robin's face, just the silhouetted contours, the line of her brow, nose and lips—and of course the hallmark fringe. A glass birdcage hovered over winding silver steps. Metallic moving platforms extended to the audience. It was stylish to the max.

'You like?'

'I love.'

'We open with "Told You So",' explained the director.

'Spotlight, then *bam*! You're up in the cage. Fade to black and in a blink you're down on the boards, free as a bird. Magic.'

'How do I get there?'

'Let us worry about that.' He gestured to the flanks of the model. 'This is your series of pulleys and platforms; it's the oldest trick there is. All you need to be is in the right place at the right time—oh, and be happy to get thrown about like a pinball.'

'Sounds like fun.'

Drummer Matt leaned back and put his hands behind his head. 'Seriously, you're gonna recreate this at every single venue?'

'Sure we are,' said Barney. 'All this, it's the *point* of Robin's show. The whole outlook: style, sex, a let's-see-what-you've-got-then stance...'

The tour was to kick off at the start of next year. They were covering multiple sites across North America, major arenas she had never imagined filling but incredibly tickets were shifting and one had sold out in hours. Her success over the Atlantic had been thanks to a recent US version of *The Launch*, which had sparked interest in its British counterpart. Word of mouth had taken her the rest of the way; an underground rumble that began via YouTube and in an overnight surge had fans addicted to her tunes. Her album *Beginnings* had been released at a time when the Billboard 100 had been saturated with manufactured groups (boy band Fraternity had held the number one spot for eleven weeks) and had offered a welcome contrast. There was no one quite like Robin Ryder. She was quintessentially British but at the same time identifiable to and representative of females worldwide.

'Did you hear about Puff City and the US track team?' Polly asked when they were done. The women grabbed a coffee in the canteen.

'No.' In spite of herself Robin's tummy flipped at the connection to Leon Sway. Why? He was nothing to her. 'What about them?'

'Jax Jackson wants to release a single.'

'Fuck off!'

'I know. My bet is he was laughed out of town before someone with half a brain realised they could make a charity gig out of it. Anyhow it's going ahead.'

'With Puff City?' She was agape.

'Yeah. You should ask them about it at your meet. Anti gun crime or something? Jax wanted to go it alone but he's been forced to rope in the rest of the team.' Polly rummaged in her purse for red lipstick. 'I wish you could smoke in here.'

'I'm surprised they said yes. Isn't Jax a bit of a dick?'

'He's a lot of a dick,' said Polly. 'But, honey, Jax and the guys are in demand. And if they've got a cause attached to it then, well, who's going to be able to say no?'

It would certainly give Leon the screw he was so obviously after, Robin thought. Not that he would be short of offers, sending bunches of hackneyed flowers all over town and relying on his looks to make up the rest. She had seen in the *Metro* that he'd returned to LA. He probably had seventeen girlfriends queuing up at home that he couldn't wait to get back to, not to mention *The Waltons* family set-up.

'D'you know what? I'd rather talk about the tour.'

Polly nodded. 'Nervous?'

'Nah.' Robin grinned. 'Not my style. Far as I'm concerned, they can bring it.'

Later that afternoon she returned to her flat, electing to walk because being cooped up in Barney's HQ all day had made her feel foggy, and she had a song that had been niggling her for ages that she wanted to get on paper before sunset.

All the way back she had the sensation of being followed. It was hard to pinpoint, an instinct she would subsequently put down to imagination, or a weary mind playing tricks, but every corner Robin turned, every street she crossed, she was conscious of footsteps trailing behind. Normally she avoided taking a route through the super-busy heart of the borough, instead cutting across a quieter park, but not today. She moved swiftly through the hordes of people, anonymous in the swarming masses, and must have managed to lose her tracker—if they were even there in the first place—because by the time she arrived home, she was alone.

# *11*

Leon landed at LAX to a feverish reception. Paparazzi were jostling over the barriers for a clean shot, lights flashing and cracking and his name repeated so many times it lost its beginning and end. *'Leon! Leon! Leon!'* He had hoped to fly back quietly and avoid the uproar, but no such luck. Something told him he had better get used to it.

'How is it being back in LA?' reporters demanded. 'What have you got to say to Jax Jackson? Can you defeat him at the 2013 Champs?' Microphones lunged and he had to shield his eyes from the glare. A woman got past the rope and clung to his shoulders, and before he could do anything to stop it she planted a kiss on his mouth.

'Step away, ma'am.' Airport security dragged her off.

Leon had been thrust into the realms of the super-famous and now it seemed like everyone wanted a piece. Being on home ground meant the hype was ready to hit new heights, beginning with this hare-brained idea of Jax's to record a single. Frankly Leon found it embarrassing. How could he say no when it was for charity? He couldn't be the only one who turned his back, especially when it was supposedly making a stand against gun crime.

Jax wanted stardom, that was the distinction between them, and The Bullet didn't care how he got it. For Leon, it was different. He trained, he ran and he focused. Yet his first steps back on American soil and he was being treated like a movie star. He'd never got into it for celebrity; he didn't care about that. He ran to win.

'Do you think you'll ever beat him?'

Leon stopped. 'Sure, I'll beat him. This isn't the final score.'

'Is The Bullet impossible to outrun?'

'Nothing's impossible.' An image of Jax's trademark gold vest clouded Leon's vision. Emblazoned on its back was the tip of a bullet in flight. 'When you're at the top, the only way is down. Jax is on borrowed time. I'm the one to watch.'

The Compton house where Leon grew up was like any other on the street, a grey one-storey villa protected behind a barred steel gate. Out front was a yard—his mom kept it nice as she could but the grass was tired and yellowing and a football lay part deflated by the trash. There was nothing remarkable about the place, nothing to suggest it had once been the scene of a brutal crime, but scratch the surface and the scars were there. They said that the years would heal, but each time Leon returned it ached as deeply as it had twelve years ago.

Paint was flaking off the gate, the catch stiff. If only they would let him buy them someplace else, his mom and sister, but they refused. Memories were all they had left.

A couple of kids rode past on their bikes. Leon turned, dipping his cap so he didn't get recognised, but even so they circled a few times at the end of the street.

'You're Leon Sway, right?' one of them asked. 'No way, this is dope! My mom said you used to live round here!'

'Tell your mom I said hi.'

'No shit, I will. You hanging for a while?'

'Maybe.'

'You're the coolest, man. How'd you get to be so fast?'

'Practice. Discipline.'

'Doesn't it get boring?'

'Never.'

'If you raced a bike who'd win?'

'Me.'

'If you raced a car who'd win?'

'Mc.'

'If you raced a lion who'd win?'

'Me.'

The kid laughed uncertainly. 'You're funny.'

'See you around.'

The boys rode off. The one who'd spoken did a wheelie and thumped the arm of the other kid, calling him a wuss for staying quiet.

Leon put his key in the lock, stopping to ready himself against the ghosts of the past. In another life Marlon would be on the other side, his arms wide open.

*Hey, little bro. Want to shoot some hoops?*

But it was this life that counted. And his brother wasn't here any more.

Marlon Sway had been nineteen when he'd died. As one of the most promising athletes on the circuit, he had been destined for greatness, the Sydney Games locked in his sights. He'd been returning from the club one night when a street fight had broken out. Somehow he had got mixed up...a gang conflict spun out of control...a stray bullet...a wrong place, wrong time... Perhaps he had tried to intervene, ever the peacemaker, but wasn't that worse? He had been caught in the crossfire. Marlon had staggered home with a punctured lung. Yards from his front door, he had collapsed on the road and his heart had stopped beating.

It had been twelve years and still Leon couldn't pick at the scab, afraid it would bleed as easily as it had when the wound was first made.

He remembered it as if it were yesterday. A deafening sound that split the world in two; the unmistakeable crack of ammo tearing the sky. Instinct had compelled him to run from their home, out on to the street, a feeling in his gut that this was bad. He hadn't known what it was to run until that moment. Time had fallen away quicker than water as his brother's body, slumped and lifeless, had lurched closer. *Be faster...be faster...*

Each and every race he ran, in Tucson, in London, in Athens, in whatever competition and wherever it was, he was there, on that rainy night in Compton when his brother was lost. The splinter of the starting pistol was all he needed. Instead of the line, he'd see Marlon. He'd hear his mom screaming, a violent, feral sound. His brother's eyes, empty. Marlon hadn't looked asleep, he hadn't looked peaceful; none of the things people said were true.

*If I'd been quicker, I could have beaten this. I could have stopped it.*

It was the need to always be faster, to make it in time

that powered Leon's sprint from that day and in all the days to come. For as long as he came in second, he wasn't fast enough. He was too late. He was tormented by the idea that had he reached Marlon sooner there could have been a chance at life, a flickering ember he could have roused...

Or at least to have been there when his brother died, so that he hadn't been alone.

Before he turned the key to his family home, Leon rested his forehead against the door. Twelve years, and it might as well be twelve days. Closing his eyes, he let the memory settle, waiting for it to scatter like light on water. He missed his brother so much.

Marlon was the reason he ran. For him he would run and run until he couldn't run any more, he would run till his heart gave up and his strength gave in. That was his destiny.

If anyone stood in his way, they would be taken down. Jax Jackson included.

'Leon, honey, is that you?'

The door clicked open and his mother emerged from the kitchen.

'Hello, Ma,' he said, squeezing her tight. 'I'm home.'

## 12

'Gorgeous.' The photographer clicked away as a stylist rushed to adjust the hem of Kristin's gown. 'And lift your arms one more time? That's it! Beautiful.'

She was shooting cover art for her new album, *Heaven*, which involved being suspended from the rafters of a studio warehouse with stirrups digging in under her arms. A shimmering halo was bolted to the back of her head and the robes had to be twenty feet long at least, pooling to the floor in swathes of frosted ivory that were meant to look celestially sylphlike but were in fact dragging her down like a lead anchor.

So this was what it felt like being an angel for the afternoon...uncomfortable.

'Smile, then, Kristin!' her mother barked from the floor. 'I am.'

'Not from where we're sitting.' Ramona White was cross-legged at the wardrobe girl's table, busy applying lipstick. 'Think of the fans. Do you think they want to see you looking miserable? You're selling a lifestyle, remember, not just a handful of ditties.'

Kristin hated when her mother insisted on coming to shoots and interviews and anything else she was perfectly capable of handling alone. She'd been years in the industry now and didn't need Ramona to hold her hand. It was humiliating; it undermined her reputation and made her appear weak and unable to make decisions, hauling Mommy along to look out for her. Doubly challenging when her mother insisted on criticising everything she did, which made Kristin invariably revert to the role of frustrated teenager storming off and slamming her bedroom door. For the sake of today, she bit her tongue.

'Almost done,' the photographer lied. Kristin knew it would be an hour at least before she could be brought back to earth and the stills hit the can. 'Everything OK up there?'

She was determined to retain her professionalism despite her mother's carping. 'Fine.'

'If we could have you gazing up, eyes nice and wide, that's it... Let's try one with hands together, in prayer... Loving it, sweetheart, that's awesome...'

'I don't like it,' snapped Ramona. 'She looks too whimsical.'

'That's what we're going for, Mrs White.'

'It's *Mz*.'

'Sure.'

'What about those poor kids, saving up their allowance to spend on this? They want to see friendly big-sister Kristin, don't they? Not some scowling pre-Raphaelite.'

'Kristin's fan base is growing and we should grow with them.'

Ramona's mouth set in a grim line. Kristin could practically hear the thoughts turning over in her head. *I've been doing this since the beginning, you moronic upstart. I created Kristin White and everything she is, every dime she's made and every record she's sold. Your fucking paycheck today comes down to me!* But her mother stayed quiet.

'Kristin, what do you think?' asked the photographer, attempting diplomacy.

'I'm happy with this approach.'

'Then look it!' crowed Ramona. The camera popped as Kristin fired a scowl in her mother's direction. She couldn't win. It was about control and always had been: the outcome was less important than the means used to reach it, and as long as Ramona had the last word and the final approval, she was content to proceed. Bunny abided by the same rules. Her sister was currently curled on a beanbag by the props closet, tapping away on her cell phone. She had a competition tonight, the last before the Mini Miss Marvellous rounds began, and according to Ramona could risk nothing in the run-up to 'the ultimate pageant of all time'. Kristin wished she could take Bunny to the movies, or bowling, or a trip to the mall where they could get milkshakes and whisper behind their hands about boys—normal things that normal sisters did. Bunny was fourteen in two weeks' time and was being made to dress and act like a forty-year-old. When would Ramona let up? Never?

Kristin's eyes brimmed with tears. As far back as she could think her life had been about pleasing Ramona, doing what Ramona wanted to do and when, and her opinion didn't matter at all. Just like now.

'I want her facing us,' concluded Ramona, 'with her arms

stretched wide. It's much more inclusive.' She resumed attending to important business on her BlackBerry.

The photographer acquiesced. As Kristin's manager, her mother's word was law. He smiled at Kristin somewhat sympathetically, making her want to burst into tears even more.

'OK,' he resumed. 'Let's try that out.'

Ninety minutes later the shoot was over. Bunny had fallen asleep and had to be shaken awake by Ramona because the competition was across town and they were yet to get her through make-up. Kristin checked her cell for a message from Scotty and was disappointed not to find one. Since returning from Tokyo they hadn't been able to see much of each other. She missed him. She couldn't explain it, but he seemed to be growing distant.

Was there someone else? There couldn't be: aside from anything else, where would Scotty find the time? Every waking hour he spent either with her or with Fenton and the boys.

'Go get 'em, kiddo.' She managed to give Bunny a fleeting hug before Ramona yanked her youngest daughter out the door. At least this meant she wouldn't be around to peruse the stills: perhaps they could salvage the earlier shots, after all.

'Your mom sure knows her mind,' the photographer commented after they'd left.

Kristin sighed. 'Tell me about it.'

Bunny White coughed violently as her mother blasted yet another flare of hairspray.

'Isn't that enough?' she enquired timidly, meeting her

bronzed-to-within-an-inch-of-its-life reflection in the mirror, and in the same flash catching Ramona's icy glare.

'I say when it's enough.'

Bunny hurt. The sequins on her ball gown were sharp and uncomfortable, and when she touched her hair it felt like candyfloss, all sticky and fossilised.

'Show me your smile.'

Bunny smiled.

'More teeth.'

She smiled wider.

'Good. Now hold it.'

She did as she was told, the muscles in her face aching despite their rigorous training. Her lipstick tasted horrible, like emulsion, and she was tired. For the last month she had been kept up each night practising her routines, and when that was done, her Q&As. Who was her role model? What was her favourite food? Where was her dream holiday? Which did she like best, strawberry or chocolate? All for the Mini Miss Marvellous showdown. Her mom wanted her to win as many titles as she could in the run-up to secure her position as the mightiest contender on the circuit. *Intimidate the competition*, she'd been instructed.

'We're ready for our princesses!' A fat woman entered the girls' dressing room, wibbling with excitement as she beckoned the entrants. 'OK, everybody, file up onstage!'

A cacophony of squeals followed, the gaggle of baby beauty queens scrambling over each other with their stick-on hair and fake dangly earrings, desperate to reach the line first.

'Elegance,' snipped Ramona, holding Bunny's shoulders in place with an iron grip. 'A lady never rushes.'

Tonight's head-to-head was freestyle dance. Ramona had chosen a medley of disco tunes to accompany her daughter's sequence, and as ever their strongest challenger was Tracy-Ann Hamilton, who strutted her stuff like a dynamo. Partway through her routine Bunny started to flag, and it was only the steel-grey glower of her mother that compelled her to continue. As she turned and twisted, jumped and spun, executing the painstakingly choreographed steps with all the dedication she could muster, the circus of surrounding faces became a gawking, gruesome carousel of grasping would-be victors, she at its centre, floundering helplessly like an animal in the road about to be shot.

'Adequate,' appraised Ramona as she came off to thunderous applause. Bunny's heart was pounding, her breath short, and she bent over to catch herself, thinking she might barf. 'You mangled the jazz axles. Why? Didn't we go through them enough times at home?'

She struggled to talk. 'I thought my shoes were going to come off. They're too big.'

'Nonsense.' Ramona knelt and roughly grabbed a stiletto, forcing Bunny to steady herself on her mother's shoulder. 'Stop leaning on me, Bunny, it's amateur.'

'Sorry.'

'These are fine. Better too big than too small. If you weren't complaining about this you'd be whining about blisters.'

'And the winner of the Freestyle Miss Pretty California category is…'

*'Come on, you bitches!'* hissed Ramona.

'Bunny White!'

'YES!' Ramona punched the air. Bunny looked up, waiting for congratulations but her mother was too busy accepting compliments from the envious parents around her. Seconds later she was being roughly pushed to the podium to collect the bouquet.

'Curtsey! *Curtsey!*' rasped Ramona from the side of the stage.

Bunny obliged, rictus smile in place. Fleetingly she wondered if Scotty would ever get to see her take the spotlight like this—maybe when she began to compete internationally, maybe then. Her heart leapt at the thought of his name alone. Where was he now? What was he thinking? All she wanted to do was curl up in bed and dream about him.

On the drive home she closed her eyes and tried to do just that. Not easy with Ramona grousing about how she could have been better, that with a little more work and taking things a little more seriously she could have been perfect, how nothing but perfection was good enough and how tonight they had been lucky…until she realised her daughter was asleep.

Before yielding to slumber, Bunny conjured Scotty's face and imagined for the hundredth time kissing his lips. He hadn't visited the house recently and this was a source of both relief and panic to Bunny: relief, because she didn't have to see him vanishing into her sister's room every day, tortured by what could be going on behind closed doors; and panic because if all that stopped then she might never ever see Scotty again as long as she lived.

Scotty was the only person in the world who could save her.

He was the only person she truly trusted.

He couldn't be taken away from her. She'd die.

## 13

As it happened, Turquoise and Robin didn't need to plan their hook-up in LA. Both stars had been booked on to America's leading talk show *Friday Later*, and when they met in the green room they greeted each other like friends.

'It's good to see you,' said Turquoise, giving her a hug. Robin made her feel like a protective older sister. Though the girl cultivated an air of invincibility, dressed in a tangerine T-shirt and skin-tight pants, her fringe falling over an extraordinary palette of make-up and a slash of flamingo-pink lipstick, Turquoise saw it for the mask it was. Robin acted as if she didn't care: just her versus the world, a one-woman army. Why had she built so many walls?

'Ditto.' Robin beamed. 'Hey, I heard you've got a movie coming up?'

Turquoise's heart caught in her throat. She still hadn't found a way to say no. Donna had insinuated that turning down the Cosmo Angel project would slam the door on future opportunities in Hollywood—major names were being attached and walking away could spell disaster. It was their only shot. The idea that Turquoise's *bête noir* could not only rob her of her youth but of the dream she and Emaline had shared was an abomination.

She'd find a way out. She had to.

'Possibly,' she said vaguely. 'It's early days.'

'Exciting, though, huh?'

She forced a smile. 'Yeah.'

Cosmo kept a tight rein over his PR and news of his involvement couldn't be broken yet: Donna had warned that tonight could bring up the proposed collaboration and had briefed her response. Their meeting in London with Sam Lucas had gone smoothly, and, as predicted, the part of Gloria, a rags-to-riches songbird, was the perfect role at the perfect time... What possible reason could she give Donna for her refusal? In the past she had made no bones about her desire to enter the movies. There was nothing whatsoever about the role—at least on paper—that she could feasibly take objection to.

'Are you OK?' asked Robin. 'You look like you've seen a ghost.'

'On air in five!' The producer passed through to check their mics. Turquoise could hear the audience being warmed up, laughter bleeding in from the studio.

'Absolutely fine.'

Robin looked unconvinced and she teamed it with a decisive nod.

The style of *Friday Later* was to keep each guest on the sofa to join in conversation with the others, so, as the biggest star with the longest airtime, Turquoise was on first.

Harry Dollar, the host, wasted no time in asking about her move into Hollywood.

'I'd rather not jinx it,' said Turquoise, with a coy expression that betrayed nothing of her ravaged nerves. 'But it's promising.'

'Can you give us a clue?' Harry appealed to the audience. 'We want to know, don't we?' Turquoise re-crossed her legs, laughing along graciously. 'I heard Sam Lucas's name on the grapevine...?'

'I couldn't say, Harry. Really.'

'But you can confirm we'll be seeing you on the big screen very soon?'

The studio lights burned. The glare of the cameras swung round to capture her response, which for a second relinquished to a flicker. 'Yes, you will.'

It was a relief when Robin was invited to join them. She talked fervently about her upcoming tour and the collaboration with Puff City.

'I'm seeing them while I'm over,' she enthused. 'It's a big deal for me—like, huge. These are the guys I had on my walls growing up. They're legends.'

Last was a raconteur comedian, who steered them mercifully towards the end of the show. Afterwards Harry kissed Turquoise and told her she was 'a woman of mystery'. If only he knew.

'D'you want to hit the town?' asked Robin.

'Sure.'

They took a car to Chilean hangout Astro off Santa Monica. Robin had invited the comedian and his entourage and as they chatted carelessly on the way Turquoise wondered if she would ever reach a point in life where she could let go so easily. Would she ever enjoy a night without the hot breath of fear hovering at her shoulder? Would she ever meet new people and feel able to open up, to embrace their company without restraint? Would she ever escape the dread of having Cosmo Angel expose her, demolishing all she had strived for against inconceivable odds, in just a few poisonous words?

If Donna had her way, in a matter of days she would be shaking hands with her costar-to-be and signing the contract as easily as she signed away her fate.

Panic flooded over her. 'Sorry...' She fumbled to collect her purse. 'I—I have to get out. Driver, pull over.'

Robin's face was etched with worry. 'What's wrong?'

'I don't feel well. Please excuse me. I've got to go home.'

'I'll come with you.'

'No. Don't. I'd rather you didn't. It's just a headache.'

'Then let's at least get hold of your car—'

'I'm fine.'

The vehicle came to a stop. 'I'll call you,' she said, before stepping out into the night, not caring if she was seen, hailing a cab like anyone ordinary and wishing with all her might she could be just a girl on the street, no one remarkable, invisible, untouchable, free.


*Cosmo Angelopoulos liked to watch. Grace Turquoise got that pretty quick, the minute she turned up at the door to his Hollywood mansion and found a six-foot black girl waiting for her inside. The girl was drugged up to the eyeballs, reclining on a velvet sofa with her legs wide apart. Wordlessly Cosmo tore off Grace's coat and pushed her to the floor.*

*'Open your mouth, cunt,' he directed. 'And look like you're enjoying it.'*

*She recognised Cosmo straight away. She had seen him in the papers, on TV, the twenty-something up-and-coming actor who was billed to take Hollywood by storm. Yes, he was staggeringly handsome. Yes, he resembled a young Marlon Brando with his brooding looks and muscular build. Yes, he had the face of a boy who would never say no to his mom. Who knew he was also a despicable pervert who liked to beat on women? But she was here to do a job, and as one of Madam Babydoll's she couldn't afford to disappoint.*

*Grace used her tongue in the way Cookie had shown her. The black girl's thighs were strong and held her in place like a vice, hands snatching down to push her in deeper. It was salty and sweet and wet, and every time she broke for air Cosmo forced her back.*

*'Keep goin', bitch,' he snarled, kneeling next to them for a front row seat. 'You like that, don't you, you greedy whore?' Grace closed her eyes and concentrated on the task.*

*'Oh, yeah...' the girl moaned. 'Yeah, baby, that feels so fine...'*

*Cosmo started to feel her up. He began by removing Grace's thong, roughly dipping his fingers in, two or three at once, which made her gasp her discomfort. They were covered in a freezing cold gel that was meant to open her up but instead she contracted against. His thumb pushed violently into her ass, forcing her to cry out.*

*'Get back to it, slut.'*

*The girl's hips tilted to meet her and Grace forced herself to keep going, despite the pain. Cosmo freed his cock and slammed into her, grunting at her rear, snatching at her breasts and pushing in deeper and deeper till it felt like there was nothing left of her to give. With a gurgling whimper he climaxed. She felt a jet of warm liquid spurt across her back.*

*If she'd thought that was it, she was mistaken. Cosmo could go all night.*

*'Your turn, bitch.' He slapped the black girl's face, twisting her pair of dark, hard nipples to bring her out of rapture. An enormous dildo appeared, its tip glistening. Obligingly the girl attached it to her waist, an obscene rubber proboscis, huge and frightening as Grace was flipped over a chair and her legs brutally spread. The hurt was like nothing she had ever experienced, tearing her in two, but still there was no mercy. The girl pounded into her, delirious, deaf to her complaints. Cosmo paced, proudly stiff once more, pausing at intervals to refresh his viewpoint. Eventually he stopped at Grace's head and drove his cock into her mouth. She could taste the remnants of his first ejaculation and gagged.*

*When it was over, she returned to Madam Babydoll's with three thousand dollars in her pocket. It was the most she had ever been paid for a job but that made no difference.*

*'He likes you,' encouraged Madam Babydoll the following week. Grace had only just recovered from the ache Cosmo had inflicted on her—but she'd never recover from the humiliation. 'You're his favourite. He wants you again. He's requested you personally.'*

*The other girls were jealous. Cosmo was the biggest catch on the books.*

*'I don't want to.'*

*'It's five grand this time, honey. You keep three and a half. It's your call.'*

*The second occasion she went he'd hired a redhead with*

*freakishly large breasts. Grace took charge of the dildo and was instructed to nail Cosmo with it while the redhead sucked him off. The ordeal took hours because Cosmo was so high he couldn't come. He made Grace call him a bad boy and tell him he needed his ass screwed to teach him a lesson. When finally he was done he was so exhausted that he had them run him a bath and put him in it, relaxing with a joint while he scoped them making out on the floor. Recovered, he took them in turn over the rim of the tub, so many times she lost count, and when Grace left the mansion at five a.m. she was sorer and more bruised than she'd ever been.*

*After that he asked for her every time. Madam Babydoll tried to switch her appointments to accommodate before realising that Cosmo would pay more and more for whatever it was he couldn't have. Soon a night with Grace reached ten thousand dollars.*

*'I said I was through with that,' she told Madam Babydoll. But in truth she had almost enough saved to get her own place, try going it alone in LA and getting out of this sordid game once and for all. One last night with Cosmo Angelopoulos, that was it; she'd endured it before so she could endure it again, and after that she'd be made. How much worse could it get? The exchange was surely worth it. She'd never need to prostitute her body again. She could meet a guy, fall in love and do it like it was supposed to be done. No one had to ever know what she'd been through or how she'd lived. A fresh start...a clean slate.*

*Deciding to go to Cosmo's that night was the worst decision she ever made.*

*The girl he'd got was young. Grace saw straight away*

*that he'd plied her with drugs—blow, pills, weed, anything
he had going—and, judging by the clothes strewn haphaz-
ardly across the floor, had already had sex with her. The
girl's eyes were glassy and stoned, she kept giggling and
slurring and when Cosmo beckoned her over to attend to
his burgeoning hard-on she weaved drunkenly before crashing to the ground.*

'I don't think she's well.'

'Shut it, bitch. Take your clothes off.'

'She needs a doctor. What have you given her?'

'What she begged for: a big hard cock.'

'She's tripping. We should call someone.'

*Brutally Cosmo slapped her. He grabbed her chin in his
hand and squeezed.* 'I said, *take your fucking clothes off.
Now. Or I'm going to make you regret it.'*

One night. *As Grace removed her stockings she repeated
the promise in her head.*

One last night and then I'll be free.

*Kneeling, she fondled the girl's breasts. The girl was out
of it, slumped on the floor, her limbs shut down. When the
girl arched her back, at first Grace thought it was with pleasure. It wasn't. She'd started to spasm, her body jumping
and seizing. Grace saw a pop of foam at her mouth, the eyes
rolling back in her head until only the whites were visible.*

'What the fuck is this?' *Cosmo cried.*

'She's fitting. Call an ambulance. Right now.'

*Grace attempted to hold her down, tilting the girl's head
as best she could to prevent her choking on her tongue.*

'Like hell I am.'

'Do it. She's in danger.'

'So am I if we get the fucking cops round!'

*Grace pinned him with a hateful stare. 'Do you want her to die?'*

*'She'll get over it. It's a bad trip, that's all.'*

*It wasn't all. The girl's body surrendered to a series of rapid tremors before suddenly, too quick, impossibly quick, it strained a final time before becoming still. Frantically Grace touched her pulse. Nothing. She felt her heart. Still. Dead still.*

No. No, no, no, no, no...

*Before she could think twice, Grace was resting the girl's head back, opening her airways and breathing into her mouth. Cosmo was useless, hanging back and swearing, freaking about the mess on his luxury shag-pile carpet and how the fuck they were going to get out of this. She tried to remember what scant first aid she'd picked up off TV, medical dramas she'd half watched, and began to establish a rhythm. Two breaths, thirty chest compressions; she didn't even know if that was right but she couldn't stop. Two more, thirty more, two more, thirty more, two more, desperation building and panic surging and then...*

*Nothing.*

*'Don't die on me, sweetheart. Come on, not here, not now...'*

*She didn't know how long she kept it up for, and only stopped when she saw the girl was grey in the face. She was dead. It was over.*

*Grace sat back on her knees. Cosmo was clothed, stalking the room. He tossed her belongings and numbly she dressed. 'Get her the hell out of here,' he ordered.*

*The word floated in Grace's throat before she caught hold of it. 'What?'*

'You whores stick together, don't you? Get out and take her with you. Far as you're concerned she never set foot in this place.'

'You heartless bastard. I'm taking her nowhere.'

'You're in this too, cunt.'

'I tried to save her.'

'Or else you killed her. I bet you finished her off right there, thumping her chest like that without a clue what you were doing!'

Grace's mouth was dry. She didn't believe him, she couldn't, but even as he uttered the words she knew they would haunt her as long as she lived.

They folded the body into the trunk of Cosmo's car. He told her that if she breathed a word to anyone he would kill her, and it had been both their faults because if she'd given him time to think then they might have been able to save the bitch. Grace didn't speak a word as they drove out to the desert. Cosmo flicked the radio on and smoked manically out of the window. All she would remember of that drive was Bruce Springsteen on the airwaves, 'Born to Run', and it seemed that her whole life had been spent doing exactly that.

She shivered in the cold night as Cosmo dug the hole. It took forever. A host of stars observed overhead as the body was thrown in, eliciting a sickening thump. Grace pleaded once more to go to the cops and he hit her so hard she was thrown across the hood of the car.

'This goes nowhere,' he told her on the ride back to town. 'Do you understand? I give you your money; you crawl back to whatever hole you came from and I never want to see you again. That bitch is nothing to me, and neither are *you. You claim to know me and you're a crazy-ass mother-fucker off the goddamn street. You even think about telling anyone any of this and you're more of a corpse than the girl I just buried. Got it? It's your fingerprints all over her, too. Never forget that.'*

Grace Turquoise quit Madam Babydoll's the next morning. She didn't leave a note, just the cut she owed. Downtown she rented an apartment and took a job in a bar. One night she was singing as she worked and invited to the stage, where as long-overdue luck would have it a visiting record producer encountered the most astonishing voice he'd ever heard.

A week later she was signed to her first label. Cosmo Angelopoulos soon became a horrifying memory, one that would wake her in the night, bathed in sweat and remembering his words. He couldn't touch her now...could he?

She wasn't to know that her flourishing stardom was going to lead her straight back into the ring. And that one day she would have to face her adversary—and then, only then, one of them would be made to pay.

## 14

Robin's tour manager had arranged a dance audition in West Hollywood. They needed to select eight principal dancers and twenty backing, and with hundreds queueing round the block from six a.m., they knew they had their work cut out.

'We'll see you in groups of thirty, three rows of ten,' Marc Delgado told them. 'When I hold my hand up like this, front row goes to the back and the next comes forward. Clear?'

The studio was a kaleidoscopic jumble of leg warmers, slashed T-shirts and hairstyles that rivalled even her own. California-tanned bellies peeked out above hip-hugging slouch pants, and smooth, powerful limbs practised stretch warm-ups with ease. There couldn't be more than an ounce of fat in the room. Robin didn't think she'd ever seen so many gorgeous people in the same place: African, Asian, Caucasian, Hispanic, each was as cute as the next.

'This is going to be tough,' she said, grabbing a coffee

and taking her place alongside Marc and Barney. Barney was flipping through the dancers' profiles.

'Jeez, where do we start?'

'Stamina,' Marc advised. 'These guys need to be able to perform night after night and week after week. Today should give you an idea of how they keep pace. We'll have the finalists moving for an hour or more, but any sign of flagging, breathlessness or ill-coordination and it's a no as far as I'm concerned.'

'Harsh!' said Robin.

Marc shrugged. 'But true.'

The routines fired up to Robin's opening number 'Told You So' and an army of bodies slipped into the choreographed routine. Marc had arranged a killer string of steps, jagged one minute, supple the next, and the dancers adhered with poise and precision.

After the first round the panel conferred, starring the names of those they'd call back and striking through any who hadn't made it. Marc explained it was a rigorous process and the dancers selected would be made to endure several gruelling cycles before decisions were made. He found Robin's determination to employ a majority of women refreshing, and unlike most stars he'd worked with she was unthreatened by their beauty. 'If you're doing me a hot show, Marc, then I want the hottest girls there are.'

Take two surrendered some formidable talent. The competition was brutal. Several dancers quit, short of air or fumbling their steps, and once the momentum was broken it was hard to get back. Robin had taken basic training when her star began its ascent, in how to cover the stage, how to move while holding her voice and how to execute a basic catalogue of struts, but not nearly enough to compete with the professionals. To be dismissing them felt cruel, but as Marc kept pointing out they had to get the numbers down somehow.

It was a thrill to be amassing her troupe. They would be like one big crew on the road, and she wasn't just picking a bunch of randoms to take the stage, she was picking people with whom she'd be content to spend time, people who might become friends.

'Like them,' Barney had counselled on the way over, 'but trust them more.'

A runner put his head round the door. Marc went to shoo him off but he gestured at Robin with a tentative, 'Sorry to disturb. Phone call for Ms Ryder.'

Robin looked up. 'Who is it?'

'The girl says it's family. I wouldn't have interrupted otherwise...'

Robin was puzzled. 'Excuse me,' she said, 'this won't take long.'

Family?

Outside the corridor was deserted, quiet apart from the shouts of kids passing on the street several storeys below. There was a booth, the phone resting expectantly on a little plastic counter. Robin scooped it up. 'Hello?'

Nothing.

'Hello?' she repeated.

She went to replace the receiver, thinking the line must have been cut off, when she began to detect a very faint breathing, so delicate it was hardly there.

'Who is it?' she demanded. 'Who is this?'

The breathing was quickening, deepening, getting louder.

Thickly she remembered the walker at her heels in London. The dodgy fan mail. And then three words, faint and rattling, so muffled that she couldn't be at all sure but she thought a female voice rasped:

'*I'm watching you...*'

Robin slammed the phone down. Her heart was in her throat and her fingers were trembling. *I'm closer than you think...*

It took minutes for her to gather herself. *It's nothing. It's nobody.* She was knackered, that was all; it was the jet lag. So what if some psycho got off on the sound of her voice? It was common enough in this industry.

Back in the audition, Barney mouthed, 'Everything OK?' and Robin nodded, smiling as brightly as she could. There was no point raising it; she'd only get told what she already knew. Besides, since when did she let herself get spooked?

She resolved to brush it off and focus on the job.

As she observed the next group fall into position, one particular dancer caught her eye. Robin checked his picture against the list. Farrell. Twenty-one years old. With his light chocolate skin and bright green eyes, he reminded her of someone.

*Leon Sway.*

Idiotically she had Googled him the previous night. She'd drunk too much champagne at a launch with Barney, and on returning to her hotel had heard him mentioned on the radio.

Countless sites had sprung up, led by an article beginning *Leon Christopher Sway, born 1988 in East Compton, Los Angeles...*which she'd meant to open but hadn't. Instead she had been drawn to the line of thumbnail shots running below and had clicked on Image Results. Most of the snaps saw the Olympian breaking through the finish in London, face to the open sky, arms stretched wide—she could think what she liked of him, but that body… In others he was alongside Jax Jackson, head to head, neck and neck, the man he couldn't beat, the photos mocked up to present the athletes locked in mortal combat. A glance showed there were hordes of blogs and fan sites devoted to him.

*Sexiest man in the world. Ultimate boyfriend. Superhuman.* The list went on.

One picture had jumped out. It was Leon with a woman, snapped at LAX. The woman was kissing him, her arms around his neck, and Leon was grinning dizzily through the adulation. Ridiculously, something in Robin had sunk. She'd snapped the laptop shut.

'I don't like him,' she said to Marc now, nodding to Farrell as the routine struck up. 'Front row, tall, grey sneakers. Let's not see him again.'

The meet with Puff City took place the following afternoon at Slink Bullion's mansion on Long Beach—he liked to keep things relaxed, apparently. As Robin's car cruised through the sweltering grid of LA, reaching the ocean with its silver, glittering harbour and wide straight roads lined with majestic palms, she gathered her nerve. As a rule she didn't let other people daunt her, but Puff City were a notorious crew. If they agreed on collaboration, not only would it be a personal triumph, it would seal her fate as the one to watch in America. With her *Beginnings* tour fast approaching, the game was on.

She pulled out her iPhone and checked her emails.

Wait till you see this place. B x

Barney had attended a lunch with record execs and had planned to meet her there, but, while normally she didn't mind going places alone, on this occasion she was glad he'd made it first. She scrolled through several unread messages before deciding she was too anxious to absorb them properly. Before she closed the account her eye fell on Turquoise da Luca's name. Robin had contacted her the morning after *Friday Later*: she'd been surprised at Turquoise's sudden withdrawal and couldn't forget the haunted look in her eyes. What was going on?

Sorry to split, Turquoise had mailed back. Run down, that's all. Let's do it next time.

The car changed lanes and peeled away from the beach, pulling up moments later at an awesome set of twisting gates. Robin's driver spoke into the intercom and the entrance swung open, revealing a lush spread of verdant gardens, through the middle of which threaded their path. At its summit was the infamous mansion: it had appeared once on *MTV Cribs*, inciting alternate waves of marvel and disgust across media forums. Did anyone seriously need sixteen bedrooms and as many en suites? Were a private gym, games room and spa really necessary? Could both an indoor and outdoor Jacuzzi swimming pool be justified when there were people starving in the world? But Slink Bullion lived by his own rules. From the streets of Brooklyn to the castles of LA, Slink had strived for every cent and couldn't care who knew it.

Seven (she had to count) vehicles were parked out front, ahead of a garage Robin suspected housed yet more: a burnished black Rolls-Royce Phantom; an ice-white Mercedes McLaren SLR with flashing alloys; a two-hundred-thousand-dollar Ferrari 458; a colossal red Hummer Pickup…and the rest. Each boasted a personalised licence plate, which put paid to any doubt that they all belonged to Slink. SL1NK A. SLNKWISE. 5LINKY.

A woman in hot pants and a sparkly bikini top met her at the door.

'Yeah?'

'I'm Robin.'

'And?'

'I've got an appointment.'

The woman looked her up and down a tad bitchily: she was Shawnella, Slink's live-in, long-suffering lover, a gorgeous black girl with legs that went on for miles.

'Baby!' she yelled into the hall. 'You got a visitor.' She blew a strawberry bubble in Robin's face and fixed her with a stare.

'What's up, Robin Ryder?' Slink came to greet her, a heavy black guy in a Red Sox sweatshirt, a baseball cap wedged over his cornrows. 'Good t' finally meet you.'

'Likewise.'

'Come on through.' He patted Shawnella's ass. Robin saw how she pouted at having to share his attention, and shot a dark grimace Robin's way before disappearing inside.

Barney had been right. This was more a palace than a mansion. Slink's dominion went on for miles. 'This is my hall of fame right here,' he informed her as they passed through a gallery covered wall to wall in awards and accolades, not a spare strip to be seen. 'I should take y'all on a grand tour but y'all be here for a week.'

Eventually they arrived at the living room—one of them. Barney Grant was seated uncomfortably on a leather couch and clutching a fat cigar he didn't want to smoke.

'Y'know my main man G.' Slink gestured to a guy in a checked shirt and cardigan, who grinned and held his hand out: G-Money, he had been part of the City since the start.

'Hey,' he said warmly, 'how's it going?'

'An' this here's my brother Principal.'

Robin got a cooler vibe off Principal 7. He was a toughened-up white kid with something to prove, lifting his chin in grudging acknowledgement and regarding her with suspicious, mistrustful eyes. 'Wassup?' he muttered sullenly.

'Y'all want somethin' t'drink?' asked Slink.

Robin clocked the fully stocked bar, next to which a second girl, this one with slightly more on but still in a state of partial undress, awaited instruction. 'A beer would be good.'

The girl popped open a bottle of Corona Light and brought it over.

'What did you think of the tracks?' asked Barney.

Slink took a seat, ankle on knee, and smiled, exposing a glinting silver tooth. 'You got it down, girl, an' I ain't even lyin'. So word up, we should make music together.'

'Last record we dropped sold a million in seven days,' put in G-Money, real name Gordon Rimeaux. Unlike the rest of the crew G-Money was clean-living, educated, had swept his act up after a difficult childhood: Robin respected him. 'That's one week, man, and that's some crazy shit right there. It's like even after all these years there's love on the streets for the City.'

'What's she bringin' to the party?' Principal folded

scrawny arms across his oversized T-shirt. 'I say we stick to the script and no messin'.'

Robin was confused. 'What script?'

'There ain't no script,' said G-Money, 'only my man Principal's not wise enough in the ways of the world to have figured that shit out yet.'

'Fuck you.'

'If the City hadn't taken you in, where'd you be? Slink took a chance, now it's you who returns the favour. 'S all in the chain, man, you pass that vibe on.'

'You wanna tell me how to live my life, asshole?' Principal stepped forward, ready for battle.

'Chill,' warned Slink, and Robin got the impression he was used to dispelling friction. 'We got a philosophy, you feel what I'm sayin'? We ride with the new school, the cool school, the anything that's true school, and that's about my girl Robin right here. G, get on down to the studio, dog, we're gonna lay out some beats.'

Principal backed off. There was a sinister gleam in his eye. As the youngest member of the group he fronted with the best of them, fuelled by anger at the life that had done him wrong. Robin didn't know his history but she guessed it made her own look like *Little House on the Prairie*. He'd take a while to warm up, but she was determined to get on his right side.

Slink's studio was in his basement and rigged with mixing consoles, drum kits, monitors and mics. It was bigger and better equipped than the booth in which she'd recorded her album back in the UK, and as Slink eased into a chair and began wiring up the track she understood this was his empire and the home he'd always had.

'Don't worry about my brother upstairs,' said G-Money. 'He's got beef with most people so don't take it personal.'

'I haven't. But thanks.'

'You just be doin' your thing.'

Robin smiled at him. 'Always do.'

'It's since hookin' up with the track team boys, he ain't too happy about that. Can't say I am either, but you gotta give it up for a good cause, you feel me?'

'Jax Jackson's idea, right?'

'Dude's a clown.'

She couldn't resist asking. 'What about Leon Sway?'

G-Money's countenance changed. It was like a cloud passing over the sun.

'None of us ever met the guy,' he said flatly. 'Guess he'd have a reason to get involved with the anti-weapon stand, though, huh?'

Robin frowned. She thought Leon's involvement with the charity venture was the stupidest, most hypocritical thing she'd ever heard. What would he know about the streets?

'How do you mean?'

But G-Money was taking a seat alongside Slink at the workstation.

'You wanna get in the live room?' Slink suggested. Barney fired her a thumbs-up. 'Drop some sounds, see what's up?'

Robin put Leon Sway from her mind. She was playing with the bigger boys now.

'You bet I do.'

# 15

Kristin's home resembled one of her video sets. It was Friday evening, and in the vast mansion grounds an ivory marquee had been erected in the style of a Disney castle, its billowing fabrics and soaring turrets home to the most perfect princess in the land. On her fourteenth birthday, Bunny White was that princess. Bunny was the star of the show—and the show, it went without saying, had been orchestrated to a military agenda by their mother.

'Those damn caterers, late as usual!' bitched Ramona, rampaging through the mansion doors and slapping Kristin's hand away from a platter of salmon tartare.

'What? I'm hungry.'

'Guests are arriving any second,' she complained. 'We've just this minute put the arrangements out and already you're troughing. I thought you were dieting.'

'I don't need to diet.' Kristin's waist was miniature in a clinging peach Marchesa gown. Her face stung at the criticism.

'Neither do I, but I do it all the same.' Ramona lived like a bird, pecking on nuts and seeds. 'It's part of the job. Image, Kristin, you should know that. Bunny does.'

'Bunny doesn't need to lose weight, either.'

'She will. Fourteen is the cut-off point for those puppy-fat excuses. It's hard work from here on in. *Alexis!*' The catering manager, no doubt hoping she could slip past unnoticed while Ramona was distracted, stilled in her tracks like a fox in the headlights.

'Yes, Ms White?'

'Where are the beignets?'

'They went out with the buckwheat blinis.'

'And have they been tasted?'

Alexis looked harassed. 'One of my girls said she ran them past you—'

'Well *I'm* not going to do it, am I? Please! If I'd sampled every single canapé from every single party I've ever thrown I'd be the size of this house!' She clamped her hands to her hips, bone on bone. 'And if *you* turned up on time to your engagements then we'd be able to avoid these eleventh-hour issues, wouldn't we?'

'There are no issues, Ms White,' said Alexis coolly. Alexis was tempted to reiterate that they'd arrived less than five minutes behind schedule, and that had only been because the ETV *Birthday Brilliant!* van and all its equipment had been blocking up the drive. The popular channel had agreed to come film because of the Kristin connection—Bunny wasn't yet prominent enough—and Ramona was determined to put on a spectacular.

Bunny appeared in the doorway. Ramona's attention

switched, as automatic and unthinking as a shark thrown fresh bait. Alexis scuttled off.

'Why aren't you wearing the wig?' Ramona demanded. 'We bought it specially.'

Bunny looked to the floor. 'I didn't want to.'

'Why?'

'It's itchy.'

Ramona rolled her eyes, exasperated. Not once did she tell Bunny how lovely she looked in her fairy-tale coral dress with delicate sash bow.

'Wow,' said Kristin, making up for it. 'You look so amazing, Bun. Really grown-up.'

Bunny smiled shyly.

'Go and put the wig on,' snapped Ramona.

'I don't want to.'

'You don't *want* to? What do you want, then? For everyone to think you look like a silly little infant? You're a woman now, Bunny.'

'No, she isn't,' countered Kristin, her anger bubbling over. 'And I don't think she should wear the wig either. It makes her look like a drag queen.'

Bunny giggled. Kristin joined in.

'Stop it!' shrieked Ramona, close to the edge. 'Don't you *ever* dare laugh at me!'

The camera crew entered, a bunch of girls in DMs and guys with shaggy hairstyles and lumberjack shirts. Ramona composed herself.

'We've done the interior shots,' said the girl in charge. 'OK if we step outside?'

'Of course,' said Ramona, eager to please, and just a

touch paranoid that they might have witnessed the tail end of her outburst.

'We've got a team out front,' the girl went on, 'so we can catch the celebrities as they arrive. Did you say you had a carpet you wanted to lay out?'

'Oh!' Ramona's bejewelled hands flew to her face. 'What am I thinking? I completely forgot!' She acted the loveable ditz but the oversight secretly slayed her.

Kristin wanted to strangle her mother. Why couldn't Bunny hang with her own friends, have a barbecue in the sun? This party wasn't for her at all; it was for Ramona. Their mother was obsessed with having the best set, the best coverage and the best guests—where 'best' stood for 'expensive' or 'most bankable'. There had been tears when Bunny had asked to invite her own friends, a request that had been swiftly declined because Ramona already had a list in place. That list comprised industry notables—celebrities known to Kristin, mostly—and none of whom meant anything whatsoever to the birthday girl.

Except for Scotty.

At least he was coming, and he'd also drawn Joey and Luke into attending, which Bunny would be thrilled about. In a few years' time Kristin hoped her sister would get with someone like Joey—a sweet, kind boy who would adore her, and who understood the pressures of the industry. It was why Scotty was such an ideal boyfriend. As well as being madly handsome and talented and sexy, he 'got' the craziness of both their lives. You couldn't explain it to someone on the outside.

'Are you excited?' Kristin asked, in an attempt to rally

spirits. Their mother had darted off and Bunny was looking crestfallen, patting her hair self-consciously.

'Maybe I *should* wear the wig,' she murmured, adolescent
gaze brimming with uncertainty and a longing for approval.
'Do you think I should? Mom says my hair's limp…and I
just want to look nice, you know?' She bit her lip. ''Specially if the boys are here…'

'You're beautiful as you are.' Kristin pulled her close.
'Enjoy it, don't let her get to you.' But Kristin suspected that
she didn't know the half of what Bunny had to endure over
the beauty pageants. At least by the time Kristin was eight
Ramona had spawned another child to focus on: poor Bunny
had been in the firing line since the day she was born.

An hour later the party was in full swing. The marquee
shone like a pearl in the fading light, bordered by the dark
silhouettes of trees, bright as a unicorn coming to rest in a
leafy glade. Twisting canopies strewn with fairy lights sparkled above the guests like stars, a fantasyland made real.
Singers, actresses and TV stars sipped pink champagne and
nibbled at miniature lobster wellingtons, while producers,
moguls and managers smoked and drank brandy, posing
for photographs with their rake-thin wives whose names no
one remembered. The pool shone ultramarine, bordered by
jasmine-scented flickering candles and next to which stood
Ramona's *pièce de résistance*: Bunny's birthday cake. It was
a fourteen-tiered monster, studded with gold flakes and silver orbs and capped with a life-size moulding of Bunny's
very own head, her golden icing ringlets tumbling down the
flanks. The head was wearing a glistening crown, which
read, a touch prematurely:

MINI MISS MARVELLOUS—WINNER!

'Bitchin', huh?'

Kristin turned. She was relieved to be extricated from a stilted conversation with a French rap star and even more relieved when she came face to face with Joey Lombardi.

'Hey!' She hugged him. Joey was Italian-American with black, curly hair and twinkling brown eyes. As one fifth of Fraternity, he was easily second favourite to Scotty; girls went crazy for him. Up close he smelled of lemon sherbet. 'How's it going?'

'Better now I've seen that.' Joey raised an eyebrow at the cake. 'It's truly a thing of wonder. Did your mother make it?'

Kristin grinned. One of the things she liked best about Joey was his sense of humour.

'If it was Bunny's actual head on top then I might consider that a serious question,' she said.

He laughed.

'Where's Scotty?' she asked, searching over his shoulder.

Joey ran a hand through his unruly hair. Kristin remembered when Scotty had wanted to leave his to its natural wave (he straightened it) and the label had told him he couldn't because curls were 'Joey's thing'. 'Beats me,' said Joey. 'I haven't seen him.'

Kristin spied Luke talking to a circle of Hollywood socialites, her mother hovering on its periphery and plunging into their conversation every so often like a wasp on food, rooting about a bit before buzzing off. Wouldn't the boys have arrived together?

She checked the time. 'He said he'd be here by now. You haven't heard from him?'

Joey shrugged. 'Nah, sorry. Can I get you a drink?'

Kristin was worried. 'What if something's happened?'

'Like what?'

'Maybe he's crashed the Lexus.'

Joey touched her arm. 'He'll be fine,' he said. 'Scott knows what he's doing. He probably got held up someplace; it wouldn't be the first time.'

'Oh?' She was surprised. Scotty had always been punctual with her.

'Sure,' Joey replied easily. 'He's drifted behind schedule on a few things recently. Said he's tired. It's nothing to write home about.'

A vague sort of dread clutched Kristin's heart.

'I think I'll call him,' she said. 'Thanks.'

Inside, she closed the door to Ramona's office and dialled Scotty. It rang and rang but there was no answer. She tried again, then once more. Nothing.

Kristin tapped the phone against her jaw. Scotty had said he'd be here, and he'd never let her or Bunny down. Something must have come up and he had forgotten to let her know, that was all, nothing to get alarmed over, just as Joey had said. And yet...

Emerging into the hall, she heard a ripple of giggles coming from the kitchen and instinctively backed up. Moments later, Luke came into frame and swaggered out on to the swarming patio, bottle of beer in hand, his hair dishevelled at the back. Kristin went to follow him out and almost ran straight into her mother.

'Mom?'

Ramona's lipstick was smudged. The top buttons of her silk blouse had been done up incorrectly. It took less than a second to work out what was going on.

'Are you insane?' Kristin cried, outraged. 'He's *twenty*!'

Ramona smirked. 'So?'

'He's Scotty's friend! He's *my* friend!'

Ramona patted her chignon. 'Well, then I suppose I'm his friend now, too.'

'How long?' Kristin whispered.

Her mother smiled coyly. Drunkenly she arched an eyebrow. 'Long enough,' she growled, and she actually put her tongue in her cheek. Ew! It was *beyond* gruesome!

'I *meant* how long has it been going on?'

Ramona sighed with exasperation. 'Oh, darling, relax!' she sang, wafting out to play the hostess. 'I *am* a hot-blooded woman, you know. What does it matter?'

Kristin was rigid with fury. It mattered a lot. Not because her mom was old and Luke was barely clear of being a teenager, not because her dislike for her mom sometimes bordered on hatred, but because Luke and Fraternity were *her* thing. She'd been made to share *it all* with her mother; from the earliest point, nothing had been hers, every move had been down to Ramona. Except for this. The boys were *hers*. How dare she steal this, as well?

'I'm leaving.' Kristin had to get away. She couldn't stand this house any more. She couldn't bear to look her mother in the eye. 'Tell Bunny I'll be back later.'

'Where are you going?' Ramona commanded. 'We need you for the ETV shoot!'

'Fuck the shoot.' She hauled open the door. 'Bunny doesn't want to do it anyway.'

'Kristin! You come back here *this instant*!'

The door slammed behind her. There was only one place

she wanted to be, only one person who could make her feel better.

If Scotty wouldn't come to her then she would go to him.

## 16

Scotty Valentine rolled over, straight into the loving arms of his manager, Fenton Fear. Fenton's chest hair nuzzled his cheek and gently he kissed the older man's collarbone.

*Bliss.* It was heaven to have Fenton in his apartment, his home...his bed. It had never happened before, Fenton was always terrified they would be seen, but on this occasion temptation had found a way. He'd only meant to drop by Scotty's to discuss a forthcoming timetable, and within minutes the men were making up for the lost weeks since Tokyo.

'You're such a handsome boy.' Fenton kissed his hair over and over. Scotty thought he would drown in happiness. 'I've missed you more than you know.'

'I do know,' Scotty said as he sighed, 'because I've felt the same.' He reached under the covers for the other man's hand, holding it tight. 'Fenton, I have to tell you...'

He stalled, frightened that the words wouldn't come back to him; that they'd just hang there, embarrassed in their solitude, and his declaration would ruin everything.

'Shh.' Tenderly Fenton stroked his back. 'You don't need to.'

Scotty could hear his manager's heartbeat beneath his cheek. When he was with Fenton it was as if the rest of the world didn't exist. They could be anywhere so long as they were together; it was cliché, but true. In Fenton's arms he was no longer Scotty Valentine, poster boy for teenage dreams and squeaky-clean advocate of healthy whole-bran pop; he was simply Scott, the man behind the media machine. He could let his guard down, be adored for the person he was, not the person he was imagined to be.

From beneath a heap of clothes on the floor, his cell buzzed for the eighth time that evening. It would be Kristin. He had promised her he would make Bunny's party but it was almost ten and things would be wrapping up by now. He'd made all her other ones over the years: he deserved a break, didn't he? Shit. Who'd have a girlfriend? Fenton never put demands on him—at least not any he wasn't happy to meet…

'Shouldn't you get that?' Fenton murmured. 'It might be important.'

Scotty tilted his head to kiss him. 'Let's pretend a little while longer.'

'Is it Kristin?'

'Probably.'

Fenton winced. No matter how many times Scotty reassured him that he felt nothing for his girlfriend, her name still twisted like barb between them.

'I don't desire her,' comforted Scotty. 'You *know* that.'

'How can you want me,' Fenton replied. It wasn't a question, merely an expression of how he felt. He wasn't after reassurance because no matter how much of that Scotty gave him, he never took it in. Scotty's affection for him was a miracle he couldn't understand.

'I'm old,' he went on. 'And I drink too much.' Fenton motioned down to his belly, covered in a downy fuzz of hairs. 'Then there's you. Exquisite. Radiant. Adonis.'

'Come here,' Scotty choked, overawed with love. Why wouldn't Fenton believe him?

The men lay together, bodies entwined, every so often sharing a sweet, fragile kiss, until Fenton's attentions grew fiercer and his mouth moved lower. Scotty hardened, stiffer and stiffer till he thought he would burst. Fenton's moustache grazed his balls, his tongue wrapped around Scotty's length, teasing the tip of his erection and using his hands in a rhythm of almost unbearable intensity that sent ripple after ripple of unfettered pleasure chasing up Scotty's spine. Delirious with yearning, Scotty groaned as his dick slid into paradise. His ardour, as always, was tinged with envy. How many other men had Fenton done this to? At his age he must have had countless boyfriends, and it tore Scotty apart to picture him for one second with anyone else. Fenton was the only man he'd been with.

'I have to be inside you,' croaked Scotty, extricating himself. Obligingly Fenton turned and Scotty set to work, dipping his fingers into his own mouth before using them on Fenton, and then, with a single, hard thrust, he entered, both of them crying out and plunging forward on the sweat-bathed sheets. Scotty gripped Fenton's buttock with one hand, snaking the other round to grasp his manager's hard-on, working it up and down as he built a rhythm, feeling his abdomen contract and the pleasure rushing through him like liquid flames...

He didn't hear the door open.

But he saw. As Fenton bucked to ejaculation beneath him he saw the shape in the entrance. It was Kristin, a sharp blank look of shock slapped across her stricken face.

'Fuck!' Fenton cried in orgasmic frenzy.

'Fuck,' Scotty replied, frozen with horror. The blood drained entirely from his face and in that second he knew it was over. Everything. Over.

# *17*

Turquoise regularly took on ten-thousand-strong audiences and thought nothing of it. She made TV appearances in front of millions and didn't bat an eye. She'd addressed royalty, politicians and the world's elite, holding her own against the most powerful on the planet.

But sitting through lunch with Cosmo Angel was a summit she could not climb.

'I'm not feeling great,' she told Donna Cameron that morning. 'Can we postpone?'

'Not really,' came the curt reply. 'This is the only opening you have.'

'I think I'm contagious.'

There was a pause before Donna said, 'Turquoise, what's up? You're never contagious. Come to think of it, you're never *ill*. I can't remember the last time you got sick. What's going on? You've been lukewarm about this project since the start. Is it Cosmo?'

'No,' she cut in. 'Of course not.' She felt tangled in a

web of lies. It was too late to back away; the decline would mean too much, the sacrifice of her future. *My little star...*

'Then help me out.'

Every excuse was a weak one. She had changed her mind. She wanted to focus on her music a while longer. She didn't feel ready, despite the role Sam Lucas described in London having her name written all over it. Only the truth could save her, and in the same blow spell total destruction. She had been abused and degraded and forced to endure untold suffering at the hands of Cosmo Angelopoulos, and it had all come to a shattering head when they had buried a young corpse in the desert one night...one dark, lonely, terrible night...

Now he had her trapped all over again.

'It's OK.' The words took all her strength. 'I'll grab a coffee, see if that sorts me out.'

'Good girl. Il Cielo, one o'clock.' The line went dead.

His wife was with him. She hadn't expected that.

When Turquoise entered the bustling restaurant it was with a mixture of distress and relief that she spotted Ava Bennett rising to meet her. Ava looked lovely in a pale shift dress, her silky white-blonde hair secured in a ponytail at the nape of her neck. It was impossible to imagine her in bed with Cosmo. Had he grown out of his perversions? He must have.

'Hope you don't mind me coming along.' Ava grinned. 'Only this is so exciting! When Cosmo told me you were on board I couldn't believe it...'

'Turquoise.' Sam Lucas stood to kiss her on both cheeks.

'Gorgeous, as always. Come and sit down. We've ordered champagne.'

Cosmo didn't stand. She was aware of his dark, brooding presence and the conflict of wills she had known would take place. To anyone else just a few seconds; to her an unspoken stalemate. Cosmo still saw her as a seventeen-year-old whore getting screwed on all fours by anything he set her up against. It didn't matter how famous she got. She was still that girl.

And he wouldn't deign to speak to her first.

'Cosmo, a pleasure to see you again,' she said hollowly. He got to his feet, an amused smirk on his face, and leaned in to kiss her. His lips hit the skin by her ear lobe, sending a grisly chill racing down her spine.

'You're glowing.' His black eyes flashed. 'Who's the lucky man?'

'Exactly what I said!' trilled Ava, but she waved him down all the same. 'Come on, don't embarrass her.'

'I'm not embarrassing her. Am I?'

'Never.'

'Sam, did you bring a copy of the script?' asked Donna, lifting her champagne for a toast. 'To the best screenplay *and* the best cast we'll see all year.'

'Well, I've got a little news on that front.' Sam shifted eagerly in his seat, like a boy on the cusp of revealing a secret he knew he shouldn't. The celebrated director had recently made a controversial comeback with the release of Lana Falcon's movie *Eastern Sky*, whose Vegas premiere had been overshadowed by scandal. Insider accounts suggested the ensuing publicity whirlwind had made Sam feel invincible, and his behaviour, at times, erratic.

Donna didn't like surprises. 'Oh?'

Turquoise liked them even less. Across the table, Cosmo slid her a smile. It was the same smile he had greeted her with all those years ago at the door to his home, whispering of all the wicked things he wanted to do to her... Her heart dropped to her toes.

'Cosmo's been working on a script,' said Sam, barely able to contain his excitement.

'Congratulations,' said Donna politely. 'What does that mean for us?'

Turquoise knew exactly what it meant. Ava caught her eye and winked. So this was the script she had told Turquoise about that time they met up in New York, the one Cosmo was keeping close to his chest. The one about the murder...

'I read it at the weekend,' enthused Sam, leaning back as a waiter came to refill their glasses, 'and I gotta say it blew my socks off. This guy's penned a masterpiece.'

Cosmo lifted his shoulders in mock humility and Ava rolled her eyes affectionately. 'Wise up, baby,' she crooned, 'you know it's good.'

'We didn't want to say anything before now because it wasn't in the can,' continued Sam. 'But, if you're game, we'd like you to take a look at this script instead.'

Donna frowned. 'What about the movie you talked to us about? What about Gloria, the singer who gets her revenge? That's what sold it to Turquoise.'

'Cosmo wanted it to be a revelation. Right, buddy?'

Cosmo took a long slow sip of the champagne and watched Turquoise over the top.

'You'll like this character even more,' he said.

'You can't change the game like this, Sam,' pressed

Donna. 'I don't care if Cosmo's come up with a magnum opus, it's not the project Turquoise and I agreed to.'

Their orders were taken, allowing time for the tension to be dispelled. Turquoise felt Cosmo's eyes on her and feared that if she tried to speak only a dry rasp would come out.

'Just hear the pitch.' Sam gestured for them to be calm. 'I know it's not what we talked about and I appreciate that comes as a shock. However, as a movie written by *and starring* Cosmo Angel it spells a fortune. With Turquoise on board? Gold dust. I know you're going to fall in love with it just as much as I have. Cosmo, over to you.'

'You mean I finally get to hear what it's about?' teased Ava.

Donna glanced at Turquoise and gave her an imperceptible shake of the head. *Don't worry; we're not consenting to anything.*

Turquoise wanted to close her ears. She wanted to run and hide. She wanted to be anywhere else on Earth but here. *Cosmo doesn't give a shit about consent.*

'The story's simple,' explained Cosmo, never once taking his eyes from Turquoise's face, 'as all the best stories are. You play a girl from the wrong side of the tracks. Momma gave her up, Daddy's long gone and the only person she can rely on is herself. She gets in with the wrong crowd, experiments with drugs and before she knows it her life's a wreck. Penniless, she's struggling to make ends meet. But, and this is the thing, she's gorgeous. The kind of girl guys want in their bed; the kind of girl they leave their wives for; the hottest body on the west coast with a smile and a pair of tits to die for. She embraces a life of vice.'

'Hang on a second,' interrupted Donna. 'You want Turquoise to play a hooker?'

*Bastard. Heartless, merciless, cold-blooded bastard.*

'Is that a problem?' challenged Cosmo, playing with her like a kitten on a string.

'Hear the rest,' Sam cut in. 'I promised you an empowerment story and that's what you'll get. Not for one second would I assume this wouldn't be a challenging role for Turquoise and that she'd have to dig deep...'

'Real deep,' echoed Cosmo.

'But it's that same rawness that will showcase Turquoise's considerable ability.'

'Go on, darling,' urged Ava. She smiled reassuringly at Turquoise, but since she herself hadn't had a clue what the script was about must have suppressed her misgivings.

'She becomes romantically involved with a client.' Cosmo patted his chest with one tanned, long-fingered hand. 'Me.'

'Isn't this *Pretty Woman*?' Ava joked weakly.

'Hardly,' snapped Cosmo, before correcting himself. 'It's darker.'

Sam nodded. 'Much darker.'

'They become involved in a killing,' said Cosmo, 'a very violent one. A minor dies while in their care.'

Turquoise thought she would be sick. *In their care?*

'They vow never to speak of it again. My character goes on to become a successful businessman, and yours grows into, of course—' and here he spread his hands wide, like the magician revealing his trick '—an acclaimed singer.'

'Victory against the odds,' Sam put in, delightedly.

Cosmo smiled, baring his teeth. 'They go their separate

ways, only my character can't forget. Yours pretends not to know him, forgetting the nights they spent together.'

'Surely she loathes him.' Turquoise spoke for the first time. 'He was a job, after all.'

'That's where you're mistaken,' Cosmo replied, running a finger across his chin, 'because this man taught her the ways of the world. He taught her to be strong, and resilient, and to toughen up; and those same things led to her becoming the star she is today.'

*Bullshit!* she wanted to cry. *Total and utter goddamn bullshit!*

Was it a joke? It had to be a joke.

Donna smoothed things over. 'Perhaps we ought to take the script away.'

'I want to hear what happens next,' Turquoise said. 'Go on. What happens next?'

Cosmo's gaze never wavered. 'What do you think happens?'

Their food was brought over. As the waiters deposited the plates Donna leaned in and murmured, 'Let's hear them out, OK? We don't have to decide now.'

'I've already decided. I'm not doing it.'

'We should read it first. This could be an opportunity, Turquoise. Sam Lucas, you and Cosmo Angel, the fact it's his brainchild—'

'This looks delicious!' Ava exclaimed.

Cosmo speared a hunk of white fish with his fork. 'While she pretends not to care,' he resumed, ignoring his wife, 'that's only a mask. This woman's conscience is secretly killing her. She might have millions in the bank, fans across the globe, all she's ever dreamed of…but she can't sleep at night. And, in spite of herself, she can't forget his touch.'

'This is meant to be enlightened?' Turquoise threw at Sam. 'She wouldn't give a crap about this guy, other than despising his guts. For God's sake—!'

Donna put a hand on her arm.

'This is the blackest point of the story,' said Sam. 'Come the end the couple resolve to go to the cops because it's the only way of clearing their conscience. But through it all your character realises that the past ten years of her life…' He turned to Cosmo. 'It is ten years?'

Cosmo seasoned his frites. 'About that.'

'The past ten years of her life have been defined by this event, and the only person to have shared that with her, however inadvertently, is this man whom, as you rightly say, she's spent so long resenting.'

'*Resenting?*' Turquoise objected. 'She was whoring for him, by definition he's a vicious sonofabitch!' She knew she was losing it but she couldn't contain herself.

Ava put down her cutlery. 'Perhaps we should talk about something else.'

'No, no.' Cosmo raised his hand. 'She has a point. But tell me, Turquoise, have you ever found yourself in that position?'

'Excuse me?'

'I think we've heard enough,' said Donna.

'Let her answer the question.' Cosmo wiped a dip of oil from the corner of his mouth.

Her voice was ragged. 'How dare you even ask?'

'The reason I do,' continued Cosmo smoothly, 'is to illustrate that we, leading our lives, can't possibly imagine what goes on behind closed doors.'

'Speak for yourself.'

'Prostitutes aren't all dirty money-grabbing whores, are they?' He was daring her, baiting her. 'They're ordinary women trying to make ends meet.'

'And the men who sleep with them?' she asked tightly.

'Aren't all *vicious sonofabitches*, as you put it. Our characters fall for each other. This is a romance that turns conventional notions of love, how men and women should meet and what the rules should be, on its head.'

'At the same time as commenting on our preoccupation with celebrity.' Sam took up the baton. 'Can money buy freedom? Can success take you so far away from a crime that you can forget it ever happened? Can love survive under desperate circumstances? You're two of the biggest stars there are—scratch that, you're the biggest. By taking on these questions you're holding a mirror up to your own lives. And the answer's sure gonna pack a punch.'

Silence. Donna turned to her. In her manager's eyes Turquoise saw a splinter of approval and it frightened her to death.

'We'll consider it,' said Donna swiftly.

'I was hoping for an answer now,' ventured Sam. 'We want to get rolling as soon as possible. Turquoise is our number one; she always has been. Cosmo even wrote a lot of it with her in mind, isn't that right, Cosmo?'

Like a lizard he drew the food from his knife. 'That's right.'

Turquoise met Cosmo's stare. In a rush she was back on his bed, tied at her wrists and ankles, naked and vulnerable.

That stare spoke of ultimate supremacy. She was a toy, and he her master. He would do with her however he pleased.

'What's your gut tell you?' Sam urged.

It told her she was done for.

'Let them think about it.' Cosmo returned to his meal, spiking his food and carving it leisurely. It was part of the fun, to keep her dangling like a worm on a hook, just how he liked it. It turned him on. Did Ava not notice?

'It's meant to be,' he concluded with the killer Cosmo Angel smile. 'We'll be here when you're ready to say yes.'

## *18*

Robin was back in London for a video shoot. They were filming for her fourth single 'You Win' and had closed off an area by Tower Bridge. Crowds were gathered on the Southbank to catch a glimpse of the star.

'Ready to go?' the director called as Robin stepped out of her robe.

With the majestic bridge in the background, historic seal of the capital with its twin golden strongholds and sky-blue suspensions, Robin's venture was deliberately grass roots. Her American tour was less than two months away and she had been advised to remind fans where her priorities lay, plus the legacy of the summer Games meant that for the first time in a while the city was pervaded by a tentative patriotism.

Her track pumped up and Robin fell into step with ease. Even when drowned out by the recording, she preferred to sing: her face didn't move right when she was miming.

*'Why does it have to be a competition? What are we*

*fighting for? Baby, this is my extradition, and still you're wanting more...'*

Every few lines they would stop and take it again, stop and take it again, until she and the director were satisfied. It was exhausting, repetitive work, characterised by fits of faltering rain during which Robin and the crew would shelter under enormous umbrellas and glance beseechingly at the sky. Each time they did, fans hollered for her—'Robin! Over here! We love you!'—and she'd wave back, driving them nuts, while thinking how weird it was that these people were standing around getting wet just to watch what had to be one of the most drawn-out and uneventful video shoots in history.

Afterwards she had three hours of back-to-back interviews lined up at a nearby hotel. No encounter was ever quite the same. From an earnest inquisition with a Sunday paper about the sentiment behind her new single, to a fun glossy mag piece where she spilled her make-up secrets, it never got boring. Robin loved all the people she got to meet, and the easy conversation they fell into as soon as they realised she wasn't a bitch who was going to sit there scowling and worrying about what angle they were getting her at.

The car arrived at six to pick her up. Barney was accompanying her to the evening's premiere at Leicester Square, a Brit action film in which Robin's friend had a supporting role.

They pulled up at the Odeon ten minutes later, Barney trying to be chilled but covertly checking his phone every five seconds because he had fallen out with his boyfriend and they were meant to be going to Barcelona at the weekend. The theatre was plastered in ginormous billboards and sweeping purple lights. Outside an army of fans huddled against the cold.

Robin received a rapturous reception as she stepped from the car and waved to her supporters. Her Grecian Versace drape dress was a stunning vision in grey lace, a departure from her usual urban style that was both sexy and sophisticated.

'Robin, can we get just a second of your time? Can you tell us about your tour? Is it good to be back in England?'

Barney steered her along the line, politely declining the queue of waiting microphones and journalists begging for a word.

Inside, the foyer was teeming. Barney peeled off to fetch them cocktails, just as Robin scanned the room and landed straight into the gaze of Leon Sway. It was like walking into sunlight. He raised a hand in acknowledgement. She ignored him.

'Robin, hi, *great* to see you.' She was joined by one of the judges from her series on *The Launch*. Barney came back with the drinks and the three of them chatted, Robin trying not to steal glances in Leon's direction, and feeling the heat of his gaze whenever his eyes fell on her. With him was Jax Jackson. Even from this distance she could sense the friction between the men. Jax was donning a gold tie, his victory statement clear, and puffing his chest out like a prize peacock. At least the cock part was accurate.

'Are we going in yet?' The idea of sitting in a dark room and switching off from all social interaction was appealing. The day had taken it out of her.

'Another one of these and I'm there.' Barney held up his empty glass. 'Anyone else?'

'I'll go,' Robin offered, heading to the bar.

She'd just had time to collect the drinks when a voice at her side said:

'Hey. You never called.'

She was struck by how crisp his scent was, nothing like aftershave, nothing chemical, just a clean skin smell. He was warm, and the fabric of his suit jacket soft, grazing against her bare shoulder. She hadn't stood this close to him before and realised how much shorter than him she was, the top of her head only just meeting his throat.

'I know,' she replied.

'You didn't come back on my messages.' He grinned. 'I left a lot of messages.'

'I know.'

'Did you like the flowers?'

'I'm not into flowers.'

'Are you into any romantic gestures?'

Robin held up the cocktails, the surly kid in her raising one finger. 'How about this?'

'*Touché.*'

Shrugging, she took a sip. 'What are you doing here?' Finally she appraised Leon properly. He was stupidly handsome.

'Got a dinner in Soho. We're not staying for the movie.'

'Good of you to come, then,' she said drily. 'What's this about Puff City?'

'You heard about that?'

'I take it you're not keen.'

Leon nicked his thumb across his top lip. 'It was Jax's idea, so no, generally speaking, I'm not keen.' A roaming photographer lurched in to snap their picture. Leon hooked an arm round Robin's shoulders, drawing her in. It happened so quickly it seemed truculent to object.

'Perfect.' The photographer was thrilled: easily the snap of the night.

'It's patronising,' said Leon.

Robin was still thinking about the photo. 'No shit it is. Can you try not to paw me in public next time?'

'Next time? Are you asking me out?'

She blushed.

'I meant the Puff City thing,' he put in. 'It's patronising.'

'To you?'

'Not to me: to kids who live with that every day. The single's anti gun crime, 'cept the only reason Jax wants to get involved is in pursuit of his own glory—that and the fact he's bored now the Games are over. He hasn't got a clue what those kids face but since he figures he's got it in him to be a hip-hop artist he'll use it as the hook to get him there.'

'But if it helps raise awareness?'

'Of Jax? Definitely. Slink Bullion? For sure. The issue? I doubt it.' His eyes twinkled. 'I like your new track, by the way.'

'You can't have heard it,' she countered. 'It's not out yet.'

'I asked to hear it.'

'Why?'

Leon regarded her sideways. 'You're not getting it yet, are you?'

'Getting what?'

'That when I want something, I don't quit.'

'Such a man,' she remarked.

'Are you so different?'

'From a man? I'd like to think so.'

'You know that's not what I meant.' He held her gaze.

Barney interrupted them. 'Ready, honey?'

Leon took her arm as she moved off. 'Come out with me tonight?'

'I thought you had a dinner.'

'I do. Afterwards. Sack this gig off.'

'I don't think so.'

'Come on. Eight o'clock, my hotel?' He gave her the name.

'Your *hotel*?'

His laugh took her by surprise. It was nice, spontaneous. 'The bar there's private but it's not *that* private. We could go public, if you prefer, but...'

'You'll get mobbed by screaming fans?' She recalled the woman he'd had slung around his neck at LAX. What was she doing even having this conversation?

'I was thinking more of you.'

'Thanks, but no, thanks. It was good seeing you, though.'

'So good that you don't want to do it again?'

'Have fun at your dinner.'

'I won't be there long, because I'm leaving to see you.' He didn't wait for a reply.

As Robin entered the theatre she tried to forget the encounter. Where did Leon get off, asking her out and then *assuming* she'd come? He thought he could get any woman, and the fact he'd concluded she was just like the rest was the only answer she needed.

A niggling voice asked: *Who are you playing against, Robin—him, or you?*

And a second one, softer, reassured her that maybe he'd try again.

* * *

Leon caught a cab back to his hotel at seven-thirty. Making his excuses hadn't been difficult: he was getting booked for countless appearances all across the world and his management accepted that some he'd have to call short.

The truth was, he couldn't wait to see Robin. Man, she got to him. He'd accepted the premiere invite when he'd heard she would be there. His team had been surprised given how skeptical he'd been about the Puff City venture; surely another PR stunt would have been way off the agenda. But the Puff City gig was different. Perhaps it was because Jax was involved, but it had danger written all over it. Leon had met the crew and hadn't liked them: they'd greeted him shiftily, unable to meet his eye. Slink wanted to record back in LA two weeks from now, and as far as Leon was concerned it couldn't be over with soon enough.

The taxi pulled up outside the Langham and a doorman welcomed him. Staying in splendour felt weird. As Leon made his way through the pristine lobby, his footsteps smacking across its gleaming floor, he couldn't help but think of his mom back in Compton, how he and his siblings had been raised with so little, with nothing, really, except love—but how when it came down to it that was the only thing that mattered.

He had to remember what he was doing this for. Leon could outpace a wild animal, but he would never escape the shadow at his heels—not unless he turned and faced it. Until the day he found his brother's killer and made that person pay, he would never be able to rest.

He reached his suite, slicing his key through the door.

Discarding his suit, he showered and dressed quickly. Downstairs, he spoke to his people about procuring a space.

Eight o'clock came and went. He ordered a second bottle of beer and waited...

And waited.

Eight-thirty passed. Nine o'clock. At nine-fifteen he realised she wasn't coming. Foolishly he had taken it for granted that she would, because despite Robin's playing hard to get there was a connection between them and it burned. He remembered her hair scented like cinnamon, the curve of her waist and her full red mouth. Standing next to her at the premiere, electricity had sparked like crazy. Touching her had been like fire. Hadn't she felt it too?

Egotism was Jax's style, not his, but even so Leon wasn't accustomed to rejection. One thing his coach always said:

*Keep your eyes on that line till you cross it. Nothing else, just the line.*

Robin was his.

At the elevators Leon was set upon by a group of women, who blushed and giggled as he signed scraps of paper. Back in his room, he settled on the bed, flipping open his iPad and typing *Robin Ryder* into the search engine.

He clicked on the first entry and scanned the article:

*Robin Louise Ryder (born Hackney, East London, 1993) is an English singer and songwriter who rose to fame after the release of her debut album,* Beginnings. *She is best known for her breakthrough single 'Lesson Learned', which held the UK number one for eight weeks and enjoyed international success and widespread critical acclaim. At eighteen Ryder was famously discovered on the UK television music competition* The Launch...

Leon scanned the document, taking in the awards Robin had claimed and the praise she had attracted—*the voice of a generation...relevant and inspiring...*—until he reached the section on her personal life. It comprised several lengthy paragraphs and numerous citations and references. Frowning, he read. With each revelation his heart sank.

*Ryder was abandoned as a newborn in one of the most controversial cases of this type in the early nineties, sparking debate between pro-/anti-abortion groups and child welfare organisations. She was found in Victoria Park, East London, by a walker, wrapped in a plastic bag and hours from death. Neither Ryder's mother or father has ever been located... Ryder entered the care system aged two but was removed from her adoptive parents after reports of violence... A series of foster homes followed before Ryder took to the streets. Ryder auditioned for* The Launch *after tackling drug and alcohol problems that she has since attributed to 'a difficult phase in my life'...*

Reaching the end of the article, Leon stared out of the window. London glittered below, a city busy building dreams as quickly as it broke them. It felt wrong reading this stuff, prying into a life that had been sad beyond measure, a life he'd had no idea she'd lived. He wanted to see her. He wanted to talk to her. He wanted to hold her.

No wonder Robin had front. Anybody would. Shock turned to empathy, gave way to compassion, and hardened to respect. He was filled with the need to protect her.

Whatever Robin had gone through before, Leon vowed she would never be lonely or frightened again. She was too special to let go.

The woman who had given her up hadn't known it, but one thing was sure:

He did.

## 19

The North London high rise had been built in the sixties, a grim lump of towering concrete, part-derelict, its lower windows smashed and filled with tarpaulin that whipped angrily in the hollow draft. Climbing from a twist of roads, the block loomed immovable, ugly, on bright afternoons casting dark and giant shadows across the metropolis. It was part of the city yet rejected by it: a place nobody wanted to live.

On the seventeenth floor, in flat 39B, Ivy Sewell and her mother disturbed no one. They saw no one, they spoke to no one; the world outside was fearsome, too much of it, too plural, too menacing. On the street they called Ivy names— *weirdo*, *loser*, *freak*—and they were right. Ivy was rotten on the inside, beyond redemption, useless. That was what Hilda had always told her. It would have been better if she'd never been born.

An orange glow seeped through the blinds in a weary, perpetual stream, illuminating the frayed sofa and mottled chair in the living room. No living went on here. Hilda was slumped on a cushion, glaring out to nothing. Occasionally a TV flickered to life. Game shows were her favourite; she liked the prizes and shiny cars and the host with his straight white smile. In a still hour, when the traffic had died and the world outside was bathed in slumber, a coarse breath escaped as she slept. But neither Sewell slept soundly. The walls knew their secrets.

Ivy went to her bedroom after midnight. Her mother would stay snoring with her mouth open, bulging ankles forced into slippers that rested like blind, foetal creatures on the tortoiseshell carpet, her head tilted back so that Ivy could detect the sparse white hairs that sprang from her chin. A hostess trolley sat stained in the corner, neglected for years, its innards fragrant with trifles of long ago. Fringed, moth-eaten lamps housed dead bulbs and the corpses of flies littered the electric fire. If Hilda woke she'd drink, a bottle, two, maybe more, drinking for the day when at last the poison killed her, watching the clock and daring it to keep on ticking so that sometimes Ivy wondered if she might not put her out of her misery herself. Ivy imagined Hilda in a bloated coffin, her face greasy and brash with the mortician's efforts, pickled in her splendour, flaccid as the chicken dinners that swam in their gravy-filled packets and whose membrane had to be pricked with a fork.

Ivy had spent her life in hope of a warm embrace or a gentle word but had been left wanting. If Hilda tried now she could not trust herself to resist wringing what life was left from her bones. *Mother.* The word meant nothing.

Ivy's bedroom was small, the window sealed, and in the corner a single mattress had split, exposing foam guts. The walls were bare, except for one. No family photos or happy memories. Instead it was covered in photographs and newspaper clippings:

ROBIN RYDER ROCKS AT HAMMERSMITH!
RYDER CLAIMS COVETED CRITICS' PRIZE!
ROBIN SOARS TO SECOND NUMBER ONE!

What was visible was only the start of it. Inside drawers and boxes there was more of the same. Every picture Ivy had seen of her twin sister, every article she had read, every recording she had heard, was pinned, taped, labelled, filed, a library of everything Robin had achieved and a reminder of everything Ivy could destroy.

She *longed* to destroy her—oh, how she did. For Robin had escaped.

It had been so delicious to introduce herself, subtly at first: Ivy's lovingly prepared album; the notepad in which she had executed her most careful handwriting; the tracking of her sister through Camden; the phone call to LA… It had been beyond delectable to hear her voice—just the two of them together, chatting like twins, the way it should be…

Turning to the cracked mirror, Ivy removed her clothes. At nineteen her body was achingly thin. Dark circles ringed her eyes, which glittered dark blue, lit by the flame of revenge. Her chest was flat, her red hair lank, and her stomach concave over her pale cotton knickers. The years had contorted her features, calcified by hatred, so that where they should have been identical they were divided by a twist of difference. Ivy's skinniness, her dyed crimson locks, the crouching hardness in her eyes and the grim set of her mouth had people glance twice, thinking she reminded them of somebody but not quite enough to say who.

She turned, the light catching the angles of her face in a new way.

There she was, a glimmer of her twin. There was the woman she could have been. Robin's life should have been hers. The injustice made her tremble.

Ivy had been too young to remember the day Hilda had returned, drunk as usual, saying she'd *got rid of the other one*. The twins' father, a bum who had drunk his way to the grave when Ivy had been six, relayed it to her one night after Hilda had passed out.

*I've done it*, Hilda had snarled. *I've thrown it away*.

But in abandoning Robin she had set her free. Ivy was the girl who had stayed, and suffered, and been beaten and bruised… The visible scars were never the worst.

*I don't want them. They've ruined my life.* Hilda had wanted to dump both babies, had only saved one because he had forced her to.

Never mind the daughter whose life she had created, who had never had a say in whether or not she was born. Ivy hadn't asked for this. She'd had no choice.

It hadn't mattered which one had been kept. Hilda hadn't cared which one she gave up. It could just as easily have been the other way around. If Ivy had escaped her mother's clutches she could have had a shot at life, had the courage and the confidence to claim what Robin had, for when Ivy sang she heard the exact same voice. They were one and the same.

Two fates decided on the toss of a coin.

Ivy clenched her fists, digging her nails into her palm. Hilda knew who Robin was. She pretended she didn't, acted as if she didn't recognise Ivy's shadow beneath that long straight fringe, in those deep blue eyes…but Ivy had seen. She knew. She'd seen how the channel changed whenever that show pervaded their TV screen. She'd seen how the radio got switched each time one of Robin's songs came on. She'd seen how Hilda drank.

Robin's reprieve had been the grossest wrong. She had been spared, a last-minute pardon from a ghastly execution. And the best part, the almost *funny* part, was that they all felt sorry for her. The stupid public actually *felt sorry for her*. Ivy had read simpering articles, fawning interviews, where Robin had been made out to be some kind of saint who had achieved against the odds. What about the odds Ivy had faced? Robin would *never* be where she was now if their fortunes had been reversed. Did she realise? Of course she didn't.

So now Ivy had to show her.

She reached out to stroke her reflection.

That meant sweet retribution against her lucky bitch twin. Ivy had done the research. Robin's tour was going to America and so was she. The plan wasn't easy, it wasn't quiet and it wasn't discreet—it was vengeance, loud, hard, messy, merciless vengeance.

She stepped out into the dark of the flat.

'Mother?' she ventured, a lonely silhouette in the doorway. There was no response.

She checked that her mother was breathing, releasing her gnarled clasp on the brandy glass and gently setting it down. Briefly she kissed Hilda's forehead and left the room.

*Watch out, Robin Ryder.* Ivy's eyes flashed in the moonlight.

*I'm closer than you think.*

*PART 2*

## 20

Jax Jackson woke at seven o' clock on a sunny morning in LA, his cock hard.

Lazily he slid his gaze over the sleeping form next to him, sheet pulled up to her waist and long glossy hair swept over a bronzed shoulder. They all looked pretty much the same from behind, so he pushed himself up on one elbow to get a better look. Cute. Jax lifted the sheet and clocked her ass. Not bad. This one would keep.

Jax swung his legs out of bed and rose to his feet, stretching his arms high till they almost touched the faux-crystal chandelier above his head. He reminded himself to get it removed—damn thing obscured the ceiling mirror. His head felt woozy and there was a taste like soil in his mouth. What had he done last night? He looked at the woman in his bed, the curve of her tits. *Oh yeah.* There'd been liquor involved, people buying him shots all over the joint, and vaguely he recalled racking up lines of coke on a naked back. Whatever, he deserved it. Jax was number one, the don, *el capitán*...

fastest man in the world! Technically he was doing them a favour, making the suckers feel special for a night.

He padded to the bathroom, slid his feet into a pair of towelling slippers and checked his reflection in the mirror. There was no getting around it: Jax Jackson was a god. Six foot one of pure dark muscle glared back at him. Sometimes he liked to imagine he'd been carved out of marble, like that Italian dude. *Sculpted*—yeah, that was the word. Raising his right arm, he bent and flexed, marvelling at the way his biceps pushed at the skin, tendons chasing up to his neck where they met the straight hard line of his collarbone. And his arms weren't even what he was famous for! Turning his attention to his powerful legs, lightly coated in tight coils of black hair, he wondered at their awesome strength. These were the legs that took the world record and knew more speed than any other man on Earth. These were the legs that saw the limit, looked it dead in the eye and broke right through it. They didn't call him The Bullet for nothing—Jax was faster than a cheetah in pursuit. OK, so his cock could do with a couple more inches, but he didn't hear the ladies complaining.

It was what he did with it that counted...and he counted, all right.

Smirking at his reflection, Jax tossed back a couple of painkillers, took a piss and stepped into the shower. He ran the water on pummel, feeling its needles drive into his skin. Only when the water was too hot to bear did Jax turn it off and step out to towel himself.

The mirror was clouded but he could just make out his immaculate reflection. With a finger he drew three shapes in the condensation, catching shards of his face with each stroke. Three numbers: 9.57. The world record for the hundred-metre sprint. *His* world record.

He made his way back into the bedroom. The girl was awake. 'Hey, baby,' she purred, sliding a slim brown leg into view. 'You wanna come back to bed?'

Jax stood at the window and pulled the blind. Sunlight flooded in and he rested a moment, bathed in its golden balm, treating the girl to the full beauty of his profile. He gave her time to drink it all in before turning to face her, a smile playing on his lips.

'You *know* what I want,' he coaxed.

The girl laughed, a high, reedy sound that flirted on the line of hysteria.

Jax crossed to the bed in two long strides, stopping so his erection was level with her face. He lifted his watch from the glass side-table and bolted it to his wrist.

The girl repositioned herself, swallowing nervously. 'I want to, baby,' she gasped, putting a hand out to touch him, 'really I do. But I don't know...it's too fast—'

'*Damn*, woman!' Jax grabbed the back of her head and lunged his face into hers. 'Course it's fast, that's the whole freakin' *point*. Let's get on it—I gotta racc today.'

The mention of Jax's sport renewed the girl's interest. She ran a finger over his jaw and dipped it into his mouth. He sucked, rolling his tongue around its tip. Guiding her head towards him, he checked his watch one last time, and only when he felt her lips close around his shaft did he press the button, feeling the seconds run down like water.

Harder and harder, faster and faster, Jax thrust against the girl's tongue, driving deeper and deeper until he detected a low moan of resistance. He was leaning over the bed now with the force of it, the girl underneath, trying to contain him. In a rush he caught sight of the end and then he was climbing, getting higher and higher and everything was flashing white and he knew he was going over, way over—

Sonofa*bitch*!

Jax came fiercely, pounding the last out of it, his eyes squeezed shut.

He pushed the girl back, bringing the watch to his perspiring face and examining it. There it was: 12.61 seconds. More than three seconds over. *Damn!*

Without looking up he said flatly, 'I gotta get movin'. Get dressed, I want you out.'

The yellow Lamborghini was his pride and joy, its bodywork second only to the contours of a woman. Jax had caught some late-night freaky TV once about a guy who stuck his dick in car exhausts, getting hot for objects or some shit, but when it came to the Lamborghini he could kind of relate— not that he'd risk getting his own crown jewels doused in diesel or whatever they put up there. (Jax was king of his vehicle but had no clue how it actually worked.)

The sign came up at speed: FOUNTAIN VALLEY ATH-LETICS CLUB. Without signalling Jax rounded off Sunset with a screech of tyres, sending up a spray of swirling gold dust. He accelerated, flicking on the radio and settling on a Turquoise dance track.

Sheesh, now there was a foxy female! They had shared a couple of nights once, a long time back when she had got paid for her efforts—and damn fine efforts they were. Not that the industry could ever discover her pre-fame dalli-ances: they wouldn't know what to do with themselves if they found out that the fierce-hot lady at the top of the music charts had once also been on top of a book of clients. Jax had needed release, Turquoise had come with a personal recommendation and, man, she hadn't disappointed. But Jax didn't like to dwell on the last of their meetings. That had been years ago, after his first international win—and he'd gone crazy...done things he shouldn't...things that made him shudder...

*Danny Fu, the Chinese gymnast.* They had been celebrating their first gold medals...

Jax shook off the memory. It was like that night had happened to another person, a different man, and on an ordinary day he never thought of it at all. How could he? Each time the details reared up a small part of him shrank and died. Fiercely he changed the frequency.

Soon he would be entering the very same industry—yeah, that was more like it. Jax Jackson, the hip-hop star! Recording with Puff City would make him immortal, unbreakable, a juggernaut...a brighter star than even Turquoise da Luca. It was about time the world got to see what else Jax was capable of. He imagined himself like Biggie without the weight, Snoop without the pigtails, Dre, only younger— screw it, all three combined to make the hip-hop god of the universe! He wouldn't just be part of Puff City, he'd rule it; he'd be the fucking *mayor*. How hard could it be? Jax could rap about cribs and Krug and cookie jars with the best of them, because, when all was said and done, he was the one living the dream.

*'It's all about the next competition.'* A familiar voice blared out of the radio. *'As athletes we're looking forward, not back. Next stop Rio. That gold is gonna be mine...'*

Jax killed the station, his good mood shattered. Who did that punk Leon Sway think he was? Freakin' kid had a death wish, standing in the line of The Bullet. Jax scowled into the rear-view mirror, flicking the bird at a truck driver who was coming up close. *Touch the paintwork on this and you die, motherfucker.*

Leon might have cut it fine in London, but there was first and there was second and nothing between counted for shit. He thought he was some hot deal: no one else *dared* give Jax front the way he did; they were way too in awe of the big man. Bring on the 2013 Championships: they would settle the score then. Leon didn't stand a chance—because the beautiful thing about Jax's life was that he never had to *try* that hard. Excellence had been with him since birth, and so while Sway was down the circuit every day pounding the crap out of the track, Jax preferred to lie in with a honey and recover from a hangover.

Jax grinned. He still won, so fuck it. Victory was a gift.

With a shriek of brakes the Lamborghini swung to a halt, huge black tyres a snarl beneath its impressive hulk. Fluid as oil the top slipped back, easing its driver into view.

'Get me out on that track, coach.' Jax flipped down his shades. 'I got energy to burn.'

# 21

Turquoise fell backwards on to the shimmering sand, her dark hair freed and cascading around her shoulders. Sparkling ocean crashed into shore, washing up the beach on a wistful sigh. The sun blazed blindingly in a clear sapphire sky.

Cosmo Angel descended on her, his bulk a vast, faceless shadow, eclipsing the light. Roughly he wedged his knee between her legs.

'We've got history,' he growled. 'It's time you faced up to that.' She could smell his breath and feel his excitement. It wasn't part of the script.

'Can we cut?' Turquoise broke away. Obligingly Cosmo rolled off, an amused sneer on his face. 'Sorry,' she mumbled, dusting her dress and blushing wildly.

'Everything OK?' enquired the director. Sam Lucas removed his cap and fanned himself against the heat. 'If I'm feeling the burn then you two sure are!'

Production had spared no expense. They were filming

in Barbados, on the shores of the Paradise Palms Hotel, a grandiose palace that shone like a mirage in the heat. It was one of the later scenes. Turquoise's character had hit big and was desperate to flee her past—only to be followed. It was as if Cosmo had lived out his private fantasy with the script he had written, picking up the thread of a real-life tragedy and fictionalising its outcome. Every time Turquoise stepped back and realised what she was doing—*acting out her own secrets*—the deceit was too much to bear. She had to stay focused on the end product and hope and pray the movie would slip quietly into oblivion.

But that wasn't going to happen.

*True Match* was set to be the biggest movie smash of the decade.

In the end, there had been no way to refuse Donna Cameron. While both women had been astonished at Sam's audacity regarding the last-minute switch, Turquoise's manager couldn't accept no as an answer.

*You employ me for my guidance*, Donna had pushed, *so here it is. Say yes.*

*Vocalists in your position would kill for this opening...*

They'd kill, would they?

Word of Turquoise's involvement had seeped through the significant channels even before anything was signed. Studios accepted her as making the transition. Sponsors supported the move. Screen moguls earmarked her for upcoming roles. Backing out would have spelled the end of her Hollywood career before it had begun...and Cosmo knew it.

'Let's go again,' said Sam, as a stylist stepped in to secure her hair once more. It was the sixth take. She couldn't bear having Cosmo this close to her, teasing her, torturing her, a sadist to the end, fully aware of what he was doing and savouring every second.

'We've got history,' Cosmo resumed, diving back into the scene like the practised player he was. The crew would put her botched attempts down to inexperience, the silly songstress who hadn't thought acting was that hard. It wasn't, compared with the facts.

'Why fight it?' Her co-star's eyes were boring down and his hand was clamped to her waist. Every fibre of her body rejected him, her skin recoiling at his touch so that it was a battle to keep from visibly trembling. It could have been ten years ago, strapped to his bed, shivering in her flimsy attire as he appraised her without pity, without feeling, without humanity. He looked the same. His aroma was the same, of musk and sweat. The way he felt, his arms coarse with hair and his flat, dry palms that raced across her chest and stomach like a starved animal, hadn't changed. Men like Cosmo Angelopoulos didn't change.

'Stay away from me,' Turquoise said coldly, playing the part and speaking the truth. 'What happened between us is over; I never want to see you again.'

'Yet here we are. I can't help myself.' Cosmo wound a loop of her hair around his fist and tugged gently. 'I'm addicted to you.'

He kissed her. The script dictated an initial resistance before submission. She couldn't do it. The instant his tongue slipped into her mouth, she gagged.

'Cut!' Sam put his hands on his hips. 'Is something wrong?'

Cosmo's eyes flashed a warning.

'No,' Turquoise replied. 'I, er, I wasn't prepared to be kissed like that.'

'It should feel authentic,' mused Cosmo, lifting his shoulders in a boyish shrug as though he welcomed her input. 'Don't you think?'

*It's authentic enough as it is, you sonofabitch.*

'Final take.' Sam consulted his watch. 'I want to get this and the pool scene in the can before sunset. OK to run with it this time, Turquoise?'

She swallowed her words along with her pride.

Cosmo had her gagged. He always had.

'I've been to a lot of beautiful places, but this is something else!' Ava Bennett stirred the peach syrup in her Bellini and crossed one tanned leg over another, parting the white material of her skirt. They were at the Paradise Palms Emerald Bar, a coral-themed heaven of sea-pinks and jewels that dripped from the ceiling like water. Shooting was over for the day.

'Can't argue with that,' agreed Turquoise, who finished off her third Kir and immediately ordered another. 'One for the road?'

'You're drinking fast.' Ava frowned. 'Tough day at the office?'

'Something like that.'

'We should get food…' Ava hailed the barman.

'I'm fine.' Turquoise preferred to get trashed. The waiter jumped to attention but she waved him away. Being out of it every night would blunt the horror, and the next morning's hangover might mean she could run through her scenes on a numb sort of autopilot.

A group of fans approached for photos. Turquoise's security was keeping their area clear but on her instruction allowed groups through every hour. When they saw movie star Ava as well they couldn't believe their luck. Ava had taken advantage of a gap in her calendar and had decided to accompany her husband on location.

One of the guys, young, good-looking, with an armful of tattoos, brazenly chanced it.

'You ladies looking for company?'

It was refreshing to be spoken to like a regular girl. Turquoise wondered if she might not go to bed with him tonight. She couldn't stand the fact that Cosmo had been the last person to touch her. After shooting she had sat in the bath for an hour, foaming and scrubbing and trying to rid herself of his touch, but no amount of washing could rinse away the shame.

Ava rolled her eyes. 'And if we said yes?' she teased. 'Trust me, baby, you wouldn't know *how* to handle it...'

The guy offered a lopsided grin. He had great cheekbones. 'Want to try me?'

Turquoise dismissed her bodyguard with a smile. 'It's OK,' she told him. The champagne was going to her head and she was starting to enjoy herself.

'Come on, let me buy you a drink,' their suitor pressed.

'In your dreams, sweetheart.'

Turquoise received her fourth from the barman. 'You can get me one.'

Ava looked shocked, but Turquoise couldn't tell if it was her acceptance of his offer or the rate at which she was putting them away. 'Um,' she said, 'I don't know if...'

'Come on, Max,' said one of the girls he was with, clearly embarrassed. 'Let's split.'

'Nah, I'm not ready yet.' Cavalier, Max slung one arm round Turquoise and one round Ava. He flashed his killer grin.

Another voice joined them.

'Come on, *Max*,' it said, threateningly calm. 'You heard the lady.'

Cosmo Angel's glare was frozen. A chill seeped down the back of Turquoise's neck. Max's arms dropped along with his jaw.

'Would you prefer to take this up with me?' Cosmo asked hollowly.

'N-no,' Max stammered, the swagger of moments before vanished, and in its place a nineteen-year-old kid about to brick himself. 'I was only messin'.'

'With *my wife*?'

Cosmo's hair was black and oiled, his brow heavy and dark. Often Turquoise imagined what life might have been like for Cosmo in another creation, one that hadn't been so compassionate: a poor Cretan kid with dusty knees, bullish and stormy-eyed and thinking the world owed him a living, lurking in neighbourhood backstreets, the self-appointed leader of a gang that intimidated girls and beat up any boy who read books and was kind to animals.

Max swallowed. 'I didn't mean anything by it, honest, I was just—'

'Get the fuck out of here, you worthless piece of crap.'

Ava put a hand on her husband's arm. 'It's OK, baby, let it go…'

'What're you still standing there for, shithead?'

Max darted out of sight.

Turquoise grabbed her purse. 'I'm going to bed.'

'Not with him, I hope,' sneered Cosmo.

'Cosmo!' Ava was appalled. 'Turquoise, I'm so sorry. Jesus—' she turned to him, trying to keep her voice down '—what the hell's the matter with you?'

*Once a whore, always a whore.* He didn't need to say it.

'Goodnight,' said Turquoise, unsteadily getting off her bar stool and heading for the elevators. Security moved to come with her.

'I want to be alone,' she commanded. 'Please.'

The elevator soared to her tower suite like a cage rattling through a labyrinth. She was the bird inside: helpless, flightless, her wings clipped by a menace she would never be able to escape. Cosmo was toying with her; it was a game to him, a sick, sadistic game, and he would play closer and closer to the line till she was ruined by madness.

With a shudder they came to a stop.

The motion jolted something in Turquoise, like a stuck wheel oiled free.

Anger crested, flooding her senses with dazzling fury.

How *dare* Cosmo? How *dare* he even look her in the eye after what he had made her do? How *dare* he inveigle his way into her life? How *dare* he return to torment her?

*How dare he?*

The doors pinged open. A steward in uniform smiled affably as she passed, but Turquoise didn't return it. Instead she charged down the corridor, jet hair flying. Hatred coursed through her veins, rendering her a blunt weapon, a loaded gun, a blister-sharp dagger, ripe to fire from a heart full of ammo...

Power. What if it didn't have to be his? What if she turned it around? She didn't have to lie back and take it; she wasn't the girl he had known. Life had made her strong.

Stronger than him.

Resolve knifed into her with ice-white clarity, and though she was drunk she had never before been thinking so clearly.

Whatever it took, whatever the price, she was bringing him down. Cosmo Angel deserved every damn thing he had coming.

## 22

Kristin's phone woke her, just as it had every morning for the past four weeks. Nausea rolled deeply, thickly, in her belly; she was accustomed to it by now as she rocked on that limbo sea between awake and asleep, one toe still dipped in the untroubled world of her dreams and one in the day that was creeping in with dismal tenacity.

Though she didn't need to, she checked the missed-caller display. *Scotty.*

Bleary-eyed, she scrolled through his attempts during the night:

SCOTTY: 12.04 A.M.
SCOTTY: 1.13 A.M.
SCOTTY: 1.44 A.M.
SCOTTY: 2.27 A.M.
SCOTTY: 3.48 A.M.

There were three voicemails, which she promptly deleted. Kristin rolled over and buried her head under the pillow,

groaning loudly and tugging it down in a bid to block out the
world. Sunlight was streaming in through the slatted blinds
of her villa, bathing her sheets in a pool of warmth that at
any other time would have been comforting but now was
hotly oppressive. She could hear the ocean building and collapsing, a rhythm that might have lulled her back to oblivion
were it not for the thoughts that crowded in, one after another, like a virus, and with each a fresh pinch of despair.

After that heinous evening (she still could not put a name
to it) Scotty had tried ten, fifteen, sometimes twenty times a
day. Though she replayed the nightmare countless times and
in varying degrees of abominable lucidity, she still could
not process what it meant.

At first, the assumption she had wanted to make: that
Scotty was being attacked. It was selfish to want that, it
would have spelled untold suffering on her boyfriend's part,
but at least it would mean his feelings for her were true…

Fifteen years of friendship, it had to be real; it *had* to…

How could it all be a fake? How long had Scotty been
lying to her, to Bunny, to *The Happy Hippo Club*, to them
all? She thought of the secrets she had told him, the con-
fidences she had shared, all the precious intimacies she'd
imagined to be a mutual exchange, but in fact she had never
known her best friend at all. He was a stranger.

Scotty had been in control of that situation, she had seen
it with her own eyes and while she denied it with her whole
heart she knew it to be true. Scotty had wanted every part
of Fenton Fear, his manager, his mentor—a bloated, hairy,
alcoholic mid-life crisis!

Oh God! Oh *God*!

Kristin gagged but all that came out was a desperate

whimper, muffled by the pillow. Memories of their nakedness haunted her, the twisted passion on their faces as re-
volting as it was shocking, and most hours she didn't know
whether to laugh or cry or shoot herself in the fucking head.
It explained Scotty's problem with sex, his avoidance and
why he'd become distant of late. It explained why he'd tried
to do that thing that day, because he'd wanted Fenton, not
her, and yet he'd been trying to pretend...

It was too grisly to contemplate!

Scotty would be beside himself—that pervert manager,
too. They'd be desperate to persuade her to hide their dirty
secret for them. Well, let them stew. Let them think about
what they had done and the devastation they had caused.
At least there was some small satisfaction to be had from
knowing that now, after who knew how long of being rid-
iculed, she was in control, and if she chose to could tear
their lives apart with a single phone call. She hoped Scotty
was in hell. She hoped he was disgusted with himself. Then
again, she thought bitterly, she was sure the lovers found
comfort in each other.

Kristin couldn't entertain the idea of speaking to him.
What would she say? How would Scotty explain himself?
Any scrap he offered would be a joke.

Try as she might there was no denying what she had witnessed. Only a second before she had turned and fled, but
enough to be certain of the absolute and unequivocal truth:
no excuses, no misunderstandings, nothing that could be in
any way mitigating. That night she'd driven aimlessly, burning like wildfire, swerving across the road and not caring if
she lived or died. Part of her had wanted to hurtle through
the crash barrier on Mulholland Drive and send the Mer-

cedes soaring like a silver comet through the star-pricked Hollywood sky.

It had been Fenton who had been star-pricked that night.

How many other nights? Had it been going on for weeks, months…*years*?

Had anybody else known? On top of everything, had he made her a laughing stock?

Kristin switched off her cell, squinting through red-rimmed eyes that were puffy from violent bouts of crying. She didn't want anyone contacting her. The day after her discovery she had booked herself the first flight to the most remote location she could find, settling on the distant shores of the Paradise Palms Hotel, Barbados.

Ramona had been furious. *'Just where do you think you're going?'* her mother had crowed as Kristin numbly packed a bag, Bunny hovering confusedly at the doorway and chewing her lip. *'Kristin! Don't you dare ignore me! Come back here right now!'*

She'd given neither an explanation. How could she? Where would she start?

*'Thing is, my boyfriend's been ass-fucking his manager. I know—rad, isn't it? I'm taking time off, you know, getting away while things calm down…'*

As was customary, a need to go to the bathroom eventually hauled Kristin out of bed. Like an animal, she reacted to her body without consideration: she ate when she was hungry, she slept when she was tired, she cried when she was sad. Now she showered and brushed her teeth robotically, her mind completely blank. She had trained herself to hold the details at bay, knowing that as soon as one macabre recollection crept in the rest would follow.

There was a knock. 'Room service!'

She opened the door to the porter, turning to the ocean view and making it clear she wasn't interested in conversation. Dutifully he deposited a tray of fruit and coffee and quietly left the room. Kristin picked feebly at a blood orange, musing on how long she could feasibly block out the world. Her label thought she'd had a mental collapse—which wasn't far from the truth—and it was only a matter of time until the press tracked her down.

They were a month from December. Fraternity were about to release their Christmas single, 'Keep You Warm', and would be slamming fans with their most romantic and pop-perfect offering yet. She'd seen the video design: Scotty and Joey and the guys bundled up against the winter in tailored coats and scarves, snowflakes on their eyelashes and rosy cheeks split by a boyish dimple as they crooned about the girls they adored, beseeching the camera, hands on hearts as they travelled a frosty wonderland thawed only by their grins.

The *fraudulence*.

It beggared belief. Scotty Valentine didn't want girls, he wanted *guys*; he didn't want soft lips, he wanted a *beard*; he didn't want a waist, he wanted *muscle*; he didn't want tits…

*He wanted an ass!*

Despairing, Kristin flung herself face down on to the bed. The tears flowed, great, heaving sobs that shook her body and sliced her throat.

Her life as she knew it was over. What was she going to do?

\* \* \*

'Bunny, get over here this minute! We haven't got all night, for crying out loud!'

The sound of her mother's voice ricocheted across the Venice Juniors Club car park, accompanied by a sharp click-clack of heels as Ramona charged towards the family Escalade. Bunny struggled to keep up. She wanted to burst out crying.

'It's my heels,' Bunny tried. 'They're really hurting...'

'I'm hardly surprised.' Ramona rounded on her daughter as the car's lights flashed and she hauled open the mammoth door. Another Mini Miss tottered past with her zebra-skin carryall and a smug lipstick-smile plastered across her face. *Little bitch!* thought Ramona, noting that the Mini Miss's mom had splurged on a wig twice the one Bunny's size and maybe that was where they were going wrong. These baby beauties were like Samson when it came to their pelts: scrimp on the hair and they were as good as done for.

'The way you were dancing I expect they'll cause you pain for days!' she carped.

Bunny climbed into the car and gazed stoically out of the window.

'I did my best,' she said miserably.

'Your best wasn't good enough,' came the tight response.

'It was the pirouette start. I told you, I never wanted to do it—'

'You *did* it,' snipped Ramona, gunning the ignition, 'because that was going to set you apart and make you *better* than the rest of those tramps! I wasn't to know you'd mess it up in such a spectacular fashion. How could you have been so careless? You were like a blundering animal out there, Bunny. After all we've worked for!'

Bunny's lip trembled. The first round of the Mini Miss Marvellous competition had been a disaster. She'd lost. Lost! Coming second wouldn't be so bad on an ordinary day, but this was important, this was the super league, and Ramona didn't see the point of being there unless they came away with the gold. Instead it had gone to her archrival Tracy-Ann Hamilton, and unless Bunny stole the limelight in the next bout it would be game over.

'Please don't shout at me,' she whispered.

Ramona rolled her eyes, shoving the vehicle into gear. 'It's not as if I take pleasure in your failure, believe me.' She grimaced, already fantasising about sabotaging Tracy-Ann Hamilton's next appearance. How she'd love to shave her bald! 'I do it because I care about you. Why else would I? Where would you girls be without me? Well? Where would you be?'

'Nowhere.'

'Exactly right.' The car roared down the freeway. 'And what thanks do I get? First your sister runs out without a word and now you. You've let me down. Both of you.'

'When's Kristin coming home?'

'God knows.' Ramona shouted an obscenity at a passing driver for pulling into her lane. 'Your sister's fame has gone to her head; it's the only explanation for this behaviour. Fancy running off like that when you've got commitments to fulfil, a job to do! Oh, don't you worry.' She laughed humourlessly. 'I'll sort her out when she gets back.'

Bunny would do anything to speak to Kristin right now. Where was she? It was unlike her sister to bail without a word, but she hadn't been answering her phone and, apart from the one message she had sent in the beginning, Bunny had heard nothing.

Night seeped in through the window in a thick black curtain. Bunny rested her head against the leather seats and watched the road rushing by. In the glass her sequinned dress sparkled and glittered in bursts of pink and green, a shield made of stars.

Her phone buzzed and she scrambled to retrieve it from her bag.

'Is it your sister?' Ramona demanded. 'Tell her she's got a Friday interview I'm yet to reschedule and a backlog of appointments I have no idea if she'll be able to—'

'It's not.'

The message was from an unrecognised number. Bunny frowned at it.

Bunny, hi, it's Scott. Can we meet?

For a second she didn't understand, and then slowly, a piece at a time, it registered. Scotty Valentine?

*Scotty Valentine!*

Hands shaking, she replaced the phone, clutching it tight in her bag.

Her number one crush wanted to hook up—at last, the two of them! Bunny's heart leapt, blind to questions why. Whatever the reason, she wasn't going to miss it for the world.

'Well?' insisted Ramona. 'Who is it?'

'Nobody.'

Her mother sighed dramatically. 'If you want me to start

checking your cell then you're going the right way about it,' she stated. 'Kristin can't bear it but what choice do I have? If you girls will insist on keeping secrets…'

Bunny bit her lip. Ramona prattled on but she didn't hear a single word.

Scotty wanted her. He had messaged her. And just like that, Kristin, the Mini Miss, her mother—everyone and everything in Bunny's world—ceased to be remotely significant. The boy she loved was all that mattered. He would never let her down.

# 23

Before she became famous, Robin had held Puff City up as the kind of group she would never in a million years get access to. They were part of that untouchable league of megastars who had been around for so long and were such an institution that they existed outside the rules of the industry. Typically private, the crew were never snapped getting debauched or vacuuming up drugs or disappearing into hotel rooms with sixteen-year-old groupies, and through this had managed to retain the air of mystery and allure belonging to only the truly legendary. Notorious behind the scenes, they relied on the rumour mill to shade in the missing pieces—and speculation was a hundred times more exotic than evidence.

It was surreal, therefore, to be in a booth, singing for all she was worth on their single. Out in the studio, Slink Bullion and G-Money listened on headphones and collaborated on the production. Slink had invited Robin to take the bridge on their charity project and she had accepted. 'Take

It Down' was a bold, brave, brilliant lament to gang culture in LA and what kids did to survive on the wrong side of the tracks. Everyone knew that Slink himself had come from challenging beginnings, and one glance at Principal 7 told the same story. This was music that came from the heart.

'You rocked it, Robin, let me get you one more time—take it a little higher on the run into *"Ain't we seen enough?"*'

Having the infamous Slink Bullion direct her was a trippy dream and she had to pinch herself to make sure it was happening. She felt fortunate G-Money was there. Slink, nice as he was, couldn't help but intimidate, the other guys drifted in and out in varying shades of indifference, while Principal 7 regarded her shiftily, creeping about in the background as if her presence offended him. Then there was Slink's girlfriend, who had answered the door to Robin so rudely on that first visit to the house and now trailed her lover like an Alsatian. Shawnella's glare was more effective than any growl in warding off threats.

Not that Robin saw Slink that way in the least. She was here for work, and some job it was turning out to be. When she'd been offered a slot she had decided not to overthink the Leon Sway connection: they would be recording on different days anyway.

The track ramped up once more and as Robin hit her falsetto she shut her eyes and dived headfirst into the emotion. When she opened her eyes, for a crazy second she thought she had magicked him there, because it was the first time in weeks that she had let herself think of Leon.

Just like that, there he was.

A marble of pleasure shot up from her stomach, and Robin stood dumb in her goldfish bowl watching the men greet each other. Leon was wearing a shirt that matched his eyes and was smiling genially. *Manners*, was Robin's first thought, because she knew he wasn't keen on the collaboration. *Must've been brought up good.* No wonder he felt like a fraud having to bleat on about hardship. Jax Jackson was there too, throwing his weight around and engaging in an impossible amount of backslapping. He sported a white vest with tons of gold jewellery and evidently imagined himself to fit right in with the Puff City vibe. Robin felt suddenly aware that she was the only girl. She looked hopefully at Shawnella but the woman sashayed off with her customary scowl, unable to compete any more for her boyfriend's attention.

Slink gestured to her to come out. She emerged to a wave of 'Hey, my man', 'How's it hangin'?', 'Dude, what's up?' and a flurry of guy hugs.

Principal 7 was hanging back as usual, the surly kid at the party, while G-Money was all about the gracious hand shaking.

'No shit, it's Lady Robin Ryder!' Jax flashed her a grin and she noticed he'd had a gold tooth put in. Seriously?

'No shit, it's you,' she replied. 'Nice dental work.'

Jax guffawed. 'We know each other,' he explained to their onlookers, and irritatingly made it sound like they knew each other and *then* some.

'Hello,' said Leon. 'How's it going?'

'Great.'

'Better than great,' Slink intervened, nodding to the booth. 'Robin's got this track down.' He put a palm flat to his chest. 'She's takin' it to a whole new place.'

'It's good to see you.' Leon smiled at her. God, his eyes were green.

Jax puffed his chest out. 'Are we gettin' goin' on this shit now or what?'

'Step this way,' said G-Money. 'It starts here.'

The recording locked down in one. Leon was relieved. It was uncomfortable having Jax breathing down his neck, and hanging with Puff City only seemed to make it worse. From their first meeting the men had put him on edge. He had hoped spending time with them might counteract it. It didn't. That white guy Principal needed to get his attitude checked. What was his beef? It was like he couldn't even look Leon in the eye.

Maybe it was because the crew had grown up not far from him in Compton. They were associated with bad memories and it was going to put a sour twist on things.

He exited the studio as it was starting to get dark. The windowless warehouse made you lose a grip on time— they'd gone in when it was day and they'd come out in the night. Robin was heading for her pick-up, a giant bag thrown over her shoulder, which made her appear even smaller than usual. Leon hurried after her.

'Hey, wait up.'

She turned but didn't stop.

'Let me get you that drink,' he said, needing to take her out because he hadn't expected her to be here and now she was… 'C'mon, you bailed on me last time.'

'I never said yes last time.'

'At least you haven't said no this time.'

'I'm about to.'

'Why?'

She came to a halt. Leon thought what a great-shaped face she had, which wasn't something that had occurred to him about anyone else before. It was delicate, the chin like the tip on a petal, and the mouth pink and full. He wanted to touch it. Kiss it.

'I'm not interested,' she said. 'There, is that good enough for you?'

'No.'

'What is?'

'What's what?'

'A good enough reason for you to stop…badgering.'

He laughed. 'Badgering?'

'Whatever.'

'Come out with me. If you still want me out of your life by the end of the night—' he held his hands up in a gesture of surrender '—I walk away. No more badgers.'

The warehouse door opened. Slink and G-Money emerged, one of them clocking the pair and hollering over their plans to hit the Boulevard.

Leon didn't take his eyes off hers. 'See? I'm tagging along. You can ignore me if you like. I'll sit in a corner by myself all night getting drunk and wishing it was just you and me.'

After a moment she said, 'Fine,' and suppressed a smile she didn't think he'd seen.

Outside La Decadence, photographers swarmed. Slink and G-Money kept a low profile as they entered, Robin trailing behind, head bowed, before she felt Leon's arms encircle her waist and draw her to him. It was enough to give the cameras the angle they needed and she gritted her teeth to stop herself making a scene. The heat of his body made her belly flutter.

'Nice little photo op,' she commented when they got inside. 'Cheers for that.'

'Pleasure.'

She scowled as Leon put in their drinks order. He was so up himself!

Their entrance caused a stir. G-Money fell into conversation with a group of star-struck teens before Slink gestured time out and they were roped into a VIP space.

'What if I don't like vodka?' Robin asked as a glass of freezing cold liquid was deposited in front of her, a twist of lemon emerging from the top.

'You were drinking it at the premiere,' Leon answered.

'Oh.' He watched her until she looked away.

The vodkas turned into shots. The music got louder. The alcohol kept coming. On one side of the booth she and Slink laid out their inspirations, the artists they had grown up with, and Robin had to bite her (by now loose) tongue from not going off on a rant about how he'd always been her number one. On the other G-Money and Leon were deep in conversation, gesturing earnestly and clinking their bottles as the room began to soften and seep, the lights blur, and Robin's body tingle with the warm contentment of being at the exact right stage of drunk. Leon was closest to her and every so often she would feel the heat of his touch as his skin brushed hers. When he raised his arm to high-five Slink over a shared joke she caught his aroma, that clean, human scent, and didn't object when his fingertips appeared on the small of her back, as if by accident, on the strip of bare skin between her jeans and her vest.

'You know how to make a guy work,' he murmured into her ear. It should have come off easy but when she turned into his green stare it was urgent with some unspoken message.

'You're giving up already?' She couldn't help it; she fancied him like mad. He was unbearably sexy. She didn't care that she was flirting, finding any excuse to touch him.

'I told you. I don't quit.'

She felt a twinge deep inside when she imagined having sex with him.

They moved against each other to the music, almost touching but not quite, lights spinning and Robin's blood humming with being happily wasted. At one point they were thrown together and Leon caught her waist, a hand on either side, and she found herself clasping his shoulders, solid as steel, and for a dizzying second not wanting to let go.

It was two a.m. by the time they left the club. Leon took her hand in his as they negotiated a path to the exit and she saw the skin of sweat on the back of his neck, and noticed that when they got outside he didn't release her fingers. She thought he might kiss her then but he didn't.

'Cold?' he asked.

'A bit.'

He didn't offer her his jacket. Instead he put his arms around her and rubbed her back very fast so that it felt like being tickled and she laughed.

A car was waiting. It took them along the ocean edge, the water a sheet of ink, the moonlight casting a pale silver spill. A cluster of night surfers were catching the waves and Robin lowered the window so that she could breathe the fresh air. She was acutely aware of Leon's thigh pressed against hers on the seat. She wanted him. God, she did.

'Can we walk?' If she didn't put some distance between them she might faint, or be sick, or throw herself at him. *Get a grip, Robin.* She never lost it like this.

'Sure.' He asked the driver to stop. 'We're not far.'

She wanted to go barefoot. The sand was cool under their soles. Leon carried her heels in one hand, dangling like a pair of hooked fish, his trainers in the other.

It was quiet, their only soundtrack the waves lapping at the shore.

'You OK?' he asked. There was a tone to his voice that she hadn't heard before, one of genuine enquiry, of concern. Warm ripples lapped at their ankles.

'Sure.'

He walked a little closer. 'You know you can talk to me, right? About anything.'

She snorted, making light of it. 'What are you, my counsellor?' But he didn't share the joke. For a screwy second Robin was filled with the need to confide about her stalker—about the bunch of withered roses that had arrived where she was staying that very morning; about the phone calls; about the sense of being watched; about her fear that each attempt came from the same determined source, and that one day that source would catch up with her.

But where would she stop? If she were to tell Leon about that, why not tell him about everything? No chance. All he could give her was sympathy, or pity, and she didn't need either of those. Nothing bad had actually happened; just a few deviations that by coincidence had come at the same time. Other celebrities dealt with it—she would, too.

She was glad when he asked: 'What do you make of the guys?'

'Slink's awesome.' Robin grinned. 'They all are. Mostly.'

'Mostly?'

'Principal's not my favourite.'

'Mine neither. But I'm kinda drunk, so don't hold me to it tomorrow.'

The word *tomorrow* made her tummy flip.

'You and G-Money get on well,' she offered quickly. 'It must be weird for you…' She was blabbing; it was the alcohol. 'I mean, don't take offence—'

'That means I'm definitely going to take offence.'

'I'm guessing you don't normally hang with people like them.'

A pause. 'What makes you say that?'

'You're rich.'

'So are you.'

'I think you're brought up nice.'

'My mom did a good job.' He was amused. 'What are they "like", anyway? Black? In case you didn't notice, so am I.'

'I'm not talking about race.'

'What, then?'

Robin struggled for the words, unsure of what she was trying to convey.

'You seem so… I can't describe it.'

'Try.'

'Clean.' She nodded. 'You're really…yeah, *clean*.'

'Thanks. I take showers most weeks, if I remember.'

The thought of him in the shower made her gulp. 'I don't mean that…'

'Me and G, we're from the same neighbourhood.'

'You are?'

'Sure. Mean streets of Compton, baby.' He gave her a friendly nudge with his shoulder. 'Why so surprised?'

'I don't know.' It just wasn't how she'd imagined him.

It started to rain. A rumble of thunder growled into the night.

Robin stopped. 'So I've got you wrong?'

'Yes.'

'How?'

'First, if you think I'm clean you should see me after a sprint.' The rain was coming down heavily, fast and wet, soaking their clothes. He didn't seem to notice. 'I'm sweaty and dirty because that's what I get like when I want to win.' For a heartbeat Leon imagined entrusting her with it—none of the stuff that was written about him on the internet but the stuff that came from his soul, the way he had loved his brother and still did with a blaze that would never dim, never die. But, he didn't. 'Second, what happened to not judging people? You think you've had my number from day one.'

'That isn't fair.' Her top was sodden. 'You brought that on yourself.'

'And you overreacted. It was just a bit of banter.'

'Don't even go there. You were way out of line that night and you know it.'

'It's not like you gave me a chance to explain.'

*'I was just messing,'* she reminded him, quoting his defence. *'I haven't had a lot of practice with this fame stuff?* Sounds lightweight to me.'

Beads of water glowed off Leon's skin. 'I'm touched you remembered it verbatim. And that's a nice American accent, by the way.'

Robin released a cry of irritation and started off down the beach.

In a flash he was with her, catching her arm.

He could feel the heat of her stare. She was watching him intently, as though she could see right into his fibre. In the dark her eyes appeared larger, huge, and he wasn't sure if it was a trick or if her face was coming closer to his, but before Leon knew it his thumb was on her chin and he was kissing her. He fully expected her to pull away, and for a moment she was totally still, just letting herself be kissed, and then to his surprise she was kissing him back, her hands on the sides of his face, and he took those hands, so small in his, and held the fingers. Water drenched their skin, drips caught in their locked tongues caught in the wet of their kisses, and she tasted sweet and delicious and her mouth was cool. Instantly he was hard.

They kissed all the way back to his Malibu apartment. The second they were inside she hauled off his T-shirt, running her hands across his chest, the muscle stiff beneath his hot, soft skin, a trail of hair vanishing into his jeans. In the bedroom he lowered her on to the sheets, wanting to kiss her and love her all over, the softness at her collarbone and her eyelashes and her hairline. He wanted to kiss her elbows and the backs of her knees.

'I can't have sex,' she told him, a muffle against his shoulder.

'OK.' He went to kiss her again, not wanting to stop.

'I mean I really can't.'

He half frowned, half smiled, and touched her nose with his. 'OK.'

'I've got my period,' she said frankly.

'I don't care.'

She looked up at him. 'I do.'

Leon kissed her softly, deeply. 'All right.'

All night he held her, and they kissed, kissing until their mouths ached, and talked about everything except the lost years: he about his burning ambition for gold; and she about her life that had got so mad that she barely recognised it any more. Leon waited for her to open up about her past but she didn't, and because of that neither did he: Marlon, the crime against his family, none of it was mentioned. For now, to have her with him was enough.

It was five a.m. the last time he looked, the ocean sighing contentedly beneath the window as he touched his lips to her closed eyes. After that they must have been asleep.

Warm sunshine woke him. The bed was empty. Leon expected to hear the shower, but the only sound was of a neighbour calling his dog down on the beach and a warm breeze blowing through the palms. Nine o'clock. He touched the pillow next to his head.

There was no note, nothing. Almost as if he'd dreamed her, Robin Ryder was gone.

## 24

Turquoise had been summoned to dinner with a visiting Donna Cameron and several VIPs who were staying at the Paradise Palms. On the terrace they were served cold champagne, succulent oysters and bright pink crab Thermidor. Conversation hummed in the air as steady as the tide and Turquoise, sun-kissed and wild-haired, wowed in a figure-clinging jade dress and heels. Ava had flown home, and fortunately Cosmo had another engagement.

'Hello, movie star.' Donna smiled, kissing her on both cheeks. 'Hollywood sure seems to be agreeing with you.'

They caught up on banalities and Donna told her there had been a flurry of interest following the project's announcement. *True Match* was the heady brew that only seldom came along. Would Turquoise be any good? Would Cosmo's script carry water? Did Sam Lucas still have what it took? The haters waiting in the wings to tell everyone it was a joke were vastly outnumbered by the throngs of fans counting the days till the film's release.

'That reminds me,' said Donna over dessert, 'one of your dancers keeps hassling me for your whereabouts. He's pretty committed. Bronx Riley?'

'Oh.'

'Since your location's under wraps I couldn't give him details.' Donna looked at her quizzically. 'Judging by your expression I did the right thing.'

Turquoise waved away the suggestion they had a connection. 'I'm too busy right now to deal with Bronx. It was a fling, it doesn't mean anything.' Even so the mention of his name tugged something loose in her chest. She quashed it. Since accepting the Cosmo project she had been ignoring Bronx's calls, deleting his voicemails. How could she see him, speak to him, *anything*, when she was spending her days re-enacting her very worst secrets? If there had ever been a chance at a future between them, now it was over.

She didn't normally disclose details of her personal life and Donna was taken aback. 'As I thought,' she said, swiftly changing the subject.

As Donna went on about movie openings already in the pipeline, Turquoise saw a flash of blonde disappearing inside the hotel lobby. Pop starlet Kristin White was staying at the hotel, though by all accounts was keeping a conscientiously low profile. Was Kristin doing rehab? It was the only explanation she could think of. Though Turquoise couldn't imagine Kristin or her squeaky-clean boyfriend Scotty Valentine staying out past midnight, let alone getting involved in the hard stuff. Ava had met Kristin several times through her work on *Lovestruck* and had always said she was friendly.

The meal wrapped early and Donna, inebriated, gushed

about Turquoise's burgeoning opportunities before excusing herself to go to bed. Under radically different circumstances Turquoise might have shared her enthusiasm, but as it was she couldn't wait to be alone.

She had a plan to draw together.

Returning to her suite, she was thankful for the deserted hotel corridors. The champagne had made her head fizzy and tired; cushion enough to protect her from the harsh reality of filming resuming first thing. At least they would soon be off this island and some semblance of normal life could resume. Being cut adrift on this location made her feel as if she were going crazy, as if everything she had achieved back in LA were an illusion and when she went back Cosmo would be standing atop the rubble of her mansion and laughing wickedly.

*You thought all this was real? Wake up, sugar, you still belong to me...*

She wondered what had dragged Cosmo away from the evening's festivities—it wasn't like him to relinquish a chance to make her squirm, and with Ava out of the way he'd have had free rein. Turquoise pictured him in his penthouse (Cosmo demanded one of seven rooftop apartments, typically occupied by Russian oligarchs or Texan oil barons), busy scheming his next ploy. If only she had the courage to expose him for what he was! She'd thought about it so many times, all the possible outcomes and what they would mean, but the facts remained the same: even if she told the truth, even if she revealed Cosmo Angelopoulos in all his wretched glory and confessed to the terrible death they had concealed, even then, even if everyone felt for her and said it wasn't her fault and what else was she supposed to have done, even then, her life, her career and all she had battled for would be ruined, if not by being branded a criminal then by being branded a whore.

The abuse of her body was not a charge Turquoise was willing to answer ever again. She had paid at the highest level—with her pride, her dignity, her ability to meet herself in the mirror and hold her head high—over the majority of her young life, and she could not accept having to surrender her adulthood to the same. Why should she? None of it had been her choosing, she had been used and exploited in the worst way, and uncovering Cosmo meant uncovering herself. They would pity her. She'd had enough of being pitied.

'Mr Angel, no! You're such a naughty boy!'

As she rounded the corner to her suite she heard a woman's excited squeal, pursued seconds later by another. Next the giggles chimed together and a group came into view.

Turquoise backed against the wall and listened. Opposite her was a mirror that looked down the hall and in its reflection she could detect Cosmo's arrogant swagger as the party swayed drunkenly towards the bank of elevators. There were five girls in all, and she saw that they were young—the oldest couldn't have been more than eighteen. Bare flesh peeped through their scant clothing and their eyes were glassy. Cosmo pushed one hard against the wall and roughly fondled her breasts. He snarled something at them and then two of the others were kissing, and when they stopped he slapped them gently across the cheek.

The elevator came and they stepped inside. Turquoise held her breath as Cosmo paused to throw a glance in her direction, but all he met was his own image. A hand reached out, seized his tie and pulled him inside, and the doors closed with a soft hush.

Turquoise stayed where she was, afraid that if she moved the approaching idea would slip through her fingers like water. To begin with it was faint, without shape or centre, then, imagining what Cosmo was doing with his women up in his invincible castle, she smiled.

Cosmo Angel was over. It was obvious what she had to do.

She received word from Donna late Friday night that they were expected to be on the Greek island of Crete the following week. Sam had been scheduled to shoot the New York scenes but Cosmo had changed his mind after a favourable weather report from Europe. On this project, at least, his word was law.

Crete was where Cosmo Angelopoulos had grown up. It stood to reason that he would want to incorporate it into his bizarre autobiopic, if for nothing else than to crash the modest village where he had struggled at school and caused trouble for the locals and kicked stray dogs in the street, all to stick them the bird and say, *Look who made it, suckers!*

The change meant that Turquoise was forced to cancel a performance at a friend's wedding, a promise that had been in the diary for months. Since it wasn't a 'legit commitment' (Donna's words) it got dismissed the instant that Cosmo issued instructions.

Early Monday they were shooting on the south of the island, close to the foot of the Samaria Gorge. Cast and crew were being put up in the finest air-conned luxury that Chania, on the north coast, had to offer, but down here it was sweltering. The land was arid and it was unseasonably hot, a cluster of brittle shrubs perishing in the heat. Tavernas were packed with hopeful fans, and the area Sam had cordoned off for the shoot provided limited shade. A rocky Libyan sea heaved behind them, rendering scant breeze.

'This is my home,' Cosmo choked, posturing against a rock as Sam's camera swung to capture his pained expression. 'It's the only place I belong...' His character was repenting his ways, trying to find his true self by returning to his roots.

'You want me to feel sorry for you?' In the script it was phrased as *'Should I feel sorry for you?'* but no one picked Turquoise up on it.

'My start wasn't the best,' he mused, draining from the words every ounce of self-pity. 'You know that. I told you I was no good, I warned you. I'm dangerous...'

*No shit you are.*

'You should have stayed away from me.'

Turquoise wanted to laugh, and had to scour the depths to summon anything remotely akin to sympathy.

'You can talk of home all you like,' she returned. 'It means nothing. Once you told me home was wherever I was, and that places had no significance.'

'How could they?' he implored, drawing out the moment. 'After where I've been?'

'And...cut!' Sam grinned. 'Superb. Turquoise, I was there with you word for word, every step of the way. You're pulling at some heartstrings with this one.'

Turquoise watched her co-star cross the perimeter and mingle with his fans. They lapped up his insincerity and crooned with pleasure when he addressed them in Greek.

Couldn't they see that there was no difference between the act they'd just witnessed and the man standing now in front of them? Couldn't anyone? Cosmo Angelopoulos was a fraud.

Tonight, he would be uncovered. What Cosmo didn't understand and had never understood over all these years was that she knew him better than he knew himself.

From across the set her assistant held up a cell phone. Turquoise padded over to receive it and was happy to see Ava's name flash up on the screen.

Hope Greece is treating you well, honey.
Trust Cosmo behaving himself? ;-)

Turquoise wondered if Ava had any inkling about her husband's infidelities. Surely she must, but then that wouldn't make sense. Ava was a strong, independent woman and wouldn't take shit from anybody, least of all a man purporting to love her.

They were all in for a surprise—and though Turquoise would never deliberately hurt one of the women she valued most in this world, now she was left with no choice.

## 25

Bunny White was no expert in applying make-up. It was ironic since she spent most of her days caked in the stuff, but Ramona was the one who perfected it, and now, armed with one of Kristin's Magic Liners and an eye like a squinting panda, Bunny had to admit defeat.

Normally Kristin would help her, but since they'd barely heard a word since she'd been away that wasn't likely to happen. Nor could it, because Kristin's very absence was the reason *why* Bunny was taking three hours with her appearance in the first place.

She pouted at her reflection and had a last stab with the lipstick. It was a strident shade, too abrasive, and she tried a subtler, brownish tone that complemented her blonde ringlets more kindly. Rummaging about in her sister's belongings, she experienced a shard of guilt, before remembering that she hadn't actually done anything wrong. Yet.

*Wanting* Scotty wasn't the same as doing anything about it, was it?

They were meeting for a milkshake at his manager's house. Everywhere else they'd get mobbed, Scotty said, and anyway Fenton Fear would be out. Bunny was glad. Fenton was friendly enough but he scared her a little. He was so…big! Like an ogre, with his massive chicken-drumstick arms and wobbly chin, and Ramona whispered that he was 'a drinker', as though this were a hazardous precursor to spontaneous combustion and he could implode at any given second, sending his freckles scattering across the walls like gunfire. Once she had seen him in shorts and his calves were wide as tennis racquets and covered in brown dots.

Never before had she felt so nervous, not even before a pageant! This was a different breed of anxiety that had butterflies in her stomach and a queasy feeling trickling through her whenever she thought of Scotty's smile. Would he greet her at the door? Would he kiss her on the cheek, as he had at home one dizzying Christmas? Would he hold her hand…?

*Of course not, Bunny! He's Kristin's boyfriend!*

It was impossible to forget the facts, and after Bunny's initial thrill at his having made contact she was forced to concede that he was probably as worried for Kristin's where-abouts as they were, hence the meeting. There were no romantic intentions whatsoever.

In the event, Scotty was already waiting on the other side of the mansion security gates when she arrived. Bunny had checked her reflection a zillion times and fretted she looked like a kid who'd raided the dressing-up box (which wasn't far from the truth) but there was only so late she could be, and, judging by Scotty's fraught expression, ill-concealed beneath his McLaren red baseball cap, that was just as well.

'Hey.' He buzzed her in. 'Thanks for coming.' There was no kiss or hug or anything. Bunny was relieved because being in such close proximity to the boy of her dreams was sending her to the cusp of a swoon (not that she'd ever swooned before, but she imagined this was how it felt). If he'd attempted to touch her she might have collapsed.

Fenton's place was modest in comparison with Ramona's efforts at The White House, but it was still impressive. Every surface hosted Fenton's accolades and evidence of his chart successes, his trophies and gold discs lovingly mounted in clean glass frames, amassed with photos of him alongside stars the world over, some from many years ago when everyone had puffy hair and square shoulders and Fenton himself looked not much older than Scotty.

'This way,' said Scotty flatly, leading them into what must have been the den. Three mammoth white leather couches dominated the space, one of which confessed to a Scotty-shaped dent and a crackling nest of half-eaten bags of Lays potato chips and rainbow-coloured candy balls. The TV was blaring and Scotty reached for the remote to kill it.

'Been watching too much crap,' he mumbled, and with the proximity of his words she caught a sour gust of breath, which wasn't quite enough to counter her strawberry-scented love for him but was troubling nonetheless.

It was when he removed his cap that she almost gasped.

He looked awful. Well, not awful as in ugly, because Scotty Valentine could never look ugly, but awful as in tired. Desperate. He looked like he hadn't gone to sleep in a month, or he'd been crying, or puking, or had become 'a drinker'. Bunny was overwhelmed with affection that until now had been selfish longing, but at this moment thought only of making *him* feel better because she couldn't see him so sad, she just couldn't! Her tongue bloated with the struggle of how to articulate the crossing of this new frontier, and no words came.

'D'you want a drink?' Scotty asked miserably. His mop of hair was scruffy and his blue eyes had lost their sparkle. *Wow,* thought Bunny, *he's really missing Kristin.* And a little piece of her expired with the knowledge.

'OK, that'd be cool,' she replied.

The promised milkshake didn't materialise. Instead he came back with lemonade for her, a beer for him. Bunny had hoped he might be able to see past her age, especially with the make-up, but given he had barely glanced at her since she'd arrived she wasn't convinced.

'I need to talk to you,' he said despairingly, sinking back into the Scotty-shaped hole and anxiously rubbing his temples. Bunny chewed her lip. In the corner of the room she noticed a marble ass bolted to the wall and struggled to remember if Fenton had a wife.

'Sit down.' He gestured a touch impatiently. Hurriedly she obeyed, settling opposite. She'd have preferred to sit next to him, maybe rest a hand on his knee if it all got too much, because every time she raised her eyes to Scotty she felt the bottom go out from under her and fly away, like being thrown off the top of a New York skyscraper.

'What's up?' she squeaked.

'It's Kristin,' he admitted, taking a slug of his beer. He burped gently and she wished he wouldn't do that, because Scotty Valentine never burped, in fact he never endured any bodily expulsions because he was a god, a prince, and thus above the mess of human biology. Only yesterday Bunny had been watching Fraternity's dreamboat Christmas single 'Keep You Warm' and lusting after his cute smile and the poetry that flowed from his lips, so the reality was faintly disheartening. But she'd forgive Scotty anything—absolutely anything.

'We've split up,' he announced, eyes flitting suspiciously across his captive audience's face. 'You knew about that... right?'

Bunny wrung her hands together. 'Is that why she's gone away?'

Scotty assessed her for the first time, as if he was trying to figure something out. 'She hasn't spoken to you?' he hazarded, visibly relieved.

'No. She just left. Mom and me don't know why, but I guess...I guess it makes sense if it's about you...' Bunny would run to the ends of the earth if Scotty ever dumped her, and toss herself into the abyss.

'OK.' He put his fingers together, resting his chin on their tips, thinking carefully. He was so sexy when he concentrated! She had no idea how he'd even got through school without being suffocated by hordes of girls. 'Do you think she's told anyone that we've split? Or—' again he squinted at her '—the reasons why?'

Bunny shrugged. 'I don't think she can have,' she replied innocently. 'Like, it was so quick. She just came back on my birthday, and...' A pause. 'You remember my birthday?'

'What? Oh. Yeah. Course.' But clearly he didn't remember that he was supposed to have made it and the fact he hadn't bothered had cracked her fourteen-year-old heart in two.

'And she started packing.' Bunny pouted. 'No explanation or anything.'

Scotty rubbed his chin. Oh, it was a handsome chin.

'I need you to do something for me, Bunny,' he said.

'OK.'

'I need you to get Kristin back.'

Bunny grimaced, hating to disappoint him. 'We've tried, only she won't listen.' Against his desolate expression, she tacked on, 'I'll ask her again to come home. Promise.'

He shot up off the couch. 'I don't mean that,' he said gruffly, running a hand through his hair. 'I mean, yeah, obviously she needs to do that, but what I'm saying is that *I* want her back. I *need* her back. With me.'

His words were torture. Kristin was so lucky and she didn't even know it!

'Why did you split up?' she asked, quiet as a mouse.

'That doesn't matter,' said Scotty quickly. 'The important thing is that it hasn't leaked to the press, and hopefully we can paper over Kristin's disappearance once we work out a plan.' He was nodding, as if formulating his next step. 'We *have* to work out a plan.' Scotty's eyes flitted to a framed photograph of Fenton, and Bunny guessed that Fenton wasn't happy about the split either. Together, Kristin and Scotty were the perfect package.

'She listens to you,' Scotty continued, coming to crouch, imploring, in front of her. 'If you tell her…' He stalled, putting a hand on each of her knees and sending sparks of electricity zooming through her bloodstream. 'Just tell her I'm sorry, I'm so sorry, and that I can explain.' His face changed, more like the old Scotty. 'It's her I love; tell her that. You just have to get her back for me, Bunny, you *have* to—I don't know who else to ask. I'm trusting you with this, OK? Do you trust me back?'

Bunny nodded. Her heart shivered. Scotty Valentine needed her! He *needed* her, and no one else would do. She gazed at him with love unadulterated, her hero, her safe place, and vowed she would not prolong his suffering, whatever it took.

What they said about losing someone was true. First, there was the shock. Grief pounced soon after, then, finally, anger set in. Anger was where Kristin was at, and though she knew acceptance would be coming, she wasn't hanging around to wait.

Five weeks she had spent weeping and feeling sorry for herself, and the thing about being miserable was that after a time it got boring.

'I'm done here,' she had told her rep the previous morning, making an early call to LA and setting the wheels in motion. 'Get me a flight home.'

'You bet. Good to have you back, Kristin.'

But they weren't getting her back. Kristin White wasn't the same girl she had been: she had shattered into a thousand pieces and had been forced to reassemble, but putting something back together rarely achieved an identical mould and parts had switched, shifted, integral parts. Over the past month she'd had endless time to work out where the fuck it had gone so wrong, and the resounding answer she'd kept coming back to was:

*I'm too good.*

All her life she'd been good, doing what was bidden, holding her temper, nodding along like a stupid dumb puppy. All her life she had tolerated other people's crap: her mom's, her record label's, her fake boyfriend's. All her life she'd borne it uncomplaining, and look where it had got her. It had to stop. How much longer could she be the fool?

Kristin showered and packed her bag. Her jet would depart in an hour. At the mirror she took a pair of scissors to her long pale hair and began cutting. She took it to her chin, satisfied as great sheets of blonde wafted to the marble floor like silk, until she was standing in a mountain of it: Rapunzel after her true love's desertion. Scooping it up, she cleared the bathroom and left a generous tip for her maid along with a note:

*Thanks for everything. I'm checking out.*

## 26

The weather in London had been uncharacteristically clear for November. Nights were cold and cloudless, and domed with stars that were normally seldom decipherable through the city smog. In flat 39B, Ivy Sewell stepped out of her bedroom and into silence.

Four a.m. The dismal hum of the North Circular droned on, and if she listened closely she could hear her mother's brittle breath as she slept. An empty bottle of brandy rocked on its side by Hilda's chair. Her neck was tipped back and she was exhaling through her mouth, eliciting an occasional whimper, as if she were being chased by nightmares. Hilda must have spent the last twenty years being chased. Never had she turned and faced her sins, content to have them pursue her to the grave and beyond. Who knew what lay past death? Hilda wore a silver cross around her neck but that didn't mean she could claim redemption.

Some things were beyond forgiveness.

Ivy was ready. Her destination: Los Angeles. Her target: Robin Ryder.

Only her sister could answer to this. Ivy could not be held responsible for what happened. Robin's ignorance was the culprit, her ability to live like a queen with no thought to the wreckage she had left behind. If Ivy had been given that exit, what could she have become? She would have been capable of anything: a life with no limits, a life hunting her own desires, a life of luck and grace, one lived for her and her alone…

A life without Hilda.

Calmly Ivy collected the cushion and squeezed it in her dry hands. It smelled musty and the dust caught in her throat, forcing her to suppress a cough.

Sickly light drained into the living room, syrup-thick.

It wasn't difficult to hold the cushion over Hilda's face. It wasn't difficult to apply the pressure that would steal the last breath from her mother's lungs. It wasn't even difficult when the struggle began and Ivy had to restrain the flailing, panicking limbs.

Suddenly, still.

Just like that, it was over. Slowly she removed the pillow, her mother's eyes and mouth wide open in terror, as empty in death as she had been in life.

Ivy straightened, the merciless soldier. She felt nothing.

How easy it was to kill. How unfortunate that was for her twin.


LA was the city of sunshine. Ivy had seen it on TV and in Hollywood films, the rich blue sky under which tanned, slim bodies skated beachfront or rode past in open-top

Jeeps. People lived frivolously here, bent on a cycle of self-gratification and excess.

It was like stepping into the movies. Only Ivy wasn't the pretty starlet dreaming of Tinseltown fame; she was the disease in the veins, the glitch in the blood. Fame would be hers, but not the hollow vanity for which this place was renowned. They said that celebrity should be a festival of achievement...could it not be a festival of destruction?

Her intent was to destroy—and oh, it would taste sweet. No drama the movies could bring would ever rival the cataclysm she was set to release.

Downtown Ivy passed through the streets as darkly and invisibly as a virus, sweating beneath her clothes, her flame-red hair matted to her scalp. Opening the door to the shop, she locked on to the nervous trainee and produced her wad of cash. She had rinsed her dead mother's savings, shocked at how much Hilda had stowed away. Not that she'd ever seen any of it, of course; the witch had kept that one quiet. Had Hilda once had wealthy relatives? Had a loser boyfriend chucked guilt money her way? Ivy no longer cared. All she cared about was that she had inherited more than even she had planned, and the reward was simple: freedom. After all this time she deserved it, and she deserved the best.

'Do you want to make a sale today?' She took a seat, slapping the money down on the table and fixing him with a dead glare. 'I'm your buyer.'

An hour later, Ivy was proprietor of a two-bed single-storey villa with its own pool. Next she purchased a car to park in the drive. She claimed a mass of new clothes to hang in the closet. She acquired a TV, a radio and laptop: all the better to carry out the final leg of surveillance.

On the day she moved in, a neighbour dropped by.

'Hi,' he said, watching her unpack, 'I'm Connor. Have you got everything you need?'

Connor was extremely short, with glasses. Every time he spoke a small pink tongue darted out and swiped his bottom lip, like something in a tree canopy that dives at prey.

'Yes.'

Connor shifted his weight. 'It's not long since I arrived here, as it goes. What do you say we hang out some time?'

'I don't think so.'

He gulped. 'Right. OK.'

Ivy went to close the door but he stopped her.

'Wait.' Behind his spectacles, he blinked nervously, like a mole surfacing from the earth. 'Would you like to come for dinner this week? I've invited the others.' He gestured round the block. 'They seem a good crowd.' Anticipating her response, he added, 'I can fit in with your dates—' and the voice sagged as her withering glare bored into him '—if you want…'

'I said no,' Ivy replied, shutting the door on his bewildered expression. People were a distraction, nuisances to be got rid of. Her focus had to be sharp, her goal untarnished.

Stepping out on to her balcony, Ivy watched the Hollywood hills like a hawk.

According to the press, Robin was set to make LA her second home. Perhaps she was already here, innocent of the calamity. It was only a matter of time before Ivy rooted her dear sister out—and the rest, devil permitting, would follow.

## 27

Robin returned to London for a string of meetings finalising the details of her tour. Barney Grant and Marc Delgado welcomed her at her label's HQ, where Marc proffered coffee and donuts and talked the band through the last push. *Beginnings* would kick off in January in a multitude of venues across North America, culminating in a live appearance at the biggest music event of the year: the ETV Platinum Awards, an annual trophy-fest held at the renowned LA Grand Palisades Arena. Major world-class artists would be there, from Turquoise to Fraternity, from Kristin White to Puff City. It would be quite a finale.

'Have you been looking after yourself?' Barney teased.

'Why wouldn't I be?' Robin withdrew a pack of gum and offered it round. Polly was already chewing but she added to it and proceeded to blow an enormous pink bubble.

'Ah, you know, all that time in the US hanging out with the A-league…'

'It's a serious question,' put in Marc. 'You need to be fit for this tour, Robin.'

'Hence why I'm now only partying six times a week.'

Marc was aghast.

'Kidding. I'm kidding!'

'We'll look out for each other, won't we?' Matt was inspecting the donuts, prodding them each in turn before grimacing on the brink of his hangover. 'Hey, I've seen some of those dancers and I'll *sure* be looking out for them.'

'I thought that guy in apricot legwarmers seemed your type,' threw in Polly.

Matt made a face. 'Hilarious.'

'This isn't a joke,' Marc said sternly, and Barney bobbed his head obediently in agreement. 'Get real, you guys. None of you has done anything like this before.'

Polly raised her hand.

'Apart from you,' conceded Marc, referencing Polly's stint on tour several years ago. 'That means you're the adult in this situation.' This elicited a ripple of classroom giggles.

When the meeting was done they jumped in a cab and headed for the Hideaway Club. Matt got chatting to a gaggle of doe-eyed girls and Robin and Polly settled at the bar. Within minutes Sammy and Belle joined them. Both girls embraced her tightly.

'Spill, then!' prompted Belle.

'About what?'

'Your LA adventure, what else?' Sammy couldn't stop smiling. The girls had met when Sammy had been a mess and a lot of people would have turned their backs—but not Robin. No one got Sammy like her best friend did. To think where Robin had come from and how far she'd travelled was incredible.

'How was Puff City?' asked Belle.

'That makes it sound like a place.' Polly was tapping at her phone.

'How *were* Puff City? For the pedants among us.'

Robin got giddy just thinking about it. 'Trippy. Weird. Amazing. Wouldn't say they all rate me, though.'

'Whoever doesn't rate you is clueless,' said Sammy loyally.

'Then Principal 7's without a clue.'

'How do you know he doesn't like you?' Belle asked.

'Just get the vibe he doesn't like anyone all that much.'

'Before Puff City he was in and out of jail every couple months,' supplied Polly.

Robin took a drink. 'What for?'

'You name it. Put it this way: it's kinda ironic he's plugging an anti-weapons single.'

'Oh, yeah,' remembered Belle, 'how was the charity thing?'

'OK.' Robin shrugged.

'Did you hook up with Leon again?' Sammy asked.

'Again? I only saw him that one time I was with you.'

'And at the premiere.'

She pretended to remember. 'All right—then, too.'

'So?' Polly joined in, with a naughty grin. 'Did you?'

Robin felt her face burn up. She had been trying not to think about Leon since running out on him in Malibu. He had tried to call her but she'd blanked his attempts. The truth was that night had scared her senseless. Robin had never been so intimate with another person, she didn't know how to be, what it meant or what happened next, and the fact they hadn't *actually been intimate* somehow made it harder. She had felt so safe in Leon's arms, and that wasn't something she was comfortable with. She didn't need someone else to make her safe, she'd spent her life ensuring *she* was that haven, just her; and now…

'You're blushing!' crowed Polly, who thought Leon was to die for. 'You like him!'

'I do not.'

'Bollocks,' said Sammy. 'I've never seen you like this about a guy. What happened?'

'Nothing.' It wasn't strictly a lie.

'Nothing my ass,' muttered Polly.

Robin threw in a decoy. 'Anyhow Jax was a twat.'

'That's no surprise,' Belle conceded, and the conversation moved on, each girl deciding they would get the juice once the others were out of the way.

They ended up getting drunk and dancing to indie star Nate Reid's new tune. At one a.m. Brit rap trio East Beatz showed up and their lead Rufio made a beeline for Robin.

'You wanna get outta here?' he slurred. Rufio was tall and tattooed with a peaked ROCK OUT cap permanently stapled to his head. He was twenty, promiscuous, and was eternally hitting the papers for some misdemeanour or other.

'What for?'

'Dunno,' he replied unoriginally.

*Rufio's the kind of guy I should be with*, she resolved through the haze, *not Leon*.

No-strings sex might make her forget—it might help her to unwind, to relax, and not to be alone at night when the fear crept in. Being back in London she was constantly looking over her shoulder, afraid to check the post, even to answer her phone. It was ridiculous.

*I can handle guys like Rufio; for starters I know what I'm getting.*

'I'm done with this place,' Rufio pronounced as a last-ditch attempt at persuasion, despite only having been there five minutes. 'Wanna check out a party in Shoreditch?'

As she climbed into the taxi she knew this was where she belonged, back home with her people. Leon didn't change anything. However she had felt with him, however his touch had seared her and his kiss was still sweet on her lips, there was no point. She hadn't got room in her life for that kind of relationship: feelings made things complicated, so it was easier not to have them at all. It was easier to be alone. It was easier.

Leon could never get where she'd come from. He could never get that even *she* didn't know where she'd come from, and that was a problem that could never be solved, not with kisses, not with words, not with anything.

'Hey.' Rufio leaned over in the cab and pulled her face towards his, slipping his tongue into her mouth and with it the astringent taste of beer. Numbly she kissed him back.

A week later she attended a fashion gala in Soho. Robin was front row as the models strutted the catwalk, among them Lori Garcia, the hot Spanish beauty who had just wed French mogul Jean-Baptiste Moreau. Conversation was stilted as she found herself wedged between a miserable, matchstick-thin TV presenter and the surly daughter of a hard-man actor.

Rufio's texts provided light relief.

*Hook up later babes*, one proposed. Rufio didn't punctuate his messages and often Robin had to read them several times before they made any sense: she guessed this one was a question rather than a statement. The omission was less problematic than the fact he had addressed her as 'babes'. She would have to put a stop to that.

Thankfully Turquoise da Luca was at the after party, on a break from shooting her movie in Greece. Robin was intrigued by *True Match* and at how Cosmo Angel would deliver as a screenwriter. Coverage had been rife and of course the media was trying to link the stars romantically, despite Cosmo being married, and by all accounts devoted to his wife, Ava.

Turquoise looked sensational. Last time Robin had seen her had been *Friday Later*, when she'd opted out of their night, and now she seemed a different woman, her jet hair secured in a chic plait and her floor-skimming bronze gown offsetting her caramel skin. But it was more than that: Turquoise had a blaze in her eyes that had been missing in LA. Perhaps shooting with Cosmo on a deserted island paradise was agreeing with her. How couldn't it?

'What's it like being a Hollywood star?' Robin teased as they hung out on the roof terrace of Covent Garden's Attic House. London was chilly and the pagoda heat lamps were ramped up to the max, casting a burned glow over the VIP guests.

'Ah, you know, I'm getting used to it.' Turquoise smiled.

'You look so well,' said Robin. 'I was worried about you before. Are you better?'

'Much.' Turquoise's eyes glittered in the night. 'That was

a crazy time, you must get that—everyone wants a piece of you and there's nothing left for yourself.'

Robin sensed that however hectic her schedule appeared it would be nothing compared with Turquoise's diary, which must be perpetually off the wall.

'Sort of,' she answered.

'It's good to try something new,' said Turquoise. 'Reinvigorating. Stepping into Cosmo's world is quite a revelation... I've learned so much about him.'

They were joined by a bunch of athletes who had recently been awarded MBEs. It wasn't long before talk turned to the Leon/Jax track rivalry.

'Jax needs to step down,' said Turquoise when the others had moved on.

'Oh?' Robin hadn't heard her speak against anyone before.

'He thinks he's invincible. The reality? Nobody is. No matter how big they become.'

'Do you know Jax?'

Turquoise waved her hand, diamonds flashing in the shadows. She lowered her tone.

'We spent the night together once.'

'You're not serious!' *Jax and Turquoise?* But Jax was a complete chump. Never mind being in a different league—Turquoise was on a different *planet*.

'It was a long time ago,' she said, with a secret smirk. 'After his first win out East.'

'Did you date?'

Turquoise grinned. 'God, no! Just one of those things.'

Robin tried to think where her companion would have

been at that point. Turquoise was only a few years older than her, so if it was Jax's first win she must have been young...

'Whenever we see each other now he avoids me like the plague,' she said.

'Why?'

Turquoise came close, a reckless glint in her eye. 'Promise not to tell?'

'Sure.'

'Jax got...*experimental*. Let's just say that he and a certain Chinese gymnast got pretty cosy...and I was lucky enough to be given a front-row seat.'

'Who was she?'

'She?' Turquoise grinned mischievously. There was a long pause while Robin figured out the omission. She put a hand over her mouth.

'You're shitting me!'

'There's more,' said Turquoise. 'Jax was so feral over his win—you've met him, you know what he's like; I mean he totally lost control, it was like he was high on his own glory or something—and that was when... Well, when the relay baton came out.'

'Jax gave it with *a relay baton*?' Robin hooted with mirth.

'Shh!' But Turquoise was laughing, too. 'Damn right he did.' She lifted her chin. 'Trust me, he was loving *every* second.'

'This is too good,' Robin spluttered, shaking her head. 'It can't be true, it can't.'

'Why not?' Turquoise challenged. 'These guys are like machines after they race. All that time without sex and all those gorgeous bodies right there in the Village. Go figure.'

Thinking of Leon in that sex-fuelled post-Games scenario, Robin experienced a pang. Of what? Jealousy? How could she be jealous when they were nothing to each other?

'The guy thinks he's indestructible,' concluded Turquoise. 'If he wants to keep shit like that under wraps he needs to go about treating people a little better. Especially women.'

Before Robin could quiz her further, Turquoise's PA intervened and drew her away. As Turquoise worked the practised charm that was second nature after years in the industry, Robin decided that in that brief exchange she had gleaned more about the singer than any number of maga zine features could ever hope to reveal. Instead of the nerve-addled creature she had encountered earlier this year, now she was unafraid, daring, undaunted by anyone.

She was fearless, and a fearless woman was a danger ous thing indeed.

# 28

At the Las Vegas Parthenon, fans were out in force for the hottest New Year's ticket in town. The titan hotel was home to the biggest auditorium in Sin City and tonight opened its doors to some of the most bankable names in America. It was the perfect set for Kristin's comeback.

Sponsored by Vegas legend Frank Bernstein and hotel magnate heartthrob Robert St Louis, the lavish production came as no surprise. Neither man did things by halves. The stage was huge, in the heyday of Vegas entertainment boasting all the big names: Siegfried & Roy; David Copperfield; the powerhouse divas of the eighties and nineties, Cher and Celine and Bette. Nowadays the impressive space saluted movie premieres and fashion sprees—and, tonight, hands-down the best New Year's gig ever to grace the Strip.

Backstage was a sea of famous faces. The star-studded cast was second to none, showcasing a host of established names as well as exciting new talent. Among them Kristin spotted Joey Lombardi waiting in the wings as a techni-

cian secured his mic. Abruptly she turned, unwilling to encounter any of the other boys. The thought of seeing Scotty
turned her stomach. She still could not eliminate the vision
she had last been presented with...

But Joey was quick. 'Hey, Kristin!' He caught up with
her, his black hair longer than when she'd seen him at
Bunny's birthday—what a lifetime ago that seemed.

'Hey.' Kristin saw a new woman reflected in his expression. Gone was her tumbling river of blonde and in its place
a sharp, choppily cut bob. She had thrown out the wraithlike
dresses and replaced them with pants and vests, showing off
her enviable figure and for once faithful to her age. She'd
embraced a new look and with it a new spirit: when she'd
declared she was moving out of The White House and getting her own place, Ramona's face had sunk as fast as her
Botox would allow; when she'd announced her split from
Scotty was down to 'an irreconcilable matter', the press had
gone mental for the reasons why; when she'd declined to
comment on her prolonged absence, her benefactors were
stricken. What had happened to their precious, malleable
little girl? She'd grown up...because she'd had to.

'It's been a while.' Joey grinned warmly. His eyes were
kind, cocoa-brown and bordered by thick, dark lashes, and
for an instant Kristin's heart softened, before she reminded
herself that they could all be in on the sordid truth. Who
knew if Fenton had enjoyed his wicked way with more than
one of Fraternity? Who knew if Joey had been made to get
to his knees? Who knew if it hadn't been part of the goddamn *audition process*?

She wanted to blurt it. She wanted to ask him. She wanted
to know.

At the same time she didn't—because knowledge was irrevocable.

'I can't miss my cue,' she said, making to leave. Starlets and their entourage jostled in their factions and she was terrified of laying eyes on Scotty.

'Can I take you out?' Joey asked, immediately abashed as though the question had emerged without his consent. 'I mean, after this?'

'Sorry, I've got plans.' Bunny was performing in the second round of the Mini Miss Marvellous tournament at the Mirage and she had promised to be there.

There was a lot to make up for. Christmas had been a sober obligation, with Bunny's rehearsal load reaching new summits and Ramona's ambitions more outrageous than ever. Kristin felt awful for having abandoned Bunny to their mother's dominion. Always she'd promised to stay close until Bunny came of age, but she'd had no choice: one more day answering to Ramona and she would have killed somebody.

She vowed to compensate by doing all she could for her sister. Recently Bunny had been uncharacteristically quiet, several times imploring her to get back with Scotty because 'whatever happened couldn't be that bad,' but, while Kristin knew Bunny adored her surrogate big brother, having her defend him was a step too far—especially when Kristin was keeping the true nature of his desires to herself in order to protect hearts like Bunny's the world over. Imagine if they found out! It wouldn't just shatter their fantasies of one day being the coveted Mrs Valentine; it would explode all the stupid myths about everlasting, unconditional love in a single, obliterating swoop.

Kristin had always prided herself on valuing her fans, and this was when it mattered. Her fans were kids—Fraternity's, too, which made it all the darker—and if fiction was what she and Scotty were selling, then fiction it should be. It didn't mean she had to believe it.

'Oh,' said Joey. 'Right. Maybe I could come with you?'

'It's not your thing.'

'It might be?' he tried, hopefully.

Fleetingly Kristin wondered if he had been employed by Scotty to win her back—not for Scotty, of course, but for his image. Or to appease Fenton, who must have undergone some kind of a coronary. Come to think of it she hadn't seen Fenton anywhere for weeks.

'Don't you have someplace else to be?' She had an image of Fraternity writhing around without their clothes on over the polished floor of some record executive.

'No.' Joey looked awkward. 'Thing is, Kristin, since you and Scotty broke up… I mean Scott's gutted about it, anyone would be, but I guess, well, for a while now, I…'

'We need you in make-up, Kristin,' an assistant interrupted them.

'All right,' she agreed, allowing herself to be dragged off. 'It's a date.'

Fraternity opened the show in spectacular fashion. As the headline act the crowd had expected to be made to wait to see them, and the surprise element only added to their passion. Fraternity fever swept through the ranks, from five- to fifty-year-olds, as adulation ricocheted across the domed arena and the boys' music was drowned out in a sea of ignorant worship. Kristin glimpsed the charade from her position at the sides and wanted to scream her anger.

They performed their Christmas single 'Keep You Warm' and Scotty played it like an ace, crooning from the cocoon of a heavy winter coat that must have been sweltering beneath the lights and reaching to clasp an ocean of outstretched hands. She could no longer accept the band or anything they stood for. His phony enactment made her gag.

People *craved* the illusion; they *welcomed* it. They didn't want real life with its pain and troubles and heartache, they didn't want agonising truths and treacherous lies, they didn't want the constituents of a hard, genuine relationship that could turn any second and rip the ground from under you. The fantasy suited them, and Kristin knew then that even if she ran onstage right this minute and revealed Scotty and Fenton's affair, just shouted it out to the crowd, she'd be met by a pool of blank, uncomprehending faces, as though *her* version were the false one, and all it would take was one voice to start chanting his name and the rest would follow, everything forgotten, an accusation they didn't and could never believe...

'*Scotty! Scotty! Scotty!*'

They called for him now like the plastic blow-up messiah he purported to be. Each was as synthetic as the next, the perfect boy-band blend that was totally and utterly bogus.

Kristin's set cut a fine contrast to Fraternity's vocoded beats. Taking the microphone unencumbered, she strummed her way through the hits that had made her, easing the crowd back in on familiar territory. Shouts of '*We love you, Kristin!*' alleviated a sliver of the hurt and made her realise that she cherished what she did. She didn't have to give it up for anyone.

*'More!'* they chanted, and she struck up the opening chords to the adored ballad from Ava Bennett's movie *Lovestruck*. As the crowd applauded, she realised she was going to have to write some new material fast, because swooning about girl-meets-guy-and-falls-in-love-for-ever had a now decidedly insincere ring to it.

Relief at the success of her run was quickly replaced by shock when afterwards she found Scotty waiting like a neglected Labrador in her dressing room.

'I don't want to see you.' Roughly she pushed past him.

'I have to talk to you,' he wheedled.

'What about?' She busied herself with pointless things in an effort to seem distracted.

'Where've you been all this time?' he spluttered, grabbing her arm. 'For fuck's sake, you could have at least *called* me? I've been going crazy!'

She rounded on him. *'And I haven't?'*

'I was building up to tell you.' Scotty came towards her, eyes full of sorrow, the bright blue eyes she used to hold so dear but that had spent too long staring into the pool of another man's reverence to ever hold any truth. 'I swear it—'

'But you want him, don't you?' she demanded sourly. 'That whole time, the whole time we were together, you wanted him. And you didn't have the decency to tell me.'

*Don't lose it, Kristin*, she told herself as her voice split. *Don't let him see you cry.*

'I'm in love with him.'

'Leave,' she told him emptily, her worst fears confirmed, and though she'd steadied herself against them, still they knocked her flat. 'I never want to see you again. I *hate* you. I never thought it was possible to hate anyone as much as I hate you.'

'I can't leave,' appealed Scotty desperately. 'Kristin, I need you.'

'What for?' she lashed.

'This can't come out,' he warned. 'You know it can't.'

'Do what you like, Scott. Your sordid trysts aren't any of my business. As your girlfriend you'd think they might have been, but what do you say we forget about that minor detail? You clearly have, you asshole.'

'Fenton and I have been going out of our skulls—'

'I'm sorry to hear that,' Kristin retorted, oozing sarcasm. 'It must have been so *hard* for the two of you. But I guess getting hard suits you both fine.'

'Fenton wants us back together. You and me.'

She barked a laugh.

'I'm serious. We'd pay you.'

Slowly she shook her head. 'Oh, Scott. What's happened to you? I thought I knew you. I thought we were friends.' Her voice wobbled. 'I thought we were family...'

'Think about it.' He was haunted, a piteous figure a million miles from his onstage persona of moments ago. If only the fans could see them both now! What a heap of artificial *bullshit*! 'Just promise me you'll think about it. Please. For the sake of whatever we had, and I know it can't seem like much, but we were close, weren't we?'

*'Scotty! Scotty! Scotty!'* echoed the cries from outside, a grisly soundtrack to his woe.

'To protect you?' she asked in a small voice.

'Yes.' He was begging her with whatever he had left.

'I'd have done *anything* for you,' Kristin choked. 'I'd have protected you with my life, Scotty Valentine. But I won't protect you from this. You can take your little deal and shove it up your ass—or up Fenton's. You never know, he might like it.'

She was still shaking from the confrontation when she arrived at the Mirage. At the entrance a fleet of photographers sailed in for fresh bait, snapping her and Joey together.

'2013 is going to be the best year of your life,' he promised as they passed through the foyer, in an attempt to counter her bad mood. 'I know it.'

'I wish I did,' she replied wretchedly.

'Kristin.' He took her arm. 'Whatever went on between you and Scott, if he was cheating on you or whatever, I swear I had no clue.' She believed him. 'If that's why you broke up, even if it wasn't, I think you're a million times the person he is.'

She squeezed his hand. 'Thanks.'

If she said anything more she might cry.

Bunny's pageant was unfolding in one of the conference suites. There was a bustle of interest as Kristin was recognised. Bunny waved at her from up on the stage, dressed in a fuchsia-pink tutu and matching fishnets, and wobbling perilously on too-big shoes. She was sporting yet another wig, this one practically as wide as she was tall, as if she'd put her finger in an electric socket. Her face was orange, her lips crimson and painted on teeny-tiny like a geisha. But her posture was most disturbing—Kristin could all but hear their mother's orders ringing between Bunny's ears: *Chin up, chest out, ass tight!* Sequins dazzled off the stage as the army of Mini Misses twinkled and scowled and smiled with profound misery. Down at the front the mothers, mostly overweight with unwashed hair, hugged themselves with fear.

'How old are they again?' Joey whispered as they took their seats.

'Fourteen going on forty.'

Ramona darted over, model-mum expression in place but Kristin could tell she was seething. Kristin had been instructed to come earlier so she could perform at the competition opening—Ramona had decided this might give Bunny a lead—but the Parthenon gig had run on. Following her image overhaul and decision to move out of The White House, anything Kristin did was at every turn grossly inappropriate and selfish.

'What time do you call this?' she hissed.

'Get lost, Mom. I'm here for Bunny, not you.' Tomorrow she had to inform Ramona that she was fired as her manager—that would be fun.

'We'll talk about this later,' Ramona snipped, unwilling to cause a commotion.

Later couldn't come soon enough with the surreal carnival-style recital playing out on the stage. First was the dance round, showcasing a parade of precocious teens, their faces made up like ghoulish dollies and their stringy hips strutting to a run of inappropriate music including an offering from Flo Rida about blowing his whistle. Bunny danced like a maniac to her slot, watched approvingly by Ramona, who nodded grimly whenever a turn or axle was completed to standard. Tracy-Ann Hamilton hovered at the sides like a little despot.

Then came the interview. When Bunny was asked who her idol was, she cited Kristin. The crowd released a collective *'Aaaah'* and heads craned to clock her response.

Joey nudged her. 'She thinks you're the best,' he whispered. 'Sibling worship. I've got that with my brother—it never goes away.' From what she could remember Joey's brother worked in construction and hadn't a dime to his name. It was sweet. Joey was sweet.

Bunny ended up winning the bout. Ramona released an animal cry and Bunny obediently curtseyed when she collected her trophy, sticky smile rigidly in place.

'Thank you so much,' she drawled, drowning beneath an elaborate bouquet. Kristin saw her mother's mouth move around the scripted words. 'I can't wait to come back next time…to take me one step closer to claiming the Mini Miss Marvellous throne!'

'Do you want to grab a nightcap?' Joey suggested as they emerged.

Kristin barely heard him. Crossing the Mirage atrium was a gorgeous shaven-headed black man, his muscular arms decorated with tattoos and his physique like a drawing of a superhero, built and stacked and bulging in all the right places.

The Olympian Jax Jackson.

A shiver of desire coursed through her for the first time in weeks.

'Hang on,' she murmured, already forgetting Joey was there. 'Give me a second.'

Without thinking, she went over to say hello. Jax stopped, his entourage loitering behind. He wore the smirk of a man rarely denied, and so unsurprised to find one of the most famous women in the world chatting him up. The old Kristin would never have been so bold, but Jax was about as far removed from Scotty Valentine as it was possible to get.

Right now that was exactly what she needed…a taste of the wicked.

'You headin' my way?' Jax enquired, and how he said 'my way' implied much more than the joint he was about to grace.

'If I'm invited,' she responded flirtatiously.

Jax grinned, exposing a gold tooth: the badge of his triumph.

'We ready to go?' Joey was next to her. She could feel him bristle, his hand on the small of her back. 'I've got your stuff.'

Jax was unaffected. 'Step this way, baby. You're in for a treat tonight.'

Kristin made her decision. She turned to Joey. 'Change of plan,' she said, feeling dangerous and reckless and loving it. 'D'you want to come?'

Joey met Jax's stare for a second before looking away.

'Nah, not my scene. Maybe I'll catch you tomorrow.' He handed over her jacket and purse.

Turning away from his crestfallen longing, oblivious to it, Kristin accompanied Jax out of the Mirage. She needed to let loose and have fun. She needed to get wild with a stranger who'd never listened to a fucking boy band in his whole entire life.

Kristin was on the edge of adventure.

Jax Jackson couldn't have arrived at a better time.

## 29

'Does it turn you on for Ava to be here?' Cosmo assaulted Turquoise between takes one day. They were filming in a mansion close to the sea; its white bricks were strung with creeping, twisting vines, and the heat was unbearable. So were his arms, locked like a vice around her.

'Why would it?'

'My wife, your best friend…and she has no idea what history we share.'

'Just because you're making some sicko documentary,' she retorted. 'Believe me, you could never come between Ava and me. You're nothing to do with our friendship.'

Cosmo guffawed. 'I doubt that, sweetheart. Ava hates being lied to.'

'I guess she'd know, being married to you.'

'Whose version do you think she'd buy? Yours, or mine?'

Turquoise knew the answer. Tight as she and Ava were, Cosmo was The Adored in that relationship. She had seen how Ava's eyes followed her husband around, and how she

visibly lifted every time he was in sight. Ava loved him—
but she didn't know him at all.

'You think you've got this all tied up, don't you?' Her eyes
flashed. He hadn't a clue. His wife had left that afternoon
following another flying visit, and conditions were ripe.

Sam summoned them for the final take of the day. Before the cameras rolled Cosmo shot her a depraved grin. 'I
remember how it felt having you tied up…'

Bitterness surged through her veins.

'Action!' called Sam.

Cosmo was through. It was time for action, indeed.


Early evening Turquoise headed to her room and gathered
what she needed. She did it calmly and without fuss, because
she had thought it through a hundred times and the outcome
was clear in her mind. Each time she wavered she put herself back in Cosmo's vile clutches, a broken, damaged, ruined seventeen-year-old so callously taken advantage of.

Cosmo's arrogance had led him straight into the honey
trap. She would have left it, moved on, but no: he'd had to
reopen the wound.

A photographer friend had loaned her the device. She
placed it neatly in her purse, closed and locked the door,
and headed down to the hotel foyer.

The man at the counter was more of a boy. They had spoken when Turquoise had checked in and he'd been taken
with her beauty.

'I was hoping it'd be you.' She smiled as she approached,
noticing the colour that flourished beneath his skin. 'Would
you be able to help me with something?'

The boy looked happy to be addressed. 'Of course, Ms da Luca,' he replied, straightening.

'It's a bit awkward, actually—' she laughed, throwing her best charm offensive '—but I seem to have left something in Mr Angel's suite... He's at a function tonight and I'd check with him myself but it's right across town.' She'd scoped Cosmo's plans and he was safely out of the way: after filming he had been on such a high that she suspected a great deal of alcohol would be involved, creating the perfect stage for her intentions.

The boy's face flickered. 'I'm afraid I'm not authorised to access Mr Angel's room, or any other in the hotel.' He looked genuinely disappointed. 'I'm sorry.'

She smiled warmly. 'Don't worry, I completely understand.' Looping a twist of hair over one ear, she frowned. 'It is a shame, though. My mom gave me that necklace before she died, and if it isn't there I don't know what I'll do. Do you think I ought to check it hasn't been stolen? What's your protocol for that? If it has that'd be terrible, because I can't think of anyone who's been in my space except the hotel staff... If I could just get in and retrieve it there'd be no need for any fuss; you know how these things can get out...'

The boy thought for a moment, before withdrawing a card from below the desk. 'All right,' he decided, without much conviction. 'If you'd like to come with me?'

Upstairs the boy swiped her in, waiting dutifully outside as though Cosmo's suite were sacred ground and stepping one foot over the threshold would turn him to ash.

Turquoise moved quickly. In the master suite she dug out the equipment, concealing it within a framed picture and casually calling out, 'Here it is!' Cosmo's quarters were insanely grandiose, a gilt-edged four-poster bed draped with linens and a giant marble bathroom boasting an oval Jacuzzi, in the centre of which was an extravagant Grecian font with a naked cherub pirouetting on top. Tucked beneath his bed she saw a briefcase. She shuddered when she thought what toys it might contain. Was it the same supply he had produced with her?

When she emerged the boy was relieved, quickly pulling the door and scoping for the billionth time that they hadn't been rumbled. Turquoise attached a delicate gold crucifix she'd brought in her pocket and breathed a thankful sigh.

'Thank you so much.' She beamed. 'I'll be sure to pass my compliments on to the manager. Am I glad to get this back!'

'You won't say what for?' the boy asked worriedly.

'Of course not,' she reassured him. 'It's our little secret.'


Retrieving the footage was risky. Next morning Turquoise slipped down for a prompt breakfast, knowing the staff would tend to Cosmo's room when he finally surfaced for his.

She waited in a lounge of plush velvet sofas for the help to come up. Did it really require six maids to do the job? The women flitted in and out of his space with fresh towels and bed sheets, all fussing to lead the charge for their Most Important Guest. She hadn't banked on there being so many, but soon began to detect a rhythm to their work, how they disappeared in twos and threes to replenish supplies and at points left the room unattended as a remaining couple chatted over their carts. When several wandered off to manage other rooms, she spied her opening and slid unseen into Cosmo's chambers.

She was in and out in less than twenty seconds, and resumed her seat in time to give a returning maid her friendliest smile. Her heart was pounding so violently she thought her body must have been shaking with the force.

Would she have what she needed? There was every chance that after his event Cosmo had returned alone and slept like a baby—but there was also the chance that he'd drunk too much and nailed fifteen hookers in one night. Given that Turquoise had waited in the bar till past midnight and still seen no sign of him, she was banking on it.

Back in her room, she took a call from Donna. Running through pleasantries was torture and she hung up as quickly as possible, promptly loading the device into her laptop.

A blank video popped up. Frantically Turquoise activated it, praying she hadn't messed up, and within seconds a blurred image of an empty room flashed to life on the screen. She forwarded through to his return until finally, to her intense relief, the deed began.

Cosmo was with four women, stumbling in ahead of them and leaning against the closed door with the undisputed bully-rights of the jailor. The quality was better than she had expected and she saw Cosmo's smile fade: on the way over he would have been the supreme charmer, the movie star these working girls felt blessed to entertain, and only now would he reveal what he truly was—a tyrant. At a guess the youngest was a minor but it was impossible to be certain. What was certain was the striking resemblance they all bore to Turquoise herself. She imagined the brief Cosmo had supplied: tall, dark hair, olive skin, green eyes…

Some were curvier than others but the common denominators were clear.

First Cosmo instructed them to undress. There was no sound but Turquoise would know that voracious expression anywhere. As the girls were commanded to make out with each other, occasionally dipping to tend to his arousal, it all seemed agonisingly familiar.

It was when Cosmo withdrew his briefcase that she knew she'd hit on gold.

The dildos he extracted were even more monstrous than she remembered, and there was resistance as two of the girls were directed to strap them on. Cosmo produced a mountain of cocaine to get the wheels oiled and Turquoise's eyes sprang with tears when she saw how eagerly—and how desperately—his company vacuumed it up. It was terrible watching their misfortune unfold, but cold hard evidence was the only way to catch a beast like him. She had no option, and if it stopped even one victim from meeting the same fate as that poor young girl buried so callously in a lonely cold desert that night, it would be worth it.

Coming up on their high, the girls took to their appointed tasks with zeal and soon the orgy became a writhing mass of limbs with neither head nor tail, one girl indistinguishable from the next and Cosmo somewhere in the midst of it all spiralling recklessly towards his private nirvana—but no heaven was worth it when it spelled hell for someone else.

Sick to her stomach, she was ready to kill the screen when Cosmo scrambled from the melee and took something else from his box of treats. Turquoise squinted, trying to decipher what it was, and when she saw she couldn't believe her eyes.

Cosmo mounted a winking golden crown to the top of

his head—it was crusted with rare and exquisite gems, its circumference peaked like icing, topped with mock sapphires and rubies and fringed with fur, an old-school king's crown like something from a deck of playing cards. The girls were so busy with each other that they failed to notice, and Cosmo stepped over them to position a large sack of what appeared to be grapes—*grapes?*—on his dresser. Taking his position on the bed, he sat upright and gazed dead ahead, his ludicrous crown jewels perched and shimmering in the half-light.

Unnervingly Cosmo was staring straight into the eye of the camera, and as Turquoise looked directly back at him she felt a chill.

Silently Cosmo issued his orders and the girls disbanded to obey. All four got to their knees, taking it in turns to crawl to the bag of fruit and extract an orb with their teeth. Like dogs they were required to return to their master, scramble to the bed and take his erection in their mouths. It took Turquoise a few seconds to fathom what was going on: the women were sucking his dick with grapes on their tongues, and judging by Cosmo's contorted face it was a sure-fire way of coaxing him to the brink of ecstasy. Each girl remained on him just a minute or so before it was the turn of the next, and the departing sweetheart returned to the bag to retrieve a second helping. With this routine, Cosmo was set to go all night.

These were someone's *daughters*, Turquoise thought furiously. Injustice crackled through her as she recalled a conversation she'd had once with Ava, in which her friend had confided her and Cosmo's wish to have a family. The hypocrisy of Cosmo's wanting kids—daughters he would protect and pay for and love, if indeed he was capable of that—was odious. Did he not consider that the girls here had fathers and mothers? Did he not see them as individuals, someone's *children*, beloveds, not things he could play with and throw away?

*Things he could allow to die?*

As Turquoise skipped through the footage, her worst fears were confirmed. Cosmo's regal routine went on for the best part of the night, with the girls wearying and beginning to protest, and whenever they did it only gave Cosmo more fuel for fun. He'd hoped they would complain, because each time they did it gave him an excuse to hit them: the king and his lowly servants, who tended to his every need, who existed and worked in fear of his wrath.

He hit them, he slapped them, he floored them. And each time he got harder.

Cosmo Angel was one seriously fucked up human being.

Turquoise reached the end of the tape and stared for a while into the blank eye of the computer screen, processing what she had seen while trying her best to forget it.

There it was. At last, after all these years, she had Mr Angelopoulos crucified in black and white—or rather full colour, for the entire world to see, should they be interested.

And, boy, she kind of thought they would.

## 30

Dawn at Fountain Valley was always peaceful. Leon squinted against the morning sun, casting pale light across the circuit, the white lanes looping towards and away from him, an endless chain with no beginning or end: his battle-ground.

Absent-mindedly he tugged at the sweatbands on his wrists. Marlon had given them to him the day he had died. *'Here,'* his brother had said, reaching into the glove box of his truck and taking something out. Leon had recognised the bands from when Marlon started training—they were black with white crests on; he would know them anywhere. *'Put these on.'*

*'But these are your lucky stripes.'*

*'And you're my lucky little brother. And if I get selected, if I go away next year you'll have to fill those out; be a man, take care of things. You promise me?'*

How different things might have been if Marlon were still alive. Maybe Leon wouldn't be here at all if things hadn't happened the way they had: maybe he'd have ended up a waster, getting stoned, dealing drugs, packing a gun. Maybe Marlon would have made the Sydney team; maybe he wouldn't. Maybe Leon could have changed the outcome if he'd reached his brother sooner…maybe not. Maybe. There were things that happened and things that didn't. That was all. All that mattered was what you chose to do with the facts.

Leon fixed on the track. Was he willing to sacrifice another four years in pursuit of the gold? That was what the super-elite required: existence in suspension, a readiness to give up your body to the physicians and psychologists and medical experts, putting things for ever on hold—family, girls, friends, the real world—while never knowing if it would pay off.

It had to. Four years chasing the next Olympics…because he would not give up. He would never give up. He had Marlon at his shoulder and for him he would keep going.

His archrival's days were over. It was time for a new leader.

The roar of an engine pulled him from his thoughts. Leon glanced up in time to see Jax arrive in the car lot, his bullet-shaped head poking out of the top of a ridiculous yellow monstrosity. The vehicle was a fiend, a massive neon thing Leon didn't know the name of.

Jax leapt from the car, already in his kit, and strode towards his opponent. He was donning his hallmark vest, the gold bullet emblazoned across his back as much a souvenir as a caution, and Teddy Simpson, the team coach, was trailing in his wake.

'So it begins,' Leon muttered, steeling himself.

'You. Me.' Jax lifted his chin. 'Let's do it.'

It was obvious Jax had a hangover. He had been partying hard, enjoying the superhero attention in London, LA and every state their PR jaunt had visited: the plane only had to touch down before Jax was unbuckling himself and getting directions to his nearest blow job. One flash of his medal was a VIP pass into anything—and anyone—he desired. With silver Leon experienced the same, but despite the accolades it wasn't enough: success wasn't about where you came so much as whether you had done the absolute best you could. If there was one extra breath you could have taken, one more push you didn't deliver, one further crush of the lungs, the final pain you could have abided and hadn't, that was real defeat.

What made the difference between silver and gold? Luck? Biology? Fortune of physicality, of owning a single gene that lifted you imperceptibly above the rest? Jax had been revealed during tests to possess a bigger lung capacity, but then the same had revealed Leon's bigger heart. What couldn't be measured, only felt in the soul, was ambition.

Leon hadn't been banking on a duel today. He'd been here since daybreak. 'Now?'

'No, next week, bozo.'

The fire caught in his belly. Desire to eliminate this man was all consuming. The Championships were this summer and he had to show his mettle. Jax was getting beat.

'A hundred metres.' Teddy stood by. 'Ready to fly?'

'You had breakfast?' Jax snarled.

Leon didn't get it.

'Prepare to eat dust.'

'Conserve your energies, Jax. It must take it out of you having such wit.'

'Fuck you,' said Jax unimaginatively.

'You want to get into this again? 'Cause I'll get into it again.'

'Be my guest, bozo.'

'Swop the pornos for a dictionary once in a while; it might widen your vocabulary.'

Teddy interceded. 'Boys…'

'You think you're so fuckin' smart?' Jax glowered.

'Pretty much.'

'Well I've got news for you.' His audience waited. 'You aren't.'

'Wow. I'm enlightened.'

'Go fuck yourself.'

'I'd sooner your girlfriend did it for me.'

Jax's mouth pursed like a walnut. 'You're a dead man,' he seethed. 'Just like your dead brother.'

Leon went for him, eclipsed at the last instant by Teddy, who wedged himself between the juggernauts. 'Jesus, you two; back the hell down!'

'Only one way to settle this,' Jax spat, privately relieved at the coach's intervention: he didn't much fancy getting floored again.

In seconds the men were crouched, strong legs in front and their hands behind the line. Leon focused on the track, waiting for his anger to subside and trying to channel it into fuel but unable to focus on anything save tearing Jax Jackson limb from limb.

Everything fell quiet.

As soon as Leon heard the pistol he was on top of the

track. That's what it felt like, as if he had fallen straight on it. The ground rose up to meet him, pushing back against every tread like a living thing, and for this handful of seconds his mind was clear. He was bursting with energy, charged with a flame, as if he could go for a thousand miles. He was back on the Compton road where Marlon had died, running to save him and save the future.

Jax was on a level, leaning into the run, winding up faster and faster till he was in full sprint, his legs turning out the treads like pistons, arms slicing through the air, cutting his way through. Leon caught sight of the finish and in an instant was consumed by the unqualified fact of it and the certainty that this was all that counted: he saw the thing he was trying to get to and he knew time was running out; that it couldn't happen again this way.

*Not again.* He had to be fast enough, had to get there in time. Had to reach it or…

Jax was pulling away. The gold bullet was in sight, drawing further; the head above it dipped as if the body it piloted were in flight. The heat in Leon's legs told him he was at his limit—he couldn't push any more. This was as good as he got, and Jax was better.

The other man's foot crashed over the line, sending up a flat cloud of chalk.

Bent over, his breathing ragged, Leon battled to slow his heart. Jax thumped him on the back, hard. Leon coughed and spat on to the ground.

'Bad luck, Sway.' Jax emptied a bottle of water over his face, neck, shoulders, blowing drops of it off his top lip, then he shook his head in a flurry like a wet dog. He watched as the younger man, palms on his knees, fought to catch oxygen.

'Know your place,' Jax growled. 'Or else.'

At the sides, he grabbed a bottle of water and popped it open. Teddy was distracted by a couple of the team showing early and falling into stretches, and Leon took a long slug, holding it in his mouth a moment before shooting it in a narrow stream on to the hot ground. When he took another he pulled the liquid into him thirstily.

On the benches, a discarded news rag was blowing on the breeze. The strapline read:

ROBIN RYDER TAMED AT LAST?

Beneath it ran a picture of Robin and UK rap sensation Rufio, one third of London posse East Beatz, spilling out of a club. Another showed them clambering into a black cab.

Leon sat down next to it, resting an elbow on his knee and his chin in his palm.

*Shit.* She was just a girl. He had other stuff to focus on, stuff that needed his attention, but the fact was her rejection still stung. Hadn't she felt what he'd felt that night? Hadn't he broken down a vital wall, or at least dislodged a part of it? Hadn't she let him in? Try as he might he couldn't forget how it had been to hold her, how small she had seemed, her skin so sweet and her lips so soft, and how different she had been in that context from the tough image she projected, the hard exterior that she had finally let fall with him.

Why had she vanished the morning after without a word, a note, anything?

Didn't she care?

Seeing her now with Rufio, Leon accepted that whatever

had gone between them was a one-way street. Robin wasn't interested, she never had been and he couldn't force her to be. Now she had hooked up with somebody else without a thought for how that might be perceived. Fine, if Rufio gave her what he couldn't, good luck to him.

Perhaps Robin wasn't the girl he'd thought she was.

The wind picked up, carrying the paper off the benches. He watched it ride on the breeze, skimming and wheeling across the track until it disappeared from sight.

## *31*

Slink Bullion was sprawled in his hot tub, sucking on a fat cigar. Through narrowed eyes he surveyed the two girls opposite him, their perfect tits bobbing at the surface of the water.

'We gotta sound this out, man.' Gordon Rimeaux, better known by his Puff City stage name G-Money, ran a hand across the back of his neck. He felt bad. Ever since Leon Sway had showed up at their door he'd felt bad. He'd barely slept a wink at night.

'Aw, quit walkin' round with a face like a slapped ass.' Principal 7 emerged on to the terrace of Slink's Long Beach mansion, his bare arms and chest mapped with artwork, and climbed in between the women. He lit his own Cuban. 'Join the frickin' party.'

Gordon hung back. He didn't want to be here but they had to work out what in fuck's name they were going to do, and if Slink and Principal refused to address the issue then he had to. How could they look Sway in the eye and act as if nothing had happened?

'Shoot, brother, I'm listenin',' Slink offered, as usual the diplomat where Principal's crappy attitude was concerned.

At the same time Principal offered, 'Girls, why don't you touch each other, work it a bit? Yeah, that's what I'm talkin' about.'

'We can't when *she's* watching,' one of them complained, pulling away and glaring, stoned, in the direction of Shawnella, who was perched on the rim in a scant bikini that was only a shade redder than her livid face. Slink had never maintained that he was a one-woman man, yet Shawnella couldn't abide the company he kept. She'd insisted on making the gig tonight, slouching about moodily in hot pants and applying lip gloss every three seconds.

Shawnella mumbled, 'Dumb sluts.'

'Damn, woman!' The cigar flew from Principal's hand, landing in the water with a sad fizz and floating across its surface like a turd. 'You tryin' to shit all over my party?'

Slink held a hand up. 'Chill, dog.'

'Party's over,' said the girl, stepping out of the pool. The other followed and they padded inside, dripping water. Shawnella shot them daggers on the way past.

'That's just beautiful.' Principal fished the cigar out and flung it after them. 'Frigid fuckin' cunts!' He sat back. 'Where's the champagne? Is this a fuckin' celebration or what?'

Slink killed the beats. 'Take control of yourself, man, for real.' He nodded to Shawnella. 'Go inside, baby, you heard the man.'

Principal scowled. Shawnella sloped off, long hair plaited like a rope down her back.

Once upon a time this might well have been Gordon's idea of a party: Puff City gigs were renowned and tonight had lived up to the hype, with Slink favouring spontaneity so that appearances would spring up across LA in warehouses and underground clubs at a moment's notice, still managing to split at the seams with followers who had uncovered the news through whispered word-of-mouth. In the nineties the crew had powered sixty-thousand-strong stadium events but these days preferred a tighter venue where fans could connect with the music. Lack of advertising meant they welcomed only die-hard disciples.

Now, he grimaced. Gordon wasn't into that scene any more. Drugs and bought women, they meant nothing, they were wrong and they belonged to another period in his life when he had been royally messed up and hadn't had a clue what shit was about. It had been a sinister time, a time he preferred not to recall…only now he was being forced to.

Shawnella emerged in the doorway, proficiently brandishing four champagne flutes, two in each hand, and a magnum of Cristal.

Filling Slink's glass, she began kneading the muscles of his back, which shone like black silk in the moonlight. 'You having fun now, baby?' she purred, confidence restored.

Slink drew on his cigar, watching as its end glowed into life. He drew the smoke in deeply. 'There ain't no reason why Sway has to know a thing,' he said, returning to the topic at hand. Shawnella released the clasp on her bikini top and climbed into the water, an attempt at distraction. It worked for Principal, at least, whose flat eyes locked on to her nipples, just visible above the line of the water, where her tits bobbed, slippery as seals' backs.

'Am I crazy or somethin'?' Gordon's voice trembled with conviction. Limbo was torture, made worse by having no one to talk to about it. 'Doesn't this mean nothin' to *any* of you? Aren't you freaking about this situation *at all*?'

'Ain't my style,' responded Slink evenly.

Principal drew his eyes from Shawnella long enough to participate. 'We gotta keep shit under control. It was way back, man. Sway's not gonna remember a thing.'

'He's not gonna remember his brother dying? Right there in front of him?'

'*Relax.*' Slink pinned him with a stare. 'I've got your back, G; you know that.' The cigar tip burned. 'Question is, have you got mine?'

'You know I do.'

'Then collect your shit. Because this ain't the kind of thing that gets us cryin' like girls to the cops, d'you feel what I'm sayin'?' A cloud of smoke eclipsed his features. 'Principal's right, we stay cool.'

Gordon looked down at his hands. When he spoke, his words were so soft he could barely be sure they were heard. 'But remember which one of us shot him.'

There was a grave silence. Slink looked at Gordon. Gordon looked at Principal. Principal looked at Slink. Shawnella stared at the water.

'He'll find out,' said Gordon tightly.

What had Slink been doing in the first place, agreeing to front the single with those guys? Inviting Leon Sway back into their lives, the same boy they had deserted years before, the boy who had been weeping in the road and clutching his brother's dead body…and who said that if Gordon hadn't bolted from the scene then a life might not have been lost that night? Maybe then he wouldn't be living with this searing guilt every damn day he woke up.

'Sure as shit he will if you don't stop pissin' confessions all over town.'

Principal smirked. 'We were kids back then, what's the big deal? Guy shouldn't have been there in the first place. It was his own fault, brother.'

'You're not my brother.' Only in their emergence did Gordon realise the words were true. He had never liked Principal: the guy had a bad vibe through and through.

Slink rose from the tub in a cascade of water, like Neptune surfacing from the waves. In lieu of a trident he wielded a bottle of Cristal.

'Never let me hear you say that again, G, or you're outta here faster than I take a dump in the mornin'. We're *all* family. Break that bond and you're out.'

It was a sentiment Gordon had heard before. Of course the crew had to stick together, put on a united front, because as soon as one stepped free of the ranks, the scandal of Marlon Sway's murder would risk being exposed. Sure, the City had a sketchy history, it was a given they hadn't always played nice, but no one suspected them of homicide—especially not in one of the most publicised cases in Compton history. Marlon had been a promising athlete, a kid with the world at his feet, still a teenager, for Christ's sake…

'Are we clear on that?' Slink's tone was measured.

Gordon nodded. He had to remember that twelve years back he'd been another man. Put him in that situation again and it would never play out that way. That fateful night had forced him to change his priorities and turn his world around…only now he had, the shame was more debilitating than ever. How long could he keep the secret?

He would keep it for as long as it took. Because Gordon knew that if he ever risked Slink Bullion's name, he'd be lying in a bloodbath of his own.

# 32

Kristin had never been with a man like Jax Jackson. Everything about him was novel, from his swagger to his dangerous streak, from his insatiable sexual appetite to his breathtaking physique. She could not take her eyes off his body. It was stupendous. Every inch polished to perfection, the glossy dark skin beneath which a powerful engine lay in wait, steadying to pounce, and the hard, long muscles that made him the biggest turbo diesel on the planet.

They had hooked up every night since Vegas. After vowing she would never get close to a man again, Kristin found herself responding to Jax like a bloom to sunlight.

He was change…and change was what she craved.

'You wanna go where no girl's gone before?'

It was Saturday night and they had returned from a gallery opening where Kristin had presented a Fresh Talent Award. The instant they were through the door to his apartment Jax was fumbling to free her from her clothes. He was ravenous, a red-blooded hot-bodied sex weapon, and she loved it.

'Wherever you want me,' she breathed.

Deftly he unfastened her halterneck. Beneath she wore no bra and he grasped her tits, running his thumbs across her nipples so she moaned, and plunging his tongue into her mouth. Swiftly he hooked his fingers into the loop of her jeans and tugged them down. His touch was in her and in a rush she was drenched, his practised groove running across that nub so she was tightening and swelling against him until she was ready to come.

'Not yet,' he murmured, kissing her neck. 'First you're gonna break my record.'

Kristin was thrown to her knees, marvelling as Jax un-buckled his suit pants and stepped out of them. His dick was straining against his underpants, a caged beast.

'Nine seconds, baby,' he rasped, exposing himself in all his Olympic glory. 'An' I'm not gonna let you come till you nail it. Understand?'

Claiming the stopwatch, holding it aloft, Jax guided her mouth towards his cock. Only when her lips closed around it did he begin to slam and grind, shouting out the count as she fought to contain his hard-on, turned on to the max by the challenge he had set before her and wanting more than anything to please him.

Jax had been her first… She longed to be his.

Feverishly he came. Stunned, Kristin wiped her mouth.

'How'd I do?' she asked coyly.

Jax caught his breath, wiping the sweat from his brow. He frowned at the digits.

'Shit,' he said after a moment, glancing down at her with

something akin to respect (which confused him, because she was female). 'Ten seconds flat.'

'Is that good?' Her eyes widened.

Jax grinned. 'Close enough.'

He threw her back on the floor and, contrary to his usual style, buried his head where she was desperate to receive him. It was all the answer she needed.


Kristin held tight to her boyfriend as they entered the Flower Girl party. Bunny's people (i.e. their mother) had advised that she launch a fragrance, and Flower Girl was a sweetly scented bouquet of sugars and spice, perfect for pre-adolescents and conjured entirely by an expensive Hollywood creative team who lived in perpetual fear of Ramona's next demand.

The terrace they'd hired was resplendent with crystal fountains and candyfloss wheels, pink petals strewn across the walkways and a twine of rose bushes in a canopy overhead, yielding white and yellow buds. Ramona had employed a troupe of eight-year-olds and had dressed them Anne Geddes–style with miniature cauliflower bonnets and dresses puffed up like dandelions.

'Sheesh,' commented Jax, het up in his suit. 'Who're all the midgets?'

'We won't stay long,' Kristin murmured in response. She was keen to support Bunny and then scram. Even standing this close to Jax was bringing her out in a fever: she just couldn't keep her hands off him. He made her feel liberated, sexy, like a real woman. Jax had shown her things and given her body pleasure she hadn't known it was capable of. He was wild and exciting—whether it was grabbing her in a toilet cubicle (last week at Basement, when they'd been partying with Puff City), or turning up unannounced at her apartment and shagging her senseless over the foot of the bed before he'd even uttered a word.

Scotty had been her forever and she had neither wanted nor imagined any other future. All her life she had assumed they would end up together, her happy ever after. But sleeping with Jax took her to new heights—he made her feel truly desired, after all that time with Scotty sensing he'd really prefer to keep his clothes on and play X-Box.

'Damn right.' Jax's hand brushed across her ass, making her tingle. Scotty had never done that: a chaste peck had used to keep her going for a week.

'Darling!' Ramona sailed over, arms flung wide to embrace her eldest daughter. Clapping eyes on Jax, she played Textbook Mom and Kristin thought what a complete phoney she was. The last time they had spoken—or, rather, yelled—had been a slanging match in the aftermath of Ramona being fired as her manager. Clearly that was, for the time, being forgotten, lest Jax think any less of them. 'Aren't you going to introduce me?'

'Mom, this is Jax,' Kristin offered reluctantly. 'Jax, meet Ramona White.'

'A pleasure,' crooned Ramona, batting her lashes. Kristin remembered the dalliance with Luke and fought the urge to push her mother into a mountain of cherry blancmange.

'You got a john round here?' replied Jax. 'I need to take a dump.'

Ramona's mouth fell open. It was a moment before she recovered herself. 'Right this way,' she said pleasantly, her lips a pinched pout of dismay, and in that moment Kristin thought Jax was just about the best person she'd ever met.

'Well,' said Ramona coolly, when he'd gone, 'what a *charming* man.'

'Isn't he?'

'Come on, Kristin, what are you thinking? It's hardly as if he's right for the image!' Swiftly Ramona glanced her up and down. 'Though with this new *look* of yours I'm frankly at sea as to what that approach is meant to be.'

'Why does there have to be an *approach*? There *is* no approach, this is just me.'

'That's precisely where you're going wrong. What are all these appearances you've cancelled? The shoots you haven't turned up for? I may not be looking after your interests any more, Kristin, but rest assured I keep well informed on the grapevine.'

'You "keep informed"? Jeez, Mom, get a life.'

'*You* should have stayed with Scott Valentine,' Ramona snapped. 'What on earth was going through your mind breaking up with him?'

Kristin's face scorched.

'You never deserved him anyway,' Ramona finished. Satisfied, she folded her arms.

'You know nothing about our relationship,' she responded frigidly. 'Nothing.'

'I know a mental breakdown when I see one.'

'Why, because *you've* had so many?'

Jax returned. Kristin leaned into the cologne she had become addicted to and saw her mother's smile crack with spiteful jealousy.

'Please excuse me,' Ramona said tightly, moving on to her other guests.

Bunny was being trumpeted at the front with her sponsors, posing for photographs with an expression tinged with worry. Kristin gave her a wave and a reassuring thumbs-up and Bunny smiled back, frowning a fraction as she clocked Jax at her sister's side.

'You wanna see somethin'?' Jax challenged, a mischievous glint in his eye. Kristin nodded, resolving to put her mother from her mind. She was shot of Ramona now and at last she was becoming her own person. Being with Jax had helped give her that.

Her lover led her through the crowd. Kristin saw how it parted for him—it literally did—and how Jax's Fastest Man title made him godly, on a higher echelon than everyone else. His world was fascinating, alien, exotic. It turned her on to hear about the hundred per cent focus he needed to race, how it felt being at the centre of the world, in front of an audience of billions, able to outrun anyone. His devotion to the cause was second to none. Regularly he could be found fretting over his rival Leon Sway: each time the titans hit the training ground it seemed the gap was getting narrower.

*'How close was it?'* she'd ask, sensing he had something on his mind.

*'It don't matter,'* Jax would flare, *'the fact is* I always win. *The fact is* he always loses. *Who gives a rat's ass about it being close? Not me. It's first and it's second, baby.'*

*'You know you're number one.'*

*'Fuckin' damn right I am.'*

In confiding in her, Jax let her see that maybe, after all,

he wasn't invincible. Kristin realised that she didn't care if he was the record holder or not, because the feelings she was developing for him were stronger than that. So far it had been about parties and screwing, but possibly they were reaching the next stage…growing towards a relationship.

And then…

Jax would seize his watch, strap it to his wrist; his ultimate wind-down…

As Kristin weaved her way through the Flower Girl party, cordially greeting acquaintances, she shivered at the thrill of their special game. How she would be positioned beneath him, would widen her eyes as he set the time, the metal glinting…9.57, the one to beat. How Jax liked to pour champagne over his rigid cock and command, *'This is the one, baby.'* How she would part her lips, desperate to leap from the blocks…

It had only been a few weeks, but there was something special between them. Trust. Wasn't it time she returned the sentiment?

'Here.' Jax pulled her to a stop behind a lofty pyramid of meringues. 'Private.' Hastily he attended to his trousers, a wicked smile pulling at his lips.

Kristin resisted. 'Wait,' she urged. 'There's something I have to tell you.'

'You're not pregnant?' Jax spluttered, blanching.

Shocked, she laughed. 'Of course not, silly.' Her smile faded. 'It's about what happened between Scotty and me. I never told you, and the thing is I feel that I should…'

Jax reached for her. 'Forget it. I'm not interested.'

'Jax, this is serious.' She kept him at bay. 'This is something I haven't told anybody, and now I'm choosing to tell you. It's driving me insane, I mean seriously, and I can't say anything to Mom or Bunny or to any of my friends, and so I have to know that you're going to hear me out.' A beat. 'Please.'

Jax tried his best not to grimace. Slumping on to a bench, he plucked a meringue from the display and tossed it into his mouth. 'Shoot,' he mumbled through shards of pink sugar.

Kristin sat down next to him. She took a deep breath and told him everything.

The following morning, Bunny woke early. She hadn't gone to bed until late and wondered what had roused her. A quick check of her cell provided the answer.

A message from Scotty had come in at 07.58:

We need to talk.

Bunny loved it when, for a delicious millisecond, she could actually believe they were going out with each other. That was the sort of text a boyfriend sent, right? She clasped the cell to her heart and gazed up at the ceiling. Her skin still smelled of the Flower Girl scent and it wrapped her up in dreams of romance and rapture. She couldn't wait to see him.

Springing from her bed, Bunny threw on her best new outfit: a baby-blue halterneck playsuit with daisies on the pockets, and wedge heels she found difficult to walk in but looked nice—and as her mom always said, *You have to suffer to be beautiful!*

Downstairs, Ramona was preparing breakfast. Bunny

had hoped her mother wouldn't be up yet and stopped in her tracks.

'Where do you think you're going?' Ramona asked archly, pecking at a punnet of blueberries and sipping Echinacea tea. Betsy the cat patrolled the hall like a Rottweiler.

'Just out.'

'Out where?'

Bunny shrugged. She was terrible at lying. Her mother's glare bored into her and she was acutely aware of the wedge heels, flashing like beacons of her illegal intentions.

'Are you meeting a boyfriend?' Ramona cried.

'No.'

Her mother didn't believe her. Ramona strode over, clipped one of Bunny's ears between her fingers and yanked her painfully to the breakfast bar. With undue force she released her, sending her thumping on to a stool.

'If you think for one second that I'm going to let you jeopardise your career for the sake of a boy then you are sorely mistaken,' Ramona cawed. 'I will not see you go the way of your sister, do you understand? I've invested my life in you, Bunny. *My life.*'

*What about my life?* Bunny wanted to scream.

'Eat,' commanded Ramona, shoving a flaccid egg white under her nose. Softening a fraction, she put in, 'We've got to keep your energy levels up for the competition.'

Bunny could hardly see her miserable breakfast through a haze of tears.

'I don't want to,' she replied.

'You don't want to eat or you don't want the Mini Miss trophy?'

'I don't know!' Bunny howled. 'Just please don't make me!'

Ramona slammed her tea down. A wash of it spilled over the sides, trickling sadly down the counter and into Bunny's lap, so that it looked like she'd wet herself.

'What is the matter with you girls, hmm? Don't you see how lucky you are? I *make* you because when you are made we achieve results! We earn money! We further ourselves! Are you so pathetic, Bunny, that the concept is beyond your grasp?' She closed her eyes. 'I should never have backed home schooling, clearly. Look what a dunce I wound up with!'

Bunny swallowed the lump in her throat. It tasted horrible. Sour.

Ramona faced the sink, shuddering as she bent over her drained teacup. Bunny watched her mother's shoulders, like the bony contours of a prehistoric bird.

'Eat your breakfast,' said Ramona calmly, without turning round.

Bunny wiped her eyes. She withdrew her cell from her pocket and scoped it under the bar, tapping out a quick missive:

Can't now. Will call you later xxx

She picked uninterestedly at her egg. Her phone vibrated.

K & J—WTF? Are they together?
Bunny, you have to come through for me. You're my only hope.

And just like that, her own hope flared. She loved it when he said her name!

*You're my only hope...*

Oh, Scotty was hers. *He was hers!* They felt the same.

Tucking her cell back into her pocket, Bunny steeled herself against her mother. So what if Ramona wanted to make her life hell? She had Scotty, and Scotty was her secret weapon. Kristin was with Jax now, and at last, at last, nothing stood in their way.

## 33

Robin's *Beginnings* tour opened at San Francisco's Supership. The space was tremendous, shaped like a vast bowl, and at final rehearsal when she shouted into the empty seats her voice swung back at her with clarity from every angle. With the stylised domino stage fronting one end, a silver platform running out into the audience and the swinging glass birdcage glinting like a pendant, her art director's vision had come spectacularly to life.

Outside, the crowd gathered and grew like an approaching storm. As she stood backstage amid the dark rigging and her posse of restless dancers it felt like the onset of gladiatorial battle. Robin prayed her audience wouldn't be baying for blood tonight.

'Are you ready for this?' Barney took her shoulders, his brow sweating.

'Course I am.' Robin smiled as confidently as she could as a sound technician checked her mic and gave her a thumbs-up. 'I'm on top of this, Barney. It's going to fly.'

The birdcage was lowered for her to step into. She managed it with some difficulty and was afraid its delicate casing wouldn't hold her though they had practised it a hundred times. Fanning from Robin's back was a plume of resplendent feathers, oily and purple and green, intricately crafted and tricky to manoeuvre without tearing. On her feet a pair of pick-sharp buckled Louboutins dictated where precisely she had to stand in order not to slip through the heel-size grates.

'You made it.' Barney smiled as the door to the cage was closed. 'This is your moment, babe. See you on the other side, yeah?'

Robin knew he wanted to say more. This was America: the Holy Grail. Barney put his fingers through the grill and clasped hers before slipping away.

Being raised to the rafters was terrifying. They had played it through tons in rehearsal but actually being here, in the dark, tens of feet above a blackened stage that in several moments would burst with light and noise and the screams of an auditorium was something you could never truly conjure outside the real event... The fact of the night rushed at her unchecked. The cage came to a stop and Robin stared at the back of the facing doors, hearing only her own breath and her own heartbeat.

Stillness descended. For an eternal instant the crowd's cheers muted and nothing beyond the certainty of right here, right now, existed.

And in that crazy calm she thought of one thing. One person.

Leon.

His face came to her without warning. His smile. His arms. The skin on his neck.

And in a bright flash the world exploded, a great torch, the biggest and brightest she had ever seen shone right into her face, and her ears were filled with the deafening roar of fans united—*her* fans, here to see Robin Ryder.

The first bass-heavy strains of 'Told You So' poured into the arena to a boom of recognition. Robin saw millions of lights, a myriad of camera phones, and from here it was like being in the heart of the cosmos, floating in space and surrounded by stars.

When the cage door swung open Robin stepped out on to the platform with ease, raising the microphone and belting out the first line:

*'I told you I would make it; I never tried to fake it...'*

She had started off with nothing—just a baby in a bin, waiting to die.

Then along came music; a way to express herself, the only articulation she had.

Tonight she had America at her feet.

The track cut and in a spark she vanished. Robin could hear the screams as the invisible platform was dropped to the stage and a second later drew back to expose her reappearance: magic, exactly as her director had said. And then she owned it, feet on solid ground as the rhythm of her opener slipped into her bloodstream and she sang with all her soul. She had skated on the periphery of this state before, being unreservedly in the zone, where time ceased to exist and the only thing that travelled through your mind was, well...nothing. No thoughts, no worries, just the fever and the flash of the instant. It felt like flying.

'You Win', her newest single, sent the masses wild, and as they took on the chant themselves she thought how bizarre it was that some scribbled lyrics she'd written in her Camden flat while partly drunk and surrounding by picked-at takeaway boxes should be adopted like this, and that this clean, wonderful moment was the outcome of that mess. The song had been a hit in the States, killing the download chart in its first week of release.

In the centre of the stage was a silver disc, which she now positioned herself on, and with both her arms high to herald the blare of the chorus, the disc released and began to climb, jettisoning her out over the crowd's outstretched arms. She reached down, directing the mic to pick up the voices that accompanied her beloved track, and took hands in hers that seemed to be their own entities, unattached to any human body, clammy, cold, hot, small, rough, yielding, so that the swaying sea of pink beneath was like a coral bed swishing on the movement of the blue tide and waving her down to the deeps.

She'd watched a documentary once about an ocean diver, who had become caught in a mass of weeds, had struggled to break free and in his fear had been starved of oxygen.

When the hand first touched hers, she felt it was bad, like an apple soft and rotten. When it held on tight, too tight, and the platform juddered to a stop, anxiety trickled through her. The disc was geared to halt at obstruction so to the delight of the fans she was suspended, tethered by the bad hand, pulling to break free but the fingers on hers were crushing. Never before had she been on the receiving end of such malicious intent. The hold was on her knuckles, her nails, her wrist, prodding and kneading the bones, curiously, darkly, insistent.

In a moment the experience was flipped, like two sides of the same coin, from euphoria to panic, light to dark, good to bad, yes to no.

*No.*

The hand was squeezing. It was strong and she could feel the thumb pushing viciously into the flesh of her palm. Somehow she maintained the words, battling off fears that this was it, that whoever had been watching her was here; they had caught up with her at last and now they wanted to hurt her. As the beat drove on and miraculously Robin kept singing, kept smiling, she thought how easily and quietly a crowd of this number could consume her, as smoothly as a pebble swallowed by the sea.

Abruptly, the hand released. With it the disc broke free and she was up again, being brought back to the security of the stage with its pulleys and trapdoors and places to hide.

*I'm OK. I'm OK.*

But not before she detected a flash of red. She thought she must be delirious, because in the instant before the woman was obscured, it was like looking in a mirror.

Robin blinked.

She was confronted by her own image…weirdly distorted, a version of herself, thinner, different hair, but the same face, same eyes, the same only…not.

It was a dream, a hallucination brought on by adrenalin. Robin searched for the woman, horror whistling through her…but she'd vanished, absorbed by the mob.

Back in the spotlight she wrapped up her final numbers,

safe with the army of dancers at her back and Polly and
Matt where she needed them.

When finally she came offstage she collapsed into Barney's arms and didn't know whether to laugh or cry or
scream or all three at once.

Next morning she was up early, ate two pieces of toast to
counteract a burgeoning hangover and drove Matt's hired
Ford Mustang to the Golden Gate. Parking on an empty
vantage point, she switched radio frequencies, striking on
one of Kristin White's new tracks, and settled back in the
driver's seat. Wasn't Kristin dating Jax Jackson now? Since
the release of their charity single Jax had been papped every
night at some club or other with a variety of similar-looking
blondes on his arm. He was an idiot. What did Kristin see
in him? It had to be contractual, a way to get both their images on track. Most of LA was.

Robin watched the cars crossing the bridge, commuters
in shirts and ties sweating with the windows down. San
Francisco was a city she had always hoped to visit, and this
a structure so renowned it felt as if she already knew it.
Yellow mist rose from the bay, hazy over the pastel water.
Sunshine gleamed off the red towers and set them alight.

The flame-haired woman glimmered once more in her
memory. Try as she might Robin could not forget how the
hand had felt, gripping hers so savagely; the face she knew
as well as her own—because it *was* her own, it was and yet
it couldn't have been—from which those cold eyes glared…
She had to be mistaken. It was fear that had done it, made
her think she was seeing things that weren't, that *couldn't*,
be there. A delusion brought on by a panic attack. It was

little wonder after the stalking campaign she had endured.
She had to get her head straight. Was she losing her mind?
She'd thought she had been dealing with the fame thing;
that she'd been managing to stay intact where so many had
fallen apart.

Was that as much of an illusion as her phantom perpetrator?

After the show her crew had been buzzing, but something
had stopped her letting go. It was as if out there she had
slipped into another world, one not Polly or Barney or anyone else could understand, one where she had transcended
flesh and bone to something else, and while that was the
drug performers craved it had scared her to death. It was
one thing to be adored in a situation as intense as that, and
another to be pinioned like a butterfly on a nail.

Her phone rang. Dragged from her thoughts, Robin
reached to collect it. Rufio.

'I'm in the shit,' he announced.

'What?'

'Fucking slow connection, hang on.' There was a muffled
pause. 'That better?'

Actually the connection was fine. Robin just hadn't believed he would dive straight into talking about himself
before asking how the biggest night of her life had gone.

'Sure,' she replied, a headache coming on. 'What's up?'

'Shit's hit. I'm shitting myself.'

'So you said.' She wondered in how many ways he could
conjugate the word 'shit'.

'Fight broke out last night, innit. Wasn't my fault but that
didn't stop the heat rocking up and cuffing me.' Rufio liked

to imagine he was in an Al Pacino movie, constantly refer-ring to the police as 'cops', 'pigs', or 'the heat'.

'You've been *arrested*?' She sat up. 'Are you OK? Where are you calling from?'

'It's cool, it's cool,' he mused, relishing how it sounded. 'I'm on bail.'

'What happened?' She could only imagine what the UK press were doing with this.

He sighed heavily. 'Some twat started on me outside the Spar.'

*The Spar?* 'Why?'

'I don't know, do I? Does there have to be a reason?'

'No...'

'Made out like I was hitting on his girl,' he grumbled. 'Total bollocks, which I told him, 'cept actions speak louder than word, innit, so I floored him.'

Robin's heart sank. East Beatz had a reputation and Rufio was the media's archetypal council-estate British bad boy, so it stood to reason—in fact it was probably *advised*—that he got into stuff like this. Right now she couldn't be deal-ing with it.

'Is he OK?' she asked tiredly. 'He's not in hospital or anything?'

'I mashed him up good,' Rufio replied, as if her question had been a slight on his potency, 'but he'll live.'

'That's reassuring.'

'I gotta go. Figured I'd give a heads-up cos your phone's gonna be off the wall. They'll want statements and shit, you know, what my girlfriend makes of it and stuff...'

'Thanks for that.' A pause. 'The tour started last night, you know?'

'Oh yeah!' Another silence. 'It going all right?'

Robin realised he'd had no idea of her itinerary. There would be coverage in the tabloids at home today but it sounded like Rufio had more serious matters to attend to.

'Fine,' she replied, electing not to expand.

'I'll keep you posted, yeah? Catch you later.'

The line went dead.

Robin sat for a moment, thinking hard. Always thinking of the same thing.

She gunned the Mustang's engine, grinding the wheels in reverse. Turning from the shimmering Golden Gate and the strident red that haunted her dreams, she realised that the one person she really wanted to talk to wasn't here. He'd tried to be, but she'd blown it.

## 34

Ivy Sewell swam a length underwater, her shape refracting beneath the ripples, silent and deadly as a crocodile. Emerging at one end, she squeezed the drips from her rope of red hair. A chill breeze licked her between the shoulder blades. She turned to the fence dividing her pool from next door's and narrowed her eyes. There was nobody there.

She was looking too deep into shadows: they hadn't found her yet.

Ivy spread her towel on the ground, slipped on her sunglasses and peered over the top at her LA stronghold. Already the London flat she'd shared with Hilda was light years away, a necessary prelude to her final destination. Idly she wondered about her mother's body being found but it failed to trouble her: they'd had no visitors, the neighbours never dropped by…who knew when the absence would be detected? Would the rats get at her first? Would she decay in her chair, the windows closed, the flat steaming with the fresh smell of rot, till only a skeleton remained? The thought made her calm. Ivy was sleeping more soundly than ever.

Blue sky scorched overhead. She smiled.

It must have been a shock for her twin to rest eyes on her after all these years. Ivy could hardly contain her thrill when she remembered seizing Robin's hand at the Supership. Amid all those people, theirs had been a shatterproof tie.

The bond was unbreakable. It was family.

'Hey.'

At first Ivy failed to hear the voice. People were white noise.

'Ivy?'

She withdrew her shades and sat up. A man's head appeared over the fence.

'I never told you my name,' she said frostily, absorbing her unwanted visitor.

Connor grinned. 'Thought you could use some company,' he commented lightly.

'I *said*,' she repeated, 'I never told you my name.'

The grin faltered. 'One of the guys in the complex told me...' He grappled under her gaze, his pink hands appearing at the top of the boundary like a pair of mouse's feet, as if holding on to something solid might steady his nerve. 'He overheard you. On the phone.'

Her job interview for the Palisades Grand—their questions had been more rigorous than she'd anticipated but she'd managed to bring them round.

'I guess he shouldn't have been eavesdropping...' Connor offered limply.

'Curiosity killed the cat.'

'Yeah.' He took her comment for jest. 'Do you want to go out some time?'

'I told you, I'm not interested.'

His eyes twinkled behind the glasses. 'You're quite the secretive one, aren't you?'

Ivy stood. She saw him pull back, in fear or desire, scoping her exposed flesh and the mane of hair that flashed in the sunlight like a warning.

'You don't want to know my secrets.' She came nearer. 'Believe me.'

Connor licked his lips. The proximity of her exhilarated him. He'd never had a girlfriend, apart from a brief encounter in college that had culminated in him losing his hard-preserved virginity in someone's parents' bedroom shortly before vomiting over the carpet. It had been too long since he had felt a woman, and Ivy, mysterious Ivy, with the blazing hair and sharp tongue, was a fine discovery indeed. He loved that she was taller than him. She reminded him of the German au pair who had looked after him as a child. Once, passing the au pair's bedroom, he had seen her undressing, naked save for a pair of high red patent heels.

Anticipation made him shudder. With a muted choke he ejaculated into his pants.

'Get out of my sight,' said Ivy, disgusted. 'And don't come back.'

Overcome with a heady brew of longing and shame, Connor retreated, certain then that he would do just about anything this woman asked.

Ivy didn't move until she heard his footsteps stumble across the yard. She resolved that if Connor insisted on getting in the way then she would be forced to dispose of him. When it came to attaining her goal, everyone was expendable.

# 35

On the other side of town, tangled in a nest of sweat-soaked bed sheets, Turquoise surrendered to the rush of her orgasm and lifted her hips to drive her lover deep.

'You're amazing,' Bronx murmured, grabbing a handful of coal-black hair and staring into her emerald eyes and wanting to say more but afraid that if he pushed her too far she'd vanish again. Turquoise cried out her climax, her throat exposed over the edge of the bed, and Bronx kissed it hungrily, burying his face and inhaling her scent.

They stayed with their arms wrapped round each other. Turquoise saw her body beached on a golden shore, blue sky above and green sea below. After months without sex she felt united, her soul and her self joined together once more.

Bronx's lips trailed down her chest, tenderly grazing her nipples and kissing the small freckle on her ribcage. Gently his fingers traced a line south, brushing across the soft hair there and making her shiver. She widened her legs, wet from having come so fiercely, and felt his touch plunge between them, pushing her apart and sliding in with a force that made her gasp. Next his mouth was on her, his tongue running across that sensitive swell over and over, sucking and teasing and tasting, a moan escaping his lips but muted in her warmth, and she widened again as she advanced on the flare of a second crescendo. Bronx increased his pace, the wet from his mouth as wet as her body until it was impossible to tell where one ended and the other began. This time it hit Turquoise with the slam of a freight train, and she pulled Bronx's head closer, her thighs gripping and shuddering as she rode the wave.

When Bronx's lips met hers she could taste the salt of her yearning. He stroked her face with such affection that she felt a hot tear slip out of the corner of her eye.

'Hey,' he breathed, 'you OK?'

'I'm fine.' She smiled, for a dangerous second filled with the need to tell him: about her history, about the murder, about Cosmo, about the tape... It would be so easy to blurt it, just to see if she could, and in a single moment of madness change her life irretrievably, like standing on the ledge of a skyscraper and thinking that one step was all it took.

That same self-preservation held her in place now. Instead she sat up, looping the ebony stream over one shoulder and turning her back to him.

Bronx propped himself up on one elbow, running a hand down her spine. 'Talk to me,' he implored. 'Please.'

She dipped her head, her face hidden.

'I know you've convinced yourself this is a bad idea,' he said gently, 'and yeah, maybe working together complicates things, but if that's what's eating you then you have my word we don't have to ever again. But I'm not an idiot, Turquoise.

I know it's more than that. Why'd you keep running out on me? Why'd you keep disappearing from my life?'

'I've been busy.'

He joined her on the side of the bed, resting his chin in the nook of her shoulder. 'I get that.' One arm snaked round her belly and hauled her in. 'But what *you* don't get is that you've got me where I can't let go. I don't want to let go. I'm hooked on you, baby, I can't pretend to be any other way. I just wish you knew how to open up to me…'

Turquoise shut her eyes. What could she say that would in any conceivable way be OK? *Y'know when I was on location with Cosmo? Actually, I was shooting my own project. It's in my interests, see, because I used to be one of his whores—a murdering whore, as it goes—and as he won't let me forget, I've been forced to take matters into my own hands…*

It might as well be an ancient language for how impossible and nonsensical it was.

'I've got to go.' Turquoise grabbed her clothes and tugged them on.

Bronx frowned. 'When can I see you again?'

'I don't know. I'll call.'

'You won't, though, will you?'

She turned, bending briefly to kiss his cheek. 'Thanks for last night.'

Before he could object, she was gone.

*True Match* had at last finished filming and Turquoise was relieved to be back in LA. Not having to see Cosmo every day made her realise what an effect he'd had on her state of mind. Her appetite had returned, she had started sleeping again, and the future, once so terrifying, had opened up, no longer on his terms but on hers.

Each morning, as soon as she woke, she would go into her office, feed an arm behind the cabinet and check it was still there: the evidence that would set her free. Always she kept a copy on her person, but the original stayed here. Back-up.

'Sam mentioned you didn't make the wrap party,' Donna Cameron said over lunch at The Ivy. The terrace was bright with flowers and the warm scent of fish and ocean air. 'You getting sick of Hollywood already?'

'Surely it's getting sick of me.' Images of Turquoise and Cosmo on location had been plastered across the national papers and gossip rags, risking, in her opinion, burning out media interest before the movie had even hit box offices.

'Never. Sam's impressed. They all are. This is the beginning of something special.'

'You're considering another project, I can tell.'

Behind her shades Donna concealed her pleasure. 'Let's just say there are discussions that need to be had. Your profile's never looked so hot.'

Turquoise wasn't convinced that the PR was altogether positive, but she'd decided not to worry over the stuff people made up. While she had been praised for a 'brave' step into the movies, she had also been slated for her 'greed' and 'dissatisfaction'. As much as they said she would excel in Hollywood as she had in the pop industry, they also vouched her venture would be a 'shameful charade' and 'an embarrassing mistake'. One morning they maintained she was giving more to the fans by embracing new frontiers, the next she was neglecting them in vain pursuit of glory. Inevitably there'd been speculation that romance had flourished onset, Brangelina-style, and that Cosmo's marriage was on the rocks, a sensation cut short when Cosmo and Ava entertained a string of demonstrative public appearances. Turquoise had called Ava the minute the erroneous story had emerged and to her relief they had laughed about it, however sour that hilarity might have felt, lodged like a hiccup in her throat.

'First,' Donna resumed, piercing the orange yolk of her egg, 'settle back into things here: we don't want the fans to think your music's coming second.'

Turquoise paused to sign her name for a passing admirer. 'I'm all for new challenges,' she agreed, 'but this is where I belong. It's good to be home.'

'It's good to have you back.'

Home wasn't just LA: it was the music. Turquoise had returned to the studio, working with a British producer to record her new album, the much-anticipated *Renaissance*. During her time away the songs had descended on her like tunes on the wind, as if they weren't being generated by her at all but gifted by a greater force, reminding her of an interview she'd read with a blues legend who believed that every guitar he picked up already contained all the songs it ever would, the melody flowing from the instrument of its own accord. Days passed where she imagined every song to already be in existence, written and complete on an unseen plane, just waiting to be discovered by the voice of its choosing.

'Take time out to relax,' Donna advised afterwards, as the women stepped on to Ocean Boulevard. 'As of the movie's release your schedule's going to be unrelenting.'

'Sure.'

Once Donna was out of sight, Turquoise dug a hand into her purse and removed her cell. She checked her inbox to make sure it was really there and she hadn't invented it.

She hadn't. The missive had come in that morning.

There it was at the top of the list: the simple, lonesome C that stood in her mind for so much—cruelty, callousness, coercion...

*Cosmo.*

Drowning her fear, Turquoise opened the message and read it.

No one runs for ever. Come to me, sweetheart.
I've got a surprise...for old times' sake.

He had named a date and hour. She clicked the phone shut.

If Cosmo wanted to invite destruction to his door, let him. She was the one with the goods and as soon as she revealed what she had against him it would put an end to this nightmare once and for all. Whatever his surprise, it would be nothing compared with hers.

Contrary to Donna's counsel she had no intention of taking a break. She had a payload to deliver, and that payload was pivotal. It changed everything.

# 36

'*You need help!*' Scotty Valentine flounced out of Fenton Fear's Hollywood mansion and charged blindly towards the tennis courts. 'You're a fucking schizoid! Can't you let me *breathe*?' The courts sat unused for most of the summer but Fenton kept them immaculate on account of the possibility he might one day embrace the sport he had always admired. Fenton could do with getting some exercise, Scotty thought bitchily, because he was fat.

He was a fat boyfriend: a fat, *old* boyfriend.

'Come back! Please!' Fenton wailed as he emerged, a towel wrapped around his sunburned gut, which was freckled from UV exposure. Normally Scotty doused his lover in Factor 50 lotion, meant for babies, because Fenton crackled like a pig on a spit as soon as show him the sun, but lately he had avoided touching Fenton at all—and Fenton knew it.

'Where are you *going*?' Fenton despaired, staggering after him.

Scotty pushed open the court gate and swept inside,

aware he was walking straight into a chicken coop but directionless in his anger.

'Wait,' Fenton gasped, 'I beg of you.' He appeared on the clay, blocking the exit, and bent to catch his breath. His hair was matted to his forehead and a pathetic look crouched in his eyes. 'I just want to make you happy,' he whimpered. 'Don't be mad at me.'

Scotty turned to face him, shielding his eyes from the glare of the sun. Appraising Fenton from the other side of the net, he couldn't believe that until recently he had been so obsessed by this man. Fenton had once been an untouchable hero, so assured, so adult, so in control, but now a different beast possessed him. His manager had become needy, governing Scotty's every move with a jealousy that bordered on the psychotic.

'I have to shout because you don't *listen*,' Scotty lashed. 'And even then you don't hear what I'm saying. How many times do I have to tell you I'm *suffocating*?' He observed Fenton gather himself, as detached now as he had once been dependent, and thought how their bodies had grown in opposite directions as the stress had taken its toll. While Fenton had piled on the pounds, gorging on fast food and squatting like a pork pie in his office as he barked impatiently at clients, the skin on his chin wibbling with exertion, Fraternity fans were reeling at Scotty's sudden weight loss, their heartthrob's cheekbones sharp and his eyes huge as they stared blankly from a vampiric grimace. On dark days Scotty considered it akin to Fenton having consumed him, swallowed him whole, his manager licking his chops as with each hour that passed Scotty felt a little more of himself slipping away.

Where had it gone so wrong? Since Kristin's discovery the men's affair, formerly so breathtaking and clandestine, had become a real, dangerous thing, and they had been living in perpetual fear, day in, day out, that they were about to wake up to the biggest media storm of the century. Like worms on a hook they dangled on her goodwill, inexplicable given the circumstances and which convinced Scotty she was biding her time, never knowing when he went to sleep at night, oppressed by the clinging web of Fenton's arms, if they would live to fight another day. And fight was truly the word—these days they couldn't stop bickering.

'It's not working,' said Scotty for the fiftieth time. 'This isn't how I want to live.'

'Never think I don't know how that feels,' Fenton choked. 'My love for you is sweet poison, a drop more every day… You're my toxic addiction, Scotty Valentine. Always you.'

'Stop saying that! I can't fucking bear it!'

'You used to love it when I expressed my affection. What's changed, darling?'

'*You* have!' Scotty struggled to express his raging emotions. 'When we first met it was an adventure, never knowing when we were going to see each other or what we were going to do, what you were going to teach me… It was a thrill—'

'The thrill of the chase, my boy.' Fenton shook his head. 'You have a lot to learn about love. It isn't all roses and surprise rendezvous… The heart mellows…'

'Fuck the mellowing! I can't even go to the bathroom by myself, for fuck's sake!'

'Is it any wonder?' Fenton spat bitterly. 'Don't think I didn't see the way you ogled that model on the "Once More

Baby" shoot last week. You could scarcely take your eyes off him! Practically drooling, you were. I'm surprised no one else picked up on it.'

'Get a life, that guy was straight as an arrow.'

'You don't deny it, then!'

'What are you now?' he spluttered. 'Just another groupie?'

'Do you make a habit of sleeping with your groupies?'

They both knew that was a false claim. It had been weeks since they'd last made love.

'This is your fault!' Fenton cried, finding his temper. 'All you had to do was find a way for Kristin to take you back and then we could have returned to how we were before.'

'What, sneaking around and hiding in closets?'

'It seems like you preferred it that way.'

'Maybe I did. At least then I didn't feel so trapped every minute of the goddamn day.'

Fenton scowled. 'If you want to go parading around in full view of everyone then be my guest. Excuse me if I thought we were trying to be discreet.'

'Discreet? You may as well lock me up in a cellar. And anyway, you try winning your girlfriend back when she's walked in on you shagging a man old enough to be your father.'

'Oh, that's right,' Fenton croaked, 'play the age card.'

'It's not a card. *It's the truth.*'

'For a sweet boy you know how to sting.'

'I'm not a "sweet boy", am I? Not any more.' Before, Scotty's pet name had been appealing; it had made him feel like an angel. Now it was pervy, like a schoolmaster who wanted to slap him on the ass with a ruler after class. Scott wasn't a baby, he was twenty-three this summer and Fenton made him feel like a kid on his grampa's knee at Christmas. Moreover the name was a fallacy, sniping as he did at Fenton and criticising him and knowing at times that the things he said were evil, all in the hope that Fenton might get sick of it and so do the hard part and call time on their relationship himself.

But Fenton had no intention of doing that. It seemed the more horrid Scotty was, the more he lapped it up, like a kicked puppy panting for treats.

Where had the man gone whom he'd respected so much?

'I've grown out of you,' Scotty concluded quietly, scuffing the baseline with his foot. 'It happens. I can apologise but I know you won't accept it.'

'Damn right I won't.' Fenton's voice shook. 'After everything I've done for you.'

'Blackmail's no reason to stay.' Scotty met his gaze. 'There's only so long we can play with fire. It ends now and with a little damage control maybe that's it, maybe no one has to know. Going to Kristin on a break-up might help change her mind.'

Fenton was deflated, like a punched balloon. 'You mean you're going back to her? You can claim it was a mistake?'

'Maybe it was.' He hadn't meant to blurt it, but now the rest followed. 'You were my first and you knew that. I held you on a pedestal. Maybe I wasn't seeing things clearly.'

Fenton laughed meanly, heartbreak sluicing through his words. 'Don't try telling me you're straight. Not after I've had you on your knees begging to—'

'Just because I don't want to be with you doesn't mean I'm not gay. You're not the only man in the world, Fenton.' He waited. 'It's time I found out what that meant.'

Fenton came to the net for one final plea. 'This isn't us,' he offered tearfully, putting his hands to prayer. 'You know it isn't. Let's start again.' When Scotty refused to meet his eye, he implored him: 'You're all I have. You're all that makes me happy.'

Scotty went for the smash. 'That's the problem.' His words were quiet, and all the more demolishing for that. 'I can't be your everything any more.'

He was along the tramlines when Fenton's voice chased him from behind, a gathered, decisive tone that he only ever used professionally. Even when Scotty had first come under his manager's wing he'd still received a special voice, a kindly, avuncular manner, but not any longer. That road was closed and there was no way back.

'If you think you've still got a place in Fraternity, you're sorely mistaken.'

Scotty stopped, swallowing hard. 'Fraternity's nothing without me.'

'Do you think I care about that?' The King of the Chart's words were as glacial as his heart. 'I've made enough off you boys to see me through ten lifetimes. It's over for you, Scotty. Walk away now and, trust me, you're as good as dead.'


Kristin was in her manager's office, consulting stills from her latest video. New single 'Open Arms' was a departure from her previous form and she was satisfied with the result, a moody rock vibe that totally gave Ramona the bird.

When she left she was surprised to find Joey Lombardi waiting for her outside, sitting on a low wall with a beanie pulled over his ears. His mop of hair was tickling the neck of his T-shirt and there was a tear in his jeans. She hadn't seen him since bailing on him in Vegas and she felt a stab of conscience: she'd totally ditched him that night.

'Hey,' he said, with an expectant smile. He held out a creased paper bag of cola gums, her favourite candy, tied with a ribbon. 'Bought you something.'

Touched, Kristin smiled. 'Thanks.' She gave him a hug. He smelled coconutty, like sun cream. 'What're you doing here? If I'd known… I've got to head over to Mom's.'

'Bunny's Mini Miss final, right?'

She was impressed he'd remembered. 'Yeah.' She checked the time. 'The results should be coming in right about now. For Bunny's sake, I hope she gets it, or Ramona'll be more of a witch than usual, and that's saying something.'

'This won't take a minute. Can I ride with you?'

Kristin had splurged on a new Audi. It was nothing compared with Jax's sick sports car, a fact her boyfriend liked to remind her of, so it was nice to be in appreciative company.

'She's beautiful,' said Joey, watching her from the passenger seat.

'Thanks.' She indicated and pulled out on to Sunset. 'What's up?'

Joey reached to scratch the back of his head and she caught a flash of dark hair under his arm. 'It's Scotty. I know he's the last person you want to think about right now, but the guys and me…we're concerned. Have you seen him lately?'

Kristin skipped a red light, her expression closed. 'Why would I?'

'He looks bad. He's lost weight and he's drinking more

than ever. It's like he's shut off from us. Some of us think there might be something harder involved.'

*Like what, his manager's dick?*

'The fact is,' Joey continued, 'you've known him for, like, ever. You know him better than anyone—'

'I thought I did.'

'No one gets what happened between you two. That's the way it should be, it's nobody else's business, but maybe this break-up's hit him harder than we thought. Kristin, if he doesn't get himself together soon then we're worried for the future of the band.'

'What does Fenton say?' The name sat on her tongue, slimy as a toad.

Joey shook his head. 'That's the other thing. Fenton's become distant, too. He works from home, like, every week, and we have to book appointments to see him now. We used to be able to just drop round, you know, if we needed something.'

'Maybe he has a house guest,' said Kristin tightly.

'Could be. Whatever it is, he's not proving much help on the Scotty problem.'

She accelerated, overtaking a Jeep. 'I expect he knows more than you think.'

Joey gave her a funny look. 'How do you mean?'

Hastily she backtracked. 'You know, just being your manager and all...'

How she wanted to splurge it. But she had to preserve those tiny hearts, hearts like Bunny's that would get blown to smithereens—and, now her anger had subsided, to preserve Scotty himself, because while he had betrayed her in a disastrous way it was no crime to be gay, and she couldn't be sure she'd have told if he'd been sleeping with another girl.

Already she was regretting having confided in Jax. She felt confident he would keep it to himself but it was impossible to know for definite.

'I said to the boys I'd see if you might talk to him?'

'I'll think about it.'

'Really?' Joey cleared his throat. 'I mean, I know how much you felt for him, how close you guys were. If it's too difficult, we'd understand…'

'It's fine.'

There was a pause before Joey added, 'It's not like you want to get back with him, though, right? It's totally over…?'

'God, no! I mean, yes, it's totally over.'

'OK.' He blushed. 'Scotty's my friend, but, well, you are, too.'

'Believe me, I'm *way* happier with Jax.'

Joey's jaw tensed. 'Right.'

She dropped him a block from home, and minutes later was winding up the regal drive of The White House.

'Bunny?' she called upon entering. An almighty thump came from above, pursued by a stampede of footsteps as someone descended the stairs. Her sister flew down so heatedly that Kristin had to back up against the wall to avoid being bulldozed.

*'You are my daughter and you will get back here immediately!'* sounded Ramona's battle cry, as her mother's stick-thin legs came stabbing down the steps after her.

'I can't do this any more!'

'Bunny—' Kristin witnessed a flash of white-blonde wig as her sister shot out of the front door and slammed it behind her. Ramona collided with her at the bottom of the stairs, and by the time they hit the street Bunny had disappeared.

She rounded on a breathless Ramona. 'What's going on? What happened?'

A hysterical laugh flew back at her. 'Isn't *that* the question?' Ramona crabbed. 'Your clever sister's only just ruined the most important afternoon of her life!'

'What?' Kristin struggled to catch up. 'She didn't win the Mini Miss?'

'Of course she didn't win!' A fleck of spittle shot from Ramona's mouth. 'Tracy-Ann Hamilton won.' The child's name alone was enough to make her tremble.

'My God, poor Bunny.'

'Poor Bunny, my ass!' her mother shrieked. 'She didn't even do her best!'

'What?'

'She sabotaged it on purpose.'

'How can you say that?' Kristin leapt to her sister's defence. 'Of course she tried her best, I know she did.'

'Then you know nothing of Bunny's life since you walked out. If that silly girl thought daydreaming over Scotty Valentine was going to win her the title instead of applying herself to our schedule then she's just had a short sharp shock of reality.'

'How can you be so cruel?' Kristin asked in wonder.

'*Me?*' Ramona rampaged. 'Who knows, perhaps if *you* hadn't thrown that perfectly eligible boy to the gutter along with everything else that's been given to you, Bunny mightn't have suffered these withdrawal symptoms!'

Kristin was incredulous. 'So now it's my fault?'

'Let's just say you wouldn't win role model of the century.'

'And you would? Jeez, Mom, don't you think Bunny might be upset? Don't you think she's disappointed? That maybe she needs a parent right now, not a *coach* or whatever the hell it is you call yourself? That maybe you should go after her?'

'She needs to cool off.'

'No, she doesn't, she needs a hug. She's fourteen.'

Ramona's face was bitter lemon. 'Talk to me about parenting skills when you're a mother yourself—if ever, at this rate.'

'Excuse me?'

'Face it: Jax Jackson is hardly husband material.'

Kristin hooted with laughter. 'That's too good,' she retaliated. 'Why don't *you* talk to *me* about husbands when you can hold on to one yourself? No wonder Dad walked out if he had to deal with this every day of his life—'

She was cut off by a stinging slap. Stunned, she raised a hand to her cheek.

Ramona was quivering. She looked as shocked as Kristin felt. Turning on a sharp heel, she strode inside and closed the door with such force that a set of Japanese wind chimes suspended in the porch crashed to the ground in a discordant jangle.

Kristin put a hand to her face, breathing heavily. Her heart was in her throat and for the first time she could taste her anger, actually *taste* it, tangy like metal. She searched both ways down the avenue, hoping for a glimpse of Bunny and finding none.

She had to locate her sister and get her out of here.

Ramona's ambition had gone beyond the point of rational return—and the trouble with climbing for the stars was that if you didn't reach them, there was a hell of a long way to fall.

# 37

Robin was getting by on three hours' sleep a night. The tour was consuming all her energy and if she wasn't performing she was rehearsing, training, on the bus or the plane between gigs, or in talks with Barney and the team about the next location.

They hit Seattle on Friday. It amazed her how the *Beginnings* set travelled seamlessly between venues, magnificent in its entirety one night then the following moved and erected identically in a completely new place, so that revisiting it felt like a continuous bout of déjà vu. Each time the crowd seemed more electric than the last, and the reviews she'd had were phenomenal: with every set she played, America fell a little bit more in love with Robin Ryder. They embraced her Britishness, her candid interviews and her inimitable flair. They loved her sense of humour. They respected her style. They gave credit for her connection to Puff City and her work on Slink Bullion's charity single, which thanks to a fortuitously coordinated series of events—the City's re-emergence, the Olympic fire and her own rise to Stateside stardom—had hit the Billboard top spot in its opening week.

Puff City were in town tonight and had agreed to guest on her closing track. The audience wouldn't know what hit them. She owed Slink big time for the favour.

When Robin opened her hotel-room door she was alarmed to discover a male figure lounging on the bed, reclining against the propped-up pillows and watching TV. Rufio was drinking from a Coke can pilfered from the mini bar and had his hand buried in a tube of Pringles. Chocolate wrappers scattered the sheets.

'Hey.'

'Shit!' She grinned, dropping her bag. 'What're you doing here?'

In spite of the fact she hadn't heard from him since that disappointing call in San Fran, she felt relieved Rufio was here. Due to her constantly moving location the threatening messages had ceased, but even so she remained anxious about being alone.

Rufio flipped a crisp into the air and caught it in his mouth. 'Celebrating,' he said, pulling her on to the bed. 'Thought I'd surprise you.'

She kissed him. 'Celebrating what?'

'Got cleared, didn't I? Shit-hot lawyer came on board and all I had to do was turn up in a suit and look sorry.' He stuck out his bottom lip. 'They fell for it.'

'Are you sorry?' Cynical, she raised an eyebrow.

'Only that I didn't get here sooner.'

Rufio held out his arms and she settled into them. It was a comfort. He ran his hands over her hips and dragged her down on top of him. 'Nice place you got here,' he teased, jabbing his hard-on into her. 'Want to shag?'

The bed looked like the aftermath of a ten-year-old's midnight feast. 'Later.' She tried to climb off but he caught her wrists. 'How'd you find me anyway?'

'Polly. And when's later?'

'I just got off the plane.'

'So?'

'So I feel rough. Now's not a good time.'

Rufio snorted, tossing a glance at his surroundings. 'Seems to me like it is.' And that observation, the *tone* of it, made Robin's heart sink. She had resisted the thought that he wasn't here because he cared about her or wanted to be with her but because she was hot property now on this side of the Atlantic and he was languishing at home with a dubious press. Recent tabloid coverage she'd caught of East Beatz had been less than favourable.

'If you're staying you have to look after yourself,' she told him, slicing open the balcony doors and letting the fresh air through. 'You know I'm working, right?'

The phone rang and irritatingly Rufio reached it first, lifting it from the side table and reclining with his ankles crossed, a debonair smirk on his face.

*'Yars?'* he said in a faux-posh accent, ribbing her newfound status but underneath the sentiment was there and he meant it. 'Robin Ryder's room—er, I mean *suite*?'

She snatched it off him. 'Barney? Hi.'

'What's he doing here?' asked Barney.

'What can I say? Rufio keeps me on my toes.'

Rufio seized the remote and started skipping channels,

settling on one of his own music videos during which the band dressed as trendy astronauts and colonised a planet.

'I thought you broke up with him.'

'What's up, Barney?'

Minutes later she replaced the receiver. 'I'm heading out.' Barney had relayed that Puff City had landed early and wanted a sound check before a TV appearance this afternoon.

'But you only just got here!' Rufio complained. 'What am I gonna do?'

'It's Seattle. You've got this whole amazing city at your feet. Think of something.'

Seattle was her biggest crowd to date. As anticipated, Puff City's appearance on her encore sent the stadium through the roof, and as well as guesting on her own track they rocked an impromptu 'Take It Down'. Given the number of people involved in the charity single it had seldom been performed live, so for the fans it was a major coup. Slink rapped over Jax's slot (easily ten times better—the guy couldn't sing to save his life) and G-Money took Leon's line.

When the gig finished they were all on a high. Rufio showed up backstage, enveloping her in a beer-scented embrace, and when Slink suggested they check out a party pad belonging to a magnate friend of his who was out of town, Robin agreed.

The penthouse was in the Seattle Highlands, a super-exclusive gated community housing some of the most incredible properties she'd ever seen. Slink's contact lived in a cream Georgian mansion, pretty as a dolls' house and giant as a castle and surrounded by verdant lawns, stone fountains and soaring, majestic yews. It boasted an Olympic-sized swimming pool whose tiles were purple, casting the water a deep lilac, spotlit from below. A rock waterfall cascaded at one end and a leafy platform overlooked the quiet Puget Sound, over which the moon cast iridescent light that rippled and danced in the fragrant night.

They had picked up the crew's entourage as well as her own dance troupe, and once through security a gang stripped off and threw themselves into the pool in their underwear.

Matt was quick to follow, hauling off his T-shirt and joining them amid a splash of squeals and laughter. 'Fucking awesome!' he crowed on a dive bomb, making the girls screech with delight. Rufio was hot in pursuit and soon the pool was filled with a tangle of slick, golden bodies, emerging every so often in a spray of water.

Robin fetched a beer, content to absorb the outrageousness of her surroundings. If someone had told her two years ago that she'd be here, now, after a mega leg of her sell-out US tour, she'd have laughed. Perhaps it was fortune's turn to pay her back.

She spotted Shawnella on a bench, scowling as she watched her boyfriend frolic. Robin made her way over. 'Hey,' she offered over the sound system, 'OK if I join you?'

Shawnella folded her arms, the movement prompting a near-total spillage of her cleavage. She was wearing a pink bikini that barely covered her nipples and matching knickers that were so high on her hips it looked like she was being sawn in half. Massive jewellery adorned her wrists and ears, and a ruby bead glinted on the skin between her top lip and her nose. Her hair was teased into dyed honey-blonde cornrows.

'This is some place, right?' began Robin. 'You been before?'

Shawnella blew out disbelief. 'Are you kidding?' She was surveying Slink with the concentration of a hawk. Robin followed her gaze and saw two gamine blondes hanging off his neck. 'He's brought just about everyone else here—I guess I'm not good enough.'

Robin faced her. 'I bet that isn't true.'

'Come *on*,' drawled Shawnella, with a look in her eye that suggested she wasn't the bimbo appendage so often dismissed at Slink's side. 'He's got, like, twenty girlfriends. I'm aware of that; I'm not blind to the facts. This is where he takes them when he wants to impress. I've been around so long he doesn't even bother.'

'If you know he's cheating, why stay? I'd never put up with that.'

Shawnella laughed with genuine amusement. Realising Robin hadn't been joking, she asked, 'You think I'm with him because I love him?'

Robin considered her reply. According to occasional mentions Shawnella received in the press, she was the 'long haul', the girl who'd been there since the start, who never quit, and, of course, like any woman dating a high-profile man, that naturally meant she was angling for a ring on her finger, if not for reasons of love then of sheer perseverance.

'You might be.'

'I'm not.' Shawnella consulted her manicure. 'See that display right there? He knows I'm seeing it, it turns him on and then later he'll want to have a fight about it. That's how it goes with Slink. We'll fight and then we'll have sex. That's how it works. He'd get bored otherwise. He's not interested in it being just us—and I accepted that ages ago. What I'm interested in is what this situation's going to do for me.'

'How?'

She peered at Robin sideways. 'When we first got together he said he'd bring me in on Puff City—like, the only female sort of thing. Look what Fergie did for the Peas. Same deal with me, except if Slink had kept his word we'd have beat them to it. Now that promise is starting to smell richly of bullshit.'

'Why didn't he go with it?'

'Either the others didn't like it or Slink changed his mind. I'm not sure which is worse. One makes him a pussy and the other makes him an asshole.'

Robin nodded to where G-Money was chilling by the pool hut, beer in hand. He didn't look as relaxed as the rest. 'I would've thought he'd have your back,' she said.

'Serious?' Shawnella replied, bored. 'G's, like, my big brother. Nothing he says carries weight these days. Slink doesn't listen to a word he says. Shit, Slink won't listen to a word *anyone* says. It's his rules or bye-bye-baby, and that's where I am.'

Robin frowned. 'G used to be wild, right?' Before he'd worn cardigans G-Money had been one of the most notorious members of the City, in the nineties spending time in prison on charges of grand theft auto and possession of weapons—little wonder he'd been all over the charity gig; it was a chance to show how he'd cleaned up his act. But Robin couldn't help being suspicious of someone who changed their ways overnight: reinvention didn't come easy.

'Sure did,' said Shawnella. 'The less said about that, the better.'

'Yeah?'

'Yeah. Besides, he ain't doin' nothin' for me.' She applied gloss, pressing her lips together with a sealing *phut* that signalled the end of the conversation.

'I'm heading in,' said Robin. 'Join me?'

'No chance. I wouldn't wanna miss the show.'

Across the lawns Robin located a Nantucket-style hut and claimed a bikini from a boxful marked OR GO WITHOUT?, which made her suspect that whoever lived here wasn't averse to throwing the occasional pool party. The knickers were scant, flimsy things and she had to rifle through to find something that didn't make her feel like she was perched on a cheese wire. A wet-from-the-pool Rufio grabbed her on the way back, hauling her shrieking over his shoulder and racing to the water, where he promptly threw her in, chasing with a flop that sent glitter dashing to the sky. Robin was immersed in an underwater lagoon and when she crashed through the surface she leapt at him, laughing and trying to push his head under.

When she began to feel cold she headed to the showers, a vast tiled space with benches running down one side. It took a while to work out how to turn the jets on. At last she located a sensor and, putting her hand before it, the sky opened up: the roof was covered in hundreds of tiny holes so that instead of bathing it was like standing in the warm rain.

Wrapping a towel around her and emerging on to the terrace, Robin spotted an open entrance to the house and decided to explore. The main wings were sealed off but the kitchen and ground floor were open and she perused photos of Slink's absent acquaintance, a portly producer she recognised from televised red-carpet events and who, judging by the array of beautiful women he'd been photographed next to, didn't appear to be married. There was the British actress Stevie Speller, a recent snap with Turquoise da Luca and another with A-list titan Cole Steel. Unsurprising, then, that he was living this kind of life.

She was about to step outside when a couple of voices, engaged in heated debate, stopped her in her tracks. They were coming from the corridor and instinctively she padded towards them. She stopped at the wall, straining to hear.

'I'm tellin' you, he's gotta let this go.' The voice was harsh, skating on a high pitch, and she recognised it as Principal 7's. 'You gotta do somethin', man, I ain't messin'.'

'Chill, dog.' That was Slink. 'It was a long time ago. You think if I went to bed with crap in my pants over every little thing I'd done wrong I'd ever sleep again?'

'He's gonna spill and it's gonna be soon. I know it.'

'An' I know G. He's cooler than that.'

'Yeah? Sway's got a hold on him. Jeez, he *likes* the guy. They're friends. Big Nate clocked them hangin' at the weekend.'

Robin frowned. Were they talking about Leon? She tried to make out the rest.

'Way he sees it,' Principal continued, 'we're the guys to blame.'

'An' he's right, I ain't arguin' different. You gotta take responsibility but I'm tellin' you, man, I've paid my dues. I've looked karma dead in the eye and I'm still cruising.'

'G wants to fess. That means us, too.'

'Relax.' Somebody exhaled heavily. 'Marlon Sway got

shot and that ain't right, but bad shit happens, what else is there to say? Unlucky, he was someone's brother and family counts, but it's over. *Over.* You think I never lost someone close to me? That life works out roses and puppy dogs and piss smells like perfume? G knows the score.'

'Maybe he needs reminding.'

'You got your hand up?'

'If that's what it takes.'

'Cool it, a'ight? Take your lead from me. No reason Sway's gonna find out.'

Robin fought to understand. What were they saying? What did they mean? Someone had died, someone close to Leon...and Puff City was responsible?

She remembered what Leon had said to her that night.

*We're from the same neighbourhood...*

*Mean streets of Compton, baby...*

Robin retreated towards the exit. She could hear no more. Outside, the party carried on, heedless and careless, empty fun she could no longer engage in.

One thing was clear: she had to find Leon and she had to warn him. She didn't know how, but she had to. She owed him that.

## 38

Pacific Heights Village looked even better in the sunshine.

As Jax Jackson swung his lemon Lamborghini into the expansive drive, he took in, with some satisfaction, the place he called home. It was an imposing white building, sweltering under the heat of an azure-blue sky, the green line of the sea visible behind, glinting like a jewel. A chain of palm trees linked around the entrance, their fronds applauding in the warm breeze. He'd worked hard for all this, worked his body till it was beat. He deserved his life, goddammit. And now even nature worshipped at his altar.

Leon Sway could go screw himself.

*Barely a hundredth in it, guys*, the coach had said after their latest *mano-a-mano*.

Fuck that shit.

Jax braked the car hard and jumped out. The fact remained that he had won. He always won. If the coach couldn't see that, it wasn't his damn problem. He ought to feel sorry for Leon, be the bigger man—Sway was too young; he couldn't handle defeat. Jax smirked to himself. He'd learned a long time ago how to cope with defeat: never let it happen.

Before making his way inside, Jax marvelled at the wheels. He'd cruise downtown in a couple hours and see if he could pick up a cute ass or two. Grudgingly he remembered Kristin. Keeping a girlfriend had its drawbacks. Who knew they took up so much time? Girlfriends were meant to be fun, weren't they? Kristin was a hot broad in the sack, but that was where it ended. All this talk about feelings and 'the future' was *not* on his agenda.

The lobby was filled with a new delivery of fresh flowers.

'What's that fuckin' *stink*?' said Jax, striding to the elevators. 'Someone taken a dump in here or somethin'?'

'Hello, Mr Jackson,' the concierge said pleasantly, with a rigid smile. 'You have a visitor.' He gestured to the bank of leather futons.

A woman in a tight navy-blue skirt suit was flicking through a magazine, crisply crossing and uncrossing long, tanned legs. Her hair was blonde and coiffed into a chic but very rigid bob, as if it weren't hair at all, but something hard, like plastic. A generous bust threatened to spill from the confines of her shirt.

'Hey, Cindy,' said Jax. 'Wanna come up?'

Cindy Shepard, PA to the big man, let her plump pink lips break into a smile. She angled her body towards him and folded one leg over the other, hoping that he might catch a glimpse of something on the way past—she hadn't worn these crotchless panties for nothing. Cindy prided herself on a personal assistance that was very...personal.

'Sure,' she purred, standing. 'I have some important business to discuss with you.'

Jax nodded in a bored way. 'Right.' He looked her up and down. 'Tits look good.' As the elevator slid open he delivered a quick wink to the concierge, who looked back with a blank expression. Jeez, fags were as touchy as girls these days.

Nailing Cindy was precisely what he needed. One woman had never been enough to satisfy The Bullet, and while it helped to have Kristin onside as a lady in the industry (becoming a credible hip-hop artist was proving trickier than he'd thought), when all was said and done Jax was a cocksman who thought 'Monogamy' was an expensive brand of toiletries.

'Get outta that suit,' he instructed the instant they were upstairs.

Cindy batted her lashes. 'You first.'

'I'm not playing games,' he ordered. 'Do it.'

Moreover he had been disturbed by Kristin's revelations concerning Scotty Valentine. The guy was *gay*? For real? With his manager, that flabby pensioner with spray-on hair? Sheesh, he thought, watching his PA unbutton her blouse, you could never be sure; had to watch your ass like it had an OPEN ALL HOURS sign bolted on to it. Why'd Kristin have to go telling him that? It creeped him out, not least because it reminded him…

*No!*

A tremor coursed through him as he thought of that fateful, shameful night. He had taken his first gold, smashed the record; he'd been on top of the world. In cruel fragments of memory he remembered being on top of an entirely different thing...

*Danny Fu.* The Chinaman who'd claimed gold on the parallel bars. A total blowout after the closing ceremony, liquor, drugs, some serious mind-altering shit, and that was the sole excuse Jax clung to. Never had he done anything with a guy before or since, it had never occurred to him because he was a red-blooded steak-eating dick-powered hetero any day of the week, and the insane confusion of that single erotic night would haunt him for all eternity.

Mercifully, his cell rang. Not so mercifully, it was his lawyer. Jax snapped it up from the side table just as Cindy was slipping off her heels.

'What's up, Logan?'

Jax winced as a torrent of abuse came streaming down the line. Turned out his gold-digger ex-wife was rinsing him for yet more alimony: there was a surprise. Last year he'd been wed for the princely sum of twenty-one hours—a lesson if ever there was not to marry a Vegas stripper in the Chapel of Love simply because it seemed like a good idea at the time.

'Chill, dog!' Jax exclaimed. 'I know this looks like a situation but I got it under control—' He turned his head from the phone as Logan delivered yet another speech about keeping him informed, taking responsibility for his actions, yadda yadda yadda.

Casually Cindy shrugged off her top, her eyes fixed on Jax, who was trying to work out whether it was in his best interests to listen to what Logan was saying or just cut him off and fuck her senseless. He felt himself stiffen when the bronzed curve of her tits came into view. Taking in that she wasn't wearing a bra, he lamented, as he did every time, that these puppies weren't the real deal. Still, you couldn't have everything.

Peeling open the thin material, Cindy threw her head back and raised a manicured finger and thumb to her left nipple. Rolling the bud, playing with it, she allowed the tip of a pink tongue to escape from her mouth and let out a gasp, as if taken by surprise. Jax looked on, interested by the display, then reached out and in one deft movement unzipped her skirt. It dropped to the floor, revealing a peach of an ass and—*now* they were talking—a pair of crotchless panties. Jax could still hear Logan going on about something or other and registered vague irritation that his attention was, once again, being fought over.

Next Cindy was down on her knees, fumbling to free his cock. He could feel her soft tits and lazily reached down to grab one, pinching a nipple with just a bit of force.

'Not while I'm on the cell,' he told her sternly, one hand covering the mouthpiece.

Undeterred, Cindy pulled him out and opened her mouth.

'JAX JACKSON!' Logan bellowed down the phone. 'Are you paying attention to me or not, you little prick? Here I am working my ass off for you day in, day out, fending off the army of suckers you've reeled in and you don't listen to a damn word I'm saying! Help me out here, Jax; you know it ain't my job to wipe your black ass the rest of my life.'

'All right, all right,' Jax conceded. With two fingers he pushed Cindy's head, dismissing her to the floor. 'I see we got a problem, big L. Throw some money at it, yeah? How much? Yeah, yeah, I realise that. Yeah, that's right. Uh-huh. Transfer the cash, then. OK. Cool. Sure thing. Ciao.'

Jax punched some buttons on his phone then one-handedly flipped it shut. He was fuming. Who did that bitch's people think they were messing with, some jackass? It was time they realised this was Jax Jackson they were ripping off. Grudgingly he admitted it'd teach him not to be taken in by a nice pair of titties and an imaginative trick with a string of pearls. Taking a wife was not for him, no sir—in fact, getting tied down in any capacity was rapidly losing its sheen.

Once he was done with Cindy he'd buzz Kristin and tell her it was over. She was sweet, but what could you do? End of the day, women were the same: no matter what they told you, they had an eye for the money. Next time he wasn't making the same mistake. Jax was a born bachelor and there was nothing else for it.

Cindy was groping around on the floor for her clothes.

'Hey, baby, what's the rush?' Jax suddenly engaged with the fact there was a half-naked blonde in his bedroom. On her hands and knees.

'You're an asshole,' said Cindy, getting to her feet and tugging her shirt on.

Jax looped an arm round her waist and pulled her to him. 'So they tell me.'

'I mean it. I come here trying to help you, trying to sort you out, and all I get is this bullshit. I'm sick of it. You can't fuck me one minute and turn me away the next.' She gave a pout. 'How dare you make me feel like some cheap… prostitute?'

Jax was reminded of the panties and dipped a finger between her legs, gratified, though not surprised, to find her wet. He applied a knot of pressure and heard her intake of breath. Sure, she'd whine on him a bit longer but he knew he'd just given her a one-way ticket to heaven and back. He had to: he was pushing so hard against his shorts it hurt.

'I'm your PA, Mr Jackson,' she breathed. 'You can't keep treating me like this.' She licked her lips. 'This is a professional arrangement.'

He kissed her hard on the mouth and after a weak show of resistance she began to respond, slowly at first and then with greater urgency.

'Stop,' she breathed, showing no sign of wanting to stop.

Jax pushed her back on to the bed and pulled her knees apart.

'Take that fuckin' shirt off,' he commanded. 'Or you're *really* gonna get in trouble.'

## 39

Over the years Turquoise had learned what it meant to be incognito. On the appointed day she asked to be dropped a short walk from Cosmo's house and tipped the driver generously, securing a cap over her ears as she watched the car trickle reluctantly round the corner.

Once it was safely out of sight she took the couple of streets to Ridgedale and met the mansion she had spent so long avoiding. It was massive, brash, unnecessarily pleased with itself: a fortress for Cosmo, never a home, and despite the fact he shared the dwelling with Ava Bennett it had the Angelopoulos stamp all over it. All the dinners Ava had invited her to, all the parties Donna had suggested they make, all the industry gatherings Cosmo had hosted and she'd declined because of the vow that she would never again set foot on his property if it meant adhering to his rules.

Now, all that changed. She had the rules, right here in her pocket.

An enormous wrought-iron gate fitted with cameras and

a system of locks greeted her with all the warmth of a snarling Doberman. ANGEL RESIDENCE, announced a gold-plated sign by the security intercom, as though Cosmo's living arrangements were blessed by divine intervention, a philosophy she had no doubt he adhered to.

Turquoise pressed. A voice from the gatehouse came on the line.

'Yes?'

'Cosmo's expecting me,' she replied, and though her breath was painful and ragged in her lungs she managed to sound professional. Slipping back into it was all too easy.

'One moment, please.'

After a brief intermission the gate clicked open and Turquoise entered, at the same time checking to make sure it was still there. Why wouldn't it be? All the same its contours calmed her, the edges of her bargaining tool, because without it she was helpless.

Her heart was thrashing. She could hear the blood in her ears.

*You've got this. He can't touch you; you're not that girl any longer.*

But there would always be a part of her that was that girl. It would never go away. How could it, when it was such a part of her life? And though she wished with all her might that her journey hadn't been what it had, that her parents had lived or that Emaline had survived or that she had never been sent to Ivan Garrick or got into the car with Denny that day, she couldn't deny it because that was the same as denying herself. All that had made her.

Walking to the portico entrance was like treading through a dream, one she had visited before on countless feverish sunsets, unable to tell what was real and what imagined. Was she even here? Was she inventing it?

A swift sharp breeze gave her certainty. Through the still, sultry day, turgid with heat, it blew like a reminder. *This is a necessary fear.*

Abruptly the door opened. And with it, everything Turquoise had rehearsed was knocked out of her in a single solid punch.

'Hey!' Ava stepped out to hug her. 'What an awesome surprise! Wow, I've missed you. I haven't seen you for so long, I was worried you'd started avoiding me!'

*Ava?* Turquoise's mouth went desert-dry. Her brain tried to unscramble something decent or acceptable to say but she found she was unable to speak.

'Are you going to just stand there?' Ava waved her through, casual and carefree in a loose silken pantsuit with a tie-waist, her feet bare. 'Come on in!'

'Thanks,' Turquoise managed, following, removing her cap and feeling the cold interior prickle through her scalp. What the *fuck* was Cosmo playing at? What was Ava doing here? Perhaps she had misread his message; if she was clever she could claim she'd dropped in on her friend on a whim and escape without having to see him—

'Ah, there she is.' Cosmo stepped out of his office, a tumbler cradled in the palm of his hand and that crocodile grin perfectly in place. 'Just in time.' At the foot of the grand staircase, winding in carved cherry wood like a corkscrew through the floors, his eyes glinted with the kick of the game. Ava was smiling. What did she know? What had Cosmo told her?

'Let me get you something to drink,' offered Ava, at last.

'No, please, I'm fine.' She waved Ava away, battling to keep her composure but feeling it slip through her grasp with every passing second. 'It's a flying visit, it's just…'

*Assume nothing.* Ava was here by mistake—it would be as much of a shock to her husband as it was to Turquoise. Cosmo wanted to talk through business, something to do with the movie. Yes, that was it. It was the line he'd choose to run, too, lest his wife find out.

'…Cosmo, I've brought the proposal you wanted to discuss.'

It was a gamble. Ava was watching her beatifically, her hands in front of her waist, the fingers touching. Behind her, mounted on the wall in an unnecessarily elaborate frame, was Sassoferrato's *The Virgin in Prayer*, and the echo was unnerving.

Cosmo examined her with dead eyes. 'What proposal?'

Hate swelled in her belly. 'We discussed this when you asked me over.' All she could think was: *It sounds like we're having an affair. Of all things, after all this time, it sounds like we're having a goddamn affair.*

It was an eternity before Cosmo spoke. He swirled the liquid in his glass. 'I don't remember,' he said blankly. 'Remind me.'

There was a protracted pause. Turquoise's face flamed furiously, from the swollen rock in her throat to the burning tips of her ears. 'Actually—' she smiled at Ava, fighting to get things back on track '—I will have that drink. A Perrier, if you've got it?'

'I'll be right back.'

'What the hell are you doing?' she hissed at him the instant his wife was gone. 'You never said Ava would be here. Are you *mad*?'

Cosmo rested against the wood panelling. The thought occurred that he had secret passageways in this place, underground corridors hidden behind bookshelves whose spines were hollow plastic; empty inside, as much a fake as he was.

'You sound jealous.' The corners of his mouth were twitching in amusement. 'What were you expecting?'

'You said you had a surprise,' she said grimly, knowing she had mere seconds before Ava reappeared. 'So do I. Evidently now is not the time.'

'What were you hoping my surprise was?'

'That you were walking the fuck out of my life and promising never to look back.'

He chuckled. 'You used to be so much sweeter. So much more…obliging.'

'You never knew who I was. You still don't.'

'Still don't what?' Ava rejoined them. Turquoise accepted the drink with shaking hands and felt her friend's gaze bore into her. Daring to meet it, she looked up, but instead of the warm regard she had become used to she encountered a frostier edge.

'I must have got my appointments crossed,' she managed weakly. 'I'm so sorry.' She went to put the drink down but there were no surfaces, and every movement she made, every word she said, in that awful, cloying silence, was beyond suspicious.

'You're not staying?' Ava asked, confused. She shot her husband a quizzical, accusatory glance. *Was it something you said?*

'Of course she is.' Cosmo went to take Turquoise's arm

and she flinched, allowing him to because she could only imagine how Ava was taking in this scene and it broke her heart to guess at her best friend's bewilderment. Ava was the innocent here; she had no idea what tensions she was witnessing. 'Come,' he said. 'Darling, are we ready?'

Turquoise didn't think she had heard correctly. 'Ready for what?'

'For your surprise,' said Cosmo, as though it were obvious. Turquoise turned to her friend but Ava's expression gave nothing away. 'See,' her nemesis continued, 'I don't keep secrets from my wife. I don't believe in it.'

'Excuse me?'

'Ours is an honest marriage. Ava knows everything about me…and so by rights she knows everything about you. Am I beginning to make sense?'

The world skewed on its axis. Frantically she turned to Ava but the gaze she received was vacant, a different Ava, not her friend at all.

'Surprise,' said Ava.

She produced something from behind her back with lightning speed, something long and dark and heavy, just a flash before it was too late, and the last thing Turquoise felt was a short hard slam to her head before the world evaporated in a sheet of total black.

## 40

Kristin flew to Alaska on Valentine's Day. It was a slog of a trip, changing at Seattle and Fairbanks to the final plane that would take her to Fort Yukon, a far-flung city just north of the Arctic Circle. Jax had been at elite-level training camp since Monday, steeling his body against the freezing air and crucl elements, and while girlfriends were discouraged—a distraction to the almost inhuman focus needed to race—she had to see him, just for the night.

This trip was a chance to put a stop to the romantic horrors of the past year and an opportunity for the word 'Valentine' to mean something new. Right now she yearned for Jax's company more than ever: following her row with Ramona, Kristin had been unable to return to The White House and was beyond worried about Bunny. Jax would listen to her, he'd hear her out, he'd make her better—and if he couldn't do that, he'd make her forget.

As the tiny plane bumped uncertainly on to the runway Kristin switched on her cell, struggled to find a signal and, when she did, located a message from Joey. Was Scotty OK? He hadn't turned up for a conference that day and neither had Fenton.

She made a mental note to get in touch with her ex in the morning. With Jax she had found strength, and despite the hurt it was time to bury the hatchet. Scotty's infidelity had wrecked her but she wished him no ill—they had been through too much together to sacrifice their friendship completely. She could only guess at what it would mean to both men if she told them she had no intention of spilling their secret. Tomorrow. Yes. She'd do it then.

Her hotel was a wooden lodge surrounded by murky, looming firs. In summer it must have been beautiful—the Yukon and Porcupine Rivers twinkling in the sunshine and the bobbing fishing boats coming into land—but winters here were long and harsh and it felt as if she had arrived in the middle of nowhere. After settling into her cosy room, warming her hands at the flickering fire and pulling the patchwork over her sheets, imagining what she and Jax might get up to when they returned here tonight, she took her car to the road and headed out to a never-ending wilderness. After several kilometres the camp came into sight.

Kristin stayed by her car, folding her arms against the chill as she watched Jax race. There was nothing else like it. As soon as he hit the track he was a beast, fast and powerful and raw, and it was *so* damn sexy. How had she ever been so devoted to Scotty's looks? Compared with Jax he was effeminate, a pretty boy, and now she knew where his preferences lay it seemed a miracle she hadn't spotted the signs before.

'Hi.' An athlete walked past her on the way to the circuit,

smiling as he placed her, a kit bag slung over his shoulder. 'You OK there?'

'Sure.' She raised a hand in acknowledgement, recognising him as Leon Sway, Jax's archenemy, and though Jax had only ever fed her disparaging lines about Leon's physique and ability she couldn't help feeling tongue-tied. His eyes were so...*green*.

'You want me to tell Jax you're here?'

'That's all right; I'll catch him after. It's a surprise visit.'

'No kidding,' he said with a smile.

She found herself blushing. Leon was lovely: he had a crescent-moon dimple in one cheek, and was taller and trimmer than his adversary, a sword to Jax's canon. 'Thanks.'

When she saw Leon powering across the asphalt minutes later, Kristin couldn't help sensing that Jax hadn't given her the full picture when it came to the conflict. It was so easy when you read or heard about someone to assume they were a certain way, but until you met them yourself it was impossible to be sure. Look at her own PR: people criticised her new look, said she'd abandoned her fans, but there was no way they could know why or how she'd taken that leap — and that her discretion was a sacrifice purely for their protection.

She decided to wait inside the warmth of the car, listening to songs on the crackly radio and flicking through a magazine, until an hour later the athletes began to disperse. She saw Jax disappear inside the club, but when the others came by minutes later, Leon knocking hello on his way past her window, her boyfriend was nowhere to be found. Where was he?

She pulled open the door, wrapped up tight and headed down to the building, calling his name. Silence. All around was deserted landscape; scarred, shrubbed plains that banked on to distant mountains and lakes still as mirrors. He couldn't have gone anywhere.

Inside, the club smelled of sweat and adrenalin, a seductive contrast to the bitter fresh air. It reminded her of the gym Ramona used to force her and Bunny to attend, all plastic notice boards and linoleum and the perpetual, antiseptic stench of chlorine. Faintly she detected muted voices and smiled to herself as she crept closer to them: she couldn't wait to throw her arms around Jax and kiss him endlessly.

At the threshold to the changing room, she hovered. Was he showering? She imagined joining him, enlaced in wafts of steam, citrusy and sharp, and Jax's rippling torso, slick with water and pristine as a carving. She heard his voice and wondered if he was on the cell.

Barely able to contain her excitement, Kristin pushed open the door.

The sight that met her eyes was as alarming as it was brutally recognisable. It was like watching her own sex life with Jax, except instead of Kristin on her knees, holding the back of Jax's thighs as he rutted back and forth with a stopwatch in his hand, there was another woman: a petite, honey-limbed, perfectly proportioned blonde.

Across the walls a museum of trophies and medals was slammed, gold and silver and bronze, so that it was like entering a cave of pirate treasure; a basement devoted to the team's victories. Jax had slung a batch of medals around the blonde's neck and a winner's plate was discarded on the floor, practically still bearing the handprint where Jax had seized it and slapped it across his lover's ass. He'd done that with her before.

This couldn't be happening to her again. It couldn't. Not again.

'That's it!' Jax was yelling, the stopwatch held aloft his head like the Holy Grail. 'Come on, come on, come on!'

'Excuse me for interrupting the party.'

Jax bucked to an abrupt halt as he clapped eyes on his girlfriend. 'Jeez, what the *fuck*—?' The blonde fell backwards and Jax brought the watch irritably to his face, more concerned with a failure to meet his record than with the fact he'd just been rumbled.

'You make me sick,' Kristin said evenly, shocked at how her composure never trembled. This was how guys were, and it wasn't her fault, it wasn't anything to do with her. 'How many, Jax? How many women? Go on, I can take it.'

The blonde was scrambling to retrieve her clothes. Nauseatingly Kristin identified her: Jax's PA, she was like a Chihuahua in a pink ruff, the way she followed him around so self-importantly but with the constant impression that she was about to pee herself.

'Whatever,' he grumbled, standing there naked as the day he was born.

'*Whatever?* That's all you've got to say?'

Incredibly, Jax shrugged. 'I was gonna break up with you anyhow. Don't go getting all heavy on my ass about it, it's not like I asked you to marry me.'

'Seriously?' She wanted to laugh. 'You're too good.'

'Not the first time I've been told it.'

'After everything I confided in you,' she spluttered, 'this is how you repay me?'

'I never asked you to spill about your fairy ex-boyfriend.'

Jax wrapped a towel around his waist. He shook the watch, checking it wasn't broken. 'As it goes I'd sooner you hadn't.'

'What, because you're not man enough to handle it?'

'I'm man enough for anything!' he roared, a claim rendered even more pointless for the overbaked passion behind it. He collected himself. 'Quit gettin' up on my back.'

'Piss off, Jax. You know what?' She threw at him the only weapon she had. 'I met Leon Sway today and that guy's got more class in his little finger than you have in your whole body. He was looking hot out there, in more ways than one. You want my prediction? It's over. You're flagging. You're not long for this, despite what the bloody stopwatch says. Sway's set to overtake you and then what? Who will you be then? Some washed up has-been who can't do anything except fuck and bitch and cheat on girls.'

Jax was apoplectic with rage.

'And if you think you've got a career carved out in my world,' she concluded, 'you can think again. *You can't sing*, Jax, except everyone's too afraid to tell you.'

Kristin slammed the door on his baffled expression and stormed back to her car.

By the time she arrived back in LA the news had already broken. Stands blared with the obliterating headlines, and it was plastered across the web like a disease.

PERV & THE PRETTY BOY

FRATERNITY GAY SEX SHOCKER

SCOTTY VALENTINE & FENTON FEAR: LOVERS REVEALED!

EXPOSED! MANAGER'S GAY SEX ADDICTION

SCOTTY VALENTINE FAKED IT TO FANS

Everywhere Kristin turned, all through the airport, all across the concourse, reporters were jostling for her reaction, desperate to get a comment because now it had become clear—searingly, splinteringly clear—why the golden couple had split in the first place.

The truth was beyond all imaginings.

She battled through the flashing cameras and demands for her attention, and was bundled into the waiting car by her PA, who had insisted on meeting her at the airport.

'How did it break?' she gasped as the vehicle sped off.

'Anonymous tip-off. Any ideas?'

It didn't take a genius to work it out. Jax's final revenge…

Kristin swallowed her outrage. All she could think about, the only thing she could focus on to get her through each second, each minute, was getting home to Bunny. She could only pray that the news hadn't reached her baby sister, and yet she knew that Bunny Google-checked Fraternity daily and would have done so even more in her hour of need.

When they pulled up at The White House, an army of paparazzi was already waiting in the drive, pushing over each other with microphones and cameras and shouting her name.

She struggled through. Inside, the mansion was cold with the blast of air con. Kristin shivered. Ramona was nowhere to be seen and instinctively she padded upstairs. A terrible urgency dragged her on, a feeling she couldn't quite pinpoint but knew was awful, unambiguously awful, and the way it was so quiet, so still, yet she wasn't alone…

Upstairs, Bunny's bedroom was wide open. She walked in, closer, always closer, not knowing what it was she was close to but compelled to see it through. Her sister's en-suite was ajar. Pink light shone through the coral curtains. Kristin pushed and suddenly it was no longer pink but red, chillingly red, bath water dyed red, full of red syrup, and at its surface the crown of a small blonde head emerged, matted at the edges, wigless, young, just a little girl.

Bunny White was as quiet and still as an angel, surely asleep…dreaming in a pool of her own blood. Her wrists floated at the surface like deadwood.

A soggy note was plastered to the stool next to her.

*It doesn't matter, Scotty. I'll always love you.*

Kristin dropped to her knees. She couldn't even cry; she had nothing left to give.

## *41*

The dinner was held at the Manhattan Regency Ballroom in New York.

Leon pulled up outside the entrance and stepped from the car, tailored to perfection in a dark suit, stiff white shirt and bow tie. He'd never worn a bow tie before and his sister had teased him ruthlessly, but it was an important night and he had to make the right impression. Following the Puff City single and the awareness of street crime it had raised, an event was being hosted in promotion of change. Politicians from every state were gathered and press had flocked from all over the country. Finally, here was a practical reason to have got involved in that charade. Needless to say, Jax hadn't bothered attending.

He took his date's hand. Lisa Carmichael was a trainee lawyer. She hung art on the walls of her redbrick apartment; she drank wine, read books and listened to old records. She worked out five days a week and had a lithe, smooth-skinned body. She was clever and kind. She supported him unconditionally. If he had been a man with boxes, she ticked every one. They had been dating for three weeks and tonight was their first appearance as a couple.

'What's up, my man?' In the foyer, Gordon Rimeaux clasped his hand and shook it. Now they were friends, Leon no longer thought of him as G-Money. 'Good t'see you.'

It had been Gordon, in fact, who had introduced him to Lisa. A couple of years back Gordon had become involved in a bout of anti-firearms promo work with the NYPD... Who knew he was so dedicated to the cause?

'Hey, Rimeaux,' said Lisa, 'you look well.'

Gordon shrugged. 'Just keepin' it real.'

'Always.'

'Did the others make it?' Leon scanned the room.

'Nah, just me.' Gordon nicked his chin with his thumbnail. 'Slink's in the studio...' He trailed off, unable to meet the younger man's eye.

Leon didn't bother asking about Principal 7 or the rest of the crew. Principal had made it clear since the start that he didn't care for the foundations of the track they had laid down; only the record sales that the extra publicity might prompt. Though Leon liked him better, Slink was the same. Gordon seemed to be the only one who cared.

Trays of champagne circulated, visiting groups of jowly white men who had enjoyed a lifetime of excess and had no clue why they were here except for the faint and niggling awareness that they *ought* to be and that they ought to get photographed doing it.

'I've been talking to Leon about his brother,' said Lisa, popping a truffle *bruschetta* into her mouth. 'We're reopening the case.'

Gordon looked blank. 'Oh, yeah?'

'There are too many loose ends.' Lisa gestured, warming to the cause. 'It was never investigated properly at the time. Talk about a depressing example of an underprivileged black kid who never gets a fair representation.'

It had been weird when Lisa had first brought up Marlon, as though Leon were a charity case she could solve out of the goodness of her heart. But what was wrong with a goodness of heart? Though his brother's story was way before her time in the law, its unanswered questions echoed through the ranks. Leon wasn't with her for the help, and he hoped she wasn't with him for the project.

'You think you can figure it out?' enquired Gordon. 'I mean—' he shifted on his feet '—it was such a long time ago, huh.'

'Even more scope to get the evidence we need,' said Lisa with confidence. 'Every year passed is going to put the perpetrator deeper in the ring—how he's lived, what he's done, who he hangs with. It's a matter of looking in the right place.'

'And you know where to look, right?' He grinned awkwardly at Leon, who had heard so many promises about finding his brother's killer that he didn't much listen to new claims.

'Not yet,' said Lisa. 'But I will.'

They were called in for dinner. The ballroom was domed, the ceilings vaulted, candlelight pooling across the intricately decorated tables. There seemed an unsavoury irony in gathering in such an opulent space, drinking and eating to their hearts' content, dressed to impress and mingling with the famous and fortunate, when the alleged reason for it all was to benefit those whose lives had been immeasurably less lucky.

The speeches were brief, some more heartfelt than others, and when they brought a black girl to the podium to talk about growing up without a father because he'd been killed in a drugs bust, everyone looked grave and nodded, patting themselves on the backs for being here and trying to make a difference, as they sipped from goldfish-bowl glasses of wine and painted patterns in their raspberry mousse with a fork.

Leon looked across the table. Gordon met his eyes briefly before glancing away.

The first night of Robin's New York gig was steeped in controversy. Reports cited a bomb-plant outside the arena, prompting security to ramp into overdrive and the place to be evacuated, even if on later inspection it was discovered only to be a discarded backpack.

'That's it, then—we're cancelled.'

Barney was fielding a stream of calls. 'Sorry, babe, it looks that way.'

The withdrawal was gutting but at least it meant she could get to Leon: Robin had planned to make it to the Regency when the night was over, in the hope of catching him there, but going now would be a sure-fire way of seeing him again. She didn't know how she'd feel about it, and had to separate her emotions from the real purpose of her visit—easy to say and harder to do, especially when she had no clue what she would say to him.

*I think Puff City were involved in your brother's death...*

No, that wasn't right.

*I know Puff City were involved in your brother's death...*

But he'd never even told her about his brother and somehow that stung like crazy. Then again, what had she ever told him of herself?

Robin took a car to the venue, where the guy on the door stood back to let her pass.

In the ballroom, guests were mingling. Formalities had finished. She didn't know if he was still here, and, scouting the room, began to suspect he wasn't. Then she laid eyes on G-Money, and in a flash remembered Slink and Principal talking about him.

*G wants to fess. That means us, too...*

What was he doing here? She knew what the gig was in aid of. Did G get some kick out of knowing something his company didn't? Of pretending he backed their cause when in fact he was more implicated than he'd ever let on?

What did he have to confess to?

G-Money was chatting with a pretty brunette in a strapless dress, whom Robin guessed was his girlfriend. His face broke into a grin and he waved her over.

'Robin! This is unexpected.' He was wearing black-rimmed glasses and a geek-chic tartan tie beneath his suit jacket. 'Did Leon invite you?'

The girl next to him bristled. 'I'm Lisa,' she cut in. 'Did we miss you earlier?'

'Oh, no,' Robin replied. 'I was meant to be doing a show at the Ring.'

'You're on tour,' she stated matter-of-factly, as though Robin hadn't known.

'That's right.' There was a hiatus.

G-Money broke it. 'Hey, brother,' he said to someone at her back, 'where you been at?'

She could feel his presence: the silent strength that came off him and the power he emitted. When she saw him, her tummy did a full-on somersault. Man, he could wear a suit. It hung off him smart and sharp, the angles of his shoulders and elbows and the clean line of his jaw above the collar. His aroma was deep. For a second she was speechless.

'Hi,' he said, coolly.

'Hi.'

Another pause, before he put an arm round Lisa's shoulders. The woman's face tilted a fraction in satisfaction and Robin felt herself burn up. How could she have missed it? Lisa wasn't with G; she was with Leon.

'What brings you here?' Leon asked. She didn't like how he asked it, as if that night where they had laughed and talked like friends had been a dream. It was her fault. She had pushed him away, possibly the best person in her life, and this was the result.

All the things she had rehearsed escaped her. How could she ask for a private word without it sounding preposterous? But she'd never been a coward and wasn't about to start.

'Have you got a second?'

'Sure.'

His agreement was a revelation—to save Lisa embarrassment, probably. He kissed his girlfriend on the cheek before steering Robin through the crowd and into an adjacent room. His face was stern, unreadable, as if she'd lost the part of him that had put up with her for so many weeks.

'I can't be long,' he said.

'Of course.' Why was this so difficult? 'I know I've turned up out of the blue...'

'You could say that. Look, Robin, if this is about us, don't waste your breath.'

His candour stalled her.

'Actually, it isn't.' It came out hard, too easy to relapse, and even as she said it she saw the conflict in his eyes. Seeing Leon with another woman had rocked her. She couldn't bear for him to think she had come to discuss their relationship: it was too humiliating.

'As a matter of fact this is far more important,' she retorted.

His face was inscrutable. 'For a while back there I kinda thought you and me were important.'

'Were we?'

'Weren't we?'

'You tell me.'

'I've tried.' He folded his arms. The movement prompted a scent of aftershave to wash over her, the same he'd been wearing on the night they'd spent together. 'So you throw it back in my face and still I'm supposed to try harder?'

'I never asked you to try.'

'You never ask anyone. You just keep going on your own because it's easier not to let people in, and I don't know if that's because you're afraid—you know what, I thought it was, but maybe that was giving you the benefit of the doubt—or maybe it's because you just don't need that in your life. Thing is, everyone needs it, Robin, that's what I'm trying to say. I've been there, and it's *not* easier—not in the long term. One day you'll wake up and realise everyone's stopped caring, because if you don't care, why should they?'

'You don't know anything about me. You don't know what I've been through.'

He pulled back so he could regard her directly. 'Good excuse.'

'What?'

'That's the one you use, right? Keep peddling out the same line and eventually you might get left alone. That'd be a happier life, wouldn't it?'

She was shaking. 'How dare you distil it to something so trivial?'

Leon relaxed the knot on his tie with a quick tug. 'Wake up, Robin: you're not the only one who's had it rough. Look around you. Except instead of accepting it these people use what strength they have left to make something good. I *saw* that in you, right from when we met, and you chose to ignore it. That's the difference between us, and I don't know, perhaps I was kidding myself for thinking it was surmountable and the result would be worth it. Because it takes two people to want that, not just one.'

'This is exactly the reason I don't get into shit like this.'

'Why, because you can't handle what it brings out in you? If you faced that instead of hanging out with some loser with a jail sentence then you might meet the problem head-on and learn how to solve it for once in your life.'

She was stunned into momentary silence. 'You're telling me I've got problems?'

'Go figure.'

Leon shouting at her was worse than anything. She realised in a horrid mix of anger and self-doubt that she wanted his approval, his protection, his shelter; she *needed* it.

'So Lisa's the answer, is she?'

'Compared with you, yeah, damn right she is. You're nobody's answer, Robin, you're just one big question I've given up trying to solve.'

His words hit her with the force of a slap. It was like being punched in the stomach.

*You're nobody's answer.*

Leon swallowed. He looked about to speak but she cut him off.

'I guess that's it, then. Good luck.'

He grabbed her wrist. 'What was it you wanted to say?'

The touch of his skin burned. 'Forget it.' She shrugged free. 'Just forget it.'

# 42

Ivy Sewell had always been a fast learner. Flipping burgers: how hard could it be?

The challenging part was putting up with the morons at the Palisades Grand's premier fast-food joint as they sweated over grills and guffawed at each other's jokes. It was fun to them—extra cash over the coming months and nothing more to it, maybe a few friendships to be nurtured over the years or buddies to join for a beer after hours. Ivy wasn't interested in any of that. She was here for one reason and one reason alone.

Vengeance.

Working at Burger Delite! was an investment. Over the spring she would keep her head down, uncomplaining as she went about her tasks salting pretzels and seeding buns and dressing salads, biting her tongue whenever she was asked an inane question about herself and inventing her backstory as easily as she squirted mustard on a hot dog.

'You wanna be manager of this place or somethin'?' Her

supervisor grinned. He was a fat old guy called Graham who needed to pluck the hairs from his nostrils.

'Just doing my job,' she replied.

'You talk too nice to be doin' this,' Graham commented, coming close so that she could feel his breath on the back of her neck. 'Here's me thinkin' you're gonna wise up one day and not come in and then what am I gonna do?'

Ivy concentrated on not shuddering. His proximity was vile. And yet she had to abide it for the sake of the cause, because if Graham let her go she would lose it all.

She threw another patty on the grill and watched as sparks of hot fat spat and burst.

'You'd survive,' she countered, thinking that was the most truthful thing she'd said since arriving. If she decided to leave, if she turned her back on the plan, they'd all survive.

But Ivy had no intention of doing that.

Graham wasn't the first man to want to get close. Her hair, tucked beneath her cap but escaping at the nape, was bright as a handkerchief in snow. Her eyes were feline and her lips were scarlet red. She knew she looked good, her similarity to Robin playing in her favour.

*You know who you remind me of?* they'd say, one after the other like clockwork, thinking they had landed the hot ticket needed to get in her knickers—and then when she feigned surprise, *C'mon, you must've heard it before...*

'Am I gonna get any service round here?' A guy with his teenage sons was hollering over the counter. They'd be watching the sell-out comedy gig, stopping by to get refreshments because that's what people did: eat, shit, and get entertained.

Grudgingly Graham sloped off. 'Yeah? What can I get

you?' His eyes kept sliding back to his employee, scoping Ivy's figure, her still profile and her private smile.

Ivy pressed the back of her spatula on to a new burger, enjoying how the meat popped and fizzed like flesh under a boot. Pieces of meat, that's all they were. She thought of her mother, a sack of blood and bones by the end, waiting to die. Everyone was waiting to die. She had the power to bring that reality close, a quickening of the inevitable.

This was the place to do it.

The Palisades Grand was LA's chief venue. Come July the arena would welcome the biggest event in the music industry calendar: the ETV Platinum Awards. Everybody who was anybody would be there, and that meant Robin Ryder. Robin would be on a high, fresh from her tour, on top of the world. And then she'd be walking straight into the scene of her assassination.

Ivy had been keeping an eye on her sister. Nothing could compare with having come face to face with her in San Francisco, but scoping all she could on the web—every update, every development—was like foreplay. The anticipation was exquisite, the purest agony, knowing as she did that the countdown had begun. Following an aborted bomb scare in New York, Robin's name was hot on the media's lips.

Just wait until they saw what was next.

Ivy laughed. She hadn't meant to do it out loud and it was enough to spark Graham's renewed attention.

'Somethin' funny?' he leered, coming over to renew the flirtation.

'Nothing that you'd understand.'

He took her response for playful banter. 'Why'n't you explain it to me over a drink?'

Men were such pathetic, predictable creatures. 'I don't think so.'

Graham chuckled. 'Give me time,' he threatened. 'I'll have my wicked way yet.'

Ivy grimaced. If it wasn't Graham in pursuit of her attentions, it was Connor—except while she could leave her supervisor at the end of the day, Connor was hanging around like a dick in the wind the minute she returned to the apartment. It was a miracle she had managed to secure all she needed amid the incessant knocks on the door. On one occasion she had opened it, the computer tucked just out of sight, its screen boasting rifles and semi-automatics and charges of ammo, an order of arsenal enough to supply an army, so that all Connor would have had to do was to peer over her shoulder...

Connor was blind, as blind as Graham, as blind as them all.

This summer, at last, they would meet the truth.

It was the end of her shift. Ivy pulled off her cap and pushed through the exit.

'Your time's up,' she called, letting the door swing shut behind her.

*PART 3*

## 43

It took a long time for Turquoise to surface. She felt herself swimming from a deep-sea bed, up and up through the fathoms towards a distant light that kept moving further and further beyond her reach. Every part of her ached, her limbs heavy and dragging her down, and it was hard to see and harder to breathe. She couldn't get a lungful; the water was too close, all around, above and below and everywhere, holding her in. On a blink it rushed in, black and cold, stinging her lids and splintering a piercing agony through her skull.

Pain shoved her into consciousness. Her eyes opened to darkness, swollen and sheer, a thick curtain she could reach out and touch. The world was invisible. Nothing could ground or place her, no light, not even a shadow, to guide her vision. Was she dead?

A rising tide that built in her chest till she wanted to scream told her she wasn't. She was alive. The scream didn't come, just a muffled cry that hit an impenetrable wall. Her lips were fused, suffocated, zipped together. Gingerly she brought her fingers up, both hands at once because she could not separate them, and missed her face as disorientation played tricks and spots burst behind her eyes. Finally she met her skin, wanting to weep at the company of it, because she was here, she was whole…and the band of tape still soldered to her mouth.

*Keep calm.*

*Breathe.*

The words looped in her head, insufficient to betray the isolation and terror of her situation. *Hostage.* Helpless. Hopeless.

But inhaling through her nose, unable to take in the oxygen her body craved, only exacerbated her fear. Her heart catapulted as she attempted to lift a corner of the tape but couldn't get the angle, because she had no strength and her wrists were tied so tightly that the cords burned and every twist arrived with a fresh bolt of agony. With a whimper she tried to sit, pushing herself up on her elbows, her stomach muscles cramping as her legs failed to deliver. Reaching her ankles, she found them bound as well. Picking frantically to free them, blind and bewildered and her lungs on fire as she fought the desperation to take a throatful of air, she accepted it was no good. *I'm going to die here. I'm going to die.*

In tantalising drips, images seeped through, half remembered, half dreamed.

The letters ANGEL RESIDENCE, gleaming in the light…

A glittering glass of water, freezing cold, and the crack of thawing ice…

Ava's smile…

The word, one word…*'Surprise'*—

Her vision was assaulted by light. A shaft came pouring in, brighter than the sun, pursued by footsteps. Turquoise squinted through the haze, willing herself to focus: the throb at the back of her head was disabling. The door closed and a softer glow was switched on.

'Hello, again,' said Ava. She was sitting primly against the wall of what Turquoise saw was a small, cell-like room. It was about twelve feet by ten, white-polished marble, bright and clinical as a hospital waiting room. Ava's legs were crossed and her hands were linked primly at the knees. Through a vapour of confusion Turquoise went to speak, before remembering she was gagged. Her tongue was woollen and stuck to the roof of her mouth.

'You've been asleep for a while. I tried to rouse you but you must have been very tired. Do you think we can talk now? Are you up to it?'

Turquoise trembled. *What are you doing? Why aren't you setting me free?*

'I know this is a shock.' Ava's voice was as calm and cool as her surroundings, and as unruffled as if the women had been catching up over lunch. Nothing about her demeanour betrayed anything out of the ordinary—just the eyes, which had lost the Ava sparkle and were now as flat and unfeeling as a reptile's. Which was the real Ava, that one or this?

'You're going to live,' she said. 'Do you hear me? Do you understand?'

From the mattress she was confined to, a single cream pad that smelled of plasticky, floral antiseptic, Turquoise nodded. She stared up, wild-eyed, at a woman she did not know.

'But first we need to teach you a lesson. You've been a bad girl. Do you know why?'

Dumbly she shook her head.

'Have a think,' Ava encouraged, leaning forwards, her almond eyes glittering with false reassurance. A plait of white-blonde hair was draped over one shoulder and she wore a familiar pantsuit—the last one Turquoise had seen her in. In pieces she recalled the journey to Cosmo's house and the alarm she had felt when her friend had opened the door.

*Her friend...*

'Is there anything you want to tell me?' Ava pressed, with the soft insistence of a parent wheedling confession from her child. 'When you're ready I'll let you speak, but I want you to be ready, Turquoise, because if you start screaming I'm going to have to punish you and you won't like that.' A beat. 'Even if you do, your cries for help will be a waste of energy. No one will hear you because we're soundproofed. You could cry until your throat burst and still they wouldn't come.' She smiled kindly. 'All right?'

Turquoise closed her eyes, tentatively stepping through the twisting corridors of memory until she landed on it. Her only defence: *the tape.* Awkwardly she lowered her bound wrists, fumbling towards her jeans pocket and diving into it. She found it empty.

'Looking for something?' Ava held up her own hand, between the fingers of which the evidence shone blackly as a jewel.

Injustice hit Turquoise in a red cloud, dazzling her vision so that when she rose and stumbled towards the other woman it was useless: she went crashing down, unable to break her fall, her knotted fists slamming against the waxy floor.

Ava clicked her teeth. 'There, there,' she crooned, 'no need to go getting silly. Cosmo's on his way and you'll want to be on your best behaviour for him, won't you? You've made him wait. He tried to come down sooner but you were far too sleepy, and that's no fun for him, is it? Understand we had to sedate you: you were quite the feisty thing.'

*Cosmo...*

'You know he doesn't like it when you disobey him.' Ava waited before delivering her blow. 'Not like the old days.' With startling strength she pushed Turquoise back on to the mattress. Her face loomed close, surveying her victim's horror with interest.

'Do you promise to be good?'

Turquoise did nothing. She prayed for the nightmare to end but knew in her soul it was no nightmare. This was real. The pain coursing through her body told her so.

Gently Ava peeled back the tape. It left a gluey residue on Turquoise's mouth that she longed to wipe but her hands were helpless. Ava did it for her.

'Water,' she gasped.

Ava obliged, crossing to a steel panel in the corner of the room, above which a faucet was fixed. She returned to her chair and held the glass out, removing it from reach every time Turquoise went for it, smiling slightly, toying with her prey until at last she got bored.

Turquoise drank the liquid thirstily, her hands shaking. With every gulp, life seeped back into her veins. Her brain was slow to catch up.

*Think, think, think...* But that was all she could think.

'Why are you doing this?' she rasped.

'Why do you imagine? I'm a loyal and faithful wife.'

'Ava, *please*, for God's sake. This is me!' Turquoise's lips were so dry she could barely force the words out, her oesophagus raw. 'Look at me. Look at what you've done!'

But the Ava who might once have heard her was gone. The blonde woman's expression gave nothing away save for perverse pleasure. She was enjoying this.

'You're right,' said Ava. 'This *is* you, Turquoise—the real you. On your back, tied up, waiting for a man to have his wicked way and then throw a bit of cash in your direction. How much do you fetch these days? A girl like you must be raking in a fortune.'

'How dare you,' she whispered. 'How *dare* you?'

'I've been pretending no more than you have, darling. The star the world knows is a fiction, isn't she? A lie. If I hadn't known better I'd have believed it, too.'

Turquoise's soul dropped through her feet. She'd assumed that Ava was ignorant of her husband's past because surely no one could abide it…unless they were as evil as him.

'Cosmo told you everything.'

'From the beginning.' Ava bared her teeth. 'People ask how we keep the strongest marriage in Hollywood alive, and there's your answer. *Honesty.* I stand by my husband and he stands by me. Truth, right to the end. We're a team, Turquoise—not that you'd know how that feels, existing alone in your frightened little bubble.'

All this time she had found comfort in knowing she wasn't by herself in her suffering, even if the man she'd shared it with was her most hated adversary. The idea that

Cosmo had never been in that state, that he'd *always* had Ava's confidence, made her weak with sorrow.

Ava licked her lips. 'Madam Babydoll sure seems a long time ago, doesn't she?'

It had been so many years since she had encountered the woman's name. Hearing it on Ava's lips was horribly uncanny. Cosmo really had shared it all.

'Oh, no,' Ava went on, seeming to read her mind, 'he didn't need to enlighten me about *that*. I was there, you see. Cosmo was the prize all of us Babydolls wanted.'

It couldn't be. It was impossible.

'After you,' mused Ava, 'there was a gap to fill.'

She wrestled to understand. It made no sense.

'For a while, Lily Rose and I were the favoured package.' Turquoise detected an edge of bitterness in her captor's voice. 'Cosmo switched to blondes, in an effort to forget what he went through with you, I suppose. That's one thing you never grasped, Turquoise. You had it the wrong way round, thinking these men owed you when in fact it was you who owed them. You were lucky to take those jobs, don't you see? We all were.'

Turquoise caught a flash of a pretty Californian girl with a tan like honey.

*The way I see it,* Lily Rose had purred, *it's an opportunity to get noticed.*

Clearly it had been for Ava, as well. Ava had taken work from Madam Babydoll? She'd known Lily Rose? She'd been there? It was too much. It couldn't be true.

'Cosmo couldn't keep his secrets for ever,' Ava elaborated. 'As soon as he told me about that unfortunate girl— you remember, Turquoise, the one you killed?—I knew that ours was an unbreakable bond. Other women would come and go but none would secure his trust like I had. He forgot about Lily, he cleaned up his act, he stopped using Madam Babydoll.' She smiled. 'We knew how to create our own entertainment. Cosmo Angelopoulos became Cosmo Angel, and I went along for the ride.'

She glared at her assailant. 'I'd hardly say he'd "cleaned up his act".'

Ava gave a private smirk. 'Which brings us to the matter of your footage.' Again she held the treasure up to the light. 'It's no shock to me, so you can forget that one straight away. In fact Cosmo and I aren't averse to sharing this kind of thing together—another badge of a contented marriage, you might say: something to bring us closer.'

Every word was poison.

'What concerns us is what you plan to do with your home movie. I'm sure you'd agree, if it ever got out there would be hell to pay.'

Turquoise said nothing. She didn't need to.

'Never go for the timid ones, there's a hint. They might prove easy targets but they always lose their nerve. Your friend at the hotel was a pleasant enough young man, and *very* eager to please—meaning, naturally, he was eager to please us, too.' Ava smiled, gratified. 'The manager called the morning you checked out. Ordinarily they wouldn't have followed it up but since a maid confirmed she'd seen you in Cosmo's suite, well, they couldn't ignore it. Of course we allayed their fears, corroborated your story and promised we were all friends.'

'I thought we were, Ava,' she whispered hoarsely. 'I really thought we were.'

'It didn't take a genius to figure out the rest,' Ava went on. 'Cosmo invited you to us on the assumption you would bring the evidence, and so you did.' She shook her head, curious. 'Did you really think you had the upper hand? That you could threaten us? Your plan was over before it got started...while ours hasn't even begun.'

Dread surged. 'You stay away from me. You just stay the *hell* away from me!'

'Oh, no, sweetheart.' Ava got to her feet. 'That's a risk you must appreciate we're unwilling to take.' Her eyes danced with the thrill of blood sport before flashing a warning. 'We have to know you won't try this again.'

The door opened. A bulky figure stood silhouetted in its frame.

'What are you going to do?' Turquoise demanded, paralysed by fright.

Slowly, wordlessly, Cosmo joined them. He knelt to her level, the spearhead of his wife hovering behind. Cosmo's eyes were pools, obscure as oil and hooded by a heavy brow, the look of a man whose dove had returned to the cote. The liquid contours of his nose, so dark and Greek and brutal, sniffed out her panic. He produced a zipped-up bag.

'I've missed our sessions,' he told her with a smile. 'Welcome home, Grace.'

## 44

Bunny White's funeral took place a week after her body had been discovered. They hadn't needed long to verify the cause of death and so arrangements were swiftly made. The coffin was ivory, gold-buckled and bound by cream ribbons, with a bouquet of pale lilies positioned on top, spelling the words PRINCESS ETERNAL.

Kristin didn't need to bite back tears because she had no more weeping to do. Her body had been sapped of its grief, she'd cried till she could no longer see, and all she had been left with was an enduring numbness. She felt as dead as her poor baby sister.

The Mercedes pulled up at the cemetery to a flashing circus of paparazzi. Even at this, the darkest hour, they were unrelenting.

'Kristin, Ramona, do you have a comment? Is Fraternity to blame? Is that why Bunny ended it? How are you?'

*How are you?*

The question was offensive in its banality. A fourteen-year-old girl had died—a beautiful, kind, sweet darling with so many years ahead of her had taken her own life—and Kristin was meant to turn and say, *Ah, you know, we're bearing up. Lovely day, by the way, isn't it?* What a fucking joke. She wanted to slap the man who'd said it but already his face had been lost in the reeling crowd. Instead she stepped from the vehicle, a stooped Ramona trailing behind, and shielded her eyes from the glare as she passed through the gates.

Inside the grounds, a more appropriate air prevailed. Hushed tones greeted them with careful, practised tact. The priest shook Ramona's limp hand and delivered a platitude that sounded like, 'She's at rest now, with God,' which prompted in her mother a wet blub of woe but Kristin to feel lonelier than ever, because Bunny hadn't been religious— none of them were—and the pretence of reaching for invented faith in their hour of need was bleak.

'Get it over with quickly,' Ramona sobbed. 'I'm not long out of the house, Father.'

'Of course,' he vowed solemnly.

Kristin regarded her mother sideways. Ramona cut the perfect mournful figure in a sleek black dress and heels, just a dazzle of diamonds at her ears and throat. Since Bunny's demise she had holed herself up in her bedroom, swooning in the limelight of her angst, and though Kristin resisted the thought she couldn't help but wonder if a tiny, infinitesimal part of their mother—no, not theirs any more, just hers—was revelling in it.

Bunny's suicide was being publicised for all the wrong reasons. In the aftermath of the Scotty/Fenton explosion, reports had flown in from across the globe of teenage girls threatening to kill themselves, making online death pacts and winding up in the ER with stomachs full of painkillers, and Kristin had no doubt that the boy-band scandal might well have tipped her sister over the edge. Yet the fact remained that Bunny had already *been* at the edge, and the person responsible for that was standing next to her with a silk handkerchief pressed rather elegantly to her nose. Ramona. The pressures of the Mini Miss title, those expectations Bunny could never have hoped to meet, had laid her vulnerable to influences beyond her control. That was what the media didn't seem able to grasp: they were quick to pin such tragedies on the controversial bent—the better, tighter, more marketable story—without examining the currents that ran silently beneath.

*What will people think?* Ramona had asked, once the initial bout of crying had subsided. Even then, even after Bunny was lost, the family's image was paramount. There was something almost admirable about it, Kristin thought: so resourceful, so ready to recover—precisely how Ramona had achieved, through her girls, all she had.

'You poor thing,' came the consolations, sad-faced Hollywood players she had met once or twice and Bunny maybe never; Mini Miss competitors and their parents; PR girls on Bunny's creative team who hung back and checked their iPads when they thought no one was looking. 'She was so young… We can't understand it… A dreadful shame…'

The hole in the ground looked way too small, the coffin too slight and the whole thing so…so *wrong*! So unfair! Kristin wanted to scream her suffering to the sky but knew it would be absorbed unanswered. *Oh, Bunny,* she wailed inwardly. *Why didn't you talk to me?*

'We're assembled here today to pay dutiful respect to our most loved and treasured Beatrice White, taken from us too soon.' Kristin kept her head bowed, stoic and still, because the minute she let the priest's words mean anything at all she'd be overtaken with anguish. 'Our departed loved one will always be present in those lives that she touched...'

Across the gathering she spotted Joey Lombardi—a courageous move given the press were baying ruthlessly for Fraternity blood—whose eyes were rimmed with grey and whose normally fresh face was tinged with sickly pallor. What was occurring in the ranks of that outrage was something Kristin had not yet brought herself to consider, but she knew the guys would be in torment. She felt a glow at his presence and his kindness in consenting to come.

'Beatrice has become a part of each of you here; she will live on eternally in your memories.' At this, Ramona stifled a sob. Kristin rested a hand on her mother's back and felt the brittle quiver beneath. 'Blessed be God, our supreme comforter...'

The worst part was the lowering of the coffin. Ramona openly bawled as the ribbons were loosened and Bunny— dear sweet Bunny was taken from them for ever and put in the cold, dirty ground. All those overblown TV dramas where a grieving relative threw herself on top of the coffin in a yowling fury suddenly didn't seem so ridiculous.

*No! This isn't right! There's been some mistake, this isn't it; this* can't *be it!* But it was it. That was all. Bunny was dead. She would never see her sister again.

Joey caught up with her when the service was done.

'Oh, Kristin,' he murmured, hugging her tight. 'I'm so, so sorry.'

Sympathy made it worse. She pulled back so she could see his face. 'How's Scotty?' she asked, longing to think of anything but this. 'How's everything?'

'Bad.' He made no bones about it. 'Scotty's place is overrun. He can't go anywhere, he can't do anything—Christ knows what it means for the rest of us. I still can't believe it.'

'I couldn't, either.'

He nodded sadly. 'Well, that whole thing makes more sense now. We just didn't get it when you guys broke up. You seemed so solid.'

'And Fenton?'

'He's being taken through the courts.'

*'What?'*

'They don't know yet when the affair began—it could've been when Scotty first emerged and that would make it criminal.'

'Oh, God…'

'Was it you?' Joey asked softly. 'Scotty says you're the only one who knew, and Fenton wouldn't have risked it leaking to the press…'

'No.' Vehemently Kristin shook her head. 'Never. Look at what it's meant…not just for them but for Bunny.' She choked on the name. 'This destroyed her. I knew it would.'

They were ushered out of the graveyard, where the press resumed in force.

'Kristin!' the reporters yelled, shoving microphones and recorders in her face. 'Who do you blame? Do you blame Scotty Valentine?'

Joey followed her into the car and slammed the door. Behind the tinted windows Kristin finally let the tears flow, burying her head in her hands.

'I don't blame Scotty,' she said at last, her voice wracked. 'I blame Jax Jackson. He's the one who let it go. I made him swear not to tell a soul and he spilled his guts to the whole fucking world. I hate him. It's his fault.'

Scotty Valentine hauled the sheets over his head and moaned. Regrettably the tranquillisers he was popping were only capable of knocking him out for a finite period of time, and when he awoke the world was still there, demanding to be faced, and nothing had changed.

'Someone kill me,' he gurgled from the den of his bed, wondering if it was possible to will yourself to death; if you tried hard enough and wanted it that much maybe you'd just stop breathing and your heart would stop beating and then it would be finished.

What kind of life was this? He couldn't even step outside his front door without being set upon. Photographers camped out at the gates of his Beverly Hills estate and shouted his name day and night with no reprieve. The phone rang off the hook. The bell went constantly. He was too afraid to check the web, deciding if he did that the backlash would be so great and so overwhelming that his head would literally implode.

Splattering his brains across the wall was one way of doing it.

Weakly, he mewled. How had it come to this?

Cautiously Scotty climbed out of bed and stood naked at the window, feeding a finger into the wooden blind to part the slats. It was enough to send the pit of lions crouched below into a feeding frenzy, their cameras bursting and sparking as his name was clamoured from the whirlwind.

Scotty gasped, retreating fearfully. The blinds clipped shut but the drone went on: a single glimpse was enough to keep them going for hours.

. His cell rang and without thinking he snatched it up.

'Scott? It's Luke. Thank God, we've been trying to get hold of you for days.'

He hung up. The shame was unbearable. Since the revelations he had spoken once, briefly, to Joey, and that was all he could stand. He couldn't face it. He was a coward.

A second later it rang again.

'Don't you think you owe us an explanation?' This time the voice was harder.

Scotty sank on to the bed. 'I'm sorry,' he mumbled. 'Everyone hates me.'

'Whatever,' Luke said impatiently, 'nobody hates you.'

'Liar!' he howled.

There was a long pause. 'We're confused, man, OK? I mean, shit. Shit! *Fenton?*'

'I don't need this,' Scotty wailed, panicking, 'not off you—or anyone else!'

'Quit being a dick, Scott, for Crissakes. It's not just about you, is it? What about the rest of us? We're up shit creek, too, you know. Sorry,' Luke mumbled, 'bad choice of words.'

Scotty blubbed.

'Come on, dude, enough feeling sorry for yourself already.'

'I'm not,' he simpered.

'We've been worried about you for months—getting sick, missing dates, turning up late to everything. Fenton, too, it's like he just…gave in. At least now we get why you've been acting so messed up.' A pause. 'Why didn't you tell us? We'd have understood.'

Scotty's head sank. 'Like hell you would.'

'Why? We're not rednecks, bud, we'd have got it.'

'With Fenton?'

Quiet. 'It was a shock. A big shock, as it goes.'

'Are you grossed out?'

'Not 'cause he's a guy...maybe 'cause he's, like, our dad...'

*'And that's meant to make me feel better?'*

'Sorry.'

'What do the others say?' Scotty asked in a miniature voice.

'Joey's cool. Doug's all right. Brett's freaked, you know what he's like, but that doesn't mean we're not at your back...' Luke added quickly, 'I mean, not like that—'

'I know what you meant,' Scotty snapped.

'We just figured you liked girls. Everyone did.'

Scotty cracked a couple more pills and downed them with a stale glass of water. He took a deep breath. Amid the wreckage of his life there was some relief to be had from finally setting those forbidden words free.

'I thought if I lived it that way, with Kristin...' He winced as he said it, pinching the bridge of his nose between finger and thumb. 'I don't know, I thought if I lived it long enough then I might learn to convince myself.'

'Come on, bro,' Luke responded gently. 'That's not the way.'

'I know that now, don't I?' he quailed. 'Now all this shit's blown up in my face!'

'It's just damage control, all right?' Luke offered, the lie thick in his voice. 'We'll get through it.' But there was no way through. Both of them knew.

'Are we over?' Scotty asked feebly.

'The rest of the world thinks so.'

'And you? What do you guys think?' He realised too late how much he cared.

'We've lost the market, Scott. I don't know.'

Exhaustion capsized him and he surrendered to its lulling drift. 'We worked so hard for this,' he said, 'and I lost it for us. I laid everything on the line for Fenton, not just my career but yours, too. I'm sorry. Will you tell the others? I'm really, really sorry.'

'Why don't you tell them yourself?'

He shook his head. 'No way, man. If I thought this was laying low then I don't know the half of it. It's a fucking stakeout here.'

'It'll get better…'

'Will it? I'm going to be in quarantine for a year until this blows over. If it ever does.'

'It won't be that bad.' But Luke's voice held no conviction.

Scotty gritted his teeth. 'I can't believe she did it.'

'Huh?'

'I knew she was mad but I never thought she'd take it this far.'

'Who?'

'Kristin. Who else? She's ruined my life…and yours, and Fenton's. I can't let the bitch get away with it.' Scotty's eyes narrowed. 'And I won't, goddammit, I won't.'

## 45

Between cities was a better time, the soporific motion of the tour bus and the gentle hum of her team's conversation steering Robin towards oblivion for a few welcome hours.

In Chicago they picked up Rufio. He had flown in from a friend's pad in New York and Robin sensed he was looking to avoid returning to the UK for as long as he could.

'Can we get food?' he demanded. 'This hangover's a bitch.'

She agreed to take him for a burger before rehearsals.

'I'm breaking up with you,' she said as he was squirting tomato sauce.

The sauce was suspended mid-air. 'Are you joking?'

'No.'

He screwed the bottle in his fist and a slurry of red burst out over his lunch, like some sort of demonic vomit.

'I'm sorry,' she said. 'It's just not the right time.'

'Because you're somebody out here and I'm a loser?'

'That's not it.'

He stared at her.

'I'm not that shallow, Rufio. You know me better than that.'

'Whatever.' He concentrated on rescuing his chips.

Robin folded her arms across the table. 'Things are hectic,' she explained, 'and recently I don't have the time or energy for a relationship, what with everything else.' It was true, but she left out the caveat that all break-up conversations did: that if it was the right *person* then none of that mattered. Rufio wasn't right for her because somebody else was, even if that person had no interest in knowing her any more.

'Is it some other bloke?' he asked, reading her mind. Made to wait a millisecond, he slammed a fist into his palm. 'I'll punch the geezer's face in—'

'It isn't.'

'Liar.'

'Come on. You can't have thought this—' she motioned between them '—was for ever.'

'Obviously you didn't.'

Robin sat back. 'Will you be all right to get home? I can organise someone to take you to the airport, if you like.'

'Fuck off.'

'Fine.'

Rufio grimaced. 'You can get my flight. Upgrade.'

'OK.'

'And I'm gonna need someplace to stay when I get into London.'

She frowned. 'You didn't tell me you'd moved out?'

'I was squatting in Mayfair. Got evicted.'

'Right.'

'So I'm homeless and I just got dumped.' He surrendered his dignity to one last plea, fixing her with a kicked-dog expression. 'Don't you have a heart?'

Her patience snapped. She had stayed with Rufio because of her own insecurities, because of some fictional attacker she'd invented in a period of stress and exhaustion, and she didn't like the woman it had made her. She was stronger than that. It was time to call it quits.

'It's not my fault you're homeless.'

'D'you know what?' Rufio seized the burger and tore into it. A blob of onion relish plopped on to the Formica counter. 'The way I see it, this is my lucky escape. Who else is going to put up with your issues, Robin? You've got complications, man. Deal with them.'

'I'm dealing with one right now.'

He didn't get it. 'Go see a doctor or something.'

'What for? I feel fine.'

'No one who gets within ten feet of you feels fine.'

'What is that supposed to mean?'

'You don't care about anyone except yourself.' He spoke through a mouthful of churning meat. 'I should've seen this break-up coming because fact is there isn't room for anyone else in your selfish existence!'

'I don't have to listen to this.' She pushed her chair back.

'Not now you're Miss America,' Rufio grumbled. 'Aren't you paying for this?'

She threw a stash of dollar bills down and walked out.

They ran a tech rehearsal that afternoon. Gossip was rife about the Fraternity/Fenton Fear shocker and while Robin hadn't caught up on the bulletins she was quickly filled in.

'Turns out the manager's been taking them all up the ass,' put in Matt.

'Do you have to be so crass?' Polly objected. 'We don't know anything yet.'

'We know he's been boning Scott Valentine—it's anyone's guess about the rest.'

'Right, so just because Fenton's gay it means he's automatically promiscuous? Oh, and a pervert? You're such a moron, Matt.'

'Isn't he in police custody? Figure that one out.'

'What happened to innocent until proven guilty?'

Barney raised an eyebrow. 'Ignore him,' he advised, 'he's just threatened.'

'By what?' Matt was admiring the female dancers onstage, warming up to their routines in figure-hugging leggings and crop tops. 'I know where my preferences lie.'

'Fortunately for us,' Barney muttered while the others resumed their squabbling.

Robin took a seat. A runner brought her a Coke and she accepted it, grateful after the new routine. Fans had discovered one of her earlier, unreleased tracks via YouTube, the high-octane 'Spinning', which by popular demand was now being incorporated into the song list. Its accompanying moves were punishing and they only had an hour more to lock it down.

She'd been aware of the Fraternity scandal breaking but it was the death of Bunny White—Kristin's sister—that disturbed her more, and how the two events were being linked in the press. Could a girl be so devoted to the *idea* of a boy, not even the boy himself, that when the illusion was shattered it all became too much? Suicide at any age was obliterating for those left behind, but in someone so young it defied logic. Robin had dismissed Kristin as picture-perfect and it just went to show that everyone had their crosses to bear: maybe if she'd had that foresight with Leon things wouldn't have ended the way they had.

Since their fight in New York she couldn't stop thinking about him. What could she do? If only she had known about his brother sooner. If only she had bothered to find out. If only she had given him half a chance, because hadn't he given her a hundred?

'Hi.'

A voice interrupted her thoughts. Robin turned to see a stacked, dark-skinned guy in a vest and jogging pants, his green eyes twinkling. It was Farrell, the dancer they'd auditioned back in Hollywood and she had point-blank dismissed on account of his similarity to Leon. She guessed they had drafted him in on the new number.

'Mind if I sit?' Farrell asked.

Robin budged up. She smiled. 'Not at all.'

## 46

Having Leon Sway and Jax Jackson side by side on the *Friday Later* couch was the ultimate publicity coup. The show's host didn't intend to let an opportunity go to waste.

'OK,' said Harry Dollar eagerly, knowing just how to press his guests' buttons, 'we all know who's fastest—but tell me, guys, who's strongest out of the two of you?'

'Hey,' countered Leon, 'Jax is only faster on a good day.' The audience laughed along. 'In fact,' Leon turned, baiting his opponent, 'you almost lost to me last week, right?'

Hostility wafted off Jax like a force field. Harry egged them on.

'Your title's under threat, then, Jax?' he pressed.

'Believe,' Jax retorted tightly, 'this guy ain't got nothin' on me.'

They looked absurd sitting next to each other, like men from different planets. Leon was in a black sweater, pants and sneakers, his hair cropped short. Jax had opted for low-slung jeans secured with a number of hanging decorative belts, a vest that showed off his bloated guns, and a cap worn sideways. He'd agreed to the slot on the understanding that it was in promo of his soon-to-be-dropped hip-hop debut, only to find his PR had ballsed up.

'How about a showdown to prove it?' Harry rubbed his hands together in gleeful anticipation, encouraging the audience to bellow their approval.

'We can't race here,' snapped Jax, too quickly.

'Strength, not speed,' clarified Harry. 'Let's see how I fare against two world-class athletes, shall we?' The crowd hollered, the host assured that this was going to spell TV gold. You could practically see the testosterone crackle between these two—and it was time to have some fun with it. Harry was a laugh-a-minute entertainer: all it took was a humorous spin and his guests were powerless to resist, because if they did the joke would be on them.

'Now I'm no Olympian—' Harry stood, shaking his muscles loose '—but I used to work out, let's see, once or twice a year?' Cue more laughter. 'So I stand a good chance, doncha think? Line up, boys.' He started jogging on the spot. 'Let's see what you've got.'

Jax revved up their onlookers by flexing his biceps and gurning appreciatively at the bulge. Spurred on by their cheers he adopted a series of rippling Strong Man poses. 'Let the kid sit this one out, Harry,' he jeered. 'We don't want him doin' himself an injury.'

It was exactly the fighting talk the show had banked on. Harry would join the others in a push-up contest, his involvement a comedy foil to the real-deal rivalry. Neither athlete could turn down the challenge, and neither could be the first man to fall.

'Leon?' Harry opened his arms wide. 'What do you say?'

Leon shrugged. 'I say it's on.'

Swiftly Jax kissed his guns before dropping to the floor. The crowd hooted as though the gesture had been for effect, but Leon knew it was done in seriousness—and anyway, Jax didn't have that sense of humour. He wasn't sure Jax had *any* sense of humour.

The trio lined up, close to the deck, face down, arms supporting their weight. Harry made a gag suggesting he couldn't hold the first position, before imitating Jax's stern game face and fixing on the ground. Leon sensed Jax's bulk alongside him, his grit determination.

A bell sounded and the competition began. As the floor advanced and receded, Leon barely felt it: he trained way too much for this to be a problem. Jax started showing off with one-arm raises, eliciting a cheer from the ranks. After a few mangled attempts the host bowed out, elated at the combat he had managed to engineer and kicking back to enjoy the show.

Jax and Leon rose and fell like pistons beneath the studio lights. The crowd bayed for their favourite to win, stamping their feet in rhythm with the compressions.

*'Go, Jax! Go, Leon!'*

Next to him Leon could hear Jax's breath start to grind. He'd returned to using both arms, his exhalations coming short and low, almost a grunt, while his triceps quivered under the pressure. Leon saw a bead of perspiration splash from Jax's forehead on to the floor.

They kept going, pumping through the repetitions, keeping pace. Jax's cap fell off and on the next descent he snarled it in his teeth, tossing it to the side like a dog with a rag.

The audience continued to shout, and Harry at the periphery urged them on like an instructor at the pool. Leon's arms were stinging but he wasn't done yet. Blood pumped through him, a furious fuel, when he remembered what Jax had said to him down at the track.

*You're a dead man... Just like your dead brother.*

Well now he was feeling very fucking alive.

Jax was groaning, a strangled cry that came from deep inside, his inbuilt mechanism to rage in the face of defeat even if it killed him.

*'Come on, big boy,'* he was telling himself, a rasping command only Leon could hear, *'show 'em what you got.'*

'Whoa, steady there, guys...' Harry clocked Jax's sweat-bathed brow. Did they have paramedics on set? The way this was going one of them was ending up in the ER.

A string of drool was looping out of Jax's mouth. He contained it, vacuuming it up like a string of spaghetti. The moisture was pouring off him now.

*'Argghhhhh!'* came the final choked outburst before Jax collapsed on the floor in a heap. Leon didn't slacken the pace. As Jax was helped up, good-natured applause ringing round the studio, Leon switched to using one arm and flashed the cameras a smile.

Coach Teddy Simpson met Leon in the parking lot. He'd been in the audience tonight and had offered his protégé a ride home.

The Ford had seen better days. Leon pulled the door a couple of times, before leaning down into the window. 'Can you open up? Door's jammed.'

Teddy reached over. 'Sorry. Freakin' car.'

Folding his height into the front seat, Leon almost squashed a bunch of half-dead flowers in the foot well. Reaching down to collect an empty 7UP can, he wedged his gear down by his feet. Teddy's clean-living discipline began and ended at the track.

'Well that was an education,' said Teddy, pulling away. 'I won't ask if Jax needs a ride.' Jax had evaporated the instant shooting was over, tearing off his mic, storming backstage and telling anyone who'd listen, *'I'm never doing this freak show ever again.'*

'I'd say he owes me a few victories, wouldn't you?' said Leon.

Teddy nicked his jaw. 'You can beat him. You know that, right? Your body's capable of it—now you just gotta convince your mind.' He knew Leon's story, knew what he was in it for, and, while he liked to keep an arm's-length relationship with the guys, you couldn't help your favourites. Sway was brave, resilient, and forgetting all that he was without doubt the fastest twenty-four-year-old on the circuit. The Bullet was quick—in twenty years of coaching Teddy had never seen anyone run like that—but there was something he didn't buy into. He sensed that even if Jax's body made it through the season, his attitude wouldn't.

Leon looked out of the window. 'Can I tell you somethin'? Off the record.'

'Shoot.'

'I got this feeling that won't shake, Teddy. I think Jax is gonna try something at the Championships. He's gonna try to bring me down.'

'You're paranoid.'

'Nah, I've learned to trust my instincts. This is real.'

'You gotta watch what you're sayin' there, kid. That's playin' with fire.'

'I know. And Jax has let on exactly what happens if I get burned again.'

'He threatened you?'

'I can take care of threats myself: I know what bullshit smells like and Jax is full of it.' A frown set in his brow. 'But Jax is biding his time; I can sense it.'

'You have to focus,' cut in Teddy. 'Concentrate on your run, nothin' else. Stay low off the blocks, keep your head down and *focus on the race*… What's Jax gonna do about it?' He tapped a finger to his forehead. 'It's what's in here that counts, kiddo, that's the untouchable stuff. You get strong up there and nobody's got a thing on you.'

They pulled off the San Diego freeway. Robin Ryder's voice came on the radio, talking about her new single. Hell, he loved that English accent. Abruptly he turned it off.

Lisa was cooking dinner in the Malibu apartment. She was across from NYC for the week running interviews, and had set up a desk by Leon's veranda, now covered in stacks of paper and clippings and sticky notes taped to the screen of her laptop. Leon couldn't get used to finding himself face to face with pictures of his brother the instant he walked in the door.

The place smelled of basil and tomato, a pan simmering on the stove.

'How was it?' Lisa wound her arms round his neck.

The show wasn't broadcast till next week. Leon considered telling her about the contest but didn't. Robin would have laughed; Lisa would think it a waste of time.

'Aw, y'know, the usual.' He brushed a lock of hair from her forehead and dismissed the instinct that he'd really rather have come back to an empty house. His girlfriend was only trying to help. Wasn't this what he had always wanted: to find Marlon's killer and bring that person to justice?

'I'm making lasagne,' Lisa said, 'your favourite. Hope you're hungry?'

'Sure am.' He squeezed her. 'Let me jump in the shower.'

Padding through to the bedroom, he registered files on the Marlon case stacked up by the bed, in piles at the window, and an old family album left open on the floor. Leon went to it and crouched, flicking through. Marlon, aged eighteen, a year before his death, his arm around Leon's shoulders; Leon's baby sister, hugging her biggest brother's knees; their mom embracing all three kids on Leon's ninth birthday party; Marlon returning from the track on a summer night, sweatbands on, the grin of victory across his handsome face...

'Oh, shit, baby, I'm sorry.'

Lisa appeared in the doorway, wiping her hands anxiously on an apron. 'I meant to put those away, I swear— damn, that was so thoughtless...' She came to retrieve them.

'Hey.' Leon stood, looping his arms around her waist. 'It's OK.'

'It's not. You don't need to come home to this. It's just I got so caught up with stuff today...' She pulled back. 'Leon, I made a breakthrough—at least, I think I did. A witness has come forward. It was a long time ago and I need to check beyond doubt that we can trust this guy, but if we can then the evidence he could provide—'

Leon put a finger to her lips, partly because he wanted

to kiss her and partly because, though he'd yearned for it, uncovering Marlon's assassin scared the hell out of him. It would mean dragging up the past, opening wounds that had struggled for years to heal and exposing his mom to yet more suffering. Would it be worth it? To see Marlon's killer behind bars, yes, but to have to go through it all again for nothing…

'Come here,' he said, closing the gap between them. She tasted of red wine.

'Mm.' Lisa sighed. 'Leon, you kiss like nobody else.'

'Good.'

'Kiss me again.'

He obliged, running his hands over her body and pulling her close. 'Time to relax,' he murmured, easing her back on to the bed. 'We've both been working way too hard.'

'Too hard, Mr Sway?' Lisa swung round and climbed aboard. 'You have no idea how hard things are about to get.'

## 47

Turquoise didn't know how long she had been there. Day-light found no way through and the hours were impossible to monitor. A lamp had been provided, casting a meagre glow, just enough by which to decipher the fundamentals of her prison: a makeshift bathroom; a cupboard; a shelf bearing a cup (plastic, not glass) and cutlery; a wooden table and chair.

She cowered, remembering being made to witness Ava bound naked to that chair, begging for more as Cosmo whipped his wife with brutish abandon. It had turned the couple on to have her there, the silent spectator, helpless and tied up as her vision was filled.

Mercifully—because someone, for once, had been look-ing out for her—she hadn't been forced to partake. But Turquoise was under no illusions: she knew they had been giving her a taste of what was in store and that next time she wouldn't be on the sidelines; she'd be at the centre of the game. *You like this, don't you?* Cosmo had sneered. *This never stopped turning you on. Forget your dirty movie, baby, how about the real thing?*

And she had lain here, frozen and powerless to escape, fixed only on erasing every snapshot the instant it assaulted her. The only weapon she had, she used: endurance. She gave them nothing, apathetic to the end. They wanted her to kick and scream and recoil from their filthy show—her fear was their aphrodisiac—but she refused to give them that. She had seen worse. She had been through worse. Cosmo and Ava could screw themselves.

How was it that the perfect Hollywood marriage, the most celebrated on the planet, resorted to this for their kicks? All that money and fame wasn't enough: when it came to it Cosmo and Ava wanted nothing more than to be on their hands and knees in a basement (Turquoise knew the cell lay beneath the Angelopoulos mansion: blackly she had heard laughter and conversation seeping through as they entertained guests) with their only company a kaleidoscope of sex toys, each other, and the girls who were made to watch...

Turquoise shuddered to consider how many women they had brought down here. Cosmo and Ava had met each other through that world and it was that world that united them now. They thrived on it, powerful beyond the law, their victims too afraid to speak out.

At the super-couple's level, no thrill could ever be enough...except this.

She wondered if anyone was searching for her. Surely they would worry, surely Donna would come by and see she wasn't home, surely Bronx would try calling...

Who else did she have? And how would they know to look for her here?

Turquoise curled up on the mattress, shivering. She was cold. The hours passed.

Some time before dawn the door swung open and Ava appeared. Dressed in a Ralph Lauren palm-green V-neck and casual slacks, her sandals pebble-smooth and her toe-nails cleanly painted, she cut the consummate housewife.

When she saw Turquoise she smiled brightly as if greeting a houseguest, stepped in and closed the door behind her. She was carrying a tray.

'Lunch,' she said kindly, settling the tray on the floor. It bore a plate of sandwiches, their crusts immaculately severed. 'You have to eat; you'll starve to death at this rate!'

Turquoise read between the lines: strength was important for the sport they had in mind. It was also important if she stood any chance of breakout, but she refused to give Ava the pleasure of watching her take food like a dog from a bowl. She turned to the wall.

'I'm not leaving until you at least drink the water,' promised Ava, perching on the chair. It was impossible to grasp that this staid, collected woman, the woman Turquoise had thought of not just as a friend but as a sister, was the one who had been strewn back on this very same apparatus, an animal surrendered to raw desire as Cosmo's whip had licked her breasts, her thighs, her ass and her legs. 'I find the water down here a little foggy.'

Turquoise watched her hatefully.

'Come,' said Ava, holding out the glass. 'Drink.'

Reluctantly she took the water, gulping it as thirst overtook, and lay down and closed her eyes. Ava could be heard making for the door, her shoes a soft pad on the hard ground, the stealthy assassin: so stealthy Turquoise hadn't seen her coming for years.

'Turquoise?' Ava said before she departed.

Turquoise opened her eyes but remained silent. The room was off-kilter. Her insides pinched and she was feeling drowsy, close to dreams...

'You won't forget this, will you?'

The door shut, leaving her in darkness.

Daylight roused her, the warm, unmistakeable glow she had been denied for what seemed an eternity, and she woke up in a dolls' house. At least it appeared that way, her possessions so familiar that in a fresh context they appeared smaller and closer. Safer. Safe.

Turquoise thought she must be hallucinating, and blinked and blinked to bring herself back, with each brief elimination terrified she would be returned to that cold, airless room, a captive in the monsters' den.

But no, it was real; she was home. Here, in her bed, miles from them.

A miracle.

The sound of her phone shocked her into a state of blinding relief.

Stumbling through her daze, she reached to pick it up. She was dressed in the same clothes she'd been in since arriving at the Angelopoulos mansion, and the mirror by her bed revealed a drawn complexion, dark shadows beneath her eyes and dry, cracked lips...but life, all the same, still alive.

'Thank God!' Donna Cameron's voice shot down the line. 'Where the hell have you *been*? I've been calling you all week!'

She fought to engage. 'What day is it?'

'What do you mean, what day is it? It's Saturday. Where were you? We were ready to bring out the search party!'

Saturday. She tried to fathom how long she'd been prisoner at Cosmo's.

'What's the matter? Is everything all right? You're not sick?'

'Everything's fine.' Her brain crawled into gear, a marvel given the circumstances. 'I, er, must have come down with something.'

'Are you better?'

'Yeah…' Turquoise rubbed her head, remembering the drink Ava had forced upon her. *I find the water down here a little foggy.* 'I think so.'

'You don't sound good. Shall I come over?'

'No!' Silence. 'I'm OK. Really. Something I ate, I guess…'

'I'm cancelling Monday's appointments. There'll be more unhappy faces but now I've got hold of you I can at least give them a reason.'

'Thanks.'

'Don't thank me, just concentrate on getting well. You didn't seem right at our lunch, either. I thought I told you to rest?'

'I did.'

'Hmm. I'll touch base tomorrow. We've got a ton of PR gigs lined up.'

Her heart dipped to her toes and dribbled out through her feet. 'For *True Match*?'

'Of course for *True Match*,' Donna teased. 'Have you

been working on any other movies? Nice of you to tell me: no wonder you've been off the radar.'

Turquoise managed a weak laugh. 'I'll be on it, don't worry.'

She hung up and stared at the wall.

A piece at a time, she assembled the picture. Cosmo and Ava had drugged her and returned her here under cover of night. Part of Turquoise was amazed at her escape; another expected it. Kidnapping one of the most famous women in the world had been a thrill more dangerous and exciting than any they had known. They'd made the most of it, they'd had their fun—and in the process had issued a warning that resounded through her like a bell. The couple weren't messing. The implication was clear. They had driven home that no matter what measures Turquoise took to reveal Cosmo's crime, they would always be one step ahead. Cosmo's name and reputation would be protected against all possible assailants, and with the support of his wife he was invincible. They would stop at nothing.

Turquoise was alone—and trapped, utterly trapped, in that isolation.

She realised how much she had invested in Ava's ignorance—that when awarded the facts, Ava would always have sided with her because Cosmo would turn out to be a different man from the one she had married. Instead Turquoise had lost not just her safety net, her ally, but a friend she had cherished beyond every other and saw now she had never known at all.

In a stupor she faltered to the shower, her legs like lead, and climbed in beneath the needles of driving water, embracing their warmth across her face, through her hair and down her aching spine. With every scrub she removed traces of Cosmo and Ava, peeling away the nightmare but still finding more to fear beneath and scouring so hard her flesh blazed pink.

On emerging she checked her body—for what, she wasn't sure: bruises, cuts, some evidence of where she had been, anything to stop the crazy suspicion that she might have imagined it. Her shaking fingers were all the evidence she needed. One thing she'd learned was to trust her own skin; it had seen her through enough.

Her heart was going like crazy and the heat had made her faint. She sat on the bed and gripped the sheets, teeth chattering, her wet hair snaking down her back.

Gathering her strength, Turquoise stood, slipped on a towelling robe and made her way downstairs. The door to her office stared back at her, wide open. She went to it.

The room was just as she had left it. Her guitar was propped up against the desk, a songwriting pad open and weighted down with a coffee cup.

Her eyes fell on the wooden cabinet.

*Be there. Be there. Be there.*

She crossed the space and knelt, carefully sliding her hand into the narrow gap. At first she fumbled for it, convinced it had vanished—they'd found it and removed it and everything was over—before she nudged something hard with the tips of her fingers. Her palm closed around it and a laugh fell from her mouth, hysterical with relief.

Withdrawing the package, she clasped it to her.

More than the value of the object was the value of its rediscovery: when all else had deserted her, it remained. She still had something on that evil sonofabitch.

Pressing it to her beating chest, she knew that however hard they tried and however afraid she became, they would never be brave enough to take it from her.

# 48

Kristin checked herself into an Italian spa a fortnight after Bunny's funeral.

'If anyone needs time out, it's you,' advised her label. 'Take as long as you need.'

She couldn't think of anything that would make things right. All the relaxation in the world couldn't dull the pain of having lost what she had, but, while despair over Bunny eclipsed everything else, Kristin's implication in the Fraternity drama—at least as far as the press were concerned—was a goldmine. Getting away was the right thing. Reporters were on her twenty-four/seven for a judgement, any juice they could squeeze about what Scotty had been like in bed, if she had ever suspected anything, what sort of a boyfriend he had been, emotionally and physically—horribly invasive and personal questions she would never have considered answering even under the best possible circumstances.

'Fine,' Ramona bleated when she said she was going. 'Leave me to perish.'

'If you need me, Mom, I'll stay.'

'Both my daughters abandoning me,' she announced, collapsing melodramatically on to a couch and nearly flattening Betsy the cat. 'What about *my* convalescence?'

It was out of the question in any case that Ramona would go because she had invited a camera crew into her house to film a documentary called BUNNY WHITE: RIP A BEAUTY QUEEN, and was required to be within shooting distance every day of the week. She said she was doing it 'to raise awareness of the pressures of fame on young women', which was the most grotesquely hypocritical thing Kristin had ever heard, but arguing with a mother in mourning was not on her agenda. Perhaps this was Ramona's way of dealing with things.

Until the previous summer, Cacatra Island, the über-exclusive Indian Ocean getaway, had been Hollywood's number one celebrity spa. Then scandal had hit, a madman storming its shores in a stunt that had culminated in murder. LA had been rocked by the repercussions. Whispers of a secret clique abounded and the island had never recovered, passing into the hands of fashion powerhouse JB Moreau and becoming, for now, a private residence.

Quick to claim the crown of The Place To Be for recovering Hollywood stars, Tuscany Bounty Fields, TBF to those with their shrinks on speed-dial, was a recuperative hub on the west Italian coast. It was zero frills, in the grounds of an old monastery and bordered by golden fields and slender cypress trees. Kristin's room was plain, a single bed made with starched white sheets, a wooden closet and desk. Her cell was confiscated and her only glimpse of the outside world was a small arched window with a view to the rolling, burnished landscape beyond. Each client was permitted a luxury, one personal possession from home, and Kristin took a photograph of her and Bunny by The White House pool last year. In it Scotty Valentine could be seen reflected in Kristin's Ray-Bans—he had been taking the picture—and somehow the three of them together articulated the impending disaster: Kristin, squinting through the heat, not seeing clearly; Scotty on the outside, eternally so, no matter how he pretended otherwise; and Bunny smiling on, blind to it all, gazing lovingly at the boy who loved neither her nor her sister nor any woman.

How had it ended in such tragedy?

Bounty Fields was a reminder that the globe turned on its axis outside LA and its vainglorious bullshit. Meditation was encouraged, as were long walks, exercise and the exploration of a library of carefully selected novels. Kristin recognised a TV starlet in the courtyard one morning after breakfast but neither girl acknowledged the other.

One morning she headed for a deserted medieval village overlooking the Casentino valley. It was one of several that had been abandoned years before when its inhabitants had left for the city, and it stood now ghostly among oaks, remote and rejected but infused with the kind of unsinkable beauty that time cannot steal. As she descended towards the cluster of part-derelict houses, the midday sun casting a glow across the hills, studded with goat herds that were alert when they saw her but unafraid, stumbling clumsily to the rusted metal jingle around their necks, it felt as if she were entering an afterlife, a precursor of heaven, so uncanny were the polished gleam and the still, calm slowness of the perfumed, nutty air.

It made Kristin believe that something virtuous existed beyond what she knew. When it came to it, this was the decision that mattered—was the world a good place or a bad?

Survival on a knife's edge: light on one side, dark on the other. When bad things happened, as they had to Bunny, did the door stay ajar? Was there a gap still wide enough for dawn to pass through? Did the sun swallow the moon, or was it the other way around?

She prayed with all her heart that Bunny had gone to a happy, better place: a place like this, with luminous hillsides and sparkling streams and a full, domed sky bursting with blue. It was the kind of thing the old Kristin would have written songs about, those fantasy realms where fairy tales existed and no harm came to the righteous. But if life didn't work that way, if there was no sense or justice, did those worlds, too, automatically expire?

Kristin settled on a grassy mound, tucking her skirt under her knees and winding the coarse stalks around her fingers. A goat watched her inquisitively, its beard wiry and grey but its eyes alert. Its hindquarters were awkward as it moved off, lopsided and rickety as old chair legs. It disappeared into a dusty half-house whose windows were punched through and whose door was collapsed on one side.

*'Benvenuto, signorina.'*

Kristin ventured into town the next day. It was a seaside port peppered with cafés and restaurants, the beachfront stalls selling braiding and jewellery and cut-price handbags.

*'Buongiorno.'*

The colours had drawn her, a rainbow of rich smooth orbs half melting in the sun and displayed in buckets as vivid as a palette, their syrups as gorgeous and thick as paint and pooling sweetly in cartons and cornets. *Gelati,* the Italians' ice cream.

'You're Kristin White.' The boy behind the counter beamed. He was dark, with rusty blond hair, an aquiline nose and a full lower lip that protruded just enough to make his good looks interesting. His name badge read: ALES-SANDRO.

*'Ti riconosco,'* he said. 'I recognise you.'

She had made a partial effort at camouflage in a floppy sunhat and shades but had been told before that she was instantly distinguishable. Most stars looked different in real life—shorter, mostly—but Kristin was by all reports as imagined.

'Will you sign?' the boy asked, producing a napkin and marker. Proudly he pointed at his nametag and awarded her another grin. *For Alessandro,* she wrote, *with love.* She considered adding, *The most colourful balls in Italy,* or something to that effect, but didn't.

On cue he gestured to the ice cream. 'Would you like…?'

She chose raspberry and chocolate and Alessandro piled the scoops high, dense as landslides that thawed deliciously down the sides of the cone. It reminded her of a weekend in LA when she and Jax had licked ice cream at the beach, watching the surf roll in and a game of volleyball unfold on the sand.

He hadn't been in touch. To know he had tried would have meant something, a scant consolation and even slighter alleviation to the dislike she now harboured for him. How could he have turned a blind eye to Bunny and the grief they had faced? How could Jax be so hard-hearted? Didn't he care at all? He had to be the most selfish man she had ever come across, and though he couldn't be blamed for Bunny's death his callous reveal of Scotty's secret was a transgression she could never forgive him for.

'Party tonight,' Alessandro offered hopefully as he passed it over, 'here. You come?'

'I don't think so.' Kristin paid him. 'This is a break from all that.'

'Is fun,' he promised, folding the note. '*Sarà divertente. Una marea de gente*, there are many people there. You and me, we go together.'

She shrugged, hoping that wherever Jax was he had a clue what he was missing.

'Maybe.'

The party was in the town square, in annual celebration of a folklore hero who heralded the arrival of spring and chased away the winter demons. Kristin had spent the afternoon reading, sleeping and gazing out of her window, convinced that any second the door would open and her sister would be there, smiling infectiously in the way Kristin preferred to remember her—how could that smile be gone, just like that, and never coming back?—and had at last decided that heading out couldn't possibly make her feel any worse. Surrounded now by music and lights, the dancing stream of locals in carnival costume whooping and wheeling, she embraced the distraction. At the gate an Italian pushed a mask into her hands. Its eyes were arched and high, crimson lips a playful smirk, the border embellished with gold.

The mask made her anonymous. Kristin wound through the festival, air hot and heady with the beat of a deep, relentless drum. Alcohol was thick on the air and she could smell a red-hot grill, meat cooking mixed with something citrusy, like orange peel.

She spotted Alessandro on the periphery, his mask pushed up on his forehead. A slick of sweat shone across his brow. When he identified her, his face split into a grin.

'You came,' he observed. 'I'm pleased.'

'Good. Do you dance?'

It didn't matter that they could barely converse. Humour wasn't bound by language and they laughed their way through the clumsily trodden steps and Kristin drank sweet beer from a plastic cup that made her feel light and wild and carefree, not the solemn and bloated sort of drunk she felt back at home quaffing Bollinger Blanc at her mother's soirées. They joined a train of revellers that wound merrily through the square. Alessandro's hands on her waist were hot and firm, and when they came to a giggling stop and he pulled her into a silent, tender kiss, she responded passionately, burying her fingers in his hair. She was free, untethered, a million miles from everything bad in her life, from memories of Bunny and the hard, cold certainties of Ramona and Scotty and Jax. She never wanted the night to end.

'You have fever?' Alessandro breathed, running his thumb past her temple. He brought it down and trailed it over her lips. 'I know how to cool you down. *Vieni.*'

Seizing her hand, he led her through the throng. The back of his neck shone darkly in the shimmering, flickering glow and she wanted to reach out and touch it. The skin looked soft, iridescent with perspiration, and she imagined how it tasted.

Through a couple of deserted alleyways they emerged on to the empty street. The store was shadowy, lit by the electric blue of the coolers, and the GELATI sign outside was extinguished. Alessandro withdrew a key, unlocked and they stepped inside, the low buzz of the refrigerators heralding their arrival. As her eyes adjusted Kristin picked out the colours in the bank of ice cream, every shade and flavour she could think of.

Alessandro released the cover and lifted it.

'You want? For free this time.'

With his finger he ran a groove through the nearest container and held it out. Wordlessly Kristin stepped to meet him, taking his hand in hers and bringing the finger to her parted mouth. The *gelato* was sugary and slid coolly down her throat.

Alessandro emitted a husky groan and pushed her up against the counter. In a flash he lifted her dress and peeled it over her head. She wore no bra and he dived for her breasts, the nipples firm and taut in the cold, taking one hungrily in his mouth and pulling. Kristin gasped. He sucked so fiercely it teetered on the brink of agony, before flicking his tongue expertly around the bud and tipping her back into an explosion of pleasure. His hardness ground against her, splitting her legs, and she zipped him loose. Alessandro's length sprang free, smooth and swollen, and she ran her fingers down his erection, clasping his balls.

Fiercely he pushed her up on the counter, the ice-cream palettes spread gloriously beneath her. She felt the freeze seal on her thighs, her breath visible in the air, ice-white as the hairs at the back of her neck stood on end, prickling in the cold.

'*Ti voglio,*' Alessandro muttered, tugging her knickers so that they caught on her knees. With a tear he ripped them off. '*Facciamo l'amore.*'

Arching her back, she surrendered her body to him, longing to be devoured. Alessandro's kiss hit her, his tongue in her mouth, and she put her hands back to steady herself, gasping as each palm hit a bucket of the soft melting glacé. His hands followed, scooping the nectar in his fist and bringing it round to her parted warmth, flattening the chill against her drenched heat. The cold struck her crisply and she stretched wider, crying for more, not knowing what she said, senseless in the state of her desire. Her whole body burned, the build sparking in her belly as if it were a living thing.

Alessandro sank to his knees, ravenous as he tasted the cream. His tongue was slick and wet amid the fruit and her own flesh, sticky and soft as his tip caressed every inch, circling her with torturous control, up, down, around, before plunging in deep, his fingers in close pursuit to deny her reprieve. Bursts of numbness were followed by glimpses of ecstasy so intense she thought she would pass out. Tears threatened, so exquisite was the sensation, and when on the cusp of her orgasm he rose to kiss her, cassis ripe and crimson on his lips so she could taste the black juices of that fruit, she shuddered and shivered in his arms.

Kristin took his hard-on in her hands, running back and forth till a rhythm built and swelled and he rocked in her grip, his face contorted with the promise of the inevitable and his hands on the edge of the refrigerator, soldered to the cold. She brought his cock to her open legs, wanting him inside her more than she'd ever craved a man in her life. Right now, this second, her sensuality was raw and uncompromised, it could not be told no. There was no way back but through. Alessandro gripped her hips and flipped her round. Thrust forward, Kristin's breasts plunged into the slick cartons, the freezing, even surface warmed instantly by her skin so that she slipped like a skater on the rink. His hand slapped her ass, sending a splinter of delectable pain across her backside, and when he did it again it stung her between her legs on that most delicate part and she shrieked in surprise at how much she loved it.

Desperate for him, she raised her ass. 'Please,' she begged, 'take me.' His hand came round to clutch her tits, dark and wet with chocolate and coffee and coconut, and he rubbed her down with it, the paint smeared across her belly, and disappearing inside her once more, finding her clitoris so she throbbed uncontrollably against his touch.

'Please!' she cried, every part of her surging. 'I can't stand any more!'

Alessandro stood with his feet parted and his grip on the underside of her ass. The ice cream was in her mouth and hair and dripping down her body in a myriad of colours. She felt like an animal fresh from the kill, the barest, most primal part of herself.

In a plunge he was inside her, filling her up, and Kristin closed instinctively around him, tightening her muscles. She reached out and went wrist-deep into a tub of impossibly buttery strawberry cream, her knee raised to drive him further until she was all but folded into the dome of delights. Alessandro shouted in Italian as he raced for his climax, faster and faster, harder and harder, slamming without mercy till they both exploded in unison, sticky and wet with sweat and joy.

*'L'Italia ti ama,'* Alessandro groaned, bent over her trembling back.

She understood that much, at least. 'And I love Italy.'

# 19

The interrogation room on the fifth floor of LA's West Bureau Police Department was hotly oppressive. An overhead fan rotated with the sluggish reluctance of a spoon through glue.

Fenton Fear gazed forlornly out of the window. He could hear car horns blaring from the street below and the hum of careless conversation as it passed on the warm breeze. Those people hadn't a concern in the world. How had he wound up in this unthinkable mess?

'We need a straight answer,' pressed his questioner, which seemed to Fenton a droll way of putting it. 'Were you or were you not sexually involved with Scott Franklin Jessop Valentine before his eighteenth birthday?'

'I can't *bloody* remember,' replied Fenton angrily. He hadn't known that Scotty's middle names were Franklin Jessop either before this blow-up. 'It was a long time ago, OK? If it was, it was only a matter of weeks—'

His lawyer cut him off. 'My client has already answered

this point,' she said. 'It's possible that Mr Valentine misled Mr Fear about his age.'

'Goddammit,' spat Fenton, 'how many times do I have to tell you it was consensual?'

'Come now.' The interrogator sat back in his chair and folded his arms over a generous gut. Handling a case of such rampant popular interest had him bobbing up and down in his seat. 'Do you expect us to believe that? Scott was your selection; he was your number one. You're telling me the attraction only sparked once he was legal? Love affairs don't work like that, do they? Passion exists by its own rules.'

'You'd know, would you?' Fenton challenged, disgusted.

'I think *you* would, Mr Fear, which is why I'm asking.'

'My client refuses to comment,' the lawyer interjected.

'It looks like he's ready to comment to me.'

Miserably Fenton slumped his elbows on the table and rested his glistening forehead on the heels of his hands. If only they could offer him the electric chair...because what did he have left to live for after this? He was a hated man, an angel fallen so sensationally from grace that he didn't even know if hell would let him pass. His career was in tatters, he was being labelled a sex criminal and he had lost the person he loved most in the world.

Curse Scotty for telling them! How *could* he? He had known fully what it would mean and the monstrous repercussions that would play out: apparently he had deemed the sacrifice of his own career worth the bludgeoning of Fenton's. Had he really hated him this much? Things hadn't ended well but what about the love that had passed before, the tenderness? Had Scotty forgotten all about that?

His young lover had responded to the threat of being cut

loose from Fraternity. Fenton hadn't meant it, Scotty was the golden child, but that had been a risk the boy was unwilling to take. Now Fenton was alone, accused of being a pervert, a sex fiend, a depraved human being...all for the simple offence of following his heart. The ignominy was unspeakable.

'I want bail,' he told his lawyer afterwards.

'We're headed for a release on recognizance, provided you're not deemed a danger to the community. There might be a home detention order.'

'"A danger to the community"? Are you kidding me? What do you think I'm planning to do, hit up the local schools with my travelling zoo of hand puppets? *Look who Uncle Fenton's got his arm up now, kids!* Give me a fucking break.'

'I wouldn't joke about things like that.'

'Do I look like I'm joking? Just do your damn job.'

'Be patient, Fenton,' she told him. 'We'll get you cleared.'

## 50

Sex with a member of her crew had its benefits. It released the pressure before the lights went down, it solved the problem of surplus adrenalin after a show, it calmed her when she woke from bad dreams—and it sure gave Robin something to do on her nights off.

Farrell was gorgeous. She tried not to overthink how much he resembled Leon Sway but the similarity was extraordinary, the only real discrepancies being the crescent-shaped dimple in Leon's cheek, the cleaner green of the athlete's eyes, and, while Farrell's body was incredible, it was the frame of a dancer, not a sprinter. When Leon had held her she'd felt shielded by his strength, even being *next to him* had electrified her in the shadow of his might. Leon's body was a machine; Farrell's, however honed, couldn't come close.

'You're real pretty, you know that?' Farrell, fresh from the shower, sank down next to her on the bed and kissed her shoulders. Her Denver penthouse suite was boutique and stylised, the bed sheets and bath tub black, the carpets cream and the fittings chrome. Dark orchids rose from elaborate vases and the view over the city was astonishing.

'Hmm.' Robin turned her head to meet his kiss, melting as his touch trailed a line down her back and peeled away the sheet. His chest was still wet and his breath minty from having cleaned his teeth. She moved on to her back and succumbed to his caresses.

'Not tired yet?' he teased, nibbling her ear lobe. They'd had sex all night, and going by Farrell's rock-hard dick pressed against her inner leg he wasn't done yet either. Lifting his washboard stomach, he loosened the towel around his waist. His majesty sprang free.

'D'you want it?' he groaned, close to her ear. 'Let me hear you say you want it.'

'I want it,' she whispered, guiding him in.

'You're so wet,' he choked. 'I fucking love how wet you are.'

They fell into momentum, their wearied muscles concerned only with the urgency to climax. With her eyes shut tight Robin could imagine for an instant she was with Leon. It was unfair but she couldn't help it; she couldn't tell herself not to feel what she felt. Farrell's shoulders were broad, pinning her down, his backside lifting and falling on top of her: he was an able lover, he knew what he was doing, but with him as with all men there remained a sliver of detachment that stopped her engaging completely. With Leon, despite the fact they had only kissed, it had been different. She couldn't put her finger on how, or why, but it had.

'Are you ready?' he breathed. She strained against him in response, raising her back and contracting her legs against the sides of his waist and then he was pounding harder, winding his hips in the way that brought her pleasure. In a searing flash she was coming, and held him to her as she rode it out, screaming his name over and over again.

Farrell finished quietly. He was a long time dismounting her, and when he did he sat on the side of the bed with his back to her.

'That was fun.' Robin propped herself on one elbow. 'D'you think we should get up now? You've given me a serious appetite—'

'Who's Leon?'

The question threw her. 'What?'

'Leon. You just said his name about sixteen times.'

She yanked the sheet up, blushing like crazy. 'No, I did not. That's ridiculous.'

'Only saying what I heard.'

Robin didn't know how to reply. Had she said Leon's name? Oh dear.

'Sorry,' she muttered. 'I didn't mean to.'

'Obviously not,' he answered tightly. 'So who is he?'

'No one.'

'Why do I doubt that?'

'Sorry,' she said again. 'It was a stupid mistake, forget it.'

Farrell turned. 'I know this is just fun—' he gestured between them '—whatever this is, but I have to know where I stand. If you're with me, you're with me. Not someone else.'

'I know.'

'So who is he?'

She got up, pulling on her vest and jogging pants. 'It doesn't matter.'

'Funny, it kinda does to me.'

'Forget it, Farrell. It was a slip.'

'Is it that sprinter? Is it Leon Sway?'

Robin ran a hand through her hair. 'If this is just fun, can't we let it go?'

'No. It makes a guy feel kinda shitty when you pull a stunt like that.'

'Which is why I've apologised. Let's move on.'

He hauled on his jeans and went about finding his T-shirt.

'Over there,' she said, pointing to a heap on the floor. She waited awkwardly while he dressed, unsure how to make it better. Finally, shoulders slumped, Farrell turned.

'I like you,' he said. 'A lot.'

'Maybe it's not just fun between us, then.'

'Maybe not to me.'

He watched her expectantly. This was her chance. She said nothing.

'I'll see you at rehearsal.' With the click of the door, Farrell was gone.


Robin spent the rest of the day in a slump. Down time was always a jolt to the system, and after this morning's disaster it was worse than usual. Welcome distraction arrived with news that Shawnella Moore, Slink Bullion's girlfriend, was in town launching a fashion line with a D-list movie star. Her arrival had attracted a ripple of media interest and, after making the necessary phone calls, Robin headed to the warehouse on Colorado Boulevard.

A gaggle of paps was hanging around outside. The appearance of Robin Ryder was an unexpected bonus to the tedious hours waiting for Shawnella and her friend to emerge, and they trailed her up the steps like hopeful puppies, fended off at the door. Barney didn't like her going without security but she knew that was a slippery slope: if she insisted on going everywhere accompanied she would lose her independence for good. No matter how she'd been frightened that was not a ransom she could accept. Yes, there were nutcases out there, but you had to assume that ninety-nine per cent of the time they intended no harm.

In any case, Robin didn't want a chaperone on this particular jaunt. What she intended to discuss with Slink's girlfriend wasn't for anyone else's ears but theirs.

A rickety lift packed with studio props took her to the sixth floor. She tugged at the door before it gave, drawing it back to reveal Shawnella posturing in a catsuit and the D-list movie star swinging her legs from a stool at the make-up hub, totally uninterested. A rail of clothes was being wheeled on to set—samples from the line, presumably: a clash of fuchsias, lilacs and blues, dresses and hot pants, playsuits and shorts, some more identifiable than others because they had holes ripped into them as if they'd been attacked by the claws of a wild animal. The materials were plasticky and iridescent in the photographer's light, sort of a nineties shell suit wet-look, and Robin couldn't think of a single person she knew who would wear them. The 'Demand Moore' collection had some way to go.

She took a seat at the back. Shawnella gave it all, slipping in and out of the costumes with the commitment and endurance of a pro, while the movie star, deigning herself to be above it while the fact remained that nobody knew her name, kicked up a fuss about having to wear 'bulgy' outfits and heels that were so uncomfortable she couldn't walk in them, which struck Robin as a dubious claim to make about your own collection.

Shawnella was surprised to see her when they broke for lunch. There was a ripple of interest as Robin was recognised. The movie star slunk towards the exit, pissed off.

'Can I take you for coffee?' Robin asked.

The elevator was bust so they had to take the stairwell, Shawnella getting a lift from one of the assistants because her shoes were pinching.

Downstairs, she was suspicious. 'What's going on?'

'It's half an hour of your time,' said Robin. 'Please?'

Shawnella hesitated and Robin added, 'It's important.'

The day was hot and the fresh air a welcome shift from the stuffiness of the studio. Robin preferred to be in an open space anyway for what she was preparing to say, so the women grabbed a drink and took it to City Park. It was perversely easier to be incognito in a public place: the more people there were, the less you got noticed.

Shawnella wasn't one for small talk, so Robin jumped straight in.

'I need to ask you something,' she began. 'It might sound mad, I might be way off the mark, but I have to know and I can't think of anybody else I can trust with this right now.'

The implied confidence secured Shawnella's attention. 'Yeah?'

She took a deep breath, deciding to just come out with it.

'Did Slink have anything to do with Marlon Sway's murder?' She searched her companion for a reaction. 'Back in 2000…the guy got shot. He died. They never found the person responsible. I've got reason to suspect Puff City know more than they're letting on.'

Shawnella blinked. It was a fraction too late. In that microsecond Robin recognised acceptance: this was a secret Shawnella had kept for her boyfriend for far too long.

'I don't know what you're talking about,' she said, the flat denial Robin had expected.

'I overheard Slink and Principal,' she explained, 'at the party in Seattle. Shawnella, they said his name; they said Marlon's name. They said G-Money was getting close to Leon and how that couldn't happen because Leon was Marlon's brother, and how G was a weak link and now he couldn't handle his conscience—'

'Then you heard wrong.' Shawnella rounded on her. 'You heard wrong.'

'How can I have? Come on, it's written all over your face. Are you going to be Slink's yes-girl your whole life? This is serious. This matters. Someone was *killed*.'

A group of children were playing nearby, splashing each other with water. A mother came and grabbed one of their fists, dragging the boy off to a wailing soundtrack.

'It ain't none of my business,' said Shawnella, getting up and walking away.

Robin leapt after her. 'This is your chance,' she said, keeping pace, 'to step up and be *you*, not just the sometime girlfriend of a guy who couldn't care less—and that's by your own admission, not mine. *Wait*. Please, would you listen to me? This is important. This is the single most important thing you or I will ever have done.'

'You're talkin' some crazy shit, girl.' Shawnella couldn't meet her eye. 'The kinda shit that's gonna get you into trouble.'

'Maybe.' Robin yanked her to a stop. 'But that's a risk I'm prepared to take.'

Shawnella narrowed her eyes. 'Why would you?' she challenged. 'Have you any idea what Slink would do if he knew you and I were having this conversation?'

It was the admission she had been waiting for. Not explicit, but enough.

'I've got my reasons.'

'I don't.'

Robin shook her head. 'You're covering for them.'

'Never.'

'You really think you don't have a reason? What about all that stuff you said to me about how Slink treats you, all the women you share him with, all the promises he's made? What about those? He's got you exactly where he wants you. He'd never imagine you'd dare do anything with the facts and that's exactly why he doesn't think twice about you knowing. He's taken that for granted—just as he's taken everything else about you for granted. Is that the way it's going to be, today, tomorrow, for ever? You're saying you're happy with that?'

Shawnella looked blank.

'We can't let it happen,' urged Robin. Now she knew, beyond any doubt, there was no way she could turn her back—not when Leon was in the dark; these men he thought he trusted harbouring a deception as huge as this. Leon was the person she did it for: the person who, in some ridiculous way, she was doing everything for.

'We have to bring them to justice,' she declared.

'It's too dangerous.'

'Bullshit. I'm not afraid.'

'I am.' Shawnella pinned her with a stare. 'You don't know them like I do.'

'Then let's do this together.'

She retreated. 'Leave it, Robin. Don't ever speak about this again, for your own sake. You have no idea what you're getting involved in.'

'It's too late.'

'It will be for you, if you don't give up.'

'I never give up.'

'Then you're on your own.' Shawnella started walking. She didn't look back.

## 51

They said that guilt was a creeper, and grew with a life of its own. For Gordon Rimeaux, what had started as a seed of discomfort had matured into a giant canopy, casting dark, broad shadows across the ground that once had been his shelter. Guilt was a killer.

'Go easy, brother,' advised his training partner. They were at LA's Bench gym and Gordon was pumping hard on the free weights, hoping that the pain and burn might come close to matching his inner chaos. No matter how hard he worked, they didn't.

He strained under another muscle-wrenching lift and in the wall mirror scoped his biceps clenching and relaxing, the beads glistening on his arms. Exercise helped him to focus on his body, not his mind.

'I'm fine.'

'You don't look fine, man,' observed his partner, 'you look tired. Rest up a while?'

Gordon had no doubt that was the truth. In recent weeks

he had been waking at two a.m., bathed in dread. It kept happening. Dreams were cruel. He'd resumed smoking grass to knock him out, but every night went the same. Sometimes he would stay out till four but those were the exceptions: more often he would surface with a jolt into the dark, heart frantically drumming and saturated with memories so steeped in shame that he could barely breathe through their aftershock. The gunshot, the kid running, the bleeding body, the mother's cry as it ricocheted off the glossy road…and their cowardly, indefensible escape.

He'd sit it out till seven and watch the sun come up over the ocean, burning endless cigarettes. When the day arrived he would pursue every diversion he could.

Lungs and ligaments straining, Gordon accepted defeat and took to the sides, snapping open a bottle of water and struggling to harness his breath.

It could not continue.

The workout dragged on, with each repetition sealing in his mind what he had to do.

He had to do the right thing.

Gordon pushed through another hour, cancelled his afternoon studio slot and went home, where he showered, ate mechanically, without appetite, and picked up the phone.

Leon answered on the fourth ring.

'Can we hook up?' asked Gordon, weirdly calm now he was actually doing it. He would go to jail. He would take all of Puff City with him. He might lose his life.

But none of that could be worse than this purgatory.

'I'm kinda tied up right now,' said Leon.

'Tomorrow, then?'

'Hey, this sounds serious!' His voice was teasing. 'What's up?'

*You'll know soon enough.*

'Lisa and I are heading to the coast for the weekend,' said Leon. 'Can it wait till next week? I'm flat-out training till then.'

Gordon clenched his fist. He would be hanging on to his balls a few days yet.

'Yeah,' he agreed, swallowing hard, 'for real. Catch you later.'

## 52

The premiere of *True Match*, Turquoise da Luca and Cosmo Angel's first joint project, took place at Hollywood's Colossus Theatre. The movie wasn't only tipped to break box office records; it was bringing together in its co-stars and director three industry superweights whose product would respond to months of conjecture.

Turquoise had hoped to arrive before the rush, slip in quietly and sit tight until the showing was done. It wasn't to be. As her car pulled up at the carpet she spotted Cosmo and Ava working the cameras, hand in hand, laughing and kissing like the perfect couple they were deemed to be. Cosmo was darkly suited and brooding while Ava looked resplendent in a floor-sweeping liquid-gold gown, a stream of blonde gliding down her back.

'Turquoise! Over here! Turquoise, this way! Smile for us, Turquoise!'

She turned for the press, one hand resting on her hip to show off the borrowed million-dollar diamonds linked around her wrists. Her dress was shoulder-baring Versace, vampish black and split to the thigh, her jet hair and red lips completing the look.

Arriving alone meant she would spawn a ton of head-lines about how such a successful and coveted woman could possibly be single. She had become used to it, and would rather have been by herself than hauling along a two-week boyfriend and forcing him to swim for his life in a shark-infested sea of speculation. Bronx had asked to accompany her—wouldn't she feel safer, he'd challenged: all that atten-tion, it had to be a lonely spotlight? But for the couples here tonight she felt no envy. Up ahead the legendary Cole Steel was posing with his young wife, Chloe French. Since the marriage Chloe had looked drawn and unhappy, older than her years, while Cole seemed to flourish like a parasite on her dejection. If Turquoise knew anything, it was that hav-ing a partner wasn't the answer.

She pushed thoughts of Bronx away. Long ago she had ac-cepted that a relationship couldn't work—not just with him, with anyone. That was OK. It was how things had to be.

Inside the theatre she felt calmer. Cosmo and Ava were several seats down, on the same row, and she swore she could smell Ava's cloying perfume…or was it the smell of the mansion that they carried with them, toxic and sweet? Each time she stole a glance in their direction she was dis-gusted, not so much by her own experiences as with to what extent they were tricking every single person in the room. Worshipped. Wanton. Wicked.

Watching the film was as uncomfortable as she had ex-pected. What she hadn't expected was how emphatically the audience reacted: every revelation generated an audible gasp, every love scene commanded reverential silence, every twist and turn conjured a fizz of shocked whispers until, finally, the credits rolled and the place erupted in applause.

'A masterpiece,' enthused Sam Lucas at the reception, pulling Turquoise under one arm and throwing the other round Cosmo. 'I've got these two to thank.'

'Did you enjoy penning your first movie?' A reporter thrust a mic in Cosmo's face.

He didn't hesitate. 'Once I knew we had Turquoise,' he replied greasily, 'it was easy. She fit the part so perfectly. People ask me how it is writing women...well, with a woman like Turquoise, it's not hard. It was almost as if she was playing a sister, or a friend, wasn't it, Sam?' Sam nodded fervently. 'Almost as if she was playing herself.'

Turquoise tightened her grip on the stem of the champagne flute until she felt she could snap it, if not with her strength then by the force of her hatred alone.

'Something like that,' she said, slaying him with a glare.

Juggling the movie's release with her own ventures was as tiring as Donna had promised. Friday night she had an appearance in Italy and dozed fitfully on the jet, exhausted after press commitments had left her with two hours' sleep. She flew the show on autopilot and took the next day to recover at a Tuscan spa resort recommended by her choreographer, before planning to return to the US the following morning to resume promotion for the movie.

Surrounded by rolling fields, burned by the sun and infused with honey scent warmed on the Italian breeze, the quiet calm of the retreat couldn't have been further from LA. Following a massage, Turquoise padded out to the pool, threw a towel on her lounger and dived cleanly into the water. Carved into the cool stone, the sparkling blue was as refreshing as a glass of cola on a sweltering day, the sunshine bouncing off its ripples as still and bright as the canopy above. Not a sound could be heard save for the occasional whistle of birdsong. She floated on her back, one by one removing distractions from her mind and casting them to the sky.

Relaxation was difficult. At least when she was working she didn't dwell on it, but as soon as she switched off, there her archenemy was. *True Match* had been favourably received and Cosmo and his wife were riding high on the adulation. For Turquoise, it meant the roles were flooding in: Donna was in talks about a sci-fi android-with-a-heart starring role and an antidote rom-com, as well as her musical ventures. She would throw herself into them because it was the only way through. Donna was convinced she needed time out but truth was that time out scared her senseless.

Working with Cosmo meant facing the past every single day of her life. Her own suffering she could deal with, she had wrestled with the horrors long enough, but recently it had been a different ghost knocking in the dark hours of the night.

The girl who'd died.

The girl they'd buried.

The girl who, while Turquoise knew in her marrow she had done everything to save, had been concealed beneath the dry, blistering desert for almost a decade now. What about her parents? What about her family, her friends? Did she have anyone who cared about her, or had her vanishing been a pebble in a lake, a few soft ripples and then still?

Turquoise endured nightmares of being buried alive, terrors from which she woke with a mouthful of sand, only to fumble through the dark, gasping for water, for clarity, and find it was all in her head. The girl visited her in dreams, sometimes the age she'd been and sometimes the age she was now. In one she had clawed her way out of the shallow grave, hair matted in stiff, gritty tendrils, ringing at Turquoise's mansion with a grin on her cracked lips.

*Surprise.*

Even now she couldn't help listening to a Missing Persons bulletin. Every time an unidentified body was found her heart skipped a beat. She searched for the girl in every homeless soul on the street and in the eyes of every woman she passed, tricked into seeing something that wasn't there. Turquoise knew how easily she could have wound up dead herself: she had slipped through its clutches too many times. It wasn't right that she forgot.

The truth gnawed at her. She had to make it right…but she had no idea how.

As she climbed from the pool she noticed a figure sitting in the shade of a pine tree, wearing a black swimming costume, a large floppy-brimmed hat and huge sunglasses. A pale blonde pigtail snaked down one shoulder and the girl's face was absorbed in a book.

Turquoise patted herself dry, wringing out her hair and securing it in a high knot.

'Kristin White?'

If she'd given herself time to think about it she might have stayed quiet: Kristin was in mourning, she'd be here in pursuit of solitude, but the name was out before she checked it.

The girl removed her shades. 'Hi.'

'Hi.'

Politely, Kristin said, 'I've heard great things about *True Match*. Congratulations.'

'Thanks.' Turquoise remembered shooting on location at the Paradise Palms—Kristin had been there, too, though they hadn't spoken. She recalled Kristin's connection to Ava, through *Lovestruck*, and decided to tread carefully.

'It's good to get away for a night,' she admitted. 'It's manic.'

'I'll bet.'

There was no one else around so Turquoise didn't need to speak loudly to be heard. 'I'm sorry about your sister.'

'Thanks.'

'I don't have a sister but I always wished I did… It was obvious how close you two were and how much she loved you. I'm truly sorry. I wanted you to know that.'

She wondered if she had overstepped the mark, because a long silence followed.

Then Kristin spoke. 'D'you know what? You're the first person who's said that to me.' She closed the book.

'Condolences?' Turquoise's brow lifted. 'I'm sure that's not true.'

'Anyone can give condolences, it's when they're from the heart that they help. It's not that people haven't said the right things, they have, but they can't understand. If they did, they wouldn't be so concerned with getting photographed at a fourteen-year-old's memorial—' she chewed her lip '—because that's the kind of attitude that makes horrible stuff like what happened to Bunny happen in the first place. Vanity, selfishness, ego—it's everywhere. So it's nice to have someone say something and actually mean it. You know?'

'Sure.' Turquoise sat down. 'I know. What are you reading?'

Kristin held it up. It was a romance, the cover soft-focus and windswept as two lovers embraced on a shore. 'Trash,' she admitted.

Turquoise had to admit the trash looked to be working wonders. She thought how healthy Kristin appeared in spite of everything, flushed and rosy-cheeked. Hadn't she just broken up with Jax Jackson? Not that *that* piece of news had come as a surprise: Jax was a rat.

'Fictional heroes sure beat the ones in real life,' Turquoise commented.

Kristin put her shades back on. 'Maybe.'

An attendant wandered out and offered them refreshments. 'Make mine alcoholic,' decided Kristin, and Turquoise thought, what the hell, if you couldn't beat them.

Over the course of the afternoon the women became slowly drunk on salty lemony margaritas, happy to be in each other's company and to have stumbled across an unlikely kindred spirit. As the sun lowered in the sky Turquoise felt young and free and far away, reassured that in this world it was still possible to find someone with whom you connected. For today, she and Kristin weren't stars, they were just friends having a drink and talking the light out of the day. Kristin opened up about her sister, the struggles she had faced with her overbearing mom and how she had been affected by the Scotty Valentine scandal. Privately Turquoise had always thought Scotty might have been gay, but then she'd had experience enough of men who swung all ways imaginable, and in any case believed that when it came to it, most guys, given the right situation, had leanings.

'You figure Jax spilled to the press?' she probed.

'It couldn't have been anyone else. He's a moron. If he'd kept it shut maybe Bunny would still be alive.'

'Agree with you on the moron front.'

'D'you know Jax?'

'A bit.'

'How?'

'It doesn't matter. We're not in touch any more.'

'Oh.'

'He's an asshole, though, make no mistake.'

'So I've learned.'

Kristin didn't press Turquoise further, instead resuming a flustered monologue about the lover in town who was responsible for her newfound glow, and how since meeting him she was eating enough ice cream to sink a ship.

'So what's your story?' she asked after an impressive soliloquy. 'Here I am going on about myself and you've barely said a word. Am I boring you yet?'

'Not at all.' Turquoise laughed.

'Go on, then, tell me about you.' Kristin drew on the straw, vacuuming up the fruity sour dregs, and settled yet another empty glass on the patio. 'Are you seeing anyone?'

'Nah, too busy.'

'*Never* too busy for sex,' Kristin challenged, a naughty glint in her eye. 'Though working with Cosmo would probably put me off, too.'

Turquoise's brow shot up. 'What do you mean?'

'He's creepy. Don't you think? No one else says so, and

yeah, yeah, I know how everyone worships the ground he walks on, but to me he's like a pervy letch.'

She concealed her alarm. 'Hmm.'

'When I did *Lovestruck* with Ava,' Kristin hiccupped, 'Cosmo was always making these really…suggestive remarks—*really* suggestive. Usually Scotty was there so he reined it in, but I always got this sense that if I were by myself he wouldn't know when to stop.'

Turquoise said nothing.

'Maybe I'm paranoid,' Kristin finished quickly.

'Maybe. Maybe not.'

'You know how some people give you this uneasy feeling? I've always felt like that about him. Bunny used to call it "the shivers". When someone makes you anxious but you can't say why, you just know you don't want to be next to them.'

Turquoise nodded. 'I get that,' she said. The margaritas were making things foggy, but even so a niggling idea was playing at the back of her mind, like a knot loosening or a key slipping into a lock. A path through the chaos—if she was brave enough to follow.

Bringing Cosmo Angel down was only half the battle.

If Turquoise wanted to be free, truly free, there was only one course of action.

She interrupted Kristin. 'Are you still in touch with Jax?'

Kristin was surprised. 'No,' she retorted. 'I never want to see him again.'

A beat. 'Would you see him one last time?'

'What for?'

'For me.'

Kristin's blue eyes narrowed. In them was compassion

and concern and in that instant Turquoise knew unambiguously that this was right.

She had dirt on Jax—the night of Olympic-baton-fuelled
passion he would sooner die than reveal—and yet she had
never used it. Perhaps she had been on the receiving end of
blackmail too many times to ever consider it a tool at her
disposal. Now, it was.

Turquoise had been played her whole life and it was high
time she became the player.

'I can't tell you what this is about,' she said, 'but I need
you to trust me. Can you?'

Kristin nodded.

'I want you to take me to him. It's time he and I had a
little conversation.'

## 53

Jax's hired sports car swung into the parking lot of the Celestial Space Centre in Colorado, half an hour late. He and Leon were fronting the newest venture by entrepreneur Reuben van der Meyde, promising to bring space to the masses through galactic tourism.

*We've conquered this world,* ran the tagline. *Bring on the next.*

'We're on,' grovelled Jax's sycophantic manager. 'The big guy's here.'

Leon had arrived on point and was already in costume, resentful of Jax because the suit he'd been given was seriously damn hot. Relieved, he was escorted to the studio.

'Please accept my apologies, Mr Sway,' a nervous assistant was saying. She was new on the job. 'We didn't realise you'd be waiting, I know you must be a very busy man.'

'Don't sweat it,' Leon answered, wiping his brow with the back of his elbow.

Minutes later Jax was being steered into the shot, donning

a spacesuit of his own. Each was padded and white, proper Moon Landings stuff, with a clear orb of a helmet. Behind them a space capsule yawned open, its interior pearly-white, otherworldly, spooky, an alien pod that according to van der Meyde would be hurtling through the cosmos come 2020.

'You guys look great,' called van der Meyde. He was a ruthless South African. Paunchy, with a fuzz of unkempt hair, he was unremarkable to look at but utterly fearsome when it came to business. And it always came to business—what worth doing didn't?

'I want that one,' Jax announced within seconds, pointing at Leon's chest. The men's suits were identical save for a gold crest on Leon's left pectoral. Leon hadn't even noticed when he'd put it on. 'Step out of it, Sway.'

'It's too late to trade,' coaxed Jax's manager, already having had a bitch of a morning making excuses for his client. 'Let's just get the job done, shall we?'

'Bullshit,' argued Jax. 'Get me into that suit or else get me one the same.'

Leon's suit had been an ordeal to get into—no one onset was prepared to remove it.

'Be reasonable, man,' Leon said. 'These people have been waiting on your ass long enough.'

Jax scowled. He was still seething about the push-up humiliation on *Friday Later*, exacerbated when days after the men had locked horns at the Championship trials and Leon had wound up in a photo finish so close to victory that it had taken a bunch of officials poring over the stills to call it. Gold had been Jax's, it always was, but Leon had never engaged with the promise of triumph so acutely. Nought to full-throttle in less than a second, he had sprung from the blocks, every muscle working for that singular goal, his lungs aflame with burning lactic acid. He had felt the guys at his sides lose a pace, he'd been closing in, gaining on The Bullet, but it wasn't enough, it was never enough...

Yet Leon had been at Jax's shoulder; he was one step closer to claiming that ultimate podium. It was the quickest time he had ever run.

Today was about Jax proving there was only one alpha dog on the scene.

'I ain't doin' this shit,' he informed his manager, tearing at the neck of his spacesuit and failing to get any manoeuvre. 'Get me outta this thing *now*.'

In the end the nervous assistant took a marker to Jax's suit and painstakingly copied the gold crest. Leon watched from the sides as her fingers shook, but minutes later everyone agreed the replica was sufficient. Nothing could assuage Jax's bad mood, however.

'One of you gets in the pod,' explained van der Meyde, 'helmet on. The other outside, keep your helmet off. Let's get it both ways, see which looks better.'

Inside the capsule it was cool and echoey. Leon ran his fingers across a panel of controls, imagining the casing tearing through space in years to come and Earth's lonely marble appearing in the window, a drop of blue in the black.

'No way,' declared Jax when the time came to swop. 'I'm claustrophobic.'

'I'd really like to see it,' said the photographer. 'It won't take five.'

'What part of *No way* don't you understand, asshole?'

Leon emerged from the pod, drawing his height up next to Jax's, and everyone knew that to have Leon standing would be the better arrangement. The suit fitted like a dream.

Eventually Jax agreed to climb in, deliberately failing to meet the photographer's stipulations in the hope that the other set would get used, but in the event his lackadaisical posturing, the casual, almost bored attitude he adopted next to Leon's *Captain America* vibe, crackled with a dynamic that all the creative directors in the world couldn't have articulated.

'I like it,' van der Meyde approved. 'I like it a lot.'

Jax snapped the helmet off and gasped theatrically for air.

'There——' his manager grinned '——that wasn't so bad, was it?'

'What the fuck ever.'

'Great job, Jax,' everyone fawned, intent on massaging his ego.

'Many a legend has gone before you,' contributed van der Meyde, who was expert in the art and correctly hazarded that this kind of comment would be right up Jax's street. 'Space has been the ultimate frontier for decades and for generations. That's what you represent: fearlessness. It's why I wanted you, Jax. You're part of the universal family now.'

Until his nervous assistant, trying to be helpful, added: 'Just think of those poor monkeys they used to send up! Oh, they were so cute in their little space outfits…!'

A grim silence descended.

Jax's face twisted. 'You callin' me a monkey? You gettin' racist on my ass?'

The colour drained from her cheeks. 'God, no,' the assistant stumbled, 'no, of course not. What I meant was… I meant…' She trailed off, horrified.

'Give it a rest, Jax,' put in Leon.

Jax rounded like a bull about to charge. 'Tell me what to do one more time, Sway,' he threatened, 'and you're dead. Y'hear? *Dead.*'

'Whatever you say.' Leon turned to go but Jax pounced on him, totally unexpectedly, like a giant polar bear. The others rushed to intervene but not before Leon had been thrown into reverse, putting an arm out to break his fall and crashing into an expensive-looking nest of equipment. Jax rolled on top of him for several seconds, unable to bend his elbow efficiently enough in the suit to facilitate a swipe. Only when Leon pushed off from the ground did Jax resume motion, thrown unceremoniously backwards into the pod.

'My God!' quailed the manager. 'Somebody do something!'

Jax's legs churned as he struggled to find the floor. The company scattered, afraid of getting caught in the conflict. Van der Meyde staggered forward, with just enough time to roar, *'Jesus Christ, not the—!'* as Jax's storming frame careered towards his rival and threw them both into a glass case containing a billion-dollar model of the entrepreneur's Celestial Voyager. The men slammed in combat, spinning on their feet as Leon grabbed the neck of Jax's suit and they crashed in a shower of glass to the ground.

'JESUS CHRIST!' bellowed van der Meyde.

Jax swung at him again, his fist impacting uselessly on the cushion of the suit. Leon threw his entire weight into Jax's core, propelling him back, thwarted by a lighting stand until at last Jax was returned decisively to the pod. There was a brief scramble, a vision of Jax making for the hatch like some tentacled freak in an *Alien* movie, his face contorted, before Leon sealed the door. He turned and was confronted by a circle of bewilderment.

'OK,' he panted. 'Are we done yet?'

By the time he was out of the centre and clear of a rigorous debrief with his lawyer, it was getting dark. Leon arrived at the airport and called his girlfriend.

'Are you home?' he asked, looking forward to seeing her. He put a finger to his nose, which was still bleeding from the fight. His head throbbed but he'd insisted he didn't need medical attention. What he needed was an easy night.

There was a pause before Lisa said, 'Leon, listen. The witness fell through.'

It took a moment for his brain to slide into gear. 'What?'

'I'm sorry. The evidence didn't clear.'

So much for winding down—the last thing he wanted right now was a reminder of the excavation underway at his apartment. Lisa was fixated on it, poring over evidence and files and articles, any detail that she might have missed the first time, and while he supported the outcome it was as if their relationship was now becoming wholly defined by the tragedy.

Was Lisa with him for him, or for his connection to the biggest case she might ever get to work on? His home was these days inundated with reminders of Marlon and the pain he had learned with superhuman discipline to accept, and even when away she rarely let up. At the weekend they had visited Lisa's parents and she had barely stopped talking about it then, either. It was becoming an obsession. He didn't know how much more he could handle. Meeting Lisa was meant to have been a fresh start.

'Can we not talk about the witness?' It came out sharper than he'd intended but perhaps that was no bad thing. 'Look, I'll call you when I land. We're about to board.'

'Sure, baby,' she said quickly, sensing his anger, 'I'll pick you up from the airport.'

'I'm not sure I feel like coming back tonight.'

There was a pause. 'Sorry. I shouldn't have brought it up. It's just I feel like we're so close, you know—'

'Lisa, please…' He handed his documents to a steward, who gestured that he'd need to turn his phone off.

'Like there's one tiny detail I'm missing and then it's all gonna slot together—'

'Just stop, OK? This is taking over our lives.'

'Shouldn't it be?' Lisa pushed. 'Leon, this is your brother's murder we're talking about. Don't you want to see his assassin get what they deserve?'

'This might be a two-month project to you,' he answered, 'and maybe you can give up your life for that. But I've been surviving this for twelve years, and finally I'm starting to think about myself, what I want. How am I meant to move forward with this…*anguish* everywhere I turn? I need to be on it for the Championships—they're important to me.'

'Once the killer's found we can all sleep easy.'

'Can we? It won't bring Marlon back. Nothing will.'

'I know how difficult this has been for you…'

'No, you don't. You can't. *Difficult?* It doesn't come close. You'll never understand what we've been through and what it's taken for us to get past it, as a family, as a whole. This is a job to you, but to me it's everything. It's my life.'

'I understand that…'

'Then cool it.' Silence. 'I'll see you soon.'

'Leon, wait—'
But he'd already hung up.

The sky was the colour of a bruised peach as the jet soared off the runway. Leon rested his head against the seat, staring out of the window and hoping not to get recognised.

He considered calling Gordon when he arrived in LA, throwing his pre-comp regime out of the window and getting drunk…but he wasn't in the mood for more drama. It was clear something wasn't right with his friend. First there had been the anxious phone call asking to meet, and then the morning after Leon had returned from the coast Gordon had shown up at the apartment unannounced. His friend had been twitchy and riled, standing on the porch and shivering through his T-shirt. He'd refused Leon's offer to come in.

*There's somethin' I gotta tell you*, Gordon had said. *Somethin' you gotta know…*

*Shoot.* Leon had waited. *I'm listening.*

*It's big, man. I don't know how to say this…*

Then Lisa had rung, demanding to meet at the library to run through an archive. Despite Leon's attempts to draw it from him, Gordon had ducked out. They'd catch up next time.

It occurred to Leon that maybe it was about Lisa. She and Gordon were close—perhaps something had happened between them. He was disappointed by how little he cared.

He closed his eyes, willing himself to sleep.

The problem was, there was nobody he really wanted to talk to… Except her.

It was getting better, possibly, some days easier than others.

Robin Ryder. Rude, opinionated, insolent, outrageous, wonderful Robin Ryder. Leon's world was based on the notion that the mind could control the body, and power stemmed first from will and belief... So why wouldn't his heart listen?

The lights in the cabin were extinguished.

Robin and he were nothing to each other now.

Whatever happened, she was on her own.

## 54

In London, PC Joanna Priestly watched as her partner Bob Stanton wobbled back to the parked police vehicle through the driving rain. He carried a supermarket bag weighted down with sandwiches and sausage rolls: sometimes she thought Stanton had got into the job purely for how it allowed him to sit in a Ford panda all day and eat.

Never mind protecting and patrolling the capital's streets, every day was the same drawn-out exercise in lethargy and inertia: sitting bored with Stanton and abiding through clenched teeth his sexist, supercilious remarks. The force hadn't turned out to be the high-octane case-crushing roller coaster Jo had imagined it to be when she had first emerged as a bright-eyed novice…far from it. Would her breakout ever arrive?

'Pissing it down out there,' huffed Stanton, ducking into the car and shaking himself like a dog. He slammed the door and rummaged in the sodden bag. 'Crisps?'

'No, thanks, I'll pass.' Jo indicated and pulled out into

the traffic. The capital was slick with April showers, its roads darkly stained.

'Where are we going?' complained Stanton through a mouthful of food. A car in front cut her up so she had to brake hard, prompting him to mutter pointedly, 'Women drivers.'

'We've got a job to do, haven't we?' Jo said tightly, ignoring the comment because Stanton wanted a rise; her anger amused him. 'I don't want to sit in a car park all day.'

'Why not?' He ripped open a crackling bag, filling the car with the tang of salt and vinegar. 'Easiest ride in the world.'

Jo kept driving, concentrating on the road. In his day Stanton had been one of the best at the station, but after a career of accolades and awards he now saw no further reason to bother. Everyone had said when they were paired how lucky she was—Jo Priestly, quietly brilliant, the young apprentice being groomed by one of the best. She didn't feel all that lucky today...or any other day, for that matter.

The radio crackled. Stanton snatched up the call. 'Yeah?'

She fought to listen through the incessant sound of munching. They had a report from a concerned pensioner up in a block in Edmonton who hadn't seen her neighbour in months.

'Guess we'd better check it out,' mused Stanton reluctantly. 'Probably another batty old bag who can't remember when she last fed her cats.'

Jo changed gear and joined the dual carriageway. She didn't want to agree, and always tried to stay fresh whenever a new challenge was presented, but going on previous experience it was likely to end in a few jotted notes and a cup of milky tea drunk out of an Arsenal mug. If the lady offered biscuits Stanton would be made for the afternoon.

The block itself was a foreboding lump flanked by the grumble and whine of traffic. St George flags were pinned across balconies and windows like plasters over cuts, and dogs barked on stairwells that smelled sourly of urine. Jo led the way.

'Oh, thank God you came,' the woman wheezed gummily as she opened the door and invited them in. 'I wasn't sure whether to ring: when you get to my age you never know what you're dreaming up!'

'Hmm.' Stanton was already waiting on his cup of tea.

'Would you like a cup of tea?'

Jo said, 'No, thank you, if we could just—' at the same time as Stanton accepted.

'And if you've got any biscuits…?' he hollered after her as she Zimmer-framed into the galley kitchen.

'Can we just get this over with?' Jo snapped.

'You females are so uptight,' he retorted, collapsing fatly into a cushioned armchair. 'What's wrong with a little liquid to oil the pipes?'

With the tea served and Stanton greedily sugaring his, Jo withdrew her pad.

'It's down the way,' the woman warbled, perching nervously on the edge of her chair and extending a gnarled finger to indicate the direction. She had a crocheted shawl wrapped round her shoulders. 'Let me see…flat 39B, it is. Hilda. Hilda Sewell. Now, I've only met her once before and that's why I'm sure there's nothing to worry about, she likes to stay indoors, you understand, but I haven't seen the daughter either…'

Jo glanced up. 'The daughter?'

'That's right. Always struck me as rather strange, she did. But, like they say, each to their own...'

'How old is she?'

Stanton shot her a look as if to say, *What has that got to do with anything?*

'Mind if I help myself?' he cut in, plunging a knife into the Battenberg cake.

The woman was thrown. 'Yes, dear, of course.'

Jo gritted her teeth. 'You were saying...?'

'Oh, her age, I'm not sure, now you ask. Twenty,' she hazarded, 'or thereabouts?'

Jo tapped the end of the pen. 'And you haven't seen the daughter at all?'

'No.'

'Do you know her name?'

'I'm afraid I don't...' the woman said nervously. 'If I saw Hilda barely at all, I saw her daughter even less. They've lived here a long time, and as you can imagine I rarely leave the place myself.' She looked confused. 'I was sure I'd know if they'd moved on. More tea?'

Stanton grunted and held his cup out. He snatched a couple more Custard Creams.

'We're going to need to take a look,' said Jo kindly. 'I'm sure it's nothing to worry about, Mrs Fletcher, but you did the right thing calling us.' She slipped the pad into her back pocket. Something about the situation—the tinkle of a tea-spoon against Stanton's porcelain china, the muffled groan of the road behind Mrs Fletcher's double glazing, the faint discourse of a Radio 4 programme filtering through from the kitchen—sent a chill down her spine.

Stanton was disinclined to leave the warmth of the arm-chair and it was only a glance at the clock—they would be knocking off shift in an hour—that prompted him to join her.

'Should I come along?' asked Mrs Fletcher, hovering at the doorway.

'No, thank you.' Jo smiled. 'We'll let you know what we find. In the meantime, try to relax and put this from your mind. No point in worrying. Rest assured we receive plenty of calls like this one and they rarely amount to any-thing sinister.'

'I'm not in trouble, am I?'

'Of course not.'

'That's a relief.' The old woman put a hand to her chest. 'I don't want any badness.'

'I'm sure it's innocent enough.'

*'I'm sure it's innocent enough?'* Stanton challenged as they made their way along the concrete platform to flat 39B. An argument was exploding several doors down, a shower of expletives straining through. 'What is this, *Midsomer Murders*? This place is about as likely to carry foul play as bloody Strangeways.'

They came to a stop by a plain door bearing the rusted number.

'Here we are.' Jo knocked.

'To hell with that,' Stanton snorted. 'I've got a pint with the lads to make.' He battered the door with his fist. 'Po-lice! Anyone home?'

No answer.

'We'll come back tomorrow,' Stanton said.

'Bullshit!' Jo was outraged. 'I'm getting a warrant.'

'You can't.'

'Then I'm taking the door off, if I have to. That old lady's not going to be able to sleep tonight unless we get answers.'

Stanton waved his arm. 'Aw, she'll be fine once she's tucked up in bed with a Nesquik and *Poirot*. Let's move.'

Jo shoved the door with her shoulder. Stanton laughed meanly at the futility of her effort until to both their surprise the door gave, caught on a weak lock.

Immediately the smell assaulted them. Jo gagged, clamping a hand over her nose and mouth. Stanton muttered, 'Christ alive, what the...?'

The smell was worse inside. Jo had never experienced anything like it. It was metallic and foul and acrid, bitter with rot. The flat was dark and unbearably still, like a tomb.

'There she is,' Jo rasped.

Not that Hilda Sewell was at all recognisable: a skeletal figure, upright, her mouth open, the skin decaying and sallow, the scalp mottled and visible through patches of bald.

'Where's the daughter?' Jo asked.

Stanton turned. 'Hey?'

'The daughter.' Finally, she was on to something. 'We need to find her.'

## 55

For Ivy Sewell, the best thing about working at the Palisades Grand was that she got to play out a version of the big night nearly every day of the week. As LA's primary arena, the Palisades attracted crowds in their tens of thousands, herded like sheep, as unthinking and unseeing as those beasts as they were steered in nervous little groups towards the food counters and through the turnstiles. Yet seeing them as animals took away some of the magic: any fool could work an abattoir and Ivy was no butcher. It took something else, something different…something *special* to kill a human, let alone dozens. Execution on an unprecedented scale had to be planned and plotted to a margin of zero error.

Watching the masses thread through every night cemented her timetable: the hour the doors opened, the crush that descended ten minutes before the support, the security networks that kept the whole thing carelessly, stupidly rolling according to the rules and regulations, where Ivy needed to be and with whom...

She had already isolated her entrance point. Three guys alternated on that spot, checking the punters' tickets and searching their bags full of gum and cameras and the occasional confiscated vodka disguised in a water bottle. Any one of them could be working that night and it was essential she made allies of them all.

Nicki Soba was on rota this evening. Small and Asian with quick, flinty eyes, he believed he was above the menial tasks of a doorman. She stepped closer to Nicki as she spoke, flashing her smile and hanging on to every dismal word he said.

'I can't wait till the season's over,' Nicki grumbled, picking his teeth.

*Oh, it will be. Over for you, over for them all...*

'Standing here every day like a fucking ape,' he complained, ushering another party through with a grimace. 'Anyone could do this job.'

'But I've seen how they respect you,' Ivy flattered. 'They listen to you.'

'Ain't got a lot of choice, have they?' Nicki straightened, unable to help being at least slightly bolstered by the compliment. 'It's my rules or they're out of here.'

'That's so powerful,' she encouraged, thinking a man like Nicki Soba would never understand how it felt to be truly, absolutely powerful: to have a crusade.

He would find out soon enough.

'Guess.' He shrugged, tilting his chin. 'One day it'll be me on the big stage.' His words surfaced like relics, overshadowed by years of defeat—instead of the confidence

Nicki had once imbued they flopped wearily out of his mouth, the routine claim bored by its own monotony, and which on good days still had the ability to make him feel inspired but on bad ones shot down the remaining scrap that clung to hope.

Ivy had done her research. 'It should be,' she agreed. 'I don't know how half these acts have made it. Nine times out of ten they're talentless. There's no justice in the world.'

'No kidding.'

'Take the Platinum Awards,' she said, 'what a farce. All those egos in one room, and the only difference between them and us is that they got the break. Not that they'd ever admit it. Makes you wonder what the world would be like if they all got wiped out.'

'Huh.' He folded his arms.

'If they all got annihilated, just vanished one day.' She let him picture it. 'The fans are such losers they'd probably kill themselves. It's not like they've got lives of their own.'

Nicki respected her attitude. 'You working that night?'

'Wouldn't miss it.'

He tilted his head, regarding her anew. 'What did you say your name was?'

'Ivy.'

A smirk. 'Like the poison?'

Her lips twisted into a smile—for once, it was genuine.

Supervisor Graham was ogling her from the burger stand, a glint of possessive jealousy in his eye. She still had the afternoon shift to get through.

'Nice talking to you, Nicki.'

She knew he'd remember her when it counted.

# 56

'Unbelievable!' Jax spat, chucking back the last of his Powerade. 'What a load of frickin' *horse* shit.' He wiped his mouth, crunched the plastic in an angry fist and tossed it with force into the trashcan. 'What's a guy gotta do to get a bit of peace in this goddamn town?'

Cindy Shepard, PA extraordinaire, came to her boss and ran her hands across his muscular shoulders. Jax had recently had another tattoo done, a self-designed gold-tipped bullet at the nape of his neck, and the skin there was raised and sore.

'Let them speculate,' she offered, rubbing down his tensions. Jax's Lamborghini had conked out on the drive back to Pacific Heights and a rampant army of questioning fans had set upon him. Was it true that a fight had broken out in Colorado? Was his Fastest Man title under threat? Could Leon Sway have what it took to beat The Bullet?

'There's no way Sway can outrun you.' She kissed the tattoo. 'You know that…'

'Do I?' Jax rounded on her, scowling. 'Maybe you're as full of BS as the rest.'

Cindy arranged her features into a sympathetic expression. It was challenging when faced with over six feet of delicious dark muscle and the hard outline of an extremely handsome cock. 'You wanna show me what you're really made of, stud?'

'I'm not in the mood,' he lambasted, batting her away. 'I say when I want you and that's when I take you. Understood?'

'Yes, sir.'

Jax stalked out to the patio, pausing to take a salty breath. He allowed the sea air to tease his open shirt and ripple over his broad chest, down past his shorts and over his bare legs, as he reflected not for the first time on the phenomenon of his own body.

Was it enough? It had to be. Leon seemed to be grasping the reins at every damn public event they were invited to. *Friday Later* had been a shambles, not to mention the altercation at van der Meyde's Celestial Centre, after which Jax had fired his manager for no particular reason and kicked over a thousand-dollar camera tripod that had swiftly been added to his list of incurred expenses. It was all Leon's fault for pushing him out of shot.

There was only one way to claw his reputation back.

The Championships. He had to retain his gold medal.

*Nobody can beat me!* Jax assured himself. *I'm the fastest in the world! I'm a machine. I'm a legend. I'm Jax Jackson. I'm going down in the fucking history books.*

Sway would have to step over his stinking corpse to reach the finish first.

'I know just what's gonna relax you,' said Cindy, joining him. She looped her arms round his waist and lowered her hands to the main attraction, which despite Jax's anger began to swell. He ought to resist it: the less sex he had, the more fury he'd pour into his run...

'You wanna get the timer out?' she purred, trailing over his hard-on.

'To hell with that,' he growled. Cindy's lips were sweet and he attacked them so zealously that their teeth knocked together. His erection was about to pop. 'I wanna get hot.'

'You are hot.' She peeled off his shirt and ran her fingers across his pecs.

'I wanna get sweaty.'

She wanted to say 'You are sweaty' but that didn't sound right.

Instead she breathed, 'Lead the way, baby.'

Jax moved towards the basement sauna he'd had installed a month ago, kissing his PA as they descended the stairs, his tongue forced deep into her mouth. Cindy responded by unbuttoning her shirt, wondering if she would ever be able to come to work and actually get anything productive done, and freeing the nipple-less bra she had going on beneath. As they fell through the sauna door Jax swooped for her breasts like an eagle on its prey, his tongue switching and flicking, bringing his lover closer and closer to rapture.

The sauna was raging hot and ripe with the aroma of scented pine. Jax steered her backwards on to one of the smooth wooden benches, where he sank to his knees to taste the moisture between her legs. Cindy's breath was shallow and frantic as she struggled to take in the heat, close as a wall, but her ecstasy was such that she couldn't bear to stop, locking her ankles around Jax's neck and pushing herself against him so that his tongue went deep. It was rare for Jax to go down on a woman and he quickly lost interest, rising majestically to his feet and removing the last of his clothes. Cindy gasped at the glory of his glossy, perspiring chest and the iron-solid dick rising proud from a bush of black hair.

Jax mounted her, the gold chain around his neck trickling and twinkling between Cindy's gasping lips as he made her beg for it.

'I want your cock,' she moaned, clasping his ass and bringing him closer, though he pulled away, taunting her, forcing her into desperation. 'Now!' she howled.

Bodies slick, their skin soldered with suction, Cindy's hands crossed her boss's belly, finding the coarse trail that ran from his navel to his groin and then to the head of his penis. She wrapped her fingers round its width and drew from them both a groan of desire, using her wrist to bring him off. Finally she raised her knees and pulled him inside, driving him in and out, back and forth, locked with him at their most essential point, the burn of the room almost unbearable as the parched air scorched her throat and she began to feel light-headed, delirious and dehydrated but totally ready to come.

'Oh, yeah, big boy!' she cried, thinking she had never been so wet inside and out, dripping and sodden and slipping around on the bench so that if it weren't for Jax's weight pinning her down she'd have slid on her back right across the floor. Treating her lover to his favourite bonus, though he never admitted it after the fact, she clasped him to her and slipped her index finger inside his asshole. With a guttural,

repressed cry, Jax tensed around her and bucked to ejaculation, squeezing and grinding through her till he was spent.

'Jesus fuck,' he mumbled, rolling off her. Cindy let the
spasms rock through her, one after the other, and reached
to touch him but he sprang to his feet.

'I need a drink.'

Jax tugged on the door—and again, and again. It didn't
budge.

'What the…?' Using his whole weight, he dragged again.
Something was stuck.

'What's the matter?' Cindy whined.

He grunted, giving it a haul.

'Jax, Mr Jackson, sir…?'

'What d'you think's the damn matter?' There was a reedy
edge to Jax's voice, a shade close to panic. 'Freakin' door's
got jammed.'

Cindy rose to his aid but he threw her off. The oxygen
burned in her lungs.

'I'm roasting to death in here,' she wigged. 'Do something!'

'What does it look like I'm doing?' he lashed, jerking the
sauna door, and, when it failed to give, slamming his bulk
against it repeatedly. 'We're trapped!'

Cindy whimpered. 'Oh my God.' Frantically she doused
the coals in water, sending a puff of searing mist rising into
the chamber.

'What the hell are we gonna drink now?' Jax spluttered,
drips flying off his lip. 'You just made the place three times
hotter, you dumb cunt!'

'Oh God,' Cindy said again, hunched over the benches,

wheezing for breath. 'We're going to die. We're going to roast in our own skins!'

'Quit freaking, that's what panic buttons are for.' Jax punched the red panel with an open palm, blinking beads off his eyelids. The coals hissed and steamed.

'Who's going to hear it?' Cindy was gasping, dread stealing what air she was able to take in. 'We're in your basement, Mr Jax Jackson, Jax, sir! We're the only ones here!'

Jax watched the blinking light. A muscle clenched in his jaw.

'Shit.'

'What do you mean, *shit*?' she shrieked. 'Come up with something!'

'Shut your pie-hole, bitch!' Jax warned. He slumped down, his back against the wall. 'I'm gonna sue whatever sons of whores installed this joke.'

'If we ever get out!'

'Save your breath,' he huffed, 'you're gonna need it.' But they were both still panting from having screwed so hard and his words fell on deaf ears.

'Nobody knows we're here,' Cindy squeaked. 'How long can we survive?'

Jax suppressed a flourish of fear, stamping it out before it caught hold. He was a champion, a superhero, and not being able to open a bastard door wouldn't be the end! Imagine! What a way for the titan to go, locked naked in his own goddamn sauna with his own goddamn secretary. How would the world recover? It was unthinkable. He pictured the paramedics recovering his slack-skinned body, flaccid as an over-boiled ham.

'Don't move,' advised Jax, standing and inflating his

chest, 'conserve energy. Stay low, heat rises. I'm gonna get us out of here.'

Cindy started crying. She lifted the empty jug and sucked desperately at the dregs of water before collapsing on the floor. 'I'm going to be sick.'

The thought of slipping about in baked vomit galvanised Jax into a second bout of action. 'Come on!' he roared, smashing against the door and wrenching the handle with all his might. 'Come on, you fuck!' He punched the wall, cracking his knuckles. *'Damn!'*

'Isn't there an axe or something?'

'An axe?'

'We'll have to smash through. Why isn't there an emergency axe?'

'I'm gonna smash you through if you don't shut your cake-hole; you're trippin' me out, girl, chill the hell down.'

'Chill? I wish! We're cooking!' Cindy surrendered to full-blown panic. 'We're going to die, don't you get it? *We're going to die!'*

'Wait.' Jax lifted his head. 'I hear somethin'.'

Silence—then, yes, distant voices, female voices, coming closer...

'HELP!' Cindy shouted, leaping up. 'HELP US!' She battered the door with her fists, so that when it suddenly opened she went hurtling, naked, through, sprawled and weeping.

'Oh,' said one of their visitors, 'it's you again.'

Jax squinted. 'What...?' he spluttered through his sweat and relief. *'Kristin?'*

What was she doing here?

'What are you doing here?'

'Interrupting, by the looks of things.' Kristin was carefree and casual in a white tee and denim shorts, her blonde hair in a topknot and her limbs long and tanned. Immediately Jax forgot all about his brush with death and returned his attention to his dick.

'You just saved our lives.' Cindy was scrabbling up, gasping her appreciation and clamping her hands ineffectively across her modesty.

'That's lucky,' said a new voice.

To Jax's considerable alarm Turquoise da Luca stepped into view. She looked like a goddess, all dark green eyes and ebony hair, her tits beautifully round in a peach silk vest.

'What's going on?' he demanded, feeling faintly worried.

'You're going to do me a favour, Jax,' said Turquoise. 'And I'd say you owe me right about now, wouldn't you?'

## 57

Scotty Valentine's first public appearance since his sexuality exploded stole the headline slot on a late-night news show. Speaking out about the scandal was deemed by management to be the only way forward: with luck they could spin it towards a generation of young fans who were carving their own identities and would welcome a positive, unafraid role model. In an ideal world they would sever ties to Fenton Fear and play Scotty as the victim, but since the label had as much to lose through Fenton's conviction as they did through the expiration of their number-one boy band, there wasn't a great deal of choice.

Millions would be tuning in to see the biggest heartthrob of twenty-first-century music account for the deception. Some believed Scotty had tricked their youngsters in an unforgivable way; others questioned whether that wasn't the nature of fantasy, gay or straight, and pitied the poor boy who was compelled to toss his private life to the lions.

Right now the poor boy was bolted to the make-up chair,

his knuckles white as they gripped the armrests. Given that Scotty hadn't left his apartment in weeks, not only did he have to contend with the horror and humiliation of laying his intimate secrets bare (he'd been briefed in every feasible question and had prepared his responses, each as evasive as the last), but he was also wrestling with agoraphobia. Every so often the ropes he had shackled it with sprang free and he thought he was going to faint.

'You feeling OK?' asked the make-up girl as she slathered foundation around his sunken eyes. 'It'll go great, Scott,' she said kindly. 'You've got nothing to be ashamed of.'

He gulped. 'I look like death.'

'Not once I've finished with you.' Though he noticed she didn't dispute it.

It was agony waiting in the green room for the other panellists to speak. One was a politician and the other a comedian, the idea being to capture a cross section of society that would give fair representation to whatever debate had been sparked that week. But Scotty understood he was no sideline commentator, he was at the centre of this examination and the audience and the nation were only killing time before the main event.

He wasn't even used to making these appearances all by himself. He'd always had Fraternity to bounce off, five of them together, and he endured a searing bolt of loneliness.

Live TV... Was there anything more petrifying?

'Now our next guest has been at the centre of a storm of controversy,' their chair announced, seamlessly changing into a lower, graver gear. Scotty consulted the time and saw that there was still an hour remaining: clearly this would be no surface-skimming interview.

'Scott Valentine has ducked out of the limelight since an exposé destroyed squeaky-clean boy band Fraternity.' People had long ago stopped calling him Scotty: he didn't warrant the cute factor any more. 'Here, at last, choosing *The State Show* to give his first candid conference, Scott answers those questions you've all been burning to ask. Please welcome him generously—' the chair stood up and the cameras swung round '—it's Scott Valentine!'

Scotty very nearly scrammed, and had to be manually shoved on to the stage by a producer. Instantly the lights were blinding and the audience's yells rang hollow in his ears. Even if he freaked out, he figured, and buckled like a weirdo to the floor, there was no way his image could be any worse than it already was. The realisation was strangely freeing.

The chair didn't take his hand; he embraced him, patting him solidly on the back. The audience continued to clap despite the cue telling them to stop. A cry rose up from the audience—'We love you, Scotty!'—followed by yet more whoops and yells.

He thought he might cry. Perhaps there was hope, after all.

Kristin sat back on her sister's bed and tuned into *The State Show*, just in time to see Scotty take to the stage and face the performance of his life.

Her ex-boyfriend looked pale and fraught, but just on the right side of disagreeable to remain appealing, in the way that only the handsome sufferer can. Directly above the plasma screen was a torn poster of the man himself, pinned up lovingly by Bunny, bronze-skinned and smiling. What a difference a year made. If her sister were here, what would she think?

Bunny's room had been cleared. Many of her belongings had been sold and the proceeds given to an animal charity (Kristin's suggestion), but her spirit remained and it was soothing to be in the space her sister had spent so much time in. Bunny's more expensive possessions had stayed with Ramona, who was moving out of her mourning-mom phase in suspicious tandem with the wrap of the TV documentary. Her mother had jetted south to Hawaii, claiming she needed time out, but managing to tip off several contacts to ensure she was photographed on a beach reading a self-help book and looking gloriously thin in a bikini.

'I can't lie,' Scotty was saying. 'The facts speak for themselves. I should never have pretended to be someone I wasn't. I accept responsibility.'

But had he been in love with Fenton? Had it been a fully-fledged relationship?

'I'm afraid I can't discuss that.' Scotty was composed, his every utterance rehearsed and analysed by a military PR team. 'Fenton and I grew close over a number of months and neither of us were thinking clearly. That's all I can say.'

'Fenton's been arrested. Are you happy?'

'I can't talk about that, I'm sorry.'

'Should he be in prison?'

'Like I said, I can't talk about that today.'

The panellists were doing their job but they would never get the juice no matter how hard they pressed. These were the lines Scotty had been given. Fenton was still languishing in jail, as much to pacify an army of irate moms across America who felt he somehow posed a menace to their misled, heartbroken daughters (more to the point, their sons?) as on any criminal suspicion. It would buy Scotty time to get the public back on side and to weave whichever story he chose without fear of it being countered. The tack was to wheel out the same phrases, refuse to meet on the same points but to seem genuinely apologetic about doing so, and to appear frank and willing without actually giving much away.

'Are you gay?' the comedian asked, in trademark style tight to the point.

'Yes.' Scotty didn't shy away from that question. 'But that isn't the mistake I made. Being gay is no mistake. The mistake I made was in lying to my fans. My fans are the most important people to me in the world. Without them, I'm nothing.'

'Why did you conceal it?'

'It was the hardest thing I ever did. When I decided to come on this show I promised myself I'd be me, not the idea of me or the boy-band fantasy or whoever that was, but just be me. So that's what you get…just a guy. And I'm sitting here now telling you it was tough. I was dealing with a lot of confusion, a lot of feelings and stuff I didn't know what to do with. Anyone who has struggled with his or her sexuality will identify. It can't be suppressed, however much you try. And I tried.' He ran a hand through his hair, still as beautiful as ever, and gave a wry laugh. 'I had girlfriends and I figured I loved them but it never felt… I don't know, it never felt *right*. Then the band got big, bigger than anyone expected, and the whole thing spun away. There was never going to be a right time to do what I needed to… Ever.'

For the first time since they'd split, Kristin felt a twinge of sympathy, untainted by envy or resentment or bitterness, just a pure tug of understanding.

'And Fenton made it easier?' the chair pressed, sensing Scotty's guard was down.

'Obviously people are going to want to talk about Fenton,' he replied, 'but I can't. I'm really not allowed to talk about him right now.'

'He must have helped you, guided you...?'

'I arrived at this decision by myself.'

'And he helped with the loneliness?'

'It *is* a lonely thing. Anyone who's been through it will tell you. That's why I want to speak out instead of hiding away. There's a whole heap of expectation, from family, from friends, and in my case from the public as a whole. Holding your hands up and saying who you are takes a lot of guts and if I can do it then I hope to inspire others...'

Kristin killed the channel and the screen extinguished to black. She'd heard enough.

Swinging her legs off the bed, she unpinned the poster of Scotty tacked to the wall, folded it carefully and placed it in the trash. She closed her eyes and breathed in through her nose, believing against all reason that she could still detect Bunny's fragrance and hairspray and all the sticky-sugar products that had defined her life: sickly, intoxicating, hated, adored, the bitter-sweetness that would always be associated with her sister.

Downstairs she took a couple of calls, one from her manager about her upcoming appearance at the ETV Platinum Awards—the ceremony was taking place in July at LA's Palisades Grand Arena: as the music industry's flagship, broadcast to millions across the globe, it was a coup to be asked to take to the stage—and a second about her album design. The new material was a far cry from the whimsical naivety of her early efforts: this was harder, raw to the bone, a coming of age that for the first time expressed who Kristin really was. It had taken her through the Scotty break-up, through Bunny and her mother and the split with Jax, finally an expression of who she had become. She loved it.

She smiled when she thought of his name. *Jax Jackson.*

What a fool he was. Giving Turquoise Jax's ultra-protected private address and accompanying her to see him had been a pleasure. In Italy Turquoise had given nothing away, but assured Kristin that she too had a cross to bear—and Jax owed her big style.

It was time Jax faced up to responsibility. And if he were put in a delicate position (though any more delicate than his sauna stunt was difficult to imagine) then the more the better. He was a cheat and a liar. Men like Jax warranted everything they had coming.

On cue a magazine cover, discarded on the kitchen counter by her mom, caught Kristin's eye. Jax was topless, his tattoos a wreath around his neck, an undiluted challenge in his dead-straight gaze to the camera. The headline read: IS THIS MAN BULLETPROOF? She picked it up. Inside, a six-page spread dominated on Jax and his archrival Leon Sway: the athletes were gearing up to the summer Championships.

*'The Olympic sprinter is naturally aggressive,'* the article read. *'He needs to be wild when he gets out on to the track, ready to kill if he needs to. Like an animal unleashed after months in a cage, it's the force and the fury that will carry him to the finish; he's got to be fired up, ready to burst with*

*pent-up frustration, so that by the day of the race he's so pumped he's ready to attack—and attack he will. That frustration can be attributed to one thing: testosterone. Athletes need the hormone in bucket-loads to perform, and months ahead of a major championship they'll be sworn off sex until after the event—when they'll really let go. There's no telling what these guys are capable of when they're preparing for the track. Jax Jackson, the fastest man ever to have lived, is no exception.*

Kristin closed the rag. Judging by the display she and Turquoise had witnessed, Jax was far from succeeding with the sex ban.

That was the problem, and precisely why his hours on the track were numbered.

Jax couldn't resist, and that would surely be his downfall.

## 58

The penultimate leg of Robin's tour took her to Las Vegas, where she was performing at the world-famous Orient Hotel. The hotel had been scene two years ago to the legendary *Eastern Sky* movie premiere, during which a stalker had broken security and gained access to its star Lana Falcon's suite. Lana would have died were it not for the owner of the Orient, Robert St Louis, coming to her rescue. Today Lana and Robert were the sweethearts of Sin City. One look betrayed how happy they were: theirs was a true love story.

'Feeling lucky?' Matt asked after the show.

'Is that a come-on?' Robin opened the door to her dressing room. Blood was coursing through her, her legs like jelly and the crash of the crowd still echoing through her ears.

'You wish.'

'Always, Matt, always.'

'C'mon, the others are up for it. This is Vegas, baby! You've got a responsibility.'

'To what?'

'Party. Aren't you a rock star?'

'My feet hurt.'

He cocked his head. 'In ten?'

She sighed. 'Fine, you win.'

'Better believe it, I'm on fire when I get in a casino.'

'On the 2p machines in Southend?'

'That was one time and I was too pissed to go on anything else. Besides, it was 10p, not 2p. I won us a quid that night, remember?'

She grinned. 'Go away, I need to get changed.'

Alone, Robin slipped into jeans, a vest and jacket, and removed the more outlandish aspects of her make-up. Satisfied she looked like herself again, she pulled together what she needed for the night and made for the door.

There was no reason it should have caught her eye...other than the handwriting.

*No*, she begged, her throat constricting. *Not you. Please, not you.*

It was a photograph, upside down so that its white belly was turned to the ceiling, bearing only her name, which was scrawled in that familiar, creepy, childlike lettering:

**ROBIN.**

She gripped the dresser.

The picture showed a woman of about fifty sitting in an armchair and regarding whoever was taking the image through half closed, or else sneering, eyes. Her surroundings were gloomy, electric light rather than daylight. On the mantelpiece a clock stared pale-faced, its hands trapped at a quarter to three. There was a painting on the wall, dark and melancholy.

The room was bizarrely familiar, even though Robin had never been there before.

Fear filled her. *I'm closer than you think.*

The red-haired doppelganger from San Francisco flashed through Robin's mind. She clung on before fading, like an imprint on wet sand.

Her stalker had found her. The grudge was back.

Robin shivered, screwing the photo up in her hand and slinging it in the bin.

The Desert Jewel casino was zinging with the clash of cash, drinks flowing and money rushing, the scent of changing fortunes ripe in the air. Robin and her crew were escorted to a private area where Barney hit the craps table at the same time as Matt hit on a blonde with insanely long legs. Polly had got there first and was already drunk on champagne, chatting up two German magician brothers whose world tour had taken them to the Strip.

'Robin, meet Steffen!' She was dragged into the fray. Steffen had statement hair, a number one on either side of a Mohawk-meets-metrosexual strip. His brother was too busy kissing Polly for her to tell what he looked like.

'It's an honour to meet you,' Steffen said with a thick German lilt.

She clinked her glass with his before downing the alcohol. She craved oblivion. All she wanted was to get so drunk she could no longer think.

'I'm surprised they let you in,' she told him.

'Why?'

'I don't know, couldn't you fix the game or something?'

He was amused. 'Let's see.'

At the roulette he had an uncanny knack but she wasn't convinced it was anything other than luck. The more vodka she had, the more attractive she found him. She didn't want to be by herself tonight.

'Let's go to a club!' screamed Polly.

Outside the stream of cars on the Strip rushed like coins through the slots, a streaky blur like an over-exposed photograph. They all piled into Steffen's private vehicle and headed to 'the sickest club in town'. Robin was so drunk she couldn't even vouch for who said it. Each time the eerie photo reared its head she slammed it back down, willing herself to forget the gloomy image and the spooky writing that had etched out her name.

*It's nothing. Just scaremongering. These people never do anything; they're cowards.*

On the back seat, packed in tight, Steffen took her hand. By the time they reached the VIP entrance of the club it had meandered up to her thigh.

In the bar, they got more and more drunk. The shots kept coming, lines being raked up in the loos and before she knew it she was kissing Steffen, she thought she kissed his brother at one point, maybe she was kissing Matt as well. It was ages since she had let go. *I need this*, she kept telling herself. *I deserve this.* The tour was almost over; she had just one more venue before her big appearance at the Platinum Awards took her back to LA.

Another shot was passed round but this one tipped her over the edge. The room lurched and she started to feel ill. She stood up and the wall skewed.

'Whoa, are you OK?' Steffen asked, rising to steady her.

'Fine,' Robin managed. Shrugging him off, she staggered

to the bathroom, through three sets of doors and two stair-wells and thinking she must have gone wrong because next she was stumbling down a passage, the walls polished and glossy as apples, and heading for a single narrow door at the end.

When she opened it, the whole of the Vegas Strip ran out before her, thousands of feet below. The room was huge and square, black as the sea at night. Its floor was transparent glass: nothing between her and the distant ground. At its centre was a lone porcelain commode, which she headed for, walking on air, flying through drunkenness, and sat on it, fully clothed, to pull herself together. Sitting on the sky with Vegas spread beneath her was as surreal as it was trippy. Only in Vegas could you go to the bathroom and feel like a god.

Music pumped into the room. Robin closed her eyes. A familiar refrain started up: the charity single she had done with Puff City and the Olympians.

The time she had sung with Leon...

Just thinking his name was a knife through her heart. She had to let him go but she couldn't. She wanted to know if he was OK. She thought about him all the time. She dreamed about him. He was the first thing she thought about in the morning and the last thing she thought about at night. She longed for him and ached for him.

She remembered almost telling him her fears that night on the beach; how she hadn't because she was too damn stubborn and stupid and hadn't wanted to let him in. She wished she had. She wanted his arms around her now more than she had ever wanted anything.

Leon might be lost to her, but Robin vowed that as soon

as the tour was done she would go to the police and tell them what she knew about Puff City. She couldn't be sure, and she'd lied to Shawnella when she'd told her she wasn't afraid. But there was no choice.

It was the only way for Leon to run free.

When the song finished and her tears had dried, she returned to the party. Steffen pulled her into his arms and soon after that she was asleep.

# 59

Shawnella Moore stomped out on to Slink Bullion's pool patio and slammed a magazine article on to her boyfriend's chest. Its headline read:

DEMAND MOORE COLLECTION STINKS, SAYS SLINK.

The impact roused him from sleep.

'What the fuck?' Slink demanded, sitting up and rubbing his eyes. The medallions around his neck dislodged with the movement, catching the sun.

'What is this?' Shawnella raged, jabbing a finger at the piece. 'How dare you slate my fashion range, after all the work I put in, you *bastard*!' She was on the brink of tears but battling against it because she refused to give him the satisfaction.

Slink scanned the piece. ''S no big deal,' he diagnosed lazily.

'No big deal? This is my project, I've worked on this collection for—'

'You seen Principal?' He waved a hand, batting her concerns away. 'Brother's meant to be here by now...'

'Did you really say that? Did you say all this stuff? That I'm an *embarrassment*? That my range is...' Shawnella consulted the paper '...*like Halloween came early*?'

'Maybe it ain't your vibe, baby, d'you feel what I'm sayin'—?'

'No, I don't "feel what you're saying". All these years I've supported you and then when I finally do something on my own you go and wreck it for me.'

He made to grab her. 'C'mere, sweet stuff, I get it, you want a little attention...'

'Too late.' Her eyes flashed. 'Only time you give me attention is when you want a hole to put your dick into.' She checked out his shorts and sure enough the goods were there.

'You're a selfish asshole,' she said witheringly. 'You always have been.'

'Selfish?' He rose to his feet. Shawnella took a pace back. 'Take a look around, and watch what it is you're sayin'.'

'You promised me the world.'

'And I gave it to you.' Again he gestured to their backdrop. His equating emotional fulfilment with the riches his cash could buy was desolate.

'You said you'd bring me in on the music,' she told him angrily.

'Aw, whatever, girl, you can't have thought I was serious...'

Her lip trembled. 'How can you be so cruel?'

*'You can't sing!'* he spluttered.

Shawnella was shaking. She threw a glance at the discarded magazine and said:

'I did somethin' on my own, without you, and fact is you don't like it. You'd sooner I was waitin' here on the bed for you to come home with my legs wide open.'

He shrugged. 'If you like.'

'But only if you don't already have some hooker in tow.'

Slink had the audacity to roll his eyes.

'Not any more,' croaked Shawnella. 'I'm better than this.'

'You threatenin' me?'

'I'm giving you the facts. I'm leaving. It's over.'

He sneered. 'A'ight. Do what you like, see if I care.'

'That's all you have to say?'

'You're overreactin',' he said, amused by her outburst. 'You'll be back.'

'Like hell I will. When we first got together you told me you loved me. How many other women have you said that to?'

He pushed past her, through the mansion doors, where he opened the refrigerator and withdrew a can. 'Ain't you got someplace to be?' he asked, bored by the confrontation.

Shawnella withdrew the only card she had left. Her ace.

'If you know what's good for you,' she breathed, laying it on the line, 'you'll fess up and you'll do it quick.'

He popped the can and took a drawn-out sip. He wiped his mouth.

'Fess up to what?'

'You know what.'

'Do I?'

'People are gettin' close, Slink.'

'My ass.'

'They are.'

'Get outta my crib, bitch, and don't come back.'

'I won't, don't you worry.'

Shawnella didn't even stay to pack her bags. This had to be a fresh start. Slink had bought all of her possessions and she didn't want any of them—except the BMW.

He exploded as she flounced out of the door and unlocked the gleaming vehicle.

'Has G said somethin'?' he boomed, striding on to the drive in his flip-flops, finally engaged. 'Who's talkin', huh? *Who's talkin'?*'

Shawnella's tyres squealed before she sped away.

'Good luck, shithead. You'll need it.'


When Leon arrived home on Sunday night, something was different. The apartment was cleared of all Marlon paraphernalia, the surfaces freshly cleaned, the wardrobe half empty and the toothbrush and bubble soak missing from the bathroom. Lisa was gone.

A note explained that she had decided to return to New York for a while. Its tone was curt and Leon knew he had offended her: the way Lisa saw it she had put her life on hold to account for the loss of Marlon's, and all she'd received in return was grief from his brother.

Regret gave way to relief. His heart had never been in it with Lisa. She was an intelligent, beautiful woman, and one day she'd make a man very happy—only it wasn't him.

He fixed dinner and watched a movie, a Cosmo Angel thriller that he fell asleep halfway through. At midnight something woke him and he cleared up, brushed his teeth in a stupor and eventually staggered to bed.

Once there, his mind wouldn't switch off. His body was tired but his brain was alert and the vacant side of the bed was cold and unforgiving. At two a.m. he admitted defeat, got up and made a drink. Leon stood at the kitchen counter, the place ghostly in the milky light of the moon, with only the wash of the ocean disrupting the still.

At Lisa's desk he took a chair, leaning forward and slipping his thumbs into the grooves above his eyes. He reread her note and wondered if wherever she was she was sleeping soundly. Perhaps she had expected a call. Perhaps he should have been on his knees, begging her to come back, promising they could work it out. He wasn't.

Alongside Lisa's desk was the Marlon case. Boxes of files and photos had been neatly stacked and arranged, taped up and returned to the grave. He lifted one on to the surface—it was heavy—and ran a pen along the seal to open it. Even though Lisa had been working with the documents for many weeks, they still released a musky, damp smell, as if reminding him of how long they had been left neglected in the dark.

Remorse shot through him. What Lisa hadn't said on the phone was the only thing that would have changed his mind: that Marlon would surely have wanted this. Marlon would have needed his assassin brought to justice and it didn't matter how much it hurt for those left behind, his brother would not be able to rest in peace until it was done.

Leon withdrew a stack of photographs and held them up to the glow of the lamp. He smiled sadly at images of his brother racing at Fountain Valley, face turned to the sky as he secured victory, clapping his teammates on the back, his grin brighter than the sun.

In one Marlon was thwarted by a rival, chasing down

the line, giving it everything he had but foiled in the last millisecond of the race. Leon remembered shooting hoops with his brother one evening in the yard, close to his selection for Sydney.

*'Can I be honest with you, bro?'*

Leon had socked the ball through the net, glad to have Marlon's confidence. *'Sure.'*

*'I'm terrified I'm not gonna make it. There's too much competition out there. I'm afraid I'm gonna let people down, like I won't be good enough.'*

Leon couldn't imagine his brother ever failing or being bad at anything. His brother was his champion; everything Marlon did was heroic.

*'I just want to make my family proud.'* Marlon had been resolute. *'Everything Mom's put into me—all that faith and belief. I have to win. D'you get it? I have to.'*

Only now did Leon understand what his brother had meant. There was no consolation in coming second. Anything save gold was a loser's badge.

His ambitions to win at the Championships and beyond were Marlon's ambitions, too…the ambitions his brother had never lived to fulfil. He would be running for both of them.

Leon had been thumbing through the prints without looking properly. Now his gaze fell on it, and he leaned in, concentrating, rubbing his weariness away to focus on it properly: a photograph taken at Marlon's funeral, his mom and sister tight to the grave and the mourners behind. Leon thought he spotted himself but it was hard to tell because the head was bowed and besides he hadn't felt there that day at all, not really, just a glimmer.

He peered closer, still not believing what he was seeing.

There, at the back of the congregation, was a face he recognised—younger, yes, and the quality was scratchy and blurred, but it was the same person...undoubtedly the same.

What had *he* been doing there?

Leon's pulse quickened, making him hyper-alert. All the wheels Lisa had ground to make progress, and it was just this one cog that had been stuck.

Now he had oiled it free.

He knew this person. And with that knowledge everything became clear.

## 60

Turquoise would never have made it through the gruelling schedule for *True Match* unless she had been certain that Cosmo's downfall was imminent. The tape was ready to hit YouTube. She could taste how sweet it would be. Cosmo and his wife had no idea. They imagined her to be silenced and she gave them no reason to suspect otherwise.

Turquoise spoke to Cosmo when spoken to, delivered on her promises and played the part to perfection. Every so often her costar would take a liberty—fondling her ass in a press queue, grabbing her when no one was looking and whispering what he wanted to do to her, all to reassure himself that she was still his pet, still the scared call-girl she had been when they'd first met. He was treading danger-ously close to the line. Cosmo couldn't guess what she had planned and the devastation about to be heaped at his door.

But there was one thing she had to do first.

The one thing Cosmo had always been too gutless to face.

She arranged to rendezvous with Jax in LA. She had

spelled out her request on the day of the sauna, in private, just the two of them. The fact was that when it came to it, Jax, much as she disliked him, was the only person she could trust. Not through any bond of affection, but through the cold reality of blackmail. If Jax revealed her—be it now, next week, in a year, ever—then she would do the same in turn. It was life-long indemnity.

Jax was throwing a launch party to mark the release of his new hip-hop single.

Afterwards, he would take her where she needed to go. There was no other way for her to get there—she couldn't go alone, and she couldn't risk a stranger.

From that point, there would be no road back.

She arrived early at Hollywood hotspot El Paradiso and was directed straight through.

Inside, Turquoise admitted that his people had done a good job. Past the gauntlet of paparazzi she emerged on to the magnificent terrace, like something out of ancient Greece. Swathes of white gauze billowed between pillars; nude sculptures of classical Olympians were set on marble plinths, impossibly chiselled and beautifully formed; deep, wide basins had been filled with glistening black olives and succulent grapes; heaps of black caviar were piled up in silver bowls and a fountain of golden champagne was positioned in each corner. There was no doubting the message behind it: Jax wanted the world to know that he belonged on a higher plane, up with the great immortals and the heroes who had conquered history, and that one day he would take his rightful place among the fables that had gone before.

Immediately Turquoise spotted Cindy Shepard, Jax's

PA, who was, considering the sauna debacle, putting in some serious overtime. Cindy's plastic bust was scarcely contained in a clinging silk shirt, surgically inflated tits straining proudly at the material. Every so often she would glance over at her boss, and with a worried expression adjust her blouse.

Jax was chatting up a pretty girl who couldn't have been more than eighteen. Hanging as she was on to his every word, he would have no problem reeling her in...

Just as he had reeled in the lover no one could know about.

Danny Fu. Turquoise wondered if he still thought about that night, the things he had done with the quiet, mildmannered Chinese gymnast when he was riding high on victory.

She turned and slammed straight into someone on his way out, a broad chest that smelled musky and delicious. She looked up and found herself face to face with Leon Sway.

Wow. This guy was stunning.

'Leon, right?' She held out her hand. Normally she didn't feel at all flushed talking to hot men—she encountered enough of them—but Leon was something else. He possessed all the power and heat of Jax but combined with a grace that propelled his physicality to a totally different level. She couldn't stop staring at him.

'Hi,' said Leon. His dimples were cute, appearing only briefly as the serious line of his brow set once more, under which eyes dark as forests glittered.

'You're leaving already?'

'Not my scene.'

Turquoise read between the lines. The athletes' rivalry was no secret.

'Hey,' she said, 'good luck at the Championships.'

'Thanks.'

'You can win it.'

His gaze flickered. 'You think?'

'Sure.'

'Jax wouldn't like you saying that.'

'Jax wouldn't like me saying a lot of things.'

Leon smiled properly this time. 'Yeah?'

A tinny shriek cut through the space. Cindy was up on a podium, testing the microphone and sending metallic squeals of feedback into the crowd.

'Greetings, everyone,' she began, tapping it and dispatching a series of loud booms. A groan rose from the assembly and someone shouted, 'Get off!'

Jax stormed towards the stage. Clocking his approach and the expression on her boss's face, Cindy began babbling into the microphone. 'And now I give you the man of the moment, he's everybody's hero, he'll be taking the charts by storm, ladies and gentlemen, I give you the one and only hip-hop icon Mr Jax Jackson—'

Jax pulled the mic away and the clanging ring reverberated around the walls. He winced at the sound. Cindy crept off-stage, attempting to incite a round of applause, which was met with a wilted smattering of claps. Nobody seemed to know what was going on.

Clearing his throat, Jax surveyed the minions before him. He breathed in deeply, channelling his inner centre podium, how it felt to receive the hundred-metre gold. It was a calming technique, helped get things in perspective.

'I wanna thank y'all for comin',' he commenced, his gaze sliding across the guests. 'When my track gets dropped next week you can bet your asses it's gonna make history.'

'Hell, yeah!' shouted Jermaine, his training partner.

Jax gritted his teeth at the disruption. The guy needed to put a sock in it.

'It's time,' he commanded, holding his arms out. Shit, with all these massive posts and grapes around, he felt like fucking Caesar or something. 'You think you've seen the best of Jax Jackson? You ain't seen nothing yet.'

Jax swallowed his distaste when he saw Turquoise waiting at their pickup point, leaning against the canary Lamborghini, her arms folded and her dark hair swirling around her face. Jeez, why'd she have to look so fine? The fire raging in his head moved down to his chest, his stomach and his groin, settling eventually in his pants. Man, this was exhausting.

To hell with Kristin for giving out his information—he should never have allowed the bitch through his doors. As soon as Turquoise had turned up at Pacific Heights he'd known she had come bearing an ultimatum. The sooner this was done with, the better.

He recalled their conversation, the grit in her eyes and her refusal to back down.

*'This is my turf, lady,'* he'd growled, *'and you're on it. I ain't doin' nothin' for you.'*

*'Oh yes you are. You know why.'*

He'd gulped.

*'Do I need to say his name? I can remind you if you need a little help...'*

Jax had thought for a millisecond about denying it, claiming temporary amnesia or total ignorance, but one dip into her icy glare told him not to bother.

*'After this, it's over,'* he'd sworn. *'You got that?* Over.*'*

Turquoise had explained. What did the broad want with a ride out to the desert?

*'You don't need to know. That's not your business. All you have to be certain of is that breathing one word of this trip to anybody will result in total exposure. Am I clear?'*

Now, approaching the vehicle, Jax opened his mouth to speak, not knowing what he was going to say but knowing he had to have the first word, whatever that was.

She beat him to it, pulling open the door the instant the lock was released.

'Let's ride.'

# *61*

She hadn't taken this route since the fateful trip with Cosmo all those years before. Jax drove fast and no words passed between them. As the city rushed past, thinning out to sporadic clusters of houses and churches, the warm wind in her hair, Turquoise remembered.

Bruce Springsteen playing on the airwaves, 'Born to Run'. The freezing cold night and the fist that wrapped around her heart each time they rounded a corner and she felt the girl's body slide across the trunk of the car. The glare of the headlights as Cosmo had dug the grave; the stars above gazing down as grim, accusing spectators to their crime. The thump of the corpse as she was tossed carelessly in, skin already turning grey, hair matted, her face the face of a baby. How she had pleaded with Cosmo and he had hit her, and hit her again.

It began to get dark. The Lamborghini blazed a trail across the badlands, carving through fists of dry shrubs and arid planes forked with dirt roads. The sky opened, a vast sweep of deepening blue across which gauzy cirrus clouds sailed on the thermals. On and on they went, further from civilisation as the light bled out of the day, wilderness stretching as far as the eye could see and mountains looming. Dark forests appeared like ink blots on a distant horizon, rocks tough as knuckles punching through the cracked earth.

They came to a crossroads.

'Keep driving.'

Though it had been dark, and Turquoise had been delirious, the place was etched in her memory. She would never forget the sickening roll of Cosmo's car as he steered them towards that end point, a spill of moonlight illuminating their path.

The track gave way to rugged banks of volcanic rock, red and black, the Lamborghini's tyres spraying up dust fine as powder. Vegetation dwindled to a sparse, patchy shroud, irregular clumps like balding hair, from behind which animal eyes that glowed in the night returned the vehicle's light. On they drove.

'You wanna get back on this tank,' commented Jax, 'we'd best be gettin' close.'

'We are. Not far now.'

Emaline had raised her to be honest, to be true, and never to fear the pursuit of her dreams. It might have taken a while for her to get here, but the old adage was right: it was better late than never. She was trying her best to make amends and in doing so her past would release her. The girl could never be brought back, but that didn't mean she had to be left.

'Here.'

'This is it?'

'This is it.'

They reached the edge of a ravine, plunging into nothingness. It was cold. Turquoise wrapped her arms around herself as the car pulled to a stop in a crunch of tyres.

They sat in silence.

'Now what?' Jax asked eventually, pissed off it had taken so long.

'Kill the lights.'

'Sheesh, lady—'

'Do it.'

With the snuffing of the bulbs they were left in swollen dusk. A fingernail moon slung loose in the indigo, so fine she could have reached up and peeled it straight it from the sky.

Turquoise released the door. 'Stay here.'

Jax exhaled impatiently and muttered something about where else was he going to go.

The ground prickled beneath her footsteps as she made her way to the spot. She didn't know what she had expected—an open grave, perhaps; proof that the girl was still living and had leapt from her interment. Or else she had been saved, or the body discovered, and all that would be left was a gaping cavity, grinning at the latecomer to the party. Perhaps the cops might have been waiting, a helicopter soaring up from some hidden approach. Cosmo would be with them, pointing his finger and shaking his head.

The reality was ordinary. The ground was indifferent. Turquoise crouched and ran her fingers across the dusty earth, stiff folds of fossilised soil coarse under her touch. In this open wasteland no one would suspect it. The gamble had paid off. The girl was still here. Turquoise could feel her calling, the silent wail that had gone unanswered.

'I'm sorry,' she whispered to the wind. 'Please forgive me. I'm sorry.'

Back then she'd wished it had been her. So many times she had wished that.

'If I could change things, I would,' she promised. Tears spilled from her eyes, the release of coming here again, arriving full circle at the scene of her life's pivot. Cosmo had only been one of her tormentors; the other had been herself.

She closed her eyes. *I'm saying goodbye. I'm letting you go.*

Behind her, the Lamborghini's engine purred to life. Her secret would be safe with Jax—today would be forgotten, gone on the wind, a never-happened dream.

For once, a coil in her past had helped straighten her present.

Turquoise withdrew her cell. She located what she needed before rising to her feet, taking in the scene one more time and returning to the car. She pulled open the door.

'What was that about?' Jax reversed fiercely, discharging a shower of grit.

'Nothing,' she replied. 'Let's go home.'

Back in LA, she supplied the anonymous information: the co-ordinates of where the girl was buried, the year she'd died, but not her name. Turquoise hadn't known her name.

# 62

Leon wished he had never gone to Jax's party. When he arrived back at the apartment, finally clear of the press, his bones were weary and his head fit to explode. He'd hated every minute, hadn't wanted to go in the first place and only had to placate Teddy and the rest of the team.

In the midst of Jax's faux grandeur it had felt like the world was closing in.

He wanted to see Robin. He wanted to talk to her about what he'd found, had to know if that was what she'd been trying to tell him when they'd fought in New York. She was the only person who could help him make sense of it.

She was the only person who made any sense.

Thinking of his brother's murderer left Leon with a cold, hard sensation deep inside, like holding a smooth pebble in a tight fist.

He was close enough to touch—and if his suspicions were right, he could not be held accountable for his actions.

Marlon had been killed in cold blood and had perished in Leon's arms.

When Leon took a life for a life, his arms would be empty.

He would walk away and leave this man to die, just as his brother had been left.

No mercy.

# 63

*Compton, LA, 2000*

Gordon Rimeaux turned eighteen a month before Marlon Sway was killed. His birthday wasn't celebrated; like all the birthdays that had gone before it passed unremarked by his father and brothers, and yet this carried no disappointment: to be disappointed you first had to have expectation, and Gordon had none. He had grown up with nothing, his future held less, he lived for the day and he didn't much care if he woke to face another.

His was a tough neighbourhood. You had to fight your ground. At sixteen Gordon had been initiated no problem: his brother was already in with Slink and his crew. That didn't earn him respect, especially from Slink's white-trash right-hand man Principal, who figured they'd all had to make sacrifices to be accepted and blood privileges didn't cut it.

Slink was five years older than him. He mixed records

and was set on getting a deal some day. Everyone decided he was the business.

Over the next couple of years Gordon moved up the ranks. His brother quit LA and it made sense he would assume his place. It was good to belong to something, to have people at your back. Slink's crew was more of a family than any he'd had.

One night, Principal showed up covered in blood. He had started a war.

Already Slink was up against a rival gang and this latest altercation raised the stakes. Gordon had seen them; they were notorious. Most of the crew had been locked up for assault or theft; one guy from his neighbourhood was bad to the core, a livid scar like a rash down one side of his face. Intimidation fired their swagger; the way they watched you, taking you in and sizing you up, their eyes staring white from the shadows of their faces.

'You put us on the spot, brother,' Slink had warned darkly. 'Now it's payback time.'

His words had sealed the fateful night that had changed all their lives irreversibly.

It was Saturday when Slink's truck pulled up in the lot. Dusk had fallen across the city and the twinkling lights of Hollywood shot an amber thread through the black.

Gordon didn't want to be there. The sun had slipped away and a chill bit his arms, chasing goosepimples across his skin. A storm was coming. He could sense it.

They were made to wait, before at last the still was shaken by the loud growl of an engine. A mean car swung into the space opposite, a lick of flames blazing in furious red across the hood. The windows were blacked out and the machine sat low to the ground, crouching as if trying not to be seen. It purred thickly, black body slick and gleaming as liquid, and Gordon squinted into the fading light, waiting to see what would happen.

Both engines died within seconds. A bad feeling took root in his chest and started to spread. The air smelled funny, like metal. It had started to rain, a steady patter. In a slam of doors, three guys emerged from the car. They looked bad: jumpy, hollow-eyed, the skin on their faces dimly lit like a dying flame through wax.

The one with the scar singled out Principal. 'You and me, let's go.'

'Fuck you.'

'Whassamatter, pussy? You afraid to get heavy without your boyfriends?'

Principal pulled a gun. 'Take care what you say.'

The others backed off. Slink stepped in. 'Put that thing down, man, take it easy.'

'What the fuck you doin'?' Gordon hissed. 'Where'd you get that shit?'

Principal took aim at his adversary.

'This ain't the way we roll.' The other crew had their hands in the air. 'We said no guns. Drop the weapon.'

'You mess with me—' Principal released the catch '—then this *is* the way we roll.'

Gordon noticed a new guy on the far side of the lot, cutting through to the residential street behind. He was tall, well built, and wore a rain-soaked beanie hat. A kit bag was thrown over one shoulder.

'C'mon, man, let's bounce.' Principal's nemesis showed his back.

'Don't turn away from me.'

The guys kept walking, and then everything swung in slow motion. The driver's side opening, two of them vanishing but Principal's adversary still there, and then Principal raised the gun and in a split second the world imploded. A flock of birds took to the sky in a ripple of dark wings. Principal misfired and caught his opponent in the leg.

'My fuckin' knee, my fuckin' knee, you fuckin' shot me, you *fuck*!'

The guy on the other side of the lot had his hands up; he was walking over, trying to make the peace. Gordon lunged. The gun flailed. He found the pistol gripped in his own hands, momentarily, as he tried to stop it firing but in that same process it blasted. A bullet tore through the air and then too fast, too terrible, a body slumped to the ground, louder than it should have been, a sack of bones hitting concrete.

The guy was felled like a tree, clutching his stomach.

'Shit, G!' Principal exclaimed. 'You shot him! You fuckin' shot him!'

'Get the hell outta here.' Slink ripped open the door to the truck. The other crew had already bolted. *'Now.'*

'No way, man,' Gordon whimpered. He dived for his casualty but strong arms restrained him, pulling him back. 'No way, man, he can't die, we've gotta help him…'

Their victim was staggering to his feet, the rain coming down in sheets of silver and gold, and Gordon could see it now: blood draining on to the road, staining it crimson in the harsh yellow light, sparkling like pink crystals. Stomach gripped, weaving, the man started to move, half running, half crawling, bent double on the axis of his pain.

'Get in, man, let's split!'

The door was open. Gordon's legs were stuck. He couldn't abandon the wounded. He had shot someone; if they didn't get help, this guy was going to die…

'Follow him,' Gordon commanded, slamming the door. They'd pick him up, take him in; to hell with the rules, he had to right a wrong.

Slink was at the wheel. 'Forget it, G, y'hear? Forget it—'

But Gordon still had the weapon in his hands. He raised it. 'Follow him now, motherfucker, or I'll put a bullet in your fucking head, I swear to God—'

'Easy, G, nice and easy…'

*'Do it!'*

When they emerged the guy was buckled on the street. That was when the screams came. They watched a smaller boy, a little kid, running from the opposite end of the street, so fast but not fast enough, and calling a name that got lost on the wind.

'Move! Move! Drive!' Principal yelled. 'Drive!'

The boy was on his knees, cradling the man's head.

The last thing Gordon saw before the street began to fill was the lost look in the boy's eyes, raised to the sky, searching, before the car screeched off.

# 64

The LAPD received their tip-off in June. Their suspect was Ivy Sewell, female, Caucasian, twenty years old. She was five-foot-seven, a redhead, blue eyes, skinny ass.

'Sure takes balls to murder your own mother,' commented Detective McEverty, tucking into a donut and glancing through the file. 'How'd they know she's here?'

'Does it matter?' said his colleague Moretti. 'If she's hard up for cash she'll be making money the usual way. I say we cruise the strip, see what we find.'

'Just like any other night, then,' teased McEverty.

'Aw, so funny.'

'Flight receipts.' The chief entered the room and slammed down a file. 'That's how we know Ivy's here. It's been confirmed in London and over here. Wake up, boys.'

McEverty and Moretti exchanged glances.

'This is Ryder's twin,' he said. 'Take a look at the pictures. Evidence suggests she plans to act fast. Ivy left too many indicators in the UK to feel secure out here. She's aware she's gonna get caught and that time's running out—meaning it's running out for us, too.'

'What indicators?' asked Moretti.

The chief flipped open the file, which was packed with photographs taken inside the London flat. Pictures and clippings of the music icon Robin Ryder covered every wall.

'Looks like a shrine to me,' commented McEverty.

'Something like it,' agreed the chief. 'This place was searched top to bottom. Whatever the broad's got against her sister, it ain't pretty.'

'We need to find her.'

'No shit, McEverty.' Moretti grabbed his jacket. 'So what are we waiting for?'

Ivy was creeping closer. With each day that passed and brought her one step nearer to retribution, her surveillance of Robin Ryder adopted a new energy. Everywhere the singer got photographed, every man she was with, every move she made and every word she uttered was diligently noted and remembered. Detail dictated the masterpiece.

Robin's tour had ended. On the morning the star arrived back in LA and headed to her villa, Ivy was waiting, a hooded figure obscured in the trees.

Next stop, the ETV Platinum Awards…and her very last performance.

Ivy watched for a long time. She watched Robin open the door and go inside. She watched her embrace the German, a souvenir brought back from Vegas. She watched as the bedroom blind was pulled and she watched until it was raised again. She watched as a second car pulled up and a black man climbed out—Leon Sway, the athlete whom Robin had got close to. With his arrival came the first twinge of jeopardy.

Leon had been hanging around Robin for months and Ivy didn't like his persistence. Men who came in and out of her sister's life were one thing; men who clung on were another.

Did Leon have feelings for her? It wasn't a concept Ivy could abide.

Feelings made people…unpredictable.

Leon was hesitant—perhaps not such a threat, after all?—as he went to the door. He was about to knock, seemed to change his mind and return to the car, then quickly paced back.

The German answered, bare chested, a towel around his waist. Ivy couldn't hear the exchange, but it was brief. Leon retreated almost immediately, hands up in a gesture perhaps of having made a mistake, and seconds later was backing out of the drive.

On instinct Ivy returned to her own car and followed. Reflex made her believe that Leon Sway was trouble. She couldn't risk him compromising her campaign.

She was willing to remove any obstacle that could stand in her way.

Any protector of Robin would perish himself.

*PART 4*

# 65

For the first time in pop music memory, a major awards ceremony was happening and Fraternity hadn't received a single nomination.

'That's it for us,' declared Joey Lombardi. 'After the promo's wrapped for *Seven Days*, the band's over. We're finished.'

Kristin ran into him at a signing in NYC: the boys still had an album to promote and were going ahead without Scotty, who was allegedly off recording solo material.

'I'm sorry,' she said once they were done. 'That sucks big time.' Brett and Doug were loping about outside, miserable and chain-smoking while they waited for their pickup; the cute, apologetic smiles having vanished the instant their sparse gathering of disconcerted fans had scattered. Die-hard devotees of the remaining four were trying their best to stay supportive but especially for the younger ones the whole affair was deeply upsetting. The guys were tinged irreparably by Scotty's transgressions and everyone knew it.

Joey ran a hand through his hair. It had gotten longer since Kristin had last seen him.

'Does it?' he countered. 'I don't know, I'm kinda relieved.'

'You are?'

'It had to end someday.' Joey smiled drily. 'We couldn't keep on going for ever. And it was starting to get weird, you know, singing all the corny stuff we did, having ten-year-old fans when we were twenty-three...'

Kristin thought of Bunny and swallowed her regret. Italy—Alessandro, mainly—had done her a world of good, but she was still finding her feet back in LA and having to get used to a city without her sister in it. The Platinum Awards were two weeks away and would spell her first big performance since her new record had launched.

'What next?' she asked softly.

'Search me...' He attempted humour. 'You got any suggestions? C'mon,' he teased, 'you're the queen of reinvention. HQ says that's the only way forward but I'm not convinced. If we're not Fraternity, I don't know what we are. I don't know what I am.'

'You're one part of Fraternity. That doesn't change.'

'But that's just it. We're all one part and so when one of us goes it doesn't work any more. We can't carry on as a foursome; it wouldn't be right.'

'So where do you go from here?'

Joey shrugged. 'It's good not having a clue. No more management monitoring our every move, no more being told what we can and can't wear, what our hair should be like, if we're allowed girlfriends...'

'Do you have a girlfriend?'

He blushed. 'No!'

'Yeah, right…' Come to think of it Joey had never confessed to having a girlfriend.

'There is this one girl.' His glance swept across her. 'It's nothing, though…'

'What do you mean, it's nothing?'

'Well, she doesn't feel the same.'

'Have you asked her?'

'Of course not!'

Kristin felt a ripple of jealousy. It took her by surprise. She changed the subject.

'Did you hear Scotty's presenting an award at the Platinums?'

'Yeah. He's sure come out of this better than Fenton, hey?'

Kristin agreed. Scotty's PR had been clever. Although a performance at the biggest event in the industry calendar was out of the question, the planned appearance—in a position of servility, no less—would remind the public that Scott Valentine might be humble but he was still a player, and one who refused to endure humiliation in the shadows.

'I'll see you there?' she asked, really hoping that she would.

'Yeah.' He touched her arm before the others called for him to go. 'Expect so.'

Scotty almost didn't recognise his former lover. In the visitors' room, a sterile, depressing space flanked by blank-faced, emotionless police officers and divided by a bank of seats on either side of a pane of glass, he tentatively took a booth and picked up the phone.

Fenton looked haggard and thin. Half the man he used to be—literally.

'Prison food no good?'

Scotty's joke fell flat: perhaps targeting Fenton's sensitive weight issues within seconds of arriving had been a bad idea. His already weak smile toppled off his chin.

Fenton stared back at him, hollow-eyed. It was worse than any rebuke or aggression. If Fenton had shouted and screamed and accused Scotty of having left him here to perish as the villain while he, Scotty, went on *The State Show* and had a PR machine pouring every hour into steering his train-wreck of a career back on track that would at least have been something. As it was, his ex-manager's silence was chilling to the core.

'How are you doing?' he asked lamely.

Another inane question. But Scotty didn't know what else to say.

'How am I doing?' Fenton repeated flatly. He was unshaven, his eyes sunken and his skin grey. *'How am I doing?'* He leaned in. 'I haven't seen my family in weeks, Scott. I've been locked in a cell. My career and my life are over. I'm eating crap. I'm sleeping on a single wooden bunk for three hours a night, too afraid to close my eyes in case any of the perverts in here decide to tear me a new asshole. I need to ask permission to take a freaking dump. I'm lonely. I'm scared. I'm furious. I'm wretched. How do you *think* I'm doing?'

Scotty bowed his head.

'Why did you come?' Fenton asked bitterly. 'You're no good to me.'

He didn't look up. He couldn't. Ever since the men had

known each other, Scotty had been reflected in his manager's eyes through a golden glow. To be regarded so hatefully made him see how much he'd relied on that refuge. It shocked him how bad it made him feel.

'I—I had to see you,' he stammered. 'They told me I couldn't, I'm not supposed to—'

'Cut the crap, Scott. Get to the point. It might look like I have all the time I want in here but I'd rather not spend it listening to you.'

Scotty steeled himself. 'I'm going against them.' He met Fenton's gaze. 'It's not right you being held when they don't know the facts—'

'No shit,' Fenton cut in. 'What's this, an attack of conscience? You sure took your sweet time getting there.'

'I'm going against the label and telling the truth,' Scotty pushed. 'I'm telling the cops. I'm telling them and everyone else that what happened between us was mutual.'

Fenton didn't speak, just kept watching Scotty through the glass.

'I could sit it out and let you take the rap,' Scotty continued, hitting his stride. 'I could play the victim, that's what they want—and I'd be lying if I said it wouldn't be easier. But I won't. It's not right you being in here. It's not OK. And I know that whatever I say now isn't going to come close to making up for what a coward I've been but I have to try, don't I?'

The other man gave nothing away. 'Why now?' he insisted. 'Why not before?'

'I was scared.'

'*You* were scared? *You?* Don't make me laugh.'

'I was.'

'Do you have a clue what this ordeal has been like for me? The charges I've faced? The names they've been shouting? What I've been accused of? You could have put a stop to it with one phone call, but did the call come? No.'

'They wouldn't let me...'

'Don't be pathetic,' Fenton snapped. 'You could have broken out; you could have grown some balls. Your management isn't the law.' Grimly he gestured about him. 'This, however, *is*. And I've been at the receiving end of it. You won't know the half of what I've gone through in the lonely hours of the night, the moment of my arrest, the heckles and the taunts and the shameful interrogations, and now you're telling me that *you* were scared? I thought I'd heard it all but that's got to take it. You always were a pitiful creature, Scotty.'

The tantrum child in Scotty wanted to bang down the phone and storm out without so much as a backward glance, but the quiver in Fenton's voice, just that slight admission of vulnerability, stopped him. Besides, every word he said was true. It *was* time to grow up and face his responsibilities— and if he was honest, the time for that had been and gone many months ago. Was it too late?

'I can't make up for what's happened,' he replied, 'but I can tell you I'm sorry and I can correct those mistakes now.'

Fenton's breath was coming in shallow rasps, overcome with the emotion of his imminent acquittal. Scotty went to hang up.

'Scott?' he said quickly.

'Yes?'

'What's it like out there? What's it like outside, in the real world?'

Scotty tried to think of the right words. 'Tough,' he admitted. 'Frightening. Exhausting. Surprising. Amazing. Bizarre. But I should have done it a long time ago.'

'So should I.'


At the station, Scotty kept his eyes locked ahead as an officer escorted him through a set of double doors and down a walkway. The linoleum floor squeaked beneath his sneakers. Through another entrance they were straight to the heart of the action, a foyer milling with uniforms, the riffle of paperwork and the buzz of the chase.

A woman came up to him, efficient and friendly, and shook his hand.

'This way, Mr Valentine.'

She led him towards a room boasting a neat brass sign, reading: INTERVIEW.

Before he was sealed on the point of his confession and the truth that would set Fenton free, Scotty caught a snapshot of a case working opposite. The detective was emerging into the hall, opening and closing the door and in doing so awarding a flash of their perpetrator. The board was covered in her image, a red-haired female, a bit younger than him, hate and violence emanating from every pore and a glint of pure evil in her eyes.

The face reminded him faintly of someone, but the glimpse was too brief to tell who.

The door to Scotty's room shut. His interviewer sat down.

All these people they were chasing, the criminals who had done terrible things, committed heinous crimes...

Fenton wasn't one of them. He was one of the good guys.

'So, I understand you have something to tell us?'

Scotty took a breath and began.

# 66

The US track team flew to Europe at the start of July. It was hard to believe that a year had passed since their last major tournament, yet each race remained as vital and as necessary as the first. For Leon, none more so than this: his chance to claim the title that belonged to his rival, an opportunity to set the record straight and to heal the wound.

Until he confronted Puff City with the facts, he could never heal the wound.

On the plane over he assured himself that they would still be waiting when he returned to LA—they had waited over a decade, after all. It had taken all his power of will to desist, but spilling too soon would throw his race into jeopardy. He would not give them the opportunity to take this from him.

How he longed to wring the life from that man's body—that liar, that criminal, that hateful, despicable *murderer...*

The race came first. He had to be patient. Thirteen years he had bided his time...what was another thirteen days? The rest would follow. He would make sure of it.

* * *

The Championships were a week-long event. The anticipation was always the hard part—for some, their event couldn't come around soon enough, it was a chance to realise the pay-off; for others, there would never be enough training or prep they could do; they'd never be ready.

Leon was ready. He wanted results and he wanted them now. This was his arrival. The guys were already thinking about Rio: a win here would signal just the beginning.

He sailed through the heats, a shiver behind Jax each time (inflamed by the suggestion that Jax wasn't really trying yet; he was conserving his energy for the main event), and opted out of interaction with the others, instead returning each night, concerned solely with his training, his diet, his sleep, his tests, and the sole, shining beacon of the hundred-metre final.

This was his time. He had to take it, or else what had he been doing with half of his life? After Marlon died he had seized the baton—he had to win for his brother, because of his brother, in spite of his brother...

It all came down to one thing.

Nine seconds.

There were two ways of looking at it. Was it a selfish pursuit, chasing down glory and expecting everyone else to fall into line? Or was it that he had made sacrifices, putting his life on hold while he became obsessed with nine seconds of time, the be all and end all?

The night before his final, Leon met with his coach, went through his paces and retired early. Some athletes wouldn't sleep at all. For those whose first competition it was, there was scarce pressure and thus a shot at enjoyment. For those with medal expectations, every minute they weren't on the track was agony. Over the years Leon had learned to discipline his nerves, reining them in on the promise of imminent release: the second he took to the starting blocks they could fly free, and then, only then, they would combine with the adrenalin that fired his run. The result had to be potent. That was the time for nerves. Like a melting pot into which every diversion was tossed, it all formed part of the explosion.

Even so, when Leon tuned into a local radio station and caught a report on the event, it burned. He lay back on his bunk with his arm behind his head.

*'Here you will see the strongest, the fastest, the most powerful men and women on Earth, the sweat and the tears, the blood, the heartache, the suffering and the joy. You will see what it means to leap into the unknown; to have worked for years and have it all come down to now. The athletes you'll witness will be broken and mended; some will be taken apart and never put back together again. We will be making the heroes of tomorrow...'*

Before surrendering to sleep, Leon's mind threw up a flash of his brother, coming home from the track and ruffling his hair as he looked down and said:

*You can do it, little bro. You can do it.*

Morning came, and Jax Jackson devoured the breakfast of champions: a bowl of wholegrain cereal mixed with raisins and nuts; two hard-boiled eggs with a buttered sesame bagel; a platter of sliced bananas topped with crunchy peanut butter and yoghurt; a handful of grapes; a glass of milk and two cups of green tea followed by a shot of coffee.

He was feeling confident. How could he not? Leon might have put the burden on back in LA but out here the guy was lagging, the gravity of the occasion getting to him just as it had in London. Jax would be sealing his gold-medal victory, no problem.

The road trip with Turquoise had cemented his resolve. For years there had been this lurking, latent terror…terror that the Danny Fu scandal would emerge and the shame would force him into an early grave—or an early retirement, and they might as well be the same thing. Now the risk had been removed, Turquoise had vowed it was done with, and his sun had slid out from its eclipse. He was burning bright, unfettered, the world number one.

Bumping into Danny the previous night had made him more grateful than ever—these international comps were always tinged with hazard. Gymnast Danny had taken a silver medal on the pommel horse—the word 'pommel' alone enough to make Jax gag—his feminine features (and they *were* feminine, *they were*!) overshadowed by defeat that any other nation would have traded for pride. Danny and his squad rejected second best.

As Jax made his way to the locker room, the gateway to battle that was scene to so many rituals and anxieties, he recalled how Danny had blanched and the men had turned from each other, disgrace coursing through their veins. Danny didn't speak a word of English and that was for the best. Jax wondered how their night together would translate as a Chinese character. Two swords crossing. A viper in a cave. A sausage in a bun.

A relay baton…

It was finished. He was free—and he was here for victory.

The locker room smelled of salt and the synthetic of the kit, a heady, addictive aroma each took with them and would never forget. Some athletes were stretching out their routines, headphones on, a pumping soundtrack guiding them towards the track. Others were crouched on the floor, head down and hands over their ears, blocking out the world while they talked themselves up to the race. Jax zipped into his kit and decided he was long past needing any security blankets. He was buzzing and ready to go and that was about all there was to it.

Only when the volunteers arrived to escort them through to the stadium did he acknowledge the first frisson of strain. He could hear the crowd baying, the drum of the event and the roar of the fans. Tension sparked in his stomach and snaked through his organs, a fizz of potency all the more strident for having been kept in check.

*This is it, baby. The King returns.*

Coach Simpson fell into step alongside him and Jax snarled at him to fuck off—he didn't need guidance now; he was on a different plane. The girl chaperoning him attempted conversation, scarcely believing she had been assigned this role to the man myths were made of. Every step arrived with a fresh punch to Jax's gut and his muscles started to twitch.

Only when he turned to tell her to quit gassing did he register that she was supremely hot, and batting her eyelashes and pouting ever so slightly. An invitation, if ever he saw one.

'You got ten seconds?' Jax growled under his breath.

The girl was shocked to have been addressed directly. 'Er, yes, yes, I have—'

'Make it nine-and-a-half.'

Was he really about to do this? It seemed he was.

Jax unstrapped the watch from his wrist, at the same time as gripping the girl's arm, checking they were out of sight, and pushing her into an empty closet.

Getting sucked off before a race was the most cardinal of sins. It was kamikaze! It was suicide! Jax needed the testosterone to burn for him like fuel out on the track but right now his need to expel was greater. He was on the cusp of another triumph; it was as good as done. This wouldn't make the slightest bit of difference.

Jax commanded the girl to the floor, her eyes wide and her mouth open, giggling with a lust for adventure…and more work experience than she had ever banked on acquiring.

'Get set,' he told her, as his erection pounced free as cleanly as a sword.

Leon saw a different man when he looked in the mirror. This one had grown up. He had arrived. Shades of his brother— the eyebrow, the jaw—were fainter now than they used to be, because Leon looked less for Marlon these days than he did for himself.

The man he saw was stronger, braver and fiercer than the twelve-year-old who had witnessed a crime in the darkest hour of his life. He didn't weep. He fought.

Alone in the locker room, Leon closed his eyes and visualised the race, a technique psych had taught him. It prepared the brain for the sudden burst of action, focusing on the end point and imagining the achievement before it was realised.

*The finish, always the finish...*

But it wasn't the line he saw; it was Marlon in the road.

He wouldn't change that. It was the thing he had always been running towards, and today, when he won, it would be no different.

'Holy *shee-it*!'

Jax grabbed the stopwatch and blinked through the riot in his head to make sure he was seeing clearly. He was! Fuck, yeah! 9.56 seconds, baby!

He'd only freaking *done it*!

'You're a genius, d'you know that?' He kissed the girl passionately on the mouth, dragging her to her feet through a dazed stumble.

'Wow,' was all she could say, unable to tether her delirious smile. 'Wow.'

Jax puffed out his chest. He didn't believe in signs or any of that superstitious crap, but if ever he had wanted confirmation that this race was in the bag then there it was.

Jax Jackson was hotter than ever! He was so hot he was on fire! They'd need a fucking fire extinguisher to put him out once he crossed that finish!

Nothing could stop him now.

He was going to win.

## 67

Turquoise had spent the morning in a casting for a new movie. This one had her name on it, a British fantasy romance about love, loyalty and friendship. Donna wanted to keep their options open and experiment with a wide canvas of characters. *True Match* had been a hard-hitting thrill ride; this one would be its tonic.

'I'll touch base as soon as I have news,' Donna promised. 'Want to grab a bite?'

'Can't,' Turquoise replied. 'There's something I've got to do.'

Donna's brow creased. 'Anything I can help with?'

'No. But thanks.'

'There she goes again.' Donna grinned. 'The woman of mystery.'

Turquoise remembered Harry Dollar calling her the same thing after her slot on his show. How far she had come since then.

'Donna, listen,' she said, touching her manager's arm. 'Things aren't going to be the same tomorrow.'

'What?'

'Hollywood. It isn't going to be the same.'

Donna's expression settled when she thought she understood. 'Honey, Hollywood adores you. They're not gonna pull out on this one, because if they do—'

'I don't mean that. I mean...' Turquoise faltered. 'I just mean...thanks. Thanks for everything you've done for me. You've always been there. Just thanks.'

Donna was worried. 'Turquoise, what's going on—?'

'I'll call you.' She climbed into her car and slammed the door.

At home, Turquoise opened the patio doors and let the sunshine in. She wanted to feel open when she did this, at peace with the world for the first time since she had left Emaline's porch eighteen years before. *My little star...* At last, she was shining.

Turquoise had pondered if, when the time came, she would procrastinate. In the event, the delay lasted mere minutes. She paced her office. She stood silent at the mirror, remembering who she was. She poured herself a cup of coffee and waited for it to go cold.

Such a quiet thing to do, all alone, unseen and unobserved at her desk—the click of a finger was all it took to let loose cataclysm. She had been telling the truth when she'd informed Donna that Hollywood was about to change. In moments the industry would be transformed by calamity. How would it cope with the death of its prince?

Already she could see it happening, impossibly huge,

unreservedly scandalous, the perfect, most fitting revenge she could think of. It would destroy the Angel powerhouse once and for all. Ultimate vengeance would be hers, and this would be how she got it.

She wondered how many people would see the footage before it got taken down.

Enough.

Turquoise withdrew the tape from its hiding place, uploaded it on to her Mac and thought of what Cosmo Angelopoulos had said to her that night.

*That bitch is nothing to me, and neither are you.*

This was a gift from both of the bitches.

*Fuck you, Cosmo.* And she set it free.

# 68

The crowd erupted the instant Jax and Leon walked out on to the track, their thunder chasing around the stadium in an ear-splitting Mexican wave.

Cameras passed down the line, introducing the athletes one by one. Leon unzipped his jacket, totally focused, bouncing on the spot to get his blood pumping. Jax swagged it out, hip-hop beats—his own—blasting from gold-plated headphones, which he lifted momentarily to absorb the masses' adulation. His gold-bullet vest gleamed in the sun.

Each athlete was obliged to applaud the fans when they heard their name. Leon gave a single brief salute when his time was up, never once taking his eyes from the finish—one hundred metres, there it was again: his old friend. Jax held his first finger up and nodded like it was a done deal—number one, for the entire world to see. He would have no problem retaining his title. Victory was in his blood.

Ahead of the start the men slipped into their individual routines. For a guy to Leon's left, back to full strength after months of injury, non-stop pacing, back and forth, back and forth, getting a feel for the ground under his feet and locked inside his own head space. On the end, a controversial twenty-year-old who had endured a four-year doping ban and was only allowed back into competition thanks to new laws, crouched low, head down, as if glancing up would let in too much of the event and the pressure would overwhelm. This was vital to them all. Leon kept his eyes on the line. The line was all that existed.

Leon's lane was alongside Jax's. He was aware of Jax throwing his headphones into a proffered box along with his kit, the girl holding it chewing her lip in brazen worship.

'Hey,' murmured Jax before the launch, an arrogant sneer pasted across his face. 'Don't it kill to know your brother should have been here?'

Leon didn't think he had heard right.

'I figure you're used to coming second,' elaborated Jax cruelly, 'seeing as you ain't as fast as him. Kid might've stood a chance of beating The Bullet…but you never will.'

*Focus on the line. Focus on the line.*

Jax wanted a reaction. He wanted sabotage. He went for the kill.

'Some say he coulda lived if you'd been faster…'

Words that sliced Leon like a knife.

He fought the urge to push Jax on to the track with his fists and beat the crap out of him; knew that would mean disqualification and that was exactly what his rival wanted. Jax was riling him, he'd done it before, and Leon knew sometimes when it came to his brother he thought with his fists before he thought with his mind, but not today, not today…

*The line... The line...*
*You can do it, little bro; you can do it...*
'On your marks...'
Quiet settled on the crowd—dead quiet.

Leon's chest was pounding, rage and injustice spiralling through him, sparking every muscle and galvanising him to action.

Before Jax fixed his stare on the hard red ground, he uttered so softly it was imperceptible to anyone save his opponent:

'Bad luck, Sway. No hard feelings, huh.'

## 69

The pistol shattered the air. Leon pushed from the blocks, fury pouring into his every tread so that he thought no matter how wild or how far he ran it could never be spent.

He was back there. The track fell away and he was on the road, slippery wet, adrenalin rioting through every vein and sinew like gasoline.

The crack of gunfire that tore at the sky...his brother clutching his stomach and staggering out on to the street, head bent, knees buckling...the lights of a car in the distance that, moments after, had melted away in the rain... the ground beneath his feet, glassy and black, his sneakers sending up a flat spray and a trickle of water coursing down his hairline, freezing cold...

His breath got ragged, scorching his lungs with acid, heart slamming with every pace, as much now as then. The voice told him to keep going, not to stop, however much it hurt.

He had watched his brother collapse, knowing the moment he went down that he would never be getting back up. *No*, Leon had thought. *Don't do that.*

Nine seconds, nine seconds, nine seconds…

It had meant everything on that night and it meant everything right now…

He was almost home. With a last push Leon broke through the pain.

But Jax was there, coming up against him, refusing to back down, pulling away in the final stretch as he always did, head dipped, the bullet visible as it powered forward as unstoppable as a train. The bullet he had to beat. The bastard he had to beat.

Just like that, Leon found his fuel injection.

He thought he had been running before, but he hadn't known what the word meant until that moment. Speed made him flat-out, optimal, ultimate. The asphalt rose up to meet him, heaving back against every stride and now he was running fast, so fast, impossibly fast, running until the blood was hot in his legs and tearing at his throat.

Time was rushing away quicker than water.

*Be faster! Be faster!*

He had held on to Marlon's slack body, his brother's eyes beginning to glaze. The wound hanging open, bright red, and Marlon's hands attempting to contain it, crimson with death. Leon had been consumed by the absolute fact of it, the certainty that the most terrible thing that would ever happen to him had just happened.

And Marlon had whispered something to him. Until today he had never been sure what it was, and now it came to him, a gentle affirmation.

*Keep going.*

He crashed over the finish line.

There was a sliver of sheer silence before the boom unleashed.

## 70

Nearly six thousand miles away, at home in Los Angeles amid the opulence of his mansion, Cosmo Angel yawned. He and his wife were entertaining guests. Ava had given the housekeeper the afternoon off and had prepared an impressive spread of Beluga caviar, saffron-infused *arancini*, white truffle mousse and Kobe beef parcels.

A couple of their guests had expressed interest in watching the hundred-metre Championships sprint, a hot topic in light of the Leon Sway/Jax Jackson rivalry. Cosmo was irritated at the disruption because he had been about to unveil his impressive collection of Japanese Samurai *shuriken*, amassed since a memorable trip there years ago, but clicked on the plasma above the fireplace graciously nonetheless.

They were in time to see the men spring from the start, and almost ten seconds later it was over. Cosmo couldn't understand the appeal himself, although as the athletes accelerated he found himself high-fiving a director to his right and felt his masculinity reaffirmed.

What was the big deal about being a sprinter? Anyone could do it. Being handsome enough to make millions of dollars from movies and be adored the world over for bringing joy and aspiration into people's homes was not, however, something anyone could do.

Disengaging from the group's polite smatter of conversation, Cosmo padded into his study, slipping his feet into a pair of Arctic-fox-fur slippers Ava had given him for his birthday. Mounted on the wall behind an impressive glass-fronted cabinet was his collection of ninja blades. He grinned at his reflection as he slid the cabinet open and withdrew his favourite *kankyuto*, running his fingertips over the dagger-sharp points.

His cell rang.

'Talk to me.' It was his manager. There was a long silence, before:

'Cosmo, are you sitting down?'

'No, but I can be.' He dropped into a plush leather chair and put his foxy feet up on the mahogany desk, smirking. It had to be an Awards nomination—he'd been waiting long enough; perhaps *True Match* had finally sealed the deal. 'Tell me the good news.'

There was another silence. Cosmo twirled the *shuriken* in his hand. 'I haven't got all day,' he said. 'Fucking get on with it.'

'Cosmo, we've got an issue. I suggest you get online… now.'

Ava called through. 'Darling, are you there?'

He rested the phone on his shoulder as he reached to click on the PC. 'Be right back!'

'This better be good,' he hissed into the mouthpiece as

he tapped the letter C into the engine. As the list of entries scrolled down, his mouth filled with bile.

*Cosmo Angel sex tape.*

*Cosmo hooker orgy.*

*Cosmo crown shagathon.*

No. No. *No!*

Blind with fear, he followed the link. The video entitled 'Kingdom Come' had been removed, but stills of it remained, snagged in the barb like rot. There he was, plain as day, reclined naked on a bed and wearing the Crown Jewels. The whores on their hands and knees rising to meet him, heads buried in his lap, his hand pushing them down.

The debauched soirée in Crete, the grape-sucking honeys...

There he was, donning the tiara, sprawled on a fourposter and high as a kite.

*Oh, baby, yeah!* someone had commented. *You can be my king any day of the week!*

'We took it down in less than ten,' his manager babbled, 'but it's too late. Millions have seen it. The papers have got hold of it.'

Cosmo blinked through the nightmare, rigid in his seat.

'It's hitting newsstands tomorrow. There's nothing we can do. Cosmo, forget whatever embarrassment you might be feeling. This is a fucking legal nightmare.'

He stared blankly at the screen, at his fully and disastrously stripped form, at his most private, sickest fantasies laid bare for all the world to see, and only then did the enormity of it register. In that moment he knew unambiguously that life as he knew it had been snuffed out.

'Cosmo? Are you listening? We've called a crisis meeting downtown. Whatever you're doing, cancel. Just get the hell out of there. The press are on their way.'

Cosmo's brain shut down. Its magnitude was incomprehensible. Its destruction was unthinkable. He clenched his fist around the *shuriken*, pricks of scarlet blood flowering and spreading through his tightened fingers.

*Grace Turquoise da Luca.*

Cosmo buckled to the floor on the altar of his sin and after that there was nothing.

## 71

The board said it all:

1. SWAY, LEON (USA): 9.5632s (WR)
2. JACKSON, JAX (USA): 9.5724s

He had won. He had won. He had done it. He had won. *I've won.*

Behind him, a strangled cry was released into the air. Jax Jackson was on his knees, imploring the sky before crashing to the ground, tight as a ball, groaning like an animal.

He had won.

By an infinitesimal margin but a margin all the same.

## 72

Robin watched Leon's race on TV. She had told herself she wouldn't but in the end she couldn't help it. She killed the channel as soon as his win was confirmed.

'You should go to him, you know,' advised Polly, curled up on the sofa with a tub of Ben & Jerry's. 'Tell him how you feel.'

Once, Robin would have denied having any feelings whatsoever, habitually on the defence. Now, she didn't bother. It was plain to see. She had even been honest enough with Steffen to give him the real reason when she had called it quits with him.

*Is it someone else?*

*Yes.*

*Are you with him?*

*I should be.*

But she and Leon were torn, and even more so now he was officially the fastest man on Earth: the new world record holder, unreachable, immortal.

She was happy for him. She was sad. It was confusing.

The girls were recovering from the *Beginnings* tour, by all accounts an unqualified success, before the ETV Platinum Awards at the weekend. After that they would be returning to the UK. For Robin, it couldn't come a moment too soon. She had plans to sell her flat, putting an end to the roller coaster of the past few months. Her new London address would stay strictly confidential. No more unwanted contact. No more fear. It was over.

'Well?' pressed Polly, holding out the tub.

Robin dug her spoon in, losing her appetite so it sat sticking out like a pitchfork.

'I don't know,' she replied glumly. 'In another lifetime.'

# 73

Ivy took up her weapons and handled each in turn, stroking their contours as one might the surfaces of a priceless ornament or the coat of a beloved pet, with tenderness and fascination. It was important that they become acquainted with each other.

The big night was tomorrow. She wondered how many lives these firearms would take as she blasted the event into outer space.

Robin Ryder would be the last to go down. By then her twin would be paralysed with fear, rendering the act all the purer. Ivy wondered what her sister would say, if she'd be incoherent with fright or able to articulate her shock. Would she recall their encounter in San Francisco? Would she make a connection to the gifts she'd received? Would Robin realise that Ivy was her flesh and blood, the might-have-been ally she'd deserted? Or, at the instant of her expiry, would she find herself lost in the empty regard of a complete stranger?

Dusk was falling. Carefully Ivy folded her Burger Delite! uniform, the costume she would never again be made to wear, and pulled the blinds, shutting out the night.

She instructed herself to savour it. Anticipation was everything.

There was a knock at the door.

Ivy frowned. She went to it, pressing her eye against the peephole.

Connor.

She stepped away, staying quiet, and chose to ignore it.

'I know you're in there,' Connor wheedled from the porch. 'I saw you come in.' She didn't respond, so he added: 'And I saw you close the blinds...'

Ivy squinted. Surrounding her was an armoury of weapons. There was no way she could conceal them before he entered her den.

'I'm waiting.' His voice seeped in from behind the door. 'I brought beer...'

Ever since she had arrived in LA, that insidious cretin had been begging her for an evening. Fine. She'd give him one. Soon he'd wish he had never stepped over her threshold.

Ivy opened the door and put her head around, concealing the interior from view. Connor was surprised, had been on the cusp of walking away, and turned with an expression of unappetising enthusiasm. He was sweating beneath his armpits and at the plump round swell of his gut, like a hog in a buttoned-up shirt.

'Hi,' she purred, smiling as she had to Graham and to Nicki Soba and to every man she could claim something from. Connor would be the last.

An early treat...an appetiser before tomorrow.

'Why don't you come in?'

# 74

'Leon, you can't leave town.' His agent was begging. 'You're hot property right now.'

'It's only a few weeks.'

'I don't care. This is big, buddy; this is the biggest it gets. I've been off the hook all morning—everyone wants a piece of you. Can't it wait a month?'

No, it couldn't. After he had paid a visit to Marlon's killer there wouldn't be anywhere to go except as far as possible from LA—maybe for good.

Leon had returned from Europe a winner. His mom and sister had met him and the three of them had held each other in Arrivals, not caring about the paparazzi shouting his name, not caring about the press requests and calls for product sponsorship and media deals. Leon had one priority: his family.

It was down to him. He had to face the man who had taken his brother's life.

Gordon Rimeaux, better known as the infamous G-Money,

the man in the photograph who had possessed the nerve, the *audacity*, to join the mourners on that unbearable day in 2000 when he knew all along that he was responsible for their loss. To think he had befriended Leon and gained his trust. Leon had spoken to him about Marlon; they'd connected, they'd talked. It was like a sick prank.

Now Gordon had to pay the price.

Leon had packed his bags. One last job to do and he was hitting the road.

'I'll call when I'm back,' he told his agent.

'When will that be?' came the spluttered reply. He began to say something else but Leon clicked the cell off and with one hand snapped it shut.


The apartment had been cleared. Aside from the bag he would carry with him, all Leon's possessions were boxed and ready to go. The Marlon evidence had been put away, sealed, left for the next person to uncover its secrets—and uncover them they would. Leon's defence, perhaps, when he came to stand trial? He envisaged them finding the photograph and understanding why he had been forced to make Rimeaux face up to his crime.

Grief consumed him. Anger, betrayal, shock and heartache—all the emotions he'd thought had been left behind had in fact just been waiting to resurface. Knowing the man responsible after all this time wasn't liberating, it didn't feel like justice or rightness or any of the things he'd invented; it was simply sad—incredibly, pointlessly, sad.

He was doing it for his mom and for his sister. What had he left to stay for? Lisa was out of his life, and Robin... well, if he was honest she had never been in his life at all.

Tonight she would be performing at the Platinum Awards and then she would be returning to England. Everyone and everything moved on, it was a fact of life, and that Leon hadn't been able to move on for thirteen years meant he was ready to make up for it.

Grabbing his bag, he took one final glance at the place he called home before opening the door. To his surprise, somebody was already waiting.

A hooded figure, hands in pockets, head bowed.

The man looked up and met Leon's gaze.

'We need to talk,' said Gordon Rimeaux. 'Can I come in?'

# 75

Kristin surveyed the dresses her stylist had laid out for tonight's big event. The Palisades Grand would right now be gearing up for a no-holds-barred star-studded spectacle, and Kristin couldn't wait to see sparks fly. Photographers would be arriving. Reporters would be vying. The red carpet would be rolled out. Excitement fluttered in her belly.

She consulted the hangers, trailing her fingers down the fabrics—silk, lace, chiffon, satin—and remembered one glowy afternoon when she and Bunny had raided their mother's closet while Ramona was out. The fabrics they had found, so exotic and sumptuous, like buried treasure, had provided hours of entertainment. They'd experimented with each combination, feeling so grown-up but laughing like girls beneath netting and jewels and scribbled-on makeup, as they'd taken each other's pictures and giggled at the results.

*Bunny.* She willed her sister to hear her. *I'll always be with you.*

For a second she wasn't alone. The sensation was so acute that abruptly she swung round, expecting to find Bunny in the doorway. The feeling remained, brimming with promise and mystery for a weird, extraordinary moment, before fading away.

Holding the chosen outfit beneath her chin, Kristin turned to the full-length mirror.

Tonight, she had someone special to look good for. How could she have missed him all this time? Imagining his face, his laugh, made her warm inside.

The realisation was a gift from Bunny. What was meant to happen, the love that was meant to be, the fiction Kristin had made a living from…that had finally turned to fact.

*And you'll always be with me.*

# 76

Leon sat with his hands together, head down, jaw tensed, concentrating. Gordon did the talking. Part of Leon wanted to slam him to the ground and part was desperate to know, to keep on listening, to find out, even though it hurt. Every word was agony.

He focused as best he could as the past began to unravel, filling in the blanks, connecting up the dots, everything that had happened from start to finish with not a detail missed. He didn't nod, he didn't react, nothing. He lost track of how long Gordon spent talking, shaking at the brink of the truth, groping for words, laying out the whole sorry story—about his past, about his family, about the gang and Slink and Principal, about their altercation with the Compton crew, about Marlon coming into the lot that night, wrong place, wrong time, about how it had been a mistake and he had never meant to take the gun, he had never handled a revolver before in his life, and how even to this day the horror of those events meant he could not be sure of exactly what unfolded and who had been responsible.

Had Principal pulled the trigger, or had he? One would have been voluntary, a tyrant bent on destruction; the other the gravest reflex of a young man's life.

Gordon told it as he remembered. He confessed nothing, except for the facts. He did not plead for forgiveness. He did not beg for absolution. He did not extract himself from it, or try to pin it on somebody else. He believed that it had been him that day who had shot Marlon and he had lived with that belief ever since.

He didn't play the martyr. He never forgot who the real victim was.

'I tried to tell you,' he repented. 'Shit, I tried so many times. It didn't happen 'cause I was a coward. I was afraid.'

Leon couldn't look at him. 'Of what,' he said, his voice disembodied.

'Not the law,' he confessed. 'Of Slink. Slink and the boys. When he brought you in on the charity gig... I mean, it was sick. I told him so. Like he wanted to play with fire or somethin', see how close he could get before it all blew up.'

There was a long silence.

'Pretty damn close, I'd say,' Leon supplied eventually.

'Man, I'm sorry.' Gordon's voice caught. 'I'm so sorry, man. I'm sorry.'

It was too much to take in. So many years, so much sorrow, so long hunting the truth and in the end the truth had walked right up to his door.

'All that time before we did the track,' Leon said carefully, 'all those years you could have said something. You could have given us that. Why didn't you put it right?'

'Put it right?' Gordon shook his head. 'How? Your brother died and that ain't somethin' that's ever gonna be right—'

'You should have told someone.'

Gordon was resigned to his fate. 'That's how I justified it,' he stated, 'but I know that don't mean nothin' to you and your family. There's no excuse. I should have said this at the start and it's like the more time passed, the harder it got. For a while I convinced myself that *I'd* been done wrong, I'd been preyed upon by the wrong people and maybe to a point some of that's true. But it don't excuse what I did. I have to take responsibility.'

At last Leon looked him dead in the eye. His intentions were impossible to read.

'I always said that when it came to this I would tear that person's heart out,' he said.

'Then do it.' Gordon didn't miss a beat. 'If you don't, Slink will.'

The intercom sounded. Leon ignored it but then a harsh banging followed, rattling the door. He went to answer and found himself confronted by a young, official-looking red-head. She was wearing a high collar that obscured her nose and mouth.

'Yes?'

The woman levelled him with dark blue eyes. Something about them was familiar, very faintly, a shadow of a shadow. She was dressed in black and carrying a heavy bag. Her face was totally still and pale.

'Can I help you?'

'It's about Robin Ryder,' the woman said flatly, in an English accent. 'I'm afraid I need to speak with you urgently. We should go inside.'

For a second Leon was unable to move. Something bad had happened to Robin. The woman peered past him, surprised, but only fleetingly, to see Gordon.

'Really,' she pressed. 'It's better if I come in.'

Though his visitor was rake-thin, her hair a different colour and part of her face hidden from view, she looked uncannily like...

But that wasn't possible.

'I need to see some ID,' he said.

Her gaze flickered. 'Of course.'

As she unzipped her bag and put her hand in, Leon's suspicion was absorbed by fear. He was assaulted by images of Robin—her laugh, her lips, so that when the stranger withdrew a metal object and lunged for him, he was too slow to react. In a flash he felt the stab in his stomach, electrifying, before he collapsed.

# 77

Ivy surveyed her afternoon's work with pride.

Leon Sway—fastest man in the world? There was a joke; he hadn't been fast enough for her—and now he was slumped, unconscious, against the wall. His friend the same, knocked cold by the stun gun. She hadn't anticipated the extra weight being there but he had posed no meaningful threat, toppling towards her the instant Leon went down, imagining himself the hero before she dealt him the exact same fate.

Could nothing stop her? She smiled, satisfied with her shrewd precognition. She had known that Robin was Leon's vulnerable point and she had punched him where it hurt.

Calmly, collectedly, Ivy closed the door, kicking the flaccid bodies inside, dragging first Leon by his shoulders into the centre of the floor and then his friend. It was hard work but the thrill carried her through. She had already taken two lives; here were two more and then countless dozens to come. With every death she gained strength.

And after a point, you got a taste for it.

She doused Leon's apartment in petrol, top to bottom, all across the walls and over the flammable stacked-up boxes, the odour of gasoline stringent and sour. Leon had buried himself inside his very own bonfire, she thought, gratified. The place was going to blow.

Ivy wished she could witness the moment the men woke up, trapped in a swirling tide of furious impenetrable fire, unable to escape or breathe or see through the inferno, perishing in their skins, panicking and disorientated as they searched for an exit, only to find themselves staring hopelessly into the blank white eye of the storm…

But she had somewhere more important to be.

Before the final act, Ivy went to Leon and crouched, leaning to touch her lips briefly to his. They were warm. These were the lips that her twin had kissed, one of the countless things in life her sister had claimed while Ivy had been denied.

Fuelled by a burst of hatred, she stood on the threshold and struck the match. In a rasp it caught. She threw it in as carelessly as an apple core and watched the place begin to burn.

Coolly she walked to her car, climbed in and switched the ignition. As the vehicle moved off she detected the smash of shattering glass, smoke starting to billow from the windows. Next stop: the Palisades Grand.

## 78

The ETV Platinum Awards was the greatest occasion in the musical calendar. Since the eighties it had been renowned for a glittering array of iconic performances, provocative costumes, show-stopping speeches and scandalous wins. It was the definitive limelight for a galaxy of stars, from up-coming talent to established icons. Each year passed with a fresh dose of drama, whether that was an underdog victory, a red-carpet shocker or a dramatic host.

This summer, all eyes would be on three stories: Kristin White and Scotty Valentine, appearing separately but for ever tied by the theatre of their break-up; Robin Ryder, now one of the biggest names in America after a knock-out smash of a tour; and Turquoise da Luca, whose stellar year with her debut movie *True Match* had culminated in one of the biggest humiliations in Hollywood history: Cosmo Angel's shattering disgrace.

In her dressing room, Turquoise applied the last of her

make-up. She employed a stylist but had always preferred to do her own paintwork.

The smile she now gave her reflection was something that money couldn't buy.

The crowd would be waiting to see how she faced the music—they couldn't know that it was she who had been responsible for Cosmo's downfall, after all—and everyone imagined she was reeling as much as the rest.

Since the YouTube outrage, Cosmo had disappeared completely from the public eye. No one had seen him. No one had heard from him. Rumour had it he'd fired and hired a whole new team, his PR machine working into the ground, but Turquoise couldn't imagine how he could possibly come back from it. The footage had been strewn across the web in seconds, gathering a pace of its own, with every click and every view sealing Cosmo's fate. The press had gone to town. The fans had been dismayed. It had sounded his death knell.

Whatever Cosmo had threatened Turquoise with now was pointless. It could never buy back his reputation. She had taken from him what he had claimed of her all those years ago when she had first arrived in Los Angeles: dignity.

Deliberately she had spared Ava. She had thought long and hard about it and, after searching her conscience, and after the event, she was glad of that decision. When all was done, she and Ava had both worked at Madam Babydoll's and she would never know what had brought Ava there in the first place. She could never forgive Ava for what she had put her through, but Turquoise had learned over the years that people were rarely what they appeared to be. Who knew what Cosmo had subjected his wife to, in order to turn her into the reprehensible robot that had fed Turquoise water and changed her sheets? Ava's treasured marriage was tarnished eternally by her husband's perversions—and that was enough.

There was a tap at the door and Donna put her head round, smiling. After her initial astonishment at Cosmo's extra-curricular pursuits had subsided—*'D'you know, I always thought there was something odd about him; that script was way too real'*—she had seen it make Turquoise more bankable than ever. World domination was a single deal away.

'You ready?' she asked as a stage assistant passed with a time check:

'Ten minutes, Ms da Luca.'

She was opening tonight's show. It was the start of the rest of her life.

'Let's do this,' she replied, getting to her feet. Her hair was piled on top of her head and her jet catsuit clung to every curve. Huge gold hoops glinted at her ears and a slash of red lipstick confirmed her as the most stunning woman there.

Outside, Bronx was waiting.

'Hey, lady.' He kissed her and took her hand. 'Ready?'

She smiled up at him. 'Ready.'

Backstage, preparing for her own introduction, Kristin watched Turquoise kick off the show with a previously unheard track, 'Secret Room'. The tens of thousands packed into the stadium were going wild, screaming her name as the bass line trembled and her voice rang out. It was a stunning performance. Turquoise was riding high.

Kristin remembered what they had talked about in Italy that fuzzy, drunken afternoon, comparing horror stories about Cosmo and Jax. She wondered what Turquoise had needed Jax for, but didn't dwell on it. She was glad he had lost at the Championships. Word was his PA sweetheart had dumped him as well, swiftly followed by her resignation after she'd discovered him seeking solace with an open-mouthed volunteer. To think that Kristin had ever attempted to break Jax's ludicrous stopwatch record was preposterous.

She had been confused then…lost. Not any more. It might have taken her years to find out who she really was, but she'd done it in the end.

'You look beautiful.'

Kristin turned at the voice she knew so well. Scotty Valentine was next to her in the wings, smartly suited, a conservative ensemble with neat hair and a stiff collar. He held an envelope in one hand, the coveted nominations, and in the other a shimmering gong that, moments after her own appearance, would be passed to the winner of the Best Video category.

'Thanks.' In a super-short lace dress teamed with sneakers, her blonde locks grown out and now in a high ponytail, her style combined both new and old Kristin. She was still the same woman. She had fought against it, against Ramona and Scotty's betrayal and her sister's suicide, pretending a rebirth so she could cast off everything that had gone before, but she couldn't deny the girl she had been for twenty-three years.

'How's it going?' he asked.

'I'm good.' The last words they had spoken had been in anger. Despite everything, Scotty had comprised an enormous part of her young life. He had faced reckonings for his actions that he hadn't deserved, a backlash and criticism that was not just demeaning but unwarranted. Appearing tonight in front of millions was testament to his courage.

It was time to bury their vendetta.

'I'm sorry about Bunny,' he said. 'I've cried a lot of tears for her.'

'It's not your fault.'

'Not sure how many people would agree with that.'

'She built you up to something you weren't. Doesn't everyone do that with their idols? In real life you were never going to be all the things she wanted. Being gay or not makes no difference.'

Scotty watched her carefully; surprised, moved, and finally grateful.

'Fenton's free,' he told her.

'I heard. I'm glad.'

'So am I.'

In the stadium, the crowd erupted in applause as Turquoise exited the stage. The cameras swung round and the host resumed the podium.

'Your turn.' He kissed her cheek. 'Good luck.'

She squeezed his hand. 'You, too.'

# 79

Dusk was falling by the time Detectives McEverty and Moretti arrived at Ivy Sewell's apartment. It was one of those faceless complexes, the kind of place ordinary people went about their ordinary lives and nothing remarkable ever happened—except for today.

Moretti rapped on the door. 'Police, open up!'

No response.

McEverty withdrew his gun and signalled the entry.

'On my count,' he directed. 'One, two, three…'

One hard kick and they were inside, weapons low, skirting the walls. It was dark, the blinds drawn, but enough clarity soaked through to decipher their surroundings.

Chaos. She appeared to have been living in a single room—everything was gathered in one space: a narrow bed, the sheets disrupted as though it had been scene to a struggle; scattered plates and mugs, brought through from an unused kitchen and left to rot; a sea of unwashed clothes from which a TV and laptop surfaced, next to each other on the floor.

McEverty kicked the laptop open and the screen flashed white before relinquishing their suspect's last visited site, an arsenal of firearms: rifles, pistols, shotguns, revolvers...

'Jesus H.,' commented Moretti.

Confident the place was empty, McEverty released the blind and flooded the room with light. 'You said it,' he murmured as an entire wall covered in Robin Ryder miscellany was revealed, a replica of the cuttings they had found in England. 'It's her, no question.'

Moretti tucked his gun away, privately pleased to discover a vacated apartment because truth was the dame gave him the jeepers. He moved to inspect the wall—shrine, obsession, whatever it was—and stumbled over a tangle on the floor. As he put his hands to the mattress to steady himself his foot slammed into something solid.

'What the...?'

He crouched and looked under the bed.

'McEverty, get your ass over here. Now.'

His partner was distracted, riffling through paperwork. 'She got a job at the Palisades Grand,' he said, glancing worriedly at the wall and then back to the documents. 'Ain't that where the ETV event's happening...?'

'I said get over here.'

McEverty obliged.

There was a body under the bed, bruised red and purple at the neck.

One look at the man's bloated corpse, mouth open in

the final gasp of his demise, told McEverty everything he needed to know.

'We gotta get moving,' he announced, radioing for backup. 'We haven't got long.'

## 80

Gordon blinked into the light. He was hot, searingly hot. There was an acrid smell in his nostrils and his lungs were tight as drums, fighting to get air. His head was throbbing and there was shooting pain in his stomach, scorching like acid.

A low groan roused him, a thread that seemed to come both to him and away from him, and when the two met he realised it was he who was making the sound.

His limbs were heavy. Opening his eyes was like hauling a portcullis.

When he did, everything was orange and furious. The walls were roaring. And the heat...the clogging, inescapable heat... In his terror he inhaled sharply, swallowing smoke. He choked and coughed, fighting to see, and in doing so met a nightmare.

The building was on fire. With a jolt he recalled where he was—Leon's apartment.

It spun back on him: his confession; their conversation; the flame-haired stranger arriving at the door... Leon collapsing at the threshold…and that was the last Gordon could summon. Now they were scorching effigies, perishing on the pyre.

*Burned alive.*

Every muscle in his body exploded. He had to get out. But it was as though he had been weighted with lead. The smoke was asphyxiating and he couldn't get clean air, his whole body crying out for oxygen. The heat went beyond heat to something entirely different, insufferably close, the pain so intense that in pockets it felt almost freezing cold, his brain tricking his body into survival. On his feet, precarious and faltering, the heat was worse.

Higher up there was a rampant soundtrack. Pops and crackles and fizzes as glass exploded and flames licked and whooshed, flicking and darting and pouncing, an energy so bent on destruction he was dwarfed by its might. The walls were a rushing lava flow, the ceiling pooled orange and gold and flashing, leaping red.

*Get out, get out, get out…*

Leon was unconscious. Through a curtain of fury Gordon deciphered the dancing, quivering promise of a door, misshapen in the fever, the taunting desert mirage. He could have dived for it, given himself half a chance. Instead he grabbed Leon's shoulders. He didn't know how he did it, he scarcely had strength to support himself, but somehow he did.

Man, he was heavy. Every muscle in Leon's body had shut down, limp and useless.

Gordon pulled, shouting out with the searing effort. His knees gave way and his arms scalded but still he didn't stop. With a hiss a sheet of glass combusted and needles of fire slashed into his skin, blood melting the instant it surfaced.

Agony chased through him, overwhelming to the point of paralysis, but he had to keep going. He couldn't stop.

Suddenly, miraculously, with a final heave they were out. Clear sky flooded his vision, a wheeling arc as he dragged Leon's body out after him, away from the wreckage. He heard sirens, people rushing towards the building, felt a pair of arms catching him as he fell.

*Is anyone else inside, sir? Is there anyone else inside?*

Gordon's chest gave way. He collapsed. The road was cool, gloriously cool, beneath his scorched, blistered skin. Jets of water sprang like fountains into the air, trucks and hoses full of water, an ocean's worth of water that Gordon wanted nothing more than to drown in.

'Leon, can you hear me?' A medic was crouching. 'Leon, wake up. Wake up.'

A blanket was shrouded around Gordon's shoulders, soothing words and a mask over his nose and mouth to help his breathing.

*Wake up*, Gordon begged. *Wake up.*

Leon coughed. He spluttered. They slapped his back, helping him sit up.

It was then that their assailant's voice hit, as if from nowhere.

Gordon remembered her words as she had stood like an ice queen on the threshold.

*It's about Robin Ryder... I need to speak with you urgently...*

And after Leon had gone down, before he had lunged and been hit by the same:

*No use to her now...are you?*

Gordon tore off his mask.

'She's going for Robin,' he wheezed. 'Robin's in danger.'

# 81

Slink Bullion and the Puff City crew occupied a VIP table beneath the stage. A firm favourite of the Platinum Awards, they had seen it all over the years and were no strangers to controversy. At the previous event Principal 7 had taken to the spotlight during another rapper's set and blasted him for having made a public slant against the model he'd been dating. The night was as much renowned for personal as for professional spectacles.

Slink tossed back another drink. That was why he was uncomfortable—not that the rest of the crew or the cameras would know: the Slink he gave them was the Slink they all knew, chilled, collected, in charge. But the Awards were the kind of arena where shit exploded, and if anyone here knew a single thing about Marlon Sway then none of them were safe. He glanced at the empty seat next to him, dread crawling up his back.

Where was G?

Kristin White departed the stage to euphoric applause.

The catwalk came right out into the crowd, studded with lights, and next to appear on the golden, glittering podium was recently outed boy-band chump Scott Valentine. Slink didn't get queers.

'And the nominations for Best Video are…'

Slink gritted his teeth. Roll on the end of the night. He couldn't wait to get out of here.

## 82

Ivy worked a half-hour on the burger stand as usual. It was vital to stay under the radar but she could barely function. Her hands shook with anticipation, her skin tingling, her mind focused on nothing save the approaching instant of her retribution.

'If I didn't know better I'd say you were keepin' secrets.' Graham was at her neck, close enough that she could feel his breath. 'You're sure lookin' fine tonight...'

'I need the bathroom.' It was a wonder she could force the words out. They trembled on her tongue as she abandoned her position. 'Give me a minute.'

On the way through she spotted Nicki Soba. He smiled. It would be no trouble getting past; all she had to do was claim she had knocked off early and wanted to witness the charade. He would award her access; she'd be able to step straight into the fray, and then...

She could shoot Robin point-blank if she wanted.

The washroom she chose was on the eleventh floor,

tucked away from proceedings. This hadn't been updated like the others, with its cracks in the walls and residual graffiti. Ivy had scoped the place a thousand times and knew every inch and nook of her fortress.

Earlier she had concealed the sack of clothes and weapons, tucked behind a loose panel beneath the bank of sinks. Withdrawing it, Ivy retreated to a cubicle and closed and locked the door, already peeling off her uniform and dragging on her own clothes.

Catching her breath, she sat.

IF NOT VICTORY, REVENGE!

It was printed in hot-pink marker on the back of the cubicle door, the lettering neat and precise. Ivy reached to touch it, her fingertips tentative, tender almost across its surface, as she might in another life have caressed a lover's cheek. Surrounding the words was a vacant loop, the only unmarked space there was amid a sea of frantically scribbled transmissions, a halo as much a protection as a warning.

Victory had never been hers. But revenge? Revenge was in her blood.

From inside the stadium she could hear the muted thrum of beats and the united roar of the fans. Ivy closed her eyes, imagining the cries were for her, urging her on, baying for the carnage she was about to unleash. She released her breath slowly, tasting salt and iron, her tongue flicking across the split in her lip where she had bitten too hard in anticipation.

Ivy shoved the bag into the trashcan, forcing it down with her fists. As the lid snapped shut, quick as a trick in disappearing the evidence, she stared indifferently at the hands that would carry out this great execution. Wrists pale and brittle, like branches in winter.

Only when the bullet entered would it be over. Only when Robin's flawless skin was ruptured, that smile erased, that heartbeat frozen, one and the same as hers and yet a universe apart, would it be finished. In front of thirty thousand disciples whose shrieks of panic would hardly be discernible from their fanatic cries of ecstasy; massacre as they tried to flee.

How delicious it had been to pay Leon a visit, how delectable to have doused the rag and struck the match. Ivy pictured the flames licking at the walls of his apartment; the quiet asphyxiation as he lurched, blind and gasping, for a way out...

*Revenge.*

It had been in her since before she was born.

## 83

It was hard to believe that this time two years ago Robin had been an ordinary girl who had never even stood on a stage. The Platinum Awards were a huge deal, broadcast globally, and now here she was, fronting before millions at the crescendo of a sell-out tour.

'Wow, check you out!' Barney grinned, impressed by her super-slim leggings and shimmering crop top that showed off her California-tanned belly to perfection, a look completed by giant wedge heels and a dramatically sweeping fringe.

He led the group in a collective hug, as he did before every gig, and, while they groaned at the cheesiness of it, secretly they embraced it. With her arms around her band mates' shoulders, Robin felt a sense of solidarity. They were her team, her family, the only family she'd ever had. She wondered what her mother would say if she could see her now, on top of the world, left to die but choosing to live, and for once it didn't sting.

Maybe it didn't matter. Maybe she didn't care.

Maybe friends were the only blood you needed.

As they made their way towards the stage Robin could hear the awards being handed out, the applause and the fans' euphoria. Beyond the rigging she caught a glimpse of the stage lights and the contagious, addictive glow of the spotlight. It was a serious place to be. Gathered at the Palisades Grand was the elite of the music industry.

Robin pictured a girl in a London bedroom, singing into the mirror as she herself had done once, dreaming of making it big one day. She pictured the girl in a flat. It was painted in astonishing detail for somewhere she had never visited. The carpet was tortoiseshell, a mess of yellows and browns; tired lamps scattered, their shades dusty and damp; a hostess trolley in one corner; and on the mantelpiece a clock trapped at a quarter to three...

The photo she had been sent catapulted towards her through the shadows.

'Are you all right?' Polly touched her arm. 'You've gone really pale.'

Robin caught herself. 'I'm fine.'

'We're on.' Matt slammed his downturned palm into the middle of the circle and the rest of them followed, releasing with a flourish. 'Let's rock!'

The woman in the picture was nobody to her, and yet the grim familiarity of her clung on...the scrawled, childlike writing on the back...

**ROBIN.**

She swallowed her terror.

The second she was onstage, she would be safe.

## 84

Scotty was shaking like a leaf. Even though his slot had been and gone, the buzz still rushing through him was intense. His first onstage resurgence was over. It was done. And instead of the jeers and boos he had envisaged, the crowd had been angelic. While he had stood waiting for the nominees' VT to run, he had even seen a group close to the podium talking among themselves, more interested in their own business than in his. Realising you weren't at the centre of everybody's universe was a liberating insight indeed.

He decided to watch the rest of the show with Joey and the guys, whose seating was towards the back—a relegated position for America's once-so-hot boy band. In the interests of retaining a low profile, an escort led him through a staff gangway. When they stopped to let a camera pass, he noticed, tacked to the wall, a security ID poster comprising palm-sized employee mug shots—you never could be too careful these days.

Amid the hundred or so gathered, one stood out.

He recognised that face…but from where?

A red-haired, hard-faced, grisly-eyed woman; he had seen her someplace before but try as Scotty might he couldn't put a finger on it. On close inspection she bore a resemblance to Robin Ryder—albeit a gone-wrong, skinny-ass, redhead Robin Ryder. But the context was familiar, too: the head and shoulders, cropped and disembodied, pinned to a board…the hollow bearing of the formally photographed… a shard of memory that was quickly usurped by Fenton's imploring expression and overtaken by the distraction of those emotions.

The woman flashed evil. He should have known where he had seen her image before and could have been able to prevent the carnage if he had…

But no, the connection was lost.

# 85

Cosmo Angel's cobalt Ferrari roared up to the sumptuous entrance of the Palisades Grand, where it ploughed through a NO STOPPING sign and screeched to a halt with a furious shriek of tyres. The photographers had a field day as Cosmo leapt out, manic and unshaven, his shirt undone, his hair a frenzied nest, murky pockets of sleep deprivation haggard beneath his eyes…a husk of the Hollywood star he had been. Cosmo hadn't been seen in public since his 'Kingdom Come' disgrace. It was quite a reawakening.

Abandoning his vehicle, he stormed towards the gate.

'Mr Angel, sir…'

'Out of my way, fuckhead.'

'Mr Angel, if you'd just—'

Cosmo grabbed the man's lapels and pulled him up, lifting him off his feet.

'Do you know who I am?' he lashed.

The cameras were going crazy. This was a pap's wet dream.

Cosmo released the man with such force that he went crumpling to the steps, and barged through, heading straight to the theatre. He was royalty, for Crissakes, it was Access All Areas! Everyone on the planet knew who Cosmo Angel was—and if they hadn't before the YouTube exposé then they'd recently received a thorough education.

He was here for one reason.

To make Turquoise da Luca pay.

Even thinking her name made him ready to bubble over with wrath.

As Cosmo stampeded through a gauntlet of guardians, each too afraid to counter not just an A-list movie giant but also a rampaging lunatic, he resolved that there was simply nothing more to lose. Turquoise's actions had crucified his career. They had slaughtered his marriage. They had slain his reputation. They had castrated him. He was a zombie, battered and butchered, and all because of what—the blackmail of some *whore*?

That was all Turquoise would ever be, no matter how far she thought she had come or how she reckoned to have left little scared Grace behind.

Grace Turquoise da Luca was a slut hooker cash-grabbing, ball-breaking bitch that opened her legs for money.

If there was nowhere to go but down, Cosmo was taking her with him.

# 86

Leon's T-shirt was torn and blackened by fire. His skin was slick, chalky with salt and smoke as he stumbled on to the street, one arm raised like a flag.

He was dizzy. He couldn't see straight. The cars skewed and tipped and weaved.

'Jesus.' The cab driver didn't recognise him. 'You OK?'

'Drive.' He climbed in. 'No questions, just drive.'

'Whatever you say.'

Leon's lungs were charred, fighting to keep up. In the back seat he shook, desert-hot then glacier-cold, his chest compressed as though he had been winded.

'D'you need the hospital?'

'Faster,' he instructed. 'Drive faster.'

Downtown they hit traffic. Leon thought of the first words she had said to him, when they had met in London; her dark eyes guarded, a warm, deep blue:

*I was handling that myself...*

That was Robin all over. Never asking for anyone, never

needing a soul. Tonight, there was no choice. She was in danger.

'Hey—!' the driver hollered as Leon busted open the door and took to the packed gridlock, chasing the ground, pushing towards that last lone goal that was beautiful in its simplicity. The more he ran, the more his body opened up to the pursuit, clean air rinsing through him and his legs falling into the rhythm that they had known for so long. He was lighter than the wind, quicker than water, flying so fast it felt as if someone were at his back, giving him what he needed as he shot past parked cars and stationary trucks, rigid with their bottled-up impatience; not like him, free as an eagle, flying, flying...

The glinting peak of the Palisades Grand soared into view, a shining prize that shimmered in the fading sun like a relic. Light bounced off its silver contours and one second he was close enough to touch, the next impossibly far away.

Leon ran and ran, he didn't know where his might came from, something bigger and braver than he was, something he didn't understand. He let it in and then it was as if the ground left his feet, the goal coming closer.

He pushed past security, a web of arms battling to rein him in but they weren't swift enough. Speed was his missile. The intruder was unrecognisable as Leon Sway, his face and arms streaked with soot, his T-shirt ripped and pitted with holes that revealed his shoulders and back. As he tore through the lobby, heavies chasing and raising support, feeling for their weapons but to no avail, the throngs parted like waves to let him through.

'Sir, stop right there, sir!'

'Stop that man!'

'Somebody get him!'

A screeching siren sounded in his wake, security alerts winging around the building.

'Police!' they hollered. 'Stop or we'll shoot!'

Never. They would have to kill him first.

## 87

The glare was too blinding. The lights were too hot. The crowd was too loud. Robin felt like she had back in San Francisco, a sitting target, exposed and vulnerable.

The throbbing bass counted her in and she missed her cue, the lyrics deserting her so that Matt threw her a fleeting quizzical look before repeating the refrain.

She couldn't get a grip on the rhythm; it was like deciphering a foreign language. At last her voice came through but she was off-pitch, the world discordant, jangly as keys, and time distilled to the moment she couldn't escape from. She was overcome with a need to flee.

Her gaze was drawn into the darkness beyond the stage, where something unknown and unseen lurked, terrifying as a monster under the bed. Beyond the pounding beat and the sound of her dwindling vocal a distant siren sounded, high and thin and so very faint that Robin thought it might be inside her own head, the shrill approach of panic.

## 88

Ivy heard the alarm go up. Nicki Soba's radio crackled with the news.

*Red alert. Security breach. Stations on guard.*

This was it. No time to waste. They were coming.

She melted into the horde of fans at the brink of the VIP pen. All attention was on the stage, and shrouded as she was in obscurity Ivy trembled with promise. The section had been cordoned off. Already she could see the goons receiving their instructions: one by the rope, another up in the circle, a third by the nearest exit.

How had they got on to her so quickly?

There was no time to think, no time to hesitate. She had a plan to detonate.

Robin had taken the spotlight, inciting the cheers that had proved the soundtrack to her shameless, blessed, cheating life.

After all these years there remained just a hundred metres between them.

*Hello. Remember me?*

As Ivy stepped forward, drawing a hand inside her coat to retrieve the butt of the firearm, she shivered at making history that could never be rewound. When all was said and done these people were no *better* than her. They didn't have the secret…she did.

That was what Robin never realised. She never stopped to think about average people or the average life she had deserted, her neglected, forgotten-about wasteland of a past, and the thing about the past was that it liked to find a way of coming back.

Now, Ivy was anything but average.

She forced herself to wait a moment, brief as it was, to savour her arrival, before raising a gun to the air and pulling the trigger.

## 89

The first bullet smashed through a giant candelabrum, amputating it from its moorings so that it hung, drunkenly suspended, precarious as a severed finger. Robin's music cut and she went to scream but the only sound she heard was the cold blare of the security alarm.

Fear and confusion crashed through the auditorium as the arena hurtled to its feet, rushing to escape the raining bullets that sprayed the crowd like cattle as they darted for survival, stumbling over jewel-encrusted gowns and thousand-dollar Armani suits.

Mayhem. Chaos. Bedlam. The whole place moved like a landslide, tipping like a rocking boat in a squall, terror ripping through Robin along with the intoxicating aroma of fear. Bodies hit the floor. Blood smeared across the tableware. Chairs were thrown. In their desperation they trampled over each other, the spike of a heel in an ear, the tear of a dress, the pushing and shoving.

Someone grabbed her. 'Fucking hell, let's *go!*'

She couldn't. Her feet were rooted.

A crimson glimmer flickered in the shadows, bright as a ribbon, a flame in the black.

Robin knew that woman. She had seen her before.

She saw her every time she looked in the mirror.

*'It's her,'* she whispered.

If ever she had doubted it, validation came when the weapon was raised and Robin found herself staring straight into the barrel of a gun.

## 90

By the time McEverty and Moretti arrived on the scene, they were too late. The Palisades was scene to mass evacuation and hysteria, the stadium spewing out a gush of stricken luminaries as camera crews rolled up and reporters took their posts, chattering into microphones as the news broke, too much to take in and even more to communicate…the coverage of flashing lights and cutthroat excitement behind which lives were still being lost.

'Am I seeing this?' McEverty was sick to his stomach.

Inside was carnage. Gunshots rang out. Armed squads were prepped to bring the assassin down amid a writhing pack of thousands, vested up and packed with ammo as they were released into the hectic fray.

'She got here first,' quailed Moretti, bending to catch his breath, his hands on his knees. 'The broad beat us to it.'

An overwrought woman, rabid with fear, was ejected from the melee. Beyond the wild hair and slashed dress he recognised her as an RnB songstress. She clutched on to him.

'Do something!' she wailed. 'You have to do something! *People are dying in there!*'

McEverty pulled his gun. 'We're going in.'

# 91

As if in a dream, Robin watched the woman approach.

Her hair was redder than before, her gaze more gleaming, ripe with destruction.

Bodies were strewn; fallen or dead, it was impossible to tell. Robin braced herself, knowing she was going to die but that she wasn't ready. This was her life. She had worked for it, she had earned it; it was only just starting to happen. This couldn't be the end.

A round of bullets sounded from the rear of the space. An army piled through, lasers crossing the massacre like ticker tape.

'Don't you know who I am?' Her accoster's voice was close enough to hear, intimate, as if they were alone in a vacuum, the still, silent plug at the heart of a tornado.

The gun came in, mere feet away now. It was near enough for Robin to see the polished metal and the pallid hand that held it.

Numbly she nodded. The woman was her age. Beneath

the surface discrepancies, they looked the same. She had known it since San Francisco. She had known it all along.

'We're family. It's nice to meet you, Robin.' Her voice was elusive, one second tight to Robin's ear and the next far away, like a message coming from the distant end of a tunnel.

Robin's tongue was thick. She couldn't speak.

'I'll do anything,' she whimpered. The words seemed to come out regardless, her basic instinct for survival. 'Please...'

'Say it.' A thin smile.

'I can't—'

*'Say it!'* The gun shook.

Robin remembered the grip of the woman's hand in hers, cold and stifling...

The messages, the roses, the scrapbook, the phone call...

The childlike handwriting on the back of the photo...

The old lady in the chair, the clock stuck at a quarter to three...

The girl in the London flat...

'You're my sister,' she choked, searching the woman's eyes for compassion, affection, anything at all. Only the gun stared back. Behind it, her attacker spoke the words she had let go of such a long time ago, believing they would never arrive.

'That's right. We're family, Robin. I'm the family you never had.'

Robin dropped to her knees. White noise flooded through her brain.

'We should have turned out the same, you and me. We would have, if you had stayed and I had gone. Only I didn't get that choice.'

She thought she would pass out. Somehow she managed to stay upright, palms in the air, begging for mercy. If she lost consciousness that would be it: she wouldn't wake up.

'It can't be,' she gasped. 'It can't be…'

'You lived while I perished.'

'I didn't have a choice.' *I don't want to die.* 'I'm like you. I'm just like you—'

'It's too late.' The blue eyes flared. 'You don't deserve this. The place you came from, the *people* you came from… You don't deserve it. I'm the one who paid the price.'

'My mother…' Robin had trained herself out of saying it, thinking it, even.

'Your mother was a drunk. She ruined me. She took me to hell and I never came back. Where were you?' Though it was a question, the words couldn't escape that horrible, dead, flat tone. 'You left me behind. I was your responsibility, and you *left me behind.*'

'Please,' she sobbed, tears pushing through the shock, 'I never knew, I swear it—'

'People like you think you can walk away.'

'It's not what I wanted,' she pleaded. 'It's not what I chose.'

'I didn't forget. I never forgot. I've been following you. I know everything. I know you better than anyone. Isn't that what sisters are for?'

From deep within, Robin found a kernel of strength. It was defiant, self-possessed, unwilling to falter or to fail. If it had seen her through this far, it would see her through again.

'Don't hurt me,' she beseeched, her arms reaching. 'We can talk about this. We can work it out—'

'No time.'

'There is, please, there is—'

'We're through.'

The gun was levelled squarely at her forehead.

'Goodnight, Robin.'

## 92

A shot was fired. Impact hit her from the side and Robin was thrown, a crack of white light before darkness spun.

Falling…falling…

Instead of impact she became aware of strong arms around her, holding her tight.

When she looked up, she came face to face with an angel.

'It's you,' she said, and thought one thing:

*I'm alive. I'm talking; I'm still here.*

Leon Sway was covering her, his body warm and the smell of his T-shirt smoky and sweet. She could hear his thrumming, pulsing heart.

Was she dreaming? No. She would know him anywhere.

His back formed a wall to the source of the bullet. Beyond she saw where her sister's missile had ripped into a life-sized replica of the Platinum Award, a silver-plated idol belting into a mic. The head had been blown to pieces—exactly where Robin's should have been.

Leon shielded her from a shower of gunfire. His body

was steel-hard, solid as armour and firm as a rock. She gripped his upper arms, his skin beneath her fingers where the fabric had torn, and through the angle of his elbow she saw her twin go down.

Ivy Sewell jerked and thrashed as she was sprayed with lead, vacant eyes staring glassily at Robin for a long, last, lingering moment until her body caved.

Leon didn't let her go. He kept whispering in her ear, again and again:

'You're safe now, you're safe, it's over; you're safe…'

A stinging tear escaped her eye.

'We made it, Robin,' Leon said. 'It's OK, we made it.'

# Epilogue

November brought with it the first snap of cold. In London the trees had lost their leaves, brittle branches silver and still. An icy spell froze the ground, the ponds sealed over, children wrapped in scarves and hats as they played in the frost-crusted park and prayed for snow. The sky was pink and blue. Fires were lit. The nights drew in.

Turquoise da Luca was filming in the capital with British director Xander Jakobson. Her costume pinched at the waist and her hair tumbled loose, a gypsy girl come to land in the Docks, her beauty matched by her fearlessness. The movie was a romantic adventure about a woman who travels back in time to change the fate of her star-crossed love affair.

'They meant it when they said you were a natural,' gushed her lead when the first scene was in the can. 'You made *True Match*.' He checked himself. 'I mean, I know that sounds bad after…you know…not to say that Cosmo wasn't—'

'I get you.' She smiled. 'Thanks.'

In her trailer, Turquoise took a call from Donna Cameron about her new single, 'Strong', which was due for release at the end of the month. Her career was hurtling to stellar heights and she cherished every moment. Since the drama of the Platinum Awards, the upsets of which were still raw, her profile had skyrocketed, as had anyone's who had been there that fateful evening and had survived to tell the tale.

Turquoise had arrived both as a Hollywood movie star and as a world-class diva. Few artists could pull off both.

Finally, she was liberated from oppression, from fear, from the clutches of Ivan and Denny and Cosmo. She had never imagined that this day would come, and while it had done so at a price, a terrible price for so many, her history no longer had the power to destroy her.

She had stopped looking over her shoulder at every turn. She had stopped waking up in the night, bathed in sweat and flattened by memories. Her deliverance was exquisite in its transparency and scope, as if the world had been laid before her and she had been unchained to explore its riches that until this point had been swathed in obscurity.

'Your flight gets in at eleven and then it's straight to the studio,' said Donna. 'Try to sleep on the plane. Are you eating OK?'

'Never been better.'

'Resting when you can?'

'Donna, I'm fine.'

'You know I'm looking out for you. I can't think of one person involved who's gone straight back to work, never mind taken on what you have. You could have been seriously hurt that night, Turquoise. You could have died.'

She could. In fact if it weren't for a kind intervention, a twist of fate, she would have been caught in the crossfire and suffered like so many. It was funny how a split-second decision could change everything. Following her performance she had craved fresh air. By the time she'd emerged the evacuation was underway and the throng was being guided out.

Luck had been a long time coming.

'I know,' she replied. She couldn't say, *I've come closer to death than that,* and instead supplied, 'It's easier to focus on the job.'

Donna hadn't been able to understand her client's stoicism the morning after the Platinums, amid the shock and wreckage, when news of Cosmo had come in. Turquoise hadn't reacted at all, just listened while the facts were disclosed.

Didn't she care? Cosmo had been her costar, her collaborator—and, yes, while he had been revealed as being as depraved and degenerate as the next monster, they had known each other, they had surely been close...wouldn't she at least feel *something*? Anything?

She didn't. There would have been no other reason for Cosmo to attend the Platinum Awards that night other than to confront her. In tracking Turquoise down until the bitter end, he had sealed his own grim destiny. There was justice in that. She felt no sympathy.

Even if she had, relief would have buried it.

Because only then had she known it was truly over.

Cosmo Angelopoulos would never darken her door again. The joy she felt at that realisation was phenomenal. She might have ruined his reputation, but as long as he was still breathing she could not have rested easy. His funeral had been well attended, though not by her. Instead she had focused on a different ceremony: one for the girl who had been exhumed in the Anza-Borrego desert. She had sent flowers incognito, unsure if they'd been received. It wasn't a crime she could ever confess to, because it hadn't been her crime. She saw that now. And she saw that the true perpetrator was dead, slain just days after his worst nightmare became a cloying, inescapable reality. Fate moved in mysterious ways.

'I'll buzz you when I land,' said Turquoise. There was a knock at her trailer door and she said goodbye before going to answer it.

'Hello,' said Bronx, stepping inside with his lazy, sexy grin.

She returned it. Now nobody need ever find out about her past, unless she chose to tell. She had chosen one person, and that was the man she had fallen in love with. Bronx had always been there, he'd never wavered, never faltered, and she could trust him with her life.

During one long, painful weekend, Turquoise had told Bronx everything. She had bared it all, every detail, right from the start, and, amazingly, here he was. He was still here.

'Don't you know I'm working?' she teased.

'You're always working. All work and no play makes Bronx a bored boy. Especially when you look so hot and your hair's a mess.'

She had traded her confession for the most precious thing in the world.

Love.

Bronx looped his arms around her waist and steered her back into the trailer.

She giggled. 'What are you going to do?'

Deeply, he kissed her. 'Everything. Always.'

She kissed him back. 'All right,' she said. 'I can live with that.'

Kristin watched Turquoise on TV the following night, promoting her new single. The women had stayed close since Italy and were hoping to collaborate on a track in the New Year. She was happy to see her friend succeed.

She had travelled to New York for a meeting about the Bunny White 'You've Got a Friend' Foundation, an organisation for kids who felt lonely or unhappy or simply needed someone to talk to. The session had gone well and she had returned to her hotel brimming with ideas and inspirations. It was positive to be channelling her grief into a meaningful outcome. Not a minute passed when she didn't think about Bunny and miss her horribly, but knowing her sister would have loved the foundation and what it stood for was some comfort. Hour by hour, day by day, she was getting there.

'How can she be so...*on* it already? It's like the Platinums didn't affect her at all.'

Next to her, one arm behind his head as he relaxed on the bed with his ankles crossed, one sock sporting a hole, Joey Lombardi drank from a bottle of Coke and frowned at the screen. Joey was visiting his brother in NYC and he and Kristin had decided to hook up. When he'd suggested coming to her hotel she hadn't known what to say.

'She's a professional,' Kristin replied, with a shrug.

'So are you, but you still took a break.'

'That's different. I wanted to.'

Since the Awards Kristin had shifted down a gear. These days she was focusing on behind-the-scenes projects that were less about fame and attention and more about making her feel as if she was achieving something worthwhile. She had hired a lawyer and finally broken free from Ramona, whose white-knuckle grip on her assets had at last been released.

Financial and career independence was priceless, and while she would never cut her mother totally loose—one absent daughter was enough—there was no reason for them to work together again. Ramona had played out the tantrum, refusing to speak to her until, in several months, she would no doubt come creeping back for a reflected splash of Kristin's celebrity. In the meantime she had moved to Europe and begun dating a Danish body builder. Kristin had heard from a mutual acquaintance that Ramona had begun training herself, ever in pursuit of the career that would make her name. The competitive spirit never waned.

Joey stretched his arm out so it snaked behind her on the pillow. She pretended not to notice. The movement hitched up his T-shirt so she caught a flash of his olive-skinned stomach, a trail of fuzz running into his jeans.

'Anyway, what about you?' Kristin mumbled, embarrassed. She sat up and focused intently on her painted toenails. 'I don't see Fraternity reforming any time soon.'

He laughed. 'No shit.'

'You're not sad?'

'Sure. I'll always be kinda sad. But it ended for a reason and now we just want to get on with the future. Brett's writing solo stuff. Doug's signed a modelling contract. Luke's taking a vacation with his girlfriend someplace…'

At least Luke wasn't off with Ramona. Cringe! Kristin had blanked most of that night from her memory so at least was now spared the detail of her mother's erroneous dalliance.

'It's cool,' Joey finished. 'I just want to see what else is out there. Maybe we'll do a Greatest Of or get together further down the line, never say never and all that, but I've been in this game since forever and it's not reality. I want to be…*normal* for a while.'

She could relate.

'And Scotty?' she asked.

Joey tensed. Neither of them wanted to talk about Scotty or the price he had paid at the Platinums…it was too sad. His first event on that scale and he had seemed so fixed, so *optimistic* when she'd spoken to him, only to have that tragedy waiting in the wings.

'I don't know. He wasn't taking calls last time I tried.'

'I think I'll go see him,' Kristin said.

'I wouldn't. Not yet. He needs time.' Seeing her worried expression, Joey sat up next to her. 'He'll be OK. Really, he will.'

'I thought I'd never get over hating Scotty, not after how he hurt me. But we were friends, you know? Best friends. It's odd knowing that I still care about him.'

Joey took a strand of blonde from in front of her eyes and tucked it behind her ear.

'Don't you think it's weird how sometimes we miss the most obvious things?'

She averted her gaze.

'Just that you can be convinced for ages about how you feel,' he murmured, 'then one day you wake up and everything changes.' He was looking straight at her.

Her heart quickened. 'I guess...'

Joey didn't take his hand away. He moved his fingers to her chin and lifted it.

'C'mon,' he said tentatively, 'why d'you really think I'm here?'

His eyes were gorgeous, deep and brown. She thought how lovely his thick hair was, how kind his smile, how good he had always been to her, through it all. Joey Lombardi had never left her side and she had seen him as a constant friend, taken him for granted when maybe...just maybe, he was the guy she had always been searching for.

'You've got to know how I feel about you,' he confessed. 'I've felt like this for years, watching you with Scotty and Jax and every guy who came along and got a piece of you because I was too slow and I didn't tell you in time—'

She cut him off with a kiss, one gentler and softer than any she had known. It was the purest, sweetest kiss and she never wanted it to end.

When at last they parted he said, 'I've waited a long time for that.'

Kristin fell into his arms. Finally, she had found her fairytale ending.


Scotty Valentine rested back in the bathtub and put his hand cautiously under the water. He felt for it, unable to become accustomed to the glaring absence, until his fingers came into contact with the smooth, yielding stump of his knee.

Where his calf, ankle and foot should have been, there was nothing. Just air. Just water.

He was lucky to have survived. Ivy Sewell had blasted his leg but it could just as easily have been his back or his chest, and then what?

While they hadn't been able to save his leg, he had been spared his future.

Living was what mattered, living each day to the fullest and not caring what anybody thought, just being himself, whether that concerned his disability, his sexuality or anything else that people cared to criticise him for. Scotty chose to see those things as badges of his strength and was honoured to bear both with pride.

There was a tap at the door and Fenton put his head round.

'Everything OK?'

Scotty smiled, gesturing for him to come in. He had moved into Fenton's waterfront Nantucket home following his release from hospital. In the aftermath of the Platinums, the ex-lovers' private drama had been rendered small fry, no longer worthy of precious column inches. Given the space and time to talk and reconnect, the men had worked through their issues and seen what it was they really wanted—and that was each other.

Fenton was Scotty's ally, his companion and his lover. For a while he had lost his way, scared and confused, unable to separate his feelings about the relationship from the fear-fuelled pressure that had haunted him every waking hour.

Now, things were different. Fenton no longer held him on a pedestal. Scotty no longer let his anxieties dictate his treatment of the man who treasured him most. They no longer had a working relationship; they had an intimate one built on confidence and affection.

'Surprise,' said Fenton, producing two flutes of champagne.

'What's this about?'

'It's our anniversary.'

'It is?' Scotty grinned. Fenton went to help him but he insisted on doing it himself, using the rail at the side of the tub while he became accustomed to the movement.

Fenton perched on the side. He touched his glass to Scotty's.

'Three months since we started over,' he said.

Scotty leaned in for a kiss. 'Three amazing months.' Time in which Fenton had exceeded what he'd thought feasible of one human being's capacity for another. His support and devotion were boundless. It was impossible to imagine feeling any closer than this.

He didn't know how he would have done it without him. His boyfriend had been his pillar. This was where it began again. No more hiding away.

'You're brave,' said Fenton.

'I've had a brave man with me,' he replied.

Fenton took his hand. The King of the Charts had resigned from the music industry and moved to Massachusetts to experience a quieter life. He enjoyed fishing, hiking and travelling to Rhode Island on weekends to visit friends, where he would cook good food and sit on the veranda smoking and watching the stars. After the cut and thrust of the pop industry it was a welcome change, and while he had misgivings about Scotty pursuing a solo career he didn't discourage it. He had lived forty years in that world and the way he saw it now—especially now, after the wreck of the Platinums—it was a ruthless place. Yes, Scotty might fail, he might crash and burn, he might live to regret it…but there was no regret worse than never having found out. Fenton could not be the one who had stood in his way.

His disability, instead of leaving him defeated, had spurred Scotty into action. Each day was seized as if it were the last. Scotty said he wanted to change the way homosexuality was addressed in the music industry, how it was represented to the market, and despite Fenton wanting to shake him and tell him it was never going to work, it was a crazy ambition, a part of him couldn't help but admire it. The past year had taught him that despite his wealth of experience he really knew nothing of what life could throw your way, the surprises and twists that could change everything overnight.

All he knew for sure was that, together, they had found a kind of peace.

Scotty half laughed, half frowned. 'What are you doing?'

The instant Fenton lowered to one knee and fumbled in his back pocket, he knew. From it, his ex-manager produced a plain silver band.

'Scotty Valentine,' Fenton asked, 'will you marry me?'

From a couch in the middle of the dining room floor, the last remaining item of furniture in the near-vacant Angel Residence, Ava Bennett spat obscenities at a rerun of *True Match*.

'Die, bitch!' she heckled, chucking a hot dog at the screen, where it hit with a splat and dribbled mustard down the image. Despite it Turquoise's performance shone through;

her beauty remained unsullied. Ava flew to her feet and slammed one of her husband's baseball bats into it, sending the picture flying into a thousand shards of broken glass.

Whimpering, she dribbled to the floor.

Life had ended. She had lost it all.

It was hard not to take that literally when surrounded by blank walls and empty floors.

The once so sumptuous Angel mansion was now a shell. Following Cosmo's death Ava had spiralled into depression, her only solace the refuge of junk food, and had ballooned to a size twenty in as many weeks. The parts had dried up. She was hunted by paparazzi, who would photograph her chowing on burgers and chips and looking enormous in slack pants, or without a bra, or guzzling a super-sized milkshake at her husband's grave, where she would peer guiltily out from beneath a cap, unrecognisable as her former self.

Cosmo had left her in a pit of debt. His addiction to prostitutes—and to gambling, it transpired, and to drink, and to online sex chat rooms—had been worse than even she had suspected. Rather than the tens of millions she'd counted on, there had been a deficit.

That, coupled with Ava's lack of work, meant she had been unable to stay above water. The bailiffs had taken everything.

Every day she was tormented by Cosmo's abrupt demise. If only he had taken her advice and steered clear of that evil whore!

No. He'd been unable to resist. If he hadn't gone to the Platinums that night, if he had only let it go, if he hadn't got caught in the butchery that had robbed him of his life, he would still be here. But Cosmo would never have let Turquoise take the last word; he would never have accepted the outcome of her revenge when his reputation languished so forlornly in the gutter. His humiliation had been insufferable. All those people witnessing his private kicks, it had been vile, a worse vengeance than he or Ava could ever have conjured in their wildest fantasies…and their fantasies got pretty wild.

Ava blubbed with fresh misery. To this day she couldn't fathom how Turquoise had possessed the nerve to execute such a heinous, despicable deed.

She had packed a box of special belongings, private possessions to keep close by.

Ava went to them now and released the cardboard flap. She fed a hand in and removed the golden crown that Cosmo had worn that night on Crete.

It glimmered.

Ava put it on and faced the mirror, her face blotchy and red.

The fat, ugly, widowed, wicked queen.

She looked at her reflection and wept.


Slink Bullion was smoking a nine-inch cigar in his mansion Jacuzzi and watching a Turquoise video on his beach-shack entertainment system. There was one smokin' hot honey. He decided to get in touch with her management about guesting on a vibe he was toying with. Seeing as he was a single man these days, *officially* single, who knew what they could share?

Puff City needed an injection of something and Slink wasn't sure yet what. It wasn't like him, he always saw the bigger picture, but since G had walked it had been a struggle.

G-Money was now living in Australia. Word was he had made his peace with Leon Sway, and Leon, for reasons unknown, had decided not to pursue it. The guy's house had burned down, admittedly; maybe he'd had deeper stuff on his mind. Slink hoped it would stay that way. Just because G got an attack of conscience and figured he'd come clean, it didn't mean the rest of them should.

No wonder he had moved to another continent.

Slink grimaced as he hauled his body from the water. He extinguished his cigar at the bar, picked up his cell and dialled Principal. No answer.

Since the Platinums, Principal had been acting like a prime pussy. Slink had got his brothers out of there, away from the danger, where his comrade had run for his life like a weasel down a dark hole. Now Principal was smoking too many drugs, governed by paranoia, not eating properly, setting himself up for an early grave.

*They came for me*, he had told Slink through dry lips the morning after the Awards, shaking as he gripped the wheel of his truck and blindly ran a red light.

*All the shit I did, man; this is payback.*

Without G, without Principal, Puff City was in trouble. The way Principal was going, he wouldn't be back any time soon.

Slink padded indoors. His hall of fame glinted back at him, wall-to-wall mounted discs and accolades. It was time for a new venture; time to shake things up.

A photograph of Shawnella caught his eye—he had stripped them down after she'd left but must have missed that one. It had been taken when they first hooked up, at a red-carpet premiere, and in it she was gazing up at him tenderly.

Slink felt a pang of regret, which wasn't an emotion he normally gave a lot of time to.

Shawnella had hit massive with her (revised) fashion range and had secured a huge following, making her a star in her own right. Plus she was looking...well, there was no other way of putting it than *damn fine*. Shawnella was also dating a producer Slink had met a couple of times and had dismissed as a limp-dicked creep, but he seemed to be giving her what she wanted. Shawnella's debut single was tipped for release in the New Year.

Snatching the picture from the wall, he cracked the frame, removed the print and tossed it in the trash. He needed to make some calls. Shawnella couldn't go killing the Billboard 100 if he wasn't anywhere close. That was cosmic disorder or some shit.

Occasionally Slink figured he was better off alone. He had never been faithful to her anyway. More often he wondered if the woman with whom he had shared ten years had been more vital to him than he cared to admit; and a little of him —scrap that, a lot—missed her.

Gordon Rimeaux stayed in LA until the end of the summer, recovering from the fire.

It took a while. He was suffering from smoke inhalation, a chronic cough, shortness of breath and headaches that lasted for days.

They kept him in hospital. They told him that if he had got out of the building sooner and left Leon behind, he would have escaped unscathed. As it was, for the first forty-eight hours it had been uncertain as to whether or not he would even survive.

In the fall he headed for Australia. Old friends lived by the coast and after staying with them for a month he decided to make a go of it, buying a modest place from which he could watch the ocean. He had to figure out the next stage of his life, but whatever it was he knew it had to be thousands of miles from Puff City.

Gordon spent a lot of his time outdoors, learning to surf, swimming and chilling on the beach. People stared at his burns but he didn't let it bother him. He grew his hair, lost weight, and with each day that passed resembled G-Money less and less and grew into the man he might have been had he never taken the gun from Principal thirteen years ago.

Yet though Gordon's body bore the scars of the fire, burns that were pale and smooth in taut patches across his arms and legs, and a sensation of weight bearing down on his chest, he felt lighter and clearer than he had since he was eighteen.

A lifetime he had carried it. Letting it go was like surfacing for air.

He had fully expected Leon to press charges. When Gordon regained consciousness it had been to the bloody aftermath of the Platinum Awards, during which the same terrorist who'd ignited Leon's place and left them for dead had opened fire at the Palisades Grand. Movie star Cosmo Angel had died, shot three times in the head. Scott Valentine had lost his leg. Countless others had been injured. It took several updates and explanations for him to piece together the picture. Yet Robin Ryder, the assassin's target, had survived.

Leon had visited him at the ward. He had stayed at Gordon's bedside for an afternoon.

'All the evidence has gone,' Leon had offered. 'It went in the fire.'

Gordon had waited for more. None came. He didn't need to say it. What happened had happened, one life in exchange for another.

Before he left, Leon had put out his hand. Gordon had taken it.

And the past was laid to rest.

Wednesday morning and Gordon stepped on to the beach. The sand was bright and hot beneath the soles of his feet, the water as he met the tide cool and crisp.

He looked out to the horizon, waded in and started swimming.

Jax Jackson was clubbing at Hollywood's Rieux Lounge when Turquoise's new single blared out over the sound system. The throngs went wild, hands in the air, bronzed arms moving in time to the music. Jax cringed, gritting his teeth.

'You wanna buy me a drink?' yelled one of the brunettes he was with. She came in so close he could smell her cheap perfume. She bit a cherry-red lower lip.

Jax was glad of the excuse to get away, even if secretly he was bitter at having to purchase refreshments. Since losing his title his entourage had drifted away, not to mention the dollars evaporating as sponsorships and contracts dwindled to oblivion. Last week he had been forced to sell the Lamborghini. It had been the only time in his life that he'd cried.

Reluctantly he signalled to the barman. The guy smiled in acknowledgement when he recognised him but Jax noticed he didn't offer any freebies.

'All the vodka you've got in the house,' he announced magnanimously, proving a point. He was still Jax Jackson, wasn't he? He was still the freaking Bullet. 'Shots.'

Looking slightly confused, the barman obliged. Jax waited for someone to come up to him, ask for an autograph, beg for a photo, anything. They didn't.

He scowled, able to taste defeat on his tongue as if he'd had it for lunch that very day. So often he replayed the chapters of his collapse: how Leon had draped the US banner across his shoulders as he ran his lap of honour; how the victor had knelt to the track and kissed it, the flag fluttering in the breeze; how Jax himself had slumped on the track in a fist of anguish so raw and enduring that an official had had to come prod him to make sure he hadn't undergone a cardiac arrest; how he'd crawled to his feet, the crowd yelling messages of support, and he'd turned his sweat-drenched face to the ranks and heckled something offensive while flashing the bird. Maybe that had been it... the final nail in the coffin.

It had been that volunteer's fault. She had spelled the beginning of the end, because if it hadn't been for her insisting on sucking him off he would have won that day and he would still be the record holder. He would still be a god. If she hadn't begged to break his record with her tongue then *he* might have actually broken it when it counted.

Man, that was deep—maybe he should become a philolosophiler or something. Phililosopher. He'd never been sure how to say that word.

It wasn't as if his hip-hop venture was proving all that lucrative either. So far it had been a total disaster. His first video 'Bulletproof' had been laughed off YouTube. He winced, recollecting the comments it had spawned. *Loser! Joker! Freak! This guy should stick to the other track—oh, wait, he's crap at that, too...*

The drinks came and reluctantly Jax handed over his AmEx, hoping the barman might clock the name and decide the order was on the house. No such luck.

Jax scoped the crowd for his people but they had got lost in the masses. He couldn't much remember what they looked like anyway, had only picked them up a week ago, the sort of taggers-on he'd never previously have entertained but now had no one else to hang with.

Normally on a night out he would be able to spot Cindy's blonde crop, but his PA had checked out as soon as she'd uncovered the volunteer blowjob. It was hardly as if it were the first time Jax had sought pleasure elsewhere. Who did she think she was, his wife? But it was the hurt, she'd claimed, of the stopwatch record: Cindy had thought that was just between them, it was *her* record as much as his, and he had 'whored it out elsewhere'. Jesus. Women.

Jax was a bachelor, born and bred; he was better off without them.

He downed four shots in immediate succession. They scorched his throat, lighting him up, making the rest of the night doable.

The Turquoise track ended. Jax spotted a pair of tits at the end of the bar and sidled over. 'Want one?' he asked, proffering the shots like a sex pest selling sweets. The girl glanced warily at him before moving away.

Jax took another shot. A headache was flourishing behind his eyes.

He had beaten his stopwatch record; he had done the hip-hop thing… What was left?

Retirement? No freaking way.

Jax might have lost his title, but he was sure as shit getting it back.

Rio de Janeiro was three years away and Jax damn well didn't intend to be driving a clapped-out X-plate SUV for the rest of his days.

Leon would have to kill him to get his hands on Olympic gold.

'Hey, baby, I thought I'd lost you.' The brunette from earlier joined him at the bar, seizing a drink. She wound her arms around his neck and steered him towards the bathroom.

Why not? Jax thought, depressed. There was nothing else to do.

Robin Ryder looked up at the London high rise. It was raining. Grey sleet drove against the building's smashed windows and mottled brickwork; behind her the relentless traffic droned, no beginning or end, a constant forbidding soundtrack. It had taken weeks for her to summon the courage, and now she was here it was like stepping into a dream.

Inside, she mounted the steps to the seventeenth floor. Dressed in a hooded sweater and jeans, she prompted no remark or attention. Robin had imagined this place so often, but never like this. The sliding door to the life she might have had.

Always in her mind it had been full of love, a caring

mother and father, a safe home that for whatever reason had rejected her and left her to die. Seeing it now, this wasn't and never had been the case. She had been the one who'd been spared. Her abandonment had been her saviour. No such mercy for Ivy.

A woman police officer met her at the top of the stairwell.

'Hi,' she said kindly. 'I'm Jo. I was the one who found your mother.'

*My mother.*

She had visited Hilda's grave—the woman in the photograph that Ivy had sent. Robin had wanted to feel something, knew that she should, but the tears hadn't come. She had carried the idea of a mother with her ever since she could remember, and she still did. Hilda Sewell solved no puzzle, no enigma; no mystery that Robin had thus far missed out on. Simply, she was a stranger.

'Are you ready?' asked Jo.

'I've had twenty years to get ready,' Robin replied. 'I hope so.'

Along the platform they came to flat 39B. Across its broken door, a tape reading CRIME SCENE—DO NOT ENTER rippled in the draught.

Jo lifted it and gestured for her to go in.

'One rule,' she advised. 'Look but don't touch.'

The flat could have been a museum, peppered as it was with ancient, dust-caked artefacts and the smell of age and rot. So this was it, the home she had craved for two decades. Cold. Dark. Steeped in sadness and regret.

Despite Ivy's rampage and the malice that had coursed through her veins, Robin couldn't help but wonder how much this life had contributed to such an outcome. Partly she understood her sister's vendetta. The way Ivy had seen it Robin had been freed.

She wished it hadn't wound up this way. She wished she could have known her sister; that they might have been close. She wished things hadn't ended how they had.

She realised how fortunate she had been, left in a park bin to die.

'Do you want to see the bedroom?' Jo asked gently.

Robin forced herself to go in and to face the images and obsessions of her own shrine. She took it in and told herself it was better to confront it, to remember it, because whatever she imagined later would be worse than the reality.

None of it could detract from or negate a career that was tipped to grow. It couldn't take away the family she had found, not through blood or obligation but through choice: the precious people in her life, Polly and Barney and Matt, Sammy and Belle...

And her boy.

'Are you OK?' he asked.

Robin turned. She nodded. 'I think so.'

Leon Sway took her hand. 'She's gone,' he said. 'She's never coming back.'

Ivy had been shot dead, executed by a raft of military that hadn't been quick enough to prevent her destruction but had been able to stop it before more lives were lost. Afterwards they had pronounced her crusade a kamikaze mission. She had known she would die. Her sole purpose was to take her long-lost twin with her.

At that, she had failed. She'd come close, but she had failed.

Ivy had tried to take Leon, but he was a survivor. He was brave and beautiful and miraculous.

He had run his heart out that night, proving it to his brother, to her, to the world...but most important, to himself.

Leon was her life, her light, her saviour.

He squeezed her hand in his. 'What do you say we get out of here?'

She brought it to her mouth and kissed it. At last, she was home.


A fortnight later, the sun woke Leon as it streamed through the blinds of his and Robin's Caribbean retreat. He turned to her, angelic in her sleep, her dark hair over her forehead, her lips slightly parted and her smooth back exposed by the fallen sheet at her waist. He traced his fingers across her shoulders, softly kissing her neck.

Contentedly, she moaned, and he climbed from the bed before she woke up. After the year she'd had, she needed to rest. St Barts was the vacation they needed.

Leon tied a towel around his waist and stepped on to the balcony. Sparkling ocean and gleaming sand stretched before him, the sunshine warm on his back. In the harbour, boats came in to dock, blue and red and bright, coarse ropes being thrown to land and tied with salty hands. There was so much life in the world, and now he was part of it.

Forgiveness had set him free. Forgiveness of Gordon and of Puff City, forgiveness of their crime and its concealment, acceptance of what had happened and a promise to move on—that was what had cut him as loose as the vessels bobbing on the water, wide green sea spread to a distant horizon, waiting to be crossed, an adventure at his fingertips.

Marlon had helped him that day. Leon was a level-headed guy, he didn't believe in ghosts or spirits or anything like that, but he did believe that he had not been alone on that run to the Palisades Grand; that something or someone had been driving him on.

He would never be so arrogant as to suggest he knew the answers. He didn't. But Marlon had looked out for him in life, and so he had done the same in death. They were brothers. Death didn't get in the way of that.

Leon inhaled the ocean air. His lungs contracted painfully; he hadn't yet been able to return to training, and with Rio on the cards he had to get back on the circuit. Three years he had to keep widening that gap. The title he'd earned wasn't one he was prepared to give up.

It was a reminder that had Gordon not stayed with him he wouldn't be around to breathe at all. Leon had come so close to exacting revenge…and for what?

What did vengeance resolve?

Nothing. Ivy Sewell's murderous rampage and eventual self-sacrifice was testament to that. In the payback game, no one came out on top. Everyone was destroyed. It offered no solutions; it came with no peace. True strength was in knowing how to let go.

'You're up early,' came a voice.

He faced her. Robin looked sleepy in the mornings, her softest time of day. She was wrapped in a sheet and leaned against the frame, golden sunshine on her face.

'There's a lot to get up for,' he replied.

'Oh yeah?'

'Starting right here.'

Passionately, he kissed her, releasing the knot on the sheet so it dropped to the floor.

'Leon, people can see!'

'Forget them,' he said, but he stepped in and pulled the shutters all the same.

'You're insatiable,' she said as they fell giggling on to the bed.

'Is that a problem?'

'Might be.'

'Then you'd better get used to it. Because the thing is...' Leon put his forehead to hers '...I'm completely and totally in love with you.'

Robin touched his chin, bringing his face to hers so she could see him properly.

'Thing is,' she whispered back, 'I'm in love with you, too.'

\* \* \* \* \*

Read on for an extract from Victoria's debut novel

HOLLYWOOD SINNERS

available now

*Venice*

'Lana, over here! Lana, Cole! How's the marriage?'

Lana Falcon adjusted her pose for the cameras, hand on hip, shoulders back, and delivered her trademark megawatt smile. She held it in place and counted the seconds, careful not to let it drop. Against the red carpet her midnight-blue gown trailed like dark water.

She took pity on the reporter, who was slightly overweight and sported a beard that looked like he had drawn it on himself.

'You're half of America's most famous couple,' he gasped, scarcely believing his luck as Lana came to the side. 'How does it feel?' The film festival was a hive of energy: paparazzi and TV crews lined the carpet in thick numbers; fans with arms outstretched reached helplessly for their heroes–catching these two together was the biggest coup of his career.

On cue Lana felt an arm slide round her waist, smooth as a

snake. She turned to the man next to her, caught the familiar line of his profile and the gleam of his teeth, the charcoal-grey of his immaculate hair. Cole Steel. Her husband.

Cameras flashed and sparked in throbs of light. He didn't blink.

'It feels great,' she told the reporter with a friendly smile. 'We're very happy.'

Paparazzi jostled for the best shot. 'Cole! Lana, Cole, let's see you together!'

'Any plans to add to the family?' The reporter was sweating now.

'Watch this space,' said Cole, with a startlingly white grin. He planted a dry kiss on Lana's neck, just below her ear. The photographers went wild.

'Let's move on,' he instructed, just loud enough for her to hear.

Lana obliged. The smell of Cole's skin lingered–sweet, slightly minty. When he took her hand it was cold.

'Tell us about your new movie!' the reporter babbled, craning the mike after her, knowing he'd already lost them. 'Tell us about *Eastern Sky*!'

Lana moved into her customary position on the carpet, a little in front of Cole, his hands at her waist, steering her forward. At twenty-seven she was Hollywood's most desirable young actress. Regularly voted one of the world's most beautiful women, she was, with her burnt-chestnut hair, wide green eyes and warm smile, a killer combination of sex siren and girl-next-door. Women wanted to be her friend. Boys wanted to take her home to their mothers. Men jacked off over her, torn between fantasies of white cotton panties and crimson-red lingerie–the fascination was that Lana Falcon could pull off either. And, boy, did they dream she did.

'Cole, Lana, this way!'

Cole guided his wife into a series of poses, his hands moving round her body with the precision and grace of a dancer.

'Beautiful!' came the approving clamour.

Somebody shouted, 'Could we get a kiss?'

Cole laughed with the press like chums. Lana observed as he shot at them with pretend pistols, firing from the first two fingers of each hand.

Lana followed direction. Tilting her chin to meet his, she saw her surroundings–the deep reds and pure, billowing whites; the rich, syrupy gold of the event's majestic lions–taper sharply into her husband's approaching features until her view was suffocated entirely by his face, and the sad rub of his lips.

Cole Steel. Hollywood's highest grossing actor and a giant of the American film industry. Cole Steel. At the top of his game after nearly thirty years and tipped here to take a Volpi Cup. Cole Steel. The husband with whom Lana Falcon lived, attended parties, posed for photographs, but had never, had never...

All around, bulbs popped and flared. As Lana pulled away she searched her husband's eyes. As a good actor he could fill them with every emotion a role required–he was at his most convincing when assuming a character. As a man, as himself, he was blank. Cole's eyes were like a shark's: flat and empty. When she looked into them, Lana saw nothing.

'Let's get on the line,' said Katharine Elliot, Lana's publicist, discreetly ushering her client forward. 'They're queuing for a word.'

'We're not done here yet,' snapped Cole through gritted teeth. His smile didn't move.

Katharine stepped back. Cole was a man she did not want to piss off.

Together he and Lana refreshed their poses, the jewel in the crown of megastars gracing the Venice carpet, floating like creatures from another world, delighting with a look or a smile.

'Assholes,' muttered Cole, clapping eyes on a young, handsome actor and his Mother Earth wife. Cole claimed not to like the man because he'd beaten him to a part last year, though Lana suspected it was more because the couple paraded a soccer team of children, a brood to which they were still adding. It was something she and Cole could never achieve.

Beyond the press pit Lana caught sight of a young female fan, her desperate face streaked with tears as she was pushed and shoved amid the throng of people trying to catch a glimpse of the action. Lana took care to catch her eye, smiling warmly and giving her a wave.

*Toughen up* she thought, remembering herself at that age. *It's the only way to survive. Trust me.* She blinked against the memories. Too often they kept her awake at night.

'It's time,' Cole told her, placing a small, pale hand on her back. The cameras followed every move. Together, husband and wife were the ultimate American love story. He, one of the greatest actors of his generation; she, the girl who had come from nothing, from tragedy, to having it all.

Linking her arm with his, Lana walked alongside, nodding and smiling her way into the Palazzo del Cinema. She glanced at her wedding ring, a great cluster of diamonds that weighed heavy on her hand. In the frenzy of snapping bulbs it winked back, as if they shared a terrible secret.

*Las Vegas*

Elisabeth Sabell, legs wrapped tight round her fiancé's waist, examined with satisfaction the ten-carat antique engagement ring on her third finger.

'Fuck me!' she gasped, clasping his muscular shoulders. 'Fuck me fuck me fuck me!' The ring caught the light as they moved together, the sheets of their mammoth four-poster bed damp with sweat. As he pounded deeper, his rhythm quickening, the marvellous jewel came towards Elisabeth's enraptured face in shuddering frames, a glorious, insistent reminder that she would, before long, be Mrs St Louis.

'Tell me what you want, baby.' The man grabbed her ass, pulling himself in further. 'Tell me what you want.'

'I want you to fuck me hard, Robert St Louis!' she cried in abandon, raking livid-pink lines down his bronzed back, lifting her foot and trailing with her big toe the dip where his spine met his ass. 'Fuck me like you've never fucked me before!'

In one deft movement he hooked an arm beneath her, flipping them round, holding on for the ride. Elisabeth, on top, ran her hands across his broad chest, wondering at the strength of his arms, the gentle slope of his biceps and the hard muscle of his stomach. Tightening her grip, she pinned him beneath her.

'Strap in, baby,' she told him, throwing her head back to gaze at the *trompe l'oeil* ceiling. 'This is as close to heaven as it gets.'

Elisabeth began to rock, grabbing his hands, reaching higher, faster, like her life depended on it. Her golden mane fell in waves down her back, her pearl-white neck tilted to the ceiling. She could feel Robert's hands on her tits, her waist, her thighs; on her throat, pressing those points beneath her ear lobes that made her knees go weak. She howled out, the pinnacle in sight.

With a final thrust they both climaxed, their bodies slick with release. Elisabeth rode the swelling tide, blinking back stars, her chest rising and falling, the pulse within her a steady, exquisite, delicious beat.

Robert St Louis moved on to his elbows and gave her a lopsided smile. He brought her face towards his and kissed her slowly, tasting her mouth.

'You're beautiful,' he told her, planting a kiss on her chin, her nose, her forehead.

Elisabeth kissed him back. Together, she knew they made a staggering couple. Robert St Louis had been the most eligible bachelor in America. Now, two years on, he was hers.

Billionaire owner of two of the city's most infamous hotels, the Orient and the Desert Jewel, he was the most handsome, and the most powerful, man in Vegas. With his dark hair, almost-black eyes, warm as melting bitter chocolate, and wicked, honest grin, he was the most devastating man she had ever laid eyes on.

'I know,' she told him, peeling herself off the bed and heading for their palatial en suite.

He watched her go. 'Your father called,' he said.

'Do you have to tell me that right after we've had sex?'

He laughed. 'Sorry.'

'And?'

'Says he's got some news–I'm gonna want to hear it, apparently.'

Elisabeth rolled her eyes. She turned the shower on. 'I'll bet he has,' she muttered.

As Elisabeth stepped under the pounding water, she reflected it was a good job she loved Robert like she did–as daughter of the legendary Vegas hotelier Frank Bernstein, Elisabeth had her future in the city cut out from the start. She was destined to marry a businessman, someone of her father's choosing. It had always been that way–Bernstein made the decisions and there was no argument. Elisabeth was thirty-two now, she had a residency on the Strip and a loving, committed relationship, but still he had the power to make her feel like a bullied little girl.

Robert called something from the bedroom.

'What?' Elisabeth yelled over the rush of water. She ran a gloop of shampoo through her blonde hair.

The door slid open. 'I said: Any ideas?' He stepped in

behind her. 'Bernstein couldn't keep a secret from you if he tried.'

'None whatsoever,' Elisabeth said primly. 'It's probably another attempt to hurry the wedding along. I wish he'd butt out. Just because he introduced us doesn't give him *carte blanche* to interfere in every aspect of our lives.'

Robert knew not to press his fiancée on the sensitive subject of her father.

'Come on,' he said instead, helping her rinse her hair, 'or we'll be late.'

The Orient Hotel, Robert St Louis's multi-billion-dollar baby and the heart of his hotel empire, was a breathtaking project. He and Elisabeth arrived an hour later in a blacked-out car, the main attractions at tonight's charity gala event.

Two soaring towers, each peak like a closed flower, flanked a colossal central pagoda. Little square windows lit with gold travelled up as far as the eye could see, thousands of feet into the sky, until they became stars themselves. Dragons crouched at the entrance, fire screaming from their open mouths. Sparking fountains and flaming torches circled the majestic structure.

Robert's doorman greeted them like royalty. 'Good evening, boss.' He dipped his head, always nervous when the top gun was in the house. 'Ms Sabell.'

Elisabeth nodded.

'Evening, Daniel.' Robert knew every last one of the Orient's staff–he had hired them all personally, from pit boss to restroom cleaner. 'How many for the gala?'

'Six hundred. They're waiting for you both in the Lantern Suite.'

Robert checked his watch. 'Frank Bernstein here yet?'

'Not yet, sir.'

'Make the most of it,' Elisabeth muttered drily as they stepped into the foyer.

Robert chuckled. 'Come on, he's not so bad.'

Elisabeth loved the Orient. It was, in her opinion, the greatest hotel in the city. She'd grown up on the Strip, knew them all like the back of her hand, but the Orient was special, it was different. Huge china urns, big as cars, squatted in the five corners of the pentagonal lobby, overflowing with jade stalks and huge leaves sprayed in gold. Gilt-edged mirrors lined the walls beneath glowing red paper lamps. Below, the marble of the floor gleamed clear as water, like standing on the surface of a silver pool, so that your reflection made it difficult to tell which way was up and which way was down. It thrilled Elisabeth to know that soon, once she and Robert were married, she would be its queen.

They swept past Reception to the waiting elevator. As they rose to the sixteenth floor, Robert took her hand.

'I'm proud you're on my arm,' he told her.

'You're on mine, St Louis.' She winked as they alighted.

At news of the couple's arrival, a reverential hush fell over the assembled investors and Vegas notables. Jowly men with ruddy cheeks and fat wallets stood next to their glamorous wives, whose priceless gems dripped from their fragrant, powdered skin.

The women watched enviously as Elisabeth let the fur drop from her shoulders, revealing a glittering kingfisher-blue gown that matched her eyes. Every last one of them wanted Robert St Louis and, seeing Elisabeth now, understood why they never would.

Her fiancé took easily to the floor. 'I'm pleased to see so many of you here,' he said, clapping his hands together and approaching the waiting lectern. 'It's a special night. The Orient has been working closely with the causes here this evening...'

Elisabeth smiled, quietly greeting one of the wives with a brief air kiss.

As she watched Robert, she felt powerful. No longer was she merely Frank Bernstein's daughter: she was part of a team that had nothing whatsoever to do with him, a team that would lay the foundations of a new Vegas dynasty. This was hers alone–she didn't have to involve her father at all.

Nothing could come between her and Robert.

If ever it did, she would fight it to the death.

*London*

Chloe French held her expression as she reclined on the leopard-print chaise longue and followed the photographer's instructions.

'That's gorgeous,' he told her, clicking away. 'Anyone ever told you you've got the face of an angel?'

They had, actually. At nineteen Chloe French was the sweetheart of London's fashion circuit—a raw, unaffected beauty and a fledgling star on her way to the top. She was tall, nearly six feet, with a sheet of jet-black hair that fell to her waist and glittering slate-grey eyes.

A make-up girl wearing too-tight denim hot pants rushed over and reapplied pink lipgloss, fanning Chloe's hair out around her and repositioning the vintage clutch.

'Thanks,' Chloe called when she scurried off.

'Stop saying thanks,' instructed the photographer, an Emo

guy with thick Elvis-Costello-style glasses, 'you're disrupting the shot.'

'Sorry,' said Chloe, cringing. The camera popped as she
pulled the face.

Chloe French had been spotted four years ago outside
Topshop on Oxford Street, feeling rough amid a horrible
winter cold and wearing an old hoody with a ketchup stain
down the front. She'd been modelling ever since. Over that
time she had worked with some of the biggest names in
fashion, but she still couldn't shake the little knots of self-
consciousness that accompanied a shoot like this. There just
seemed to be so much fuss.

Consulting his assistant on the stills, the photographer
grinned. 'That's the one.' Chloe's slight awkwardness, so
unlike the other models he was used to working with, came
off brilliantly on camera as coy vulnerability.

'Have you got what you need?' she asked, sitting up. 'I'm
meeting Nate.' She beamed at the mention of her rock-star
boyfriend.

'And all the world's press?' The photographer made a
face, remembering the last time Nate Reid had come to the
studio. He'd been trailed by a troop of devoted paparazzi,
supposedly unintentionally, though nothing about Chloe's
boyfriend appeared to be without intention.

She laughed. 'Don't worry, Nate's discreet.'

'He is?' The photographer raised an eyebrow. 'I can't open
a London paper without seeing you two.'

Chloe shrugged. 'For a musician.'

'Yeah, the Pied fucking Piper,' he muttered, remembering
the cameras dancing at Nate's heels.

On cue the studio door opened and a rakish figure appeared in the doorway, a wiry silhouette crowned with artfully tousled hair.

'Nate!' cried Chloe, jumping up and running over.

'Great,' the photographer said with a roll of his eyes, 'just what we need.'

Nate Reid, frontman with The Hides, held out his arms to embrace her. Nate was the epitome of rock and roll–or at least he liked to think he was. As the hottest property in British music, he wasn't conventionally good-looking, a little on the rangy side and quite short, but what he lacked in stature he made up for in charisma. With piercing green eyes, a fuck-you attitude and an anarchic reputation, he was, in Chloe's eyes, everything that was wonderful in the world.

'Hey, babe,' said Nate, kissing her deeply. She tasted of cherries.

Chloe smiled down at him–she tried not to let the height difference bother her.

'Are you done yet?' he asked, a tad irritably. 'I've been waiting.'

Chloe gave a hopeful expression to Emo-guy.

'Yup, we're done,' he said, busy with the stills.

When she turned back she was just in time to catch Nate scoping out one of the other models, before his eyes slid swiftly back to her.

'Let's go,' she said, linking his arm tightly.

Unsurprisingly, the press had caught wind of Nate's arrival. As the couple emerged on to the street, a circus of shouting and flashing bulbs erupted. Nate held up a hand as they bustled through to the waiting car, as if the whole thing was a massive inconvenience. He parcelled Chloe away and turned to the paps, treating them to a couple of clean shots.

'You heading out tonight, Nate?' one of them asked. 'Chloe going with you?'

'Classified information, boys,' said Nate, editing out the tip-off he'd fed through earlier. He turned to get in the car.

'Is it true Chloe's moving to LA?'

Nate gritted his teeth. 'Not true.'

'There's talk that—'

He climbed in and slammed the door.

An army of lenses swooped in on the windows, clicking insistently, aimlessly, in the hope of catching a killer shot. The car moved off.

'You're so patient with them,' Chloe said, tying her hair back. 'I can never be arsed.'

''S no big deal.'

She kissed his cheek. 'Come on, I've got the house to myself this afternoon.'

Nate brightened. He was a little worn out after a marathon bedroom session that morning, but he'd never been able to resist Chloe. 'Sounds good, babe.'

Chloe gazed across at her boyfriend and felt her heart swell. Nate Reid was her hero–the night they'd met was proof of that.

So what if she caught him checking out other girls from time to time, it didn't matter. It was her he was committed to and that was the important thing. Right? Relationships required work–she knew that from her own experience. You couldn't just give up if you loved someone. And she loved Nate Reid. Nothing, and no one, was going to change that.

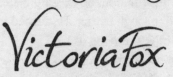

# Welcome to Paradise.

*Only the rich are invited…only
the strongest survive.*

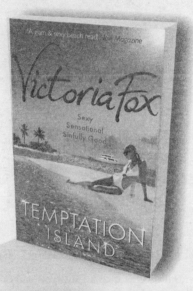

Three women drawn unwittingly to the shores
of Temptation Island, all looking for their own
truth, discover a secret so shocking there's no
turning back. It's wicked, it's sensational.
Are you ready to be told?

*'A juicy tale of glamour, corruption and ambition'*
*—Jo Rees*

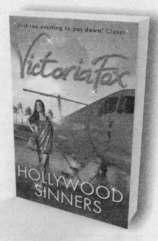

**Power. Revenge. Lust. Greed. Betrayal.**

Scandal circles like a vulture—dirty secrets are about to be exposed! For from the deepest desires come the deadliest deeds...and these Hollywood A-listers are about to pay for their sins...

**Sexy. Sensational... Sinfully good.
If you love Jackie Collins, then you'll devour Victoria Fox!**

M201_HS

Join

*Victoria Fox*

on some other mini–adventures in her

*Short tales of Temptation*

Available as eBooks

M331/STOT

# WHAT DID YOU MISS OUT ON BECAUSE YOU FELL IN LOVE?

Kate Winters might just be 'that' girl. You know the one. The girl who, for no particular reason, doesn't get the guy, doesn't have children, doesn't get the romantic happy-ever-after. So she needs a plan.

What didn't she get to do because she fell in love?

What would she be happy spending the rest of her life doing if love never showed up again?

**This is one girl's journey to take back what love stole.**

M327_LIAT